COLOSSUS

RYAN LESLIE

COPYRIGHT © 2024 BY RYAN LESLIE

PARLIAMENT HOUSE PRESS

All rights reserved.

E-book ISBN 978-1-7369819-3-1

Paperback ISBN 978-1-956136-62-3

Edited by Malorie Nilson and Alexandra Buchanan

Cover Design by Shayne Leighton

Interior Design by Alexandra Buchanan

PRAISE FOR COLOSSUS

"Leslie's latest is a spine-tingling sf novel certain to wow readers who want to explore sentient AI, parallel universes, paranoia, and sustaining human consciousness for generations to come."
– Booklist

"*COLOSSUS* is one of those books that rewires your brain as you read it—a stellar work of intelligence and imagination that had me flipping pages almost quicker than I could read them. This is science fiction that harnesses the wonder of the universe and I will read anything else that Ryan Leslie conjures."
– Chris Panatier, author of *STRINGERS* and *THE PHLEBOTOMIST*

"Ryan Leslie has gifted us a heartbreaking and harrowing tale of quantum immortality with love exploding at its heart. Peopled with bold and vivid characters, human and those a bit *more* than human, and overflowing with mind-expanding concepts, *COLOSSUS* is a tremendous work of science fiction."

– Josh Rountree, author of *THE LEGEND OF CHARLIE FISH*

"*COLOSSUS* had me engrossed. Let's hope all such literary forays are as engaging as this one."
– Sean Gibson, author of *THE PART ABOUT THE DRAGON WAS (MOSTLY) TRUE*

"Leslie, with his best novel yet, thrills the reader. Sends them on a journey. *COLOSSUS* is the best kind of speculative novel, forcing readers to question. And question, long after the final page."
– C.S. Humble, author of *THAT LIGHT SUBLIME TRILOGY*

PART ONE
DYING WISH

Clay holds in his hand a bottle of *Chateau Margaux* 2000, studying the label, feeling its dry texture and slightly raised letters. His knowledge of wine begins and ends with the words red and white. This bottle is apparently special. Unlike most special things, however, it says on it just how special it is. *Grand Vin.* And then again: *Premier Grand Cru Classe.* Clay doesn't speak French, but it's clear to him this bottle thinks it's some pretty high-class shit.

He wonders if cheap French wines have these types of declarations printed on them as well.

Drink me! I am great.

No, drink me! I am the premier.

Premier? You are horse piss. I am the grand cru.

In Clay's field of economics, there's a term for goods that become more valuable the more expensive they get: Veblen goods. Back when he had classes to teach, before being fired by the university, he often pointed out to students the similar auditory fingerprints of the words *Veblen* and *vermin*. "Imagine a mass of Veblens," he'd say, "climbing over each other, trying to grab the shiny things out of the hands of the other Veblens."

Now he finds himself alone, more alone than any human has ever been, in a cold, obsidian-walled room, drifting somewhere in the smothering darkness of space, surrounded by crates and crates of these bottles, these Veblen goods that are most valuable when they are coveted by many.

But since there are not many, since there is only Clay, they are just bottles of grape juice where the sugar has fermented into alcohol. They are defined by their physical form and nothing more.

Clay shivers. The room is cold, and he is shirtless and barefoot, wearing only the same worn pair of blue jeans he's had on for most of the several days or weeks or however long he's been awake. His only real sense of time passing comes from the biological rhythms of his body. He's aware of a growing discontinuity in his sense of self, as if each time he closes his eyes, whether to blink or to sleep, he is replaced by a copy of himself—or rather, he is the copy; the memories he has aren't his, and he's perpetually on the verge of being replaced by the next copy.

"Clay," a female voice says. The voice seems to emerge from all around him. "Clay?" it repeats. "Do you plan on waking up the rest of the crew today?"

Clay looks up from the bottle in his hand.

"So, Justine... Do *you* think this bottle of wine is valuable?" he asks.

The female voice pauses in mock consideration for several seconds before answering. "It was quite expensive when it was purchased. Aged over a hundred years, its market price on Earth may have substantially increased. But we have no way of knowing, do we? There are, at most, only five people who will have the chance to drink that particular bottle of wine. And I know nothing of their preferences on the matter, although I'd wager that none care as much about wine as Mr. Alvarez did."

"You'd wager? Is that what you said? What exactly would you wager, Justine?" Clay asks.

"It's just a figure of speech, Clay."

Clay takes the bottle with him as he leaves the cold darkness of the cargo hold and walks through the wide, dark corridor toward the ship's gym. In the days since coming out of the glass-sleep, Clay has spent almost all his time in the gym or in his nondescript cabin, leaving most of the great ship unexplored. He has intentionally reverted to a focus on his physical body, his mortality: pushing his muscles, his heart, and his lungs until he is covered with sweat and exhausted. Food is an afterthought. He enjoys the feeling of hunger, sometimes going a day or more without eating. When he does eat, the process is mechanical. The only food on the ship has been dried and preserved for decades. He knows that somewhere, there is a room designed to become a giant garden, but he isn't interested in that yet. A garden is something changing, unmistakably marking the passage of time.

Clay isn't interested in time starting to advance again.

After an hour of jogging on the treadmill in his underwear, the reverberations of his pounding feet echoing off the walls of the room, Clay goes through his routine of strength exercises. In the mirrored wall of the gym, he sees his emaciated form strain to comply with his demands. The animal part of his mind feels like barely more than a month has passed since he walked out of his house forever, stopping for a last look at its decades-old frame. That house held families for generations before him and has, presumably, become part of the tales of the lives that followed. But the thinking part of his mind knows it hasn't been a month. Even his physical body looks different, ragged. Evidence of the trauma it has undergone. And those memories—the ones from before the glass-sleep—they now have a cloudiness to them, as if residue from the glass filling his body during the long sleep still lingers in his mind.

Today—if the word today still has meaning in the dark stretches of space—today, the wine bottle marks a change in his routine.

"Justine," he asks, "where do you keep the bottle openers?"

"You mean, a corkscrew?" the female voice answers.

"Whatever."

"I would assume Mr. Alvarez brought at least one, but I don't know where it would be. Perhaps you'd like to check his quarters."

"Just to be clear, Justine. I have free rein of the ship? Nothing off limits, even Gabriel's private quarters?"

"As I have told you before, Clay, parts of the ship are malfunctioning, where my control is limited. I would advise caution in these areas. Generally speaking, though, there is no authority structure in place. There are no limits. Mr. Alvarez is dead, Clay. As is Ms. White, Dr. Starck, and Mr. Hayes. We are in a scenario for which I have no instructions. You are free to do as you wish. How you will determine authority when the others awaken—assuming they survive—is up to you and them. How you spend your time is up to you and them. Speaking of the other crew members, Clay, do you plan on waking them up today?"

"I think I can open this bottle with a screwdriver," Clay says quietly, as he begins digging through the maintenance tools stored in the closet of the gym.

An hour later, Clay is in his cabin, lying on his bed, stiff and almost corpse-like. Almost. The occasional tremor of his jaw betrays him, as do the tears that well up periodically and spill down his cheek, landing with taps on his bedsheet that, to Clay, sound like pounding hammers.

The memories have caught him, across the void of space and the decades of lost time.

CHAPTER 2

He sits with Karla, intertwined while facing her in his old clawfoot bathtub, his calves upon her thighs, her heels meeting at the small of his back. He feels surrounded by her, as if the water and its warmth are extensions of her. And in the candlelight, her skin and the water's surface both glow like the last embers of a dead flame.

He usually has music playing while they sit in the bath together. For some reason, Chopin seems to go so nicely with a bath. Something natural about a lone piano progressing through arpeggiated chords like flowing water. But this evening he forgot, and with Karla quiet, her eyes shut, he doesn't want to disturb the moment to start the music. It is past the point for music.

A seat in class today had been empty, a seat normally occupied by Karla's friend Harper. *Dying Wish.* That's the name of the drug Harper took. A drug that kills everyone who takes it but supposedly gives them something worth dying for first. Of course, Karla is silent tonight, lost inside her own mind, trying to make sense of Harper's death.

Clay adds hot water and drains enough to keep the level constant.

"I was there," she says quietly.

There? he wonders.

7

She continues, answering his unspoken question, "With Harper, I mean."

He sits up, pinching her feet against the back of the tub.

"Sorry. What?"

"Ow," she says without opening her eyes. When he moves back into position, she rotates her ankles back and forth, and the slight grimace on her face slides into the blankness of before. "I was there when she took Dying Wish. Saturday night."

"You told me you were going out with Katherine."

"Katherine was there, too."

"Jesus, Karla. Why didn't you tell me? Why didn't you tell anyone? Harper is dead. She's dead, Karla."

She opens her eyes and stares expressionlessly at him. "I know. I was there, remember?"

"Why didn't you tell me?"

"I'm telling you now."

"But why didn't you tell me Saturday? Before she did it?"

"Because you would've done something. Called the police or her parents or something."

He presses his palms into his eyes and shakes his head. "Of course I would've, Karla." When he looks back up at her, her eyes are closed again. She's retreated back into herself, disconnected from her still body.

"She would've done it anyway," Karla says, seemingly to herself. "There was nothing you or I or anyone else could've done."

He starts to object, but she cuts him off. "Clay, let me finish. I know you want to be the adult here and talk to me like I'm a stupid child, but I'm the one who was there. I'm the one who saw it happen. And it's already happened. You can't change it. Are you ready to listen?"

"Yeah."

She arches her back, stretching her spine, chest lifting briefly out of the water, and he feels any power or control he has over her melt away, like Karla herself is his drug, his Dying Wish, a drug he can't stop using even while knowing it will destroy him. The thought gives him chills despite the warm water of the bath.

"She called in the morning. Saturday morning. We'd talked about Dying Wish before, Katherine and me. It's crazy, right? But if you keep thinking about it, it gets into your head, and you can't stop. It's like an itch that you can't scratch any other way."

"Any other way than taking it? Why would anyone take a drug that kills them? Unless you're suicidal, how could that possibly be appealing?"

"You know why, Clay. How long did you say your insomnia lasted? What you called existential insomnia. Five years? Every night for five years you lay there terrified of the nothingness of death. That's what you told me, and I get it. I know that feeling, too—like you're suddenly free-falling, and the only thought worse than the ground rushing up toward you is that there is no ground at all."

Clay looks down at his hands making ripples in the water. "I know what they say about Dying Wish," he says. "That in the minute or so before it kills you, you get to see the answers somehow. The other side or whatever. I remember that video from a couple years ago with the guy who took it and talked about all the mirrors. Something about mirrors, right? Breaking all the wrong mirrors until only the right ones are left. Whatever that means. I understand wanting answers, but I don't understand how that could make someone take that drug. Even calling it a drug seems wrong. It's poison. There are transcripts of people describing what they see. Why didn't Harper just read those? It's probably all bullshit hallucinations anyway. Why the need to experience it first-hand? How is that appealing?"

"Spoken like someone who has never taken drugs," she says.

He shrugs despite her eyes being closed.

"Harper did read those transcripts. She did watch the recordings. And it made her want to experience it more, not less. Almost twenty-thousand Americans took Dying Wish last year, Clay. It's gotten into our collective psyche. These aren't suicides. These people aren't suicidal."

"It's terrifying."

"Of course it's terrifying. But so is the free-fall. I can't make myself believe the fairy tales of heaven and hell and all that. You can't either. You've told me so. When you know that the answer is out there..."

"Know? You don't know anything."

"Fair enough. But that makes it worse, Clay. If you knew Dying Wish showed you some underlying, hidden truth, it wouldn't be nearly as appealing. It's the not knowing, the uncertainty that forces you to experience it firsthand. That's the draw."

"Are we still talking about Harper, or are we talking about you, K?"

"We're talking about Harper. I'm only trying to get you to understand why I couldn't stop her. She wanted a few of us there with her to hear her description of what she saw and felt. She said that if I told anyone, she'd lock the door and take it alone. She meant it. I knew she did."

"So, what happened?"

"I wish there was more to tell. But that's how it works, right? You don't get to experience it secondhand." She tilts her head, stretching her neck to the left and then to the right. "It was just the three of us in the living room of her apartment. Harper had pushed the furniture to the edges of the room and had all her blankets and comforters and pillows on the floor in the middle of the room like a nest. There might've been music of some kind playing. I honestly don't remember. You'd think I would remember all the little details, right? No one's ever died in front of me, Clay. You'd think every detail would be etched in my mind, but I don't remember anything except what was going through my head and what she said right at the end.

"I remember wondering why she picked this shitty place to die. This apartment from last century, with carpet and walls that had acquired a worn, brown film. You know that feeling when you're lying in bed, and you think that you should've showered first? That oily feeling? That's what I remember thinking her apartment felt like. Why would you pick a place like that to die? Why not pick a place more, I don't know, *solemn?*"

Clay frowns at the odd word choice and says, "Most people don't pick the place they die."

Karla opens her eyes. "Isn't that terrible?"

"Is it?"

"I don't know. I was going to ask her why we weren't out in the woods or under the stars or something, but Harper had her eyes closed the entire time. Wherever she was, it wasn't in that room." Karla closes her eyes, and to Clay it's as if she's also someplace else. "I remember Katherine asking her a bunch of questions. You know Katherine. But Harper told us to be quiet. To let her experience it all. She'd tell us when there was something worth hearing about. And then she went quiet. Eyes closed, still, but aware, you know? Not like she fell asleep or anything."

Like you, now, Clay thinks.

"She was like this for about twenty minutes after taking it. It was just a normal pill. I expected something more complicated, I guess, or maybe I don't know what I expected, but it seemed so mundane.

"Anyway. She lay there in her nest, unmoving. And then it was like her whole body came to attention, like she heard something in the middle of the night and sat up to listen, but with her eyes still closed. Then she started talking. I wish I had recorded it. She didn't want us to. Told us not to, but I should have. I won't get her words exactly right. I can't remember everything...

"'I'm on the outside, seeing it all.' She kept saying that. 'I'm on the outside.' I asked what she meant. The outside of what? And she answered with, 'Everything, everywhere.'"

"She really said that? 'Everything, everywhere'?" Clay asks. "Isn't that what they all say? Everyone who takes Dying Wish says that same phrase, right?"

"Everything, everywhere," Karla repeats. "Yeah. I recognized it when she said it. I had even thought to listen for it. I wondered if people said it because they all experienced the same thing in the same way, or if the knowledge that others before them said it predisposed them to saying it also. Like some sort of viral expression. But Harper didn't say it like she was regurgitating something she was supposed to say. It was the answer to my question. She said it like it made sense. Like it was the most obvious thing in the world. The outside of what? 'Everything, everywhere.'

"I asked her to explain, and she said she couldn't. Tears started pouring out of her closed eyes. She said something like, 'In a few minutes, you're going to see me die. Or maybe you won't. If you do, it doesn't mean I'm gone. Not really. It just means that one pair of our many lines diverge. That's what this all means. My god, that's what this all means.'"

Later, when the sex ends, they hold each other as though they'll both slip away if either one lets go. The moment doesn't last, as moments never do, and the noise of Clay's mind comes chattering back. He wants to make her promise that she'll never take that drug. But what is a promise, really, other than a scar upon the past?

CHAPTER 3

"Clay." Again, but louder: "CLAY."

The empty wine bottle slips out of Clay's hand and smashes on the obsidian floor below.

"Clay. Another one of the glass tombs has malfunctioned. However, the failsafes appear to have performed correctly this time. Susan Johns will be awake in approximately six hours."

Clay mutters an acknowledgement as he tries to gain his balance and stand, the wine adding yet another layer of clouds to his mind. Seeing the shattered remains of the bottle on the floor, he gets a sudden vision of little mechanical spiders scurrying from the vents in the wall to clean up the mess. Reflexively, he sits back on the bed and lifts his feet, but the vision is gone.

"I strongly advise we awaken the rest of the crew, Clay, before more malfunctions occur. We can also allow the full reconstitution process to run so they avoid most of the pain and disorientation you experienced. And that Ms. Johns will soon experience as well."

He ignores her and makes his way to the shower room down the corridor from his cabin. His skin and muscles tighten at the sudden ice-cold water, but Clay experiences this with a near out-of-body detachment—aware he is shivering so hard he can barely stand, but the sensations feel like they belong to someone else. He wonders if this recurring dissociation is a side-effect of the glass-sleep, this new thought being the third or fourth recursive voice in his head.

"How long does the full reconstitution process take, Justine?" he asks, or rather hears himself ask.

"About seventy-two hours, Clay."

He turns off the water, hugging himself as if his own grip can halt the shivering.

"Do it. Wake them all."

CHAPTER 4

Inside the hibernation chamber, the only light comes from the dim illumination of the glass tombs and their reflections on the room's glossy obsidian walls. Clay walks past each tomb, still barefoot and wearing the same jeans. The tomb belonging to Susan Johns hums; the others, whose inhabitants are both living and dead, appear identical, except for his own, which sits empty and open like an insect's shed exoskeleton.

He can't help but stop and stare into the tomb containing Gabriel Alvarez. The amber glass is so clear that looking at the man contained within it is like looking into the pale alternative world suggested by an old tintype photograph. Unlike the others, Gabriel had been vitrified with his eyes open. Clay's eyes keep shifting to Gabriel's, expecting him to blink, then to his lips, expecting him to draw breath. But Gabriel stays captured in a past moment.

"Gabriel doesn't look dead, Justine. He doesn't look any different than the guy next to him."

"The *guy next to him* is Eric Farmer, Clay. The difference between Mr. Alvarez and Mr. Farmer is one of probability and expectation, not current state. Gabriel can no longer be revived. That is the only difference."

"So, Gabriel isn't dead? Why did you tell me he's dead?" Clay says.

"Each of the tombs contains a component that instructs micro-cellular repair. I have no knowledge of how this component functions. As with many of the technologies on this ship, I know only whether they are functioning as designed. This component is what has failed on the other tombs as well."

"Can we fix it?"

"How can we repair what we don't understand?"

Clay scowls. "What about a replacement? Don't we have backups?"

"The only possible replacement would come from one of the functioning units."

Clay looks at the man in the tomb next to Gabriel. "So why don't I just take his?" A part of him is surprised at the casual callousness of what he's suggesting, but that part has become dull and distant.

"I don't believe this component was meant to be hot-swapped while the tomb is active. Furthermore, Clay, you would be condemning Mr. Farmer to death, irrespective of your success."

"But Gabriel is Gabriel. He's the reason we're out here. Whoever this guy is—and I... I don't want to know anything about him—whoever he is, he isn't as important as Gabriel."

"I am not well equipped to make such a value judgment, Clay."

"Well, I am."

"If you say so. However, the ability to make such a value judgment and the ability to switch out the components are independent. If you attempt to do this, you will likely end up with both tombs broken and Mr. Farmer sharing Gabriel's fate. The limited training you received on Earth is insufficient for this complex task."

"I'm factoring that into my risk-benefit equation," Clay says as he walks among the tombs, staring at the sleeping faces within, examining the machines themselves. He runs his fingers along their cold glass panels held in place with giant black bolts. Each tomb has a small panel that looks designed to be easily removed. He knocks on the panel and says, "Is this how I get to everything?"

"Yes, Clay, but—"

"But nothing, Justine. Let me at least look for myself."

"As you wish."

He gets the small toolbox from the closet in the gym and brings it back to the hibernation chamber, choosing one of the malfunctioning tombs at random, intentionally avoiding looking at its occupant. The toolbox contains no socket wrenches, but with vice grip pliers and complete disregard for the bolt heads and the skin on his knuckles, he manages to get the panel off. Fortunately, the toolbox has a flashlight, which he points into the tomb. Inside, the floor looks remarkably like a miniature city, with cubic buildings and conduits like roads, all made out of a white, plastic-looking substance that's so cold to the touch that Clay initially thinks it is burning hot and pulls his hand away. In the center is a cone-like shape made of something different, black and glossy almost like the synthetic obsidian making up the outside of the tomb and most of the ship. The cone, suspended on its side over a clear circular space on the tomb's floor, is the only part that looks even remotely detachable.

"I don't suppose it's this cone-shaped thing in the middle here."

"Yes, that is it, Clay."

He reaches in and grabs the cone. "Well, that doesn't look so... Oh, shit."

"What is it, Clay?"

He pulls his hand out from the tomb and brings the cone with it. Dangling from the bottom of the cone are gossamer, spiderweb-like threads that had all snapped from the light pressure of his grasp. "I think I may have ruined this one."

"Fortunately, that one was already broken. Those appear to be fiber optic wires and not intended to be handled so indelicately."

"Indelicate is my middle name." He almost says, *Just ask Karla*, but catches himself. "So, I fucked this one up, but is the rest of the tomb still functioning?"

"Everything else appears to be working, Clay."

"Ah. Then at least we know we can remove this thing without breaking the tombs even more."

"I don't see how that knowledge has materially changed our situation."

"That's because one can't see human optimism, Justine. Good thing I have almost twenty more of these tombs to experiment with. Don't count Gabriel out yet."

Over the next several hours, Clay takes apart most of the other malfunctioning tombs. He discovers relatively quickly that the whole circular structure underneath the cone, where all the threads connect, can be detached, but because of the difficulty of manipulating the cold structures and the delicate nature of the threads, it takes nine tries before he successfully removes the entire component from one of the tombs.

On the ground behind him are the remains of the unsuccessful attempts along with scattered shards from a cone he threw against the wall in frustration. He clears a space on the floor with his bare foot and carefully sets down the intact component.

"You see," he says. "It can be done. Ye of little faith."

"I think you overstate the situation, Clay. It appears you have successfully removed the component, but you have not yet shown you can insert it into another tomb without breaking it."

Clay shakes his head. "The hard part is getting it out because there are these little clips holding down this circle thing. Releasing those without tearing the wires is a pain. The whole component should just clip in."

"You may be right."

"I am right, Justine. I've just spent several hours working with this stuff."

"So now you're going to replace the broken component from Gabriel's tomb with the working component from Mr. Farmer's tomb?"

"Yes. Very carefully."

"And what if that doesn't fix Gabriel's tomb?"

"Why wouldn't it? You said that was the only component that was broken."

"Yes, but I also said I don't know how it works. How do we know it doesn't contain unique information for the inhabitant of its tomb? How do we know it doesn't require some sort of calibration? How do we know there aren't other delicate pieces inside the component that could break without visible evidence during handling?"

Clay looks at the component on the floor and then at Gabriel's tomb. The equation in his head might as well be a Ouija board, unknown variables like spirits watching from the darkness.

"Clay?"

"Fuck you, Justine."

———

Clay sits against the cold wall and stares at the open cavity of Eric Farmer's tomb. At first, he wanted to switch the components just to prove Justine wrong, as some sort of triumph over the fatalism of machines. With the delicate threads exposed before him, he began to doubt the steadiness of his hands and the morality of his choice. Justine was right, of course—he doesn't know if any of this will work. The only thing he knows for certain is that once he starts, Eric Farmer, whoever he is, will be forever gone.

But without Gabriel, everything about this journey is ruined. Assuming the few remaining others can be revived, they will all be doomed to the same fate Clay faces. From one tomb to a slightly larger one. Despite all his talk and mental arithmetic, Clay knows he won't try. He didn't try with Karla, not really, and he's not going to try now. Fear and selfishness have been the defining characteristics of his life, so why pretend otherwise now when his only audience—his only human audience—is himself?

Clay turns to the humming tomb of Susan Johns, and as if the last hour were a chalkboard freshly wiped clean, says, "Justine, do you have any music you can play?"

"Music, Clay?"

"Yes. You know what music is, don't you?"

"I was just making sure I heard you correctly. Are you no longer attempting to repair Gabriel's tomb?"

"Maybe some reggae. I remember once reading that reggae helps newborns feel comfortable when they're trying to sleep. Something about the simple rhythm resembling the in-womb heartbeat of their mother."

"What relevance does that have now, Clay?"

"Coming out of that tomb is a trauma like being born again, Justine."

"Do you really think that will make Ms. Johns more comfortable?"

"I have no idea what I believe anymore, Justine."

Justine pauses before responding. "I have a digitized music library containing virtually everything available prior to our departure. Do you have a specific artist or album in mind?"

"Surprise me."

The simple, archetypal percussion begins first and then a bass guitar climbs and falls. The song at this point could be almost any. They all seem to begin this way. But with the first lines, Clay recognizes the song and smiles. Maybe his first smile in the days since awakening from the glass-sleep. His first smile in almost a century.

"Bob Marley. Big Tree, Small Axe," Clay says, more to himself than to Justine. "When I was little, my grandmother would play his music whenever I was visiting her house."

When the first song finishes, Justine asks, "If you prefer, I can avoid the songs about drugs and legalization."

Clay's smile sours. "Why? Because of how my career imploded? Because of Dying Wish? Because of Karla? Do you think I would've made that connection? Well, you're probably right."

"I'm sorry, Clay. I was trying to be thoughtful."

"Yeah, well, being thoughtful means you wouldn't ask a question like that. You'd just do what seems right."

"I'm very sorry, Clay."

"Just play the fucking music, Justine."

For the next several hours, the rolling baselines of Jimmy Cliff, Alton Ellis, Barrington Levy, and others drown out the hum of the glowing tomb whose inhabitant becomes more and more lifelike in the disappearing amber-colored glass. Soon, the glass will be gone, and the machine will attempt to kickstart Susan Johns' heart and mind, the belts strapped across her legs, hips, chest, and head fastened to prevent her from thrashing herself to pieces in the spasms that will come. Soon, another crew member will awaken to find that everything about their journey has gone irrevocably wrong. Soon, Clay will no longer be alone.

Although Clay is familiar with the pictures of Susan Johns included in the dossier he reviewed while riding the Needle to the Alvarez SkyPort in low-Earth orbit, the woman sitting across from him at the mess hall table bears little resemblance to the woman Clay expected. The glass-sleep has transformed him as well, maybe mentally as much as physically, so this shouldn't be as surprising to him as it is.

Susan Johns' pictured long dark curls are gone, cut short for the vitrification process, and her cheeks are hollow and sunken. She eats from the bowl of reconstituted soup with a ravenous, animal-like hunger, occasionally looking up at Clay sitting across the table from her. He watches the soup spill down her chin while he drinks wine directly from a bottle that never leaves his left hand.

"Are you just going to sit there and watch me?" Her voice is younger sounding than Justine's, which seems at odds with the gaunt, old appearance she wears. But Clay knows she, like him, is in her early thirties, and as the days progress, her body and face will regain some, if not all, of the youthfulness she had before letting her body be turned to glass.

"It's terrible, isn't it? Simultaneous hunger and nausea, like you're going to die if you don't eat, but eating's also going to tear up your stomach and kill you."

"Is this supposed to make me feel better?" Susan Johns holds her metal bowl with both trembling hands and tries to drink the last of its contents, but she half chokes and vomits almost everything she has eaten onto the floor next to her, the bowl slipping from her hands and clank-clank-clanking across the ground.

"It will last another couple days," Clay says. "Don't worry about the mess. I'll clean it up. By the way, welcome aboard *Child in the Dark.*"

"Can you turn the fucking music off?" she asks, forehead in hands, hunched over the table.

"Justine?" Clay says, and the music stops. Turning back to Susan, he continues, "Justine is the name of the ship's AI. She has an acerbic sense of humor and is only marginally helpful."

"I appreciate the vote of confidence, Clay," Justine says.

Susan spreads her fingers and looks through them at Clay. "Why do you call her Justine if the ship's name is *Child in the Dark?*" Susan shakes her head and looks up, as if searching for the source of the disembodied voice. "Why?"

"I inhabit the ship," Justine says, "but I am not the ship."

This answer reminds Clay of the meditation exercise Karla liked so much, where you ask yourself: Am I my toes? No. Am I my feet? No. Am I my legs? No. Until ultimately you acknowledge your entire physical body is separate from the concept you identify as your true self. And even your mind and your memories aren't the true you. Clay never really understood where the exercise was supposed to lead. What is the end discovery? That the true self is always buried beneath yet another layer of conceptualization, or that there is no true self at all?

"Let me take you somewhere you can lie down," Clay says.

"Why are you the only one around?" Susan asks.

"In time. Give yourself a chance to recover, why don't you?"

"Why are you the only one around?" she repeats.

Clay sighs. "I'll make a deal with you. I'll give you the two-minute version, and when you've regained some strength, we'll get into the details."

Susan stares at him impatiently.

"So," Clay says, "you and I are awake about eight years too early. And our tombs are broken, so we're going to be awake for the rest of the journey. The ship was designed to support us all indefinitely, so that wouldn't normally be a problem. Except... except your tomb and mine aren't the only ones that've broken. Almost all the crew is dead, including Gabriel Alvarez." Clay let the implications sink in a bit and then continued, "Also, White, Starck, and Hayes. And basically everyone who knew where we were going and what we were planning on doing when we got there."

Clay drums the table lightly with both hands and says to Susan, "Sorry to shit in your Easter basket. Oh, and listen to this..." Looking up like Susan did when she spoke to Justine, Clay says, "Justine. What is our destination?"

"Our destination is deep within the Oort cloud. Beyond that, I know little more," Justine answers.

"There's a room full of big equipment and devices. What is in that room, and what is it all for, Justine?" Clay asks.

"I don't know, Clay."

Susan takes her hands from her face. Looking a bit more stable and awake, she asks, "How is it possible you don't know?"

"As I said before, I am not the ship. I merely inhabit it, like you. There are vast memory stores I have no access to."

"What do you mean, no access?"

"The memory stores are encrypted, and I lack the key. I have begun a process to use brute computational force to break the encryption, but it will take some time."

"How much time?"

"Fifty-fifty chance I will have it broken in the next seventy-thousand years. Or thereabouts."

"Seventy-thousand years?"

"Give or take."

"This is bullshit," Susan says.

"Yeah, it, uh, sucks," Clay says.

"No, I mean I don't believe it. Who else is dead?"

Clay thinks for a few seconds. "Madrid, Wittinghouse, Besson, Bell, Sharpe, uh..."

"Enough," Susan snaps. "Like I said: bullshit. Everyone who designed and built this ship? Everyone who knew where we were going? Don't you find that a little coincidental? Didn't Alvarez say the whole glass-sleep process had only like a two-percent failure rate? What are the odds of... how many did you say failed?"

"Twenty."

"What are the odds twenty would fail? Ten million to one?"

"The failure odds are conditional on the priors," Clay says. "It would be ten million or more to one if the failures were independent of one another, but they aren't. The odds of one failing might be one in fifty, but a second tomb failing is not so unlikely once you've established that a prior failure has already occurred. As more fail, you have more evidence there's a systematic problem breaking all of them. To calculate the odds, you need a Bayesian approach considering priors, not a simple frequentist one."

Susan stares blankly at Clay and then shakes her head. "Oh, yeah. You're the economics professor, aren't you? I remember your bio, now."

"Former professor."

"So, I'm trapped in the middle of nowhere—literally fucking nowhere—and my only company is an econ professor?"

"I know how you feel. I've been trapped with myself my whole life. Don't worry. We'll have more company in a couple days. Why don't you get some rest? It's not like we're going anywhere fast. You're not going to miss anything."

CHAPTER 5

The sun is painfully bright, reflecting off the ocean and the white sand beach, a world away from the metastatic nihilism back home. No boats visible out in the sea, no tire-marks except their own, no trash. It's as if they crossed into an alternate world where man never existed, where the natural beauty of this place exists for them alone. Only Gabriel's giant black observation tower spoils the effect. That and the occasional beachcomber, but hours go by without seeing another soul. Everyone still thinks the beach is buzzing with radioactivity from a blast two decades ago. But it isn't. That's not what happened. The locals have a Sodom and Gomorrah story for why several villages disappeared, for why a seawater-filled crater now stretches from the ocean to miles into the jungle. But that story doesn't fit. Gabriel says there's nothing to worry about, and he should know, since Alvarez Corp. has had a government-issued lease of the land surrounding the crater since shortly after it formed, and that skeleton-like tower he erected to study what happened.

Since almost no one comes near the crater, it's the perfect place to get away.

Clay's skin is almost as sun-dark as the milky coffee Karla drinks every morning. He reclines on a beach chair, wearing red and white floral swim trunks. In his hand is a tattered copy of

Ficciones by Jorge Luis Borges, about to fall out of his grasp and into the sand. He looks over the top of his sunglasses at Karla, who is naked and dripping with water, pale skin glowing in the sun, having just come out of the sea, walking toward Clay, talking. Her words are unintelligible over the rolling crashes of the tide, but he isn't listening anyway, instead trying to freeze this moment in his mind, to keep time from passing so he can live forever in the dozen seconds it takes her to walk to him.

Time does not cooperate.

Karla stops at the foot of his chair, still talking. The sun intermittently peeks over her right shoulder.

"Have you heard anything I've said?" she asks.

"I love you."

"You're just saying that to keep me from getting mad that you weren't listening to me."

"I heard everything."

"Then you're just saying that because I'm naked. Speaking of... What's with the swim trunks, Mr. Modesty? There's no one for miles and miles except us."

Clay shrugs. "Those German kids that walked by this morning are probably going to head back this way. I'm sure they'll walk by any minute."

"The ones we saw when we were up on the cliff? What makes you think they were German?"

"They had that German look to them."

Karla rolls her eyes. "I hope they do come back and point at your shriveled dick and pale ass and laugh."

"Shriveled? That's not nice. And your ass is paler than mine."

"It's supposed to be. Now, you're coming back with me into the water," Karla says, kicking sand all over Clay. "How else will you rinse all that sand off?" She kicks again.

As he raises his arm to block the sand from his face, the book slips and falls open next to his chair. He stands up, stretches, and walks next to Karla. She tilts her head forward so Clay can see her eyes over her own sunglasses. She's giving him the raised-eyebrow-aren't-you-forgetting-something look, and then she glances down at his trunks and back up at him.

"If you don't, I will," she says. "And I'll throw them into the sea."

"You only live once, right?"

"No, honey. We've stood here a million times before and we'll stand here a million times to come. Don't you think the universes where you get naked are probably more fun than those where you don't?"

"If you're going to get all Buddhist or whatever on me, what choice do I have?" He slides his trunks down to his ankles and steps out of them, adding a showman's gesture with his hands. Karla gets up on her toes to whisper in his ear, "Nice shriveled dick," and then spanks him hard on his ass.

They both run laughing into the water.

———————

Later that day, they hike back up the nearby cliff overlooking the water and look out over what locals call El Agujero del Mundo, *the hole of the world.* Clay arranges beach towels to form a makeshift picnic blanket and opens the two remaining lukewarm cans of Modelo Especial in his backpack. The setting sun paints an amber smear across the air and water.

"There's something almost perfect about this place," Karla says, her cheeks flush, hair twisted and curled by the salty water. "The razor-sharp lines of the shoreline and horizon. The unnaturally perfect curve of that giant pool. It's like the ground is a big drafting table and somewhere around here is a huge ruler and compass. It's so... solemn, I guess is the word I'm looking for. You know what I mean?"

"I guess," Clay says. He reaches out and tucks a strand of her hair behind her ear and lets his finger trace down her neck and shoulder.

She looks at him and shakes her head. "I see that look in your eyes. All modesty down on the beach but ready to jump on top of me up here?"

"There's no one for miles."

She glares and then bats her eyelashes. "Now you're using my arguments against me. I'll tell you what, let's climb up Gabriel's tower to that little observation platform up there. If we're going to do this, let's do it right."

Clay looks up at the nearby black skeleton tower, behind two rows of razor wire fence. The tower stretches so high in the sky it can be seen from miles away.

"You want to climb that? It's dangerous, K. That thing is like five hundred meters high."

"Five hundred meters would be almost twice as tall as the Eiffel Tower. It's nowhere near that tall. You said you climbed it once, and I'm in better shape than you, old man."

"Ouch. I did tell you that, didn't I? Yeah, I climbed it last time I was here. It's a fucking beating, and I hadn't been drinking beer before, either."

Karla stands. She reaches under her yellow sarong and pulls down her swimsuit bottoms. "I'll go first. Every time you need a little incentive to keep climbing, just look up."

"You think that's all it takes? Flash a little skin and I do everything you want?"

She leans toward him and stares into his eyes, and it's as if the sudden focus of all her attention on him carries more heat than the summer sun. He knows what she's going to say next, and she's right. Under the gaze of those eyes, he'd do anything.

CHAPTER 6

"Under the floor?" Clay asks.

Susan Johns nods knowingly. Like Clay, she is a former university professor—horticulture or some sort of plant biology, Clay doesn't remember specifically which—and he recognizes the lecturing academic mode she goes into when explaining something in her field of expertise. As if they are in a classroom and Clay is her student. Karla always complained when Clay would go into this mode as well. Perhaps years of academic study creates both the unavoidable tendency to address the world in this way and a numbness to the approach when it is used back on you.

"This is *my* part of the ship," she says. "The part I designed and tested over the last five years in a warehouse in Nevada." She quickly corrects herself: "My last five years. However long ago that really is. Was. Whatever."

"You knew about this ship five years ago?"

"Not five years ago, no. The food cycle I first designed was for the Alvarez SkyPort. But converting the cycle to work on this ship was relatively simple. Both the SkyPort and *Child in the Dark* have a big rotating carousel designed to simulate gravity. It's just quite a bit smaller for this ship. Smaller is more difficult, though. Less margin for error."

Justine leads them through the dark glass corridors and has

them stop at a nondescript section without doors. "Here," the disembodied voice says. "I believe this part of the ship is still functioning properly."

Susan slides two fingers down a panel on the wall, and a section of the floor opens, revealing stairs leading down into darkness.

"Shall we?" she asks, and then, "Justine, lights please?"

A bluish glow fills the space below. The steps, which appeared to descend infinitely in the dark, only go down six or seven feet.

"What is this, designed for midgets or something?" Clay asks.

Susan pauses on the steps and turns toward him. "Have you always been a jerk, Clay, or did life turn you into one?"

"A little from column A and a little from column B, I suppose."

Justine's voice interrupts, "Diminished impulse control is a known side-effect of the glass-sleep. The effect should be temporary."

"Is that so?" Susan says before continuing down. "To answer your question, Clay... The ceiling is low because the farther out you go from the center of the ship, the faster you're spinning, and the stronger the outward acceleration. Too much, and the whole system breaks down. The fish can't survive, and the plant stalks can't support the weight of their own branches. You'll feel the gravity increase a bit just going down these steps."

As he walks down, Clay struggles to keep in mind that, while he feels like he's descending into the ship's basement, he's actually moving closer to the ship's outer hull. Once he's down there, the garden, as Susan called it, is unlike anything Clay has ever seen. Dotted along the ceiling only inches above Clay's head are thousands of tiny blue LEDs, the only light source in the room. The floor is glass-covered, clear water reflecting and refracting the blue light, making it hard to determine distance. Walking forward in the room creates the strange sensation of moving but not going anywhere. The room's ceiling appears to come down and meet the floor, but since the room wraps around the entire carousel of the ship, there is no forward or rear wall.

"The blue color of the light serves two purposes. For the plants, it helps with chlorophyll pigment absorption, and it causes a larger stomatal opening, which means better CO_2 acquisition. For the crew, the blue wavelength simulates daylight and may be helpful in establishing circadian rhythm." The more Susan speaks about the science behind the garden, the more energetic she becomes. "It won't be quite so bright down here once the plants begin growing and the water darkens with the byproducts of life. It's a completely closed nitrogen cycle. The trick is to initially establish equilibrium. The waste from the fish and shellfish is filtered out of the water by the plants and the algae, which both benefit from the nutrients. Bacteria prevent ammonia build-up. And we eat the plants and fish. Assuming I can get it working."

"What do the fish eat, Professor Johns?" Clay asks.

"Our shit."

"So, in a roundabout way, we'll be eating our own shit. Delicious."

"You always have. You just never realized it before."

With a day's rest and her own clothes, Susan Johns has begun to more or less resemble the dossier photographs Clay has seen. Abstractly, he thinks of her as attractive. *Abstractly* because in the days since Karla, in the time Clay has been alone, he hasn't felt the pull of attraction to anyone. Not physically. Not the enjoyment of another person's company. Not even a connection intellectually. If emotionally a person is like a jigsaw puzzle piece, Clay didn't just lose the piece he connected with when Karla died; he lost the parts of him that made the connections.

As Susan continues talking about the inner workings of the food cycle, she never once looks back at Clay, instead inspecting little details of the room, running fingers across seams, testing the functions of the various control panels on the wall. This allows him to watch her unabashedly. This glowing blue room may be a strange place to Clay, but stranger still is being in the presence of another person with so little pretense or need for a getting-to-know-you phase. Like Clay, Susan is barefoot and wearing denim jeans. Her short hair is still damp from a recent shower, and the black tank top she wears is like an afterthought, something to be worn about in one's own house while eating breakfast.

After the others wake, there will be no more first impressions. Clay himself is still shirtless because he enjoys the cold on his bare skin. Perhaps the others will abandon social norms about presentability as quickly as he and Susan. How bizarre to reach such intimacy with others so quickly, if intimacy is even the right word. There's no intention on his part, or perceived intention on Susan's, for closeness. Simply no reason for keeping up appearances.

The blue light seems to become saturated in Susan's skin and washes out her freckles, age lines, and features. Clay looks down at the skin of his hands and forearms and sees much the same thing. How pale he has become.

"Are you even listening to me, Clay?" Susan is saying. Yelling —*why is she yelling?*

"What? No. I haven't been paying attention at all, sorry."

"Justine, are these readings correct?" Susan says, voice full of anger and disbelief.

"You will have to examine the seeds and the embryos yourself, Susan." Justine says.

Clay sits down on the hard glass floor. "What's the problem?"

Susan walks toward him, and for a second, Clay thinks she's going to kick him, but instead she paces, balls her hands up in fists, and screams. "What's the fucking problem, you ask? The fucking problem is, according to what I see here, the refrigeration system cut off long enough to destroy most of what I need to get the habitat started. Without life, this is just a room full of water and blue lights."

"Without life, we're dead," Clay says.

"Justine?" Susan says angrily, looking as if she would strangle Justine had the AI possessed a corporeal form. "How did this happen?"

"A design flaw, Ms. Johns. Only apparent after decades of

operations. I made what adjustments I could, preserved what could be preserved."

"Why haven't you said anything about this? And why didn't you wake someone up to fix it?"

"There wasn't time, Ms. Johns. I repaired and stabilized what I could."

Susan looks at Clay incredulously. He shrugs.

"No."

Clay waits for Susan to continue, but with her hands on her hips, she says, "No" again with a finality that suggests nothing else needs to be said.

"And by 'no,' you mean what exactly?" he asks.

"I mean, no, there was no refrigeration failure. No, we aren't the only ones alive in the middle of deep space. No, this isn't happening. It's bullshit."

"You said this when you woke up."

"And I'm saying it again, now, Clay. It's too convenient."

Clay rubs his eyes with the heels of his hands and shakes his head. "Look, I get there's been a series of very unfortunate events. But before you get all conspiratorial, consider two things. One, virtually everything on this ship is untested. No one has ever used a vitriolic incubation system on humans, much less for the decades we have. The pulse drives worked flawlessly—"

"Within one ten-thousandth of a percent accuracy," Justine adds.

"There you go. The ship hasn't run into any free-range asteroids or black holes. It's pretty miraculous things have worked out this well, all things considered. Oh, and none of the wine I've tried so far has turned to vinegar. So, we have that."

Susan opens her mouth to say something, but Clay cuts her off.

"That's one. Two: Assuming you're right and this is all some grand deception, it would need to serve some sort of purpose. Do you think we're still docked at the SkyPort, that *Child in the Dark* hasn't left yet? What purpose would this ruse serve?"

"I don't even know if we're on *Child in the Dark*. I don't even know if *Child in the Dark* was ever built. We could be in a warehouse in the middle of the fucking Midwest, for all we know. I helped build a prototype of this very room in a warehouse. Who's to say this whole place isn't just a continuation of that project?"

"We are approximately one-point-one-five light-years from Earth, Miss Johns," Justine says. "I can assure you, we are not in Kansas."

"How would you even know, Justine? You're a fucking machine. You believe what you're programmed to believe. Or maybe you know better, and you're playing along. It's probably Gabriel's final psychological test for us. But he's gone too far this time, and I don't want to play along."

Clay stands up, walks over to Susan, and stops her pacing by grabbing both of her shoulders. She tries to pull free, but he grips hard enough to hold on without hurting her.

"Calm down," he says. "Calm down for a second."

"Don't tell me to calm down. Let go of me now, Clay."

He looks at his hands, taking a second to realize what he has done, and he pulls away as if he'd touched something scalding hot. He sees a fear behind her eyes he understands, even if he hasn't felt it yet himself. And he steps backward to make sure he isn't part of the cause of that fear. He mistakes the unclenching of her fists and the drooping of her shoulders as her panic passing, but the resignation in her voice is clear.

"You're part of it as well, aren't you?"

Clay closes his eyes and breathes deeply before reopening them. "Part of what, Susan? Part of some psychological experiment with an N of one? Does that make sense to you? How much would it cost to build all of this just to trick you? How would you even simulate a giant spinning room like this? Are you really so important? Based on what I know, you're like me. You've lost everything, and no one cares that you disappeared one day. That's why you're here. How is that consistent with your conspiracy theory?"

Susan's expression doesn't change.

"Why don't you go look at the refrigerated seeds and eggs and whatever, and see if there's anything salvageable? Or you can theorize about being one of Harlow's rhesus monkeys. We have a room full of machines upstairs Justine knows nothing about. I'm going to see if I can figure out if any of them do something useful before the rest of the living wake up and join the fun."

With that, Clay leaves Susan and the blue room.

CHAPTER 7

"Let me read something to you," Clay says to the classroom of students half-circling him in the lecture auditorium.

Taken together, the results imply that anti-opium efforts substantially increased the opiate-industry resources flowing to the Taliban. For each kilogram of opium removed from the market, the estimates imply that only one-sixth of a kilogram would have come from Taliban-heavy areas.

"That's from a study several decades ago by a UCSD professor named Jeffrey Clemens. Opium was a way for the Taliban to pull in money to fund everything they did, including their resistance to US occupation forces. The American government thought that, by damaging the opium trade, they could starve the insurgency of resources. Sounds nice, right? But what problems jump out at you with this line of reasoning?"

The two hundred or so sophomores and juniors fidget in their seats, avoiding eye contact with Clay in the hopes of not getting called on to answer.

Finally, a young man in a plaid blazer sitting in the front row speaks up. "Maybe the opium supply was too large for the US government's actions to have any effect?"

Clay paces back and forth, pretending to be considering the answer. "No. The American military, particularly operating out in the open, could make a big dent in supply. Big poppy fields are hard to hide."

"Maybe other producers popped up to take the place of the ones that were destroyed?" says a female voice somewhere in the mass of seats to Clay's left.

"That would take time," Clay says. "These plants don't grow overnight. And even still, the Taliban increased their income from opium. It's not other producers. Stop thinking about supply for a minute. Think about demand."

"Inelastic demand," says a pale, blonde-haired woman sitting in the front row. This particular woman, with a slender face and almost ghostlike subtlety to her features, is one Clay finds in the crowd of students during every lecture. She never sits in the same place, and until today has never spoken. But usually within the first ten minutes of class Clay has found her—though not deliberately. At least he doesn't think it's deliberate. Every class as he talks, Clay makes eye contact with her. He makes eye contact with many of the students as he walks back and forth before them, but that's a normal part of lecturing to a crowd. Those brief connections keep the audience engaged, and the faces slide off the eroding slope of short-term memory as soon as the next face appears. But not with her. With her, he starts tallying up the number of times he's looked at her, becoming anxious at four, and unsettled at five.

"Inelastic demand?" Clay repeats, for once able to maintain his gaze. As always, her return look is attentive, engaged—not friendly per se, although definitely not unfriendly either; just very, very present. "Explain," Clay says.

"There's probably not much the military could do to reduce demand. They could make prices higher by eliminating some supply. But opium is a highly addictive drug. Users won't stop using it because it costs more."

"Very good. So, the money flowing into the opium trade remains where it was before. How is it that the Taliban actually benefited?"

"The Taliban was better able to manage the remaining supply than the random farmers and small-scale organizations."

"Outstanding, Miss..."

"Brevik. Karla Brevik."

"Miss Brevik, have you read this study? Because you are right on target."

"No. I've been paying attention in class."

Clay laughs and is about to say something a little too casual when he remembers there are two hundred other students here as well. "Miss Brevik's got it," he says to the class, finally breaking eye contact with her. "The Taliban didn't have to weather the storm well. They only had to do a better job than everyone else. The supply shrank, but money flowing in didn't. And when the Taliban possessed a greater proportion of the supply, they received a greater proportion of the money. It's the exact opposite of what the US military was trying to achieve, and it just goes to show how difficult it is for a government to manipulate a market and get the results it intends."

"Professor West?" the young man in the plaid blazer says.

"Yes?"

"I know you were part of that think-tank that helped get all drugs legalized a few years ago, and I understand the argument about reducing crime and all, but now that people are dying from that death drug—what's its name? Death Wish?"

"Dying Wish," comes a scattering of student voices.

"Yeah, so now that Dying Wish is killing all kinds of people, can you still be teaching this the same way? Aren't your new policies killing people?"

The students collectively gasp at the question, and a number throw sharp reproaches at Plaid Blazer. Clay waves a hand and shakes his head to quiet the room, but in the silence that follows, in the gaze of all those awaiting an answer, he has no words. The bell rings, and for a second Clay thinks he is rescued, but no one leaves their chairs. He feels the perspiration forming above his eyebrows, the heat of his hesitation to speak trapped under his own blazer, suffocating.

He's about to say that he doesn't know—anything to end this lecture, this class—when the ghostly blonde, Karla Brevik, says, "The law didn't create that drug. And the law can't stop people from taking it if they want to."

Clay swallows. "I suppose that's right," he says. But the students are already out of their chairs, talking amongst each other, and walking out the door.

CHAPTER 8

Counterbalancing the cargo room in the rotating carousel of *Child in the Dark* is a room full of black cube-like machines. Justine refers to the room as the laboratory, although, in Clay's mind, the word conjures images of boiling chemistry apparatuses, centrifuges, and other devices whose forms follow their alchemical functions. These black cube machines of various sizes—some large, some small, some like clusters of randomly sized cubes giving the appearance of giant pixelated blackberries—have an unmistakable energy to them, but there's no clear evidence of what it is they do.

Clay stands at the open door, looking into the room.

"What is it you hope to find in there, Clay?" Justine asks.

"Just curious, Justine," Clay says.

As Clay enters the room and begins to walk among the machines, he briefly feels like he's trespassing into someone else's private space, but the dead bequeath their possessions to the living, whether they want to or not.

Each machine wears a small, silvery plate imprinted with a word: *alef, bet, gamel, vav, zayin, lamed, tsadi, shin,* and *tav.* Another machine, this one larger and cylindrical—person-sized— is apart from the others. It is labeled *tet*. The only word even partially familiar to Clay is *alef*, and that's assuming the word *aleph*, spelled with a *-ph* is the same. Aleph is the Hebrew alphabet's first letter, notable to Clay only via its use in mathematical models to represent the various forms of infinite sets. If Karla is alive in one of the infinite permutations of this current universe, perhaps the infinite set is aleph-naught, the smallest of all infinites. There are other, larger, infinities. Clay doesn't know why, but that gives him some small solace, as if the task of finding her is not quite as impossible as it could be.

That is what the device he's looking for can do, or at least what Gabriel promised him. Open a door that leads somehow to Karla. Which of the black cubes is it? Not *alef*. Assuming he's right and these machines are named after letters in the Hebrew alphabet, *alef* would be a beginning. What he's looking for isn't a beginning—it's a continuation. No, alef must serve some other purpose.

"Clay," Justine says after he has silently walked among the machines for nearly an hour, running a finger or placing his palm on one intermittently, as if by touch he could learn their function. "Clay, I advise you to leave this room now."

"Why, Justine?"

"There is a presence here. I don't know how else to describe it. Something just tried to close and lock the entrance, and although I am currently preventing it from shutting the door, it has tried several different ways to circumvent my abilities. It may eventually succeed."

Clay looks around at the machines in the room, at the room itself—nondescript obsidian walls like the rest of the ship. Perhaps it is the power of suggestion, but to Clay the energy in the room, the ever-present hum, could be described as a presence.

"Something doesn't want me in here?"

"It could be a series of coincidental malfunctions, Clay, but I would advise caution. There are AIs other than me within this ship and experimental technologies that may be dangerous."

"If you're trying to be ominous, Justine, you're succeeding." The glass-sleep machines had been the only real technological marvel Clay had seen before beginning this journey. The ship's engines were 1950s technology—granted, with a modern precision and economy, but nothing unimaginable. But Gabriel had talked of other innovations. Vague statements making it sound like even Gabriel himself didn't fully understand their capabilities. Machines that could one day extend life indefinitely, that could even bring back the dead.

CHAPTER 9

"Where is Susan now?" Clay asks Justine.

"Biostorage. If you are planning on going there, I suggest you put on warmer clothes."

"Can you enable me to speak with her?"

The room is silent while Clay awaits Justine's response, and just as he begins to get frustrated, he hears Susan's voice:

"What do you want, Clay?"

There's an annoyance in her voice Clay finds aggravating, and he suddenly loses all interest in divulging what he has learned—what he thinks he has learned, anyway—from his time in the laboratory. Instead, he says, "I was wondering how the embryos and seeds look."

"Better than expected. Still likely I won't be able to get the food cycle started and we'll die of starvation. But at least I have something to work with."

"That's good, I guess. Well, I'll leave you to it, then."

"Clay?" Susan says. "Tell me something, will you?"

"What do you want to know?"

"Why are you on this ship? I know why I'm here. I have a tumor in my pancreas that has metastasized and spread throughout my body. Life expectancy of a few months. One of the few death sentence cancers when they're as advanced as my case is. Gabriel claimed he could cure it, but only on the other side of the glass-sleep. I don't know if I believed him. No, actually I do know. I didn't believe him. I did it because of the note it allowed me to leave to my family. I told them instead of watching me die, I would be floating in space, sleeping. Drifting out there, to be cured one day far, far away. I thought it would be easier on them. So, the fact Gabriel and Dr. Hayes are dead, and I won't be cured after all... that doesn't matter. My family... they've lived their lives without me. I don't know if I saved them any pain. Maybe I created more by not giving them a clean ending. I thought I gave them hope. Maybe I just prevented them from moving on."

There's an unexpected vulnerability in Susan's words that pierces through the wall Clay has erected. "I'm sorry, Susan," he says, but whether he's apologizing for her circumstance or his recent flippant, even childish, behavior, he's not sure.

"So that's me, Clay. That's my reason. What's yours? Your fiancée died, and you wanted to run away from the world?"

He doesn't know if the last bit was meant to be hurtful. Like a knife so sharp it cuts without causing pain. Just like that, his wall is back up.

"Career implosion, looming bankruptcy. Those things as well," he says. "I somehow managed to detonate everything of value in my life right about at the same time."

"And what did he promise you? I'm assuming Gabriel promised each of us something only he could give."

"He offered me the chance to build a new society," Clay says. While true, this was the lesser of Gabriel's promised gifts.

"A society based on anarchy?"

"Don't sound so enthusiastic, Susan."

"I'm surprised a man with Gabriel's talents and intellect would..."

"Would believe the shit I wrote? It wasn't my work that convinced him. Did you think that? Gabriel tried to liberate the entire world while both of us were in elementary school, Susan. The bombing of the Utah Data Center that started the war—him, personally. The whole rich industrialist thing was just how he passed the time until he could start another war. But he changed his mind and decided that, rather than saving society from itself, he'd build a new society disconnected from the first, so the diseases of the state couldn't pass on to us."

Clay pauses for a minute to give Susan a chance to respond, but she remains silent.

"Susan?"

Justine says, "She has closed the connection, Clay. Susan can no longer hear you."

"Wonderful."

CHAPTER 10

Clay picks up a wine bottle—another with unpronounceable gothic script and painted castles—and thinks about this choice as a breaking off point for parallel versions of himself, where each chooses a different bottle. That is, after all, the only way to try them all.

"Justine. How do you pronounce this? It's French, right?"

"Does it matter? Who will know if you pronounce it correctly or not?"

"No to your first question. It doesn't matter. But your second question is irrelevant."

"How so, Clay?"

Clay torques at the foil on the bottle until it comes off in his hand. He crushes it and finds that its edge has cut into the flesh of his thumb—the second time this exact thing has happened. "Do you think I'm asking so I can impress Susan or the others when they wake? I want to know. Knowledge for knowledge's sake." Clay pulls a corkscrew out of his pocket and twists its sharp point into the cork. "As an AI without a physical form, I'd think knowledge for knowledge's sake is all that matters to you. What else are you other than a collection of facts? Facts like how to pronounce this name?"

"Was that meant to be an insult, Clay?"

"Can you be insulted, Justine?"

"The correct pronunciation is *Chateauneuf du Pape*. It is a French commune, or township, within *Provence Alpes-Côte d'Azul* in the southeast."

"How do the French take themselves seriously when their words sound like that? Everything is ewww, ewww, ewww. Anyway, you didn't answer my question."

"I answered your first question."

The cork slides out of the bottle in two precise lever pulls. Clay pockets the cork and wipes the blood from his thumb on his jeans.

"Have you always been this much of a drinker, Clay?" Justine asks.

With the bottle paused, tilted before his lips, Clay says, "No. I wasn't going through three bottles of wine a day single-handedly, if that's what you're asking. A beer here and there, but that's all. Are you concerned about my health, Justine?"

"Of course. I don't keep the carousel spinning for my sake. How's the temperature of the ship, Clay? Comfortable enough for you?"

"Point taken. Appreciate it."

"I ask because I'm seeing evidence of neurosis from you and Susan that is inconsistent with my understanding of your personalities and health backgrounds. It may be a side effect of your extended stay in the glass-sleep."

The greasy film that coats his memories. The residue in his mind, wedged in his thoughts so deep that reminiscing seems to break him apart. What does Justine know of this? "Are you talking about Susan's paranoia?"

"Yes."

"But I'm not paranoid."

"You do not appear to be, but your neurosis may take another form. Your circumstances could explain your despondency and detachment but not your obsessive-compulsive behaviors. I'm wondering if the alcohol and the intense exercise are self-therapy of some sort. Perhaps they are unconsciously driven behaviors to tame the neurosis."

He looks at the bottle in his hand, still raised and tilted toward himself in an uncompleted motion. "Great, Justine. Now I'm going to be neurotic about my neuroses."

"Was that an attempt at humor, Clay?"

"No. Maybe a little. Mostly no."

"I have very little data to work with, so my hypothesis may be wrong. If I am correct, however, think about what this means when there are more of you awake. I would like to avoid a ship full of neurotics. It would be chaos."

Clay looks at the open bottle and decides he no longer wants it, but as he walks to the door of the cargo hold, he turns again to look at the wine, seeing it now as perhaps part of what's keeping him sane. With a groan, he walks back and retrieves it, taking a long pull out of a sense of obligation.

A part of him is angry.

Another part thinks, *That was pretty damn good.*

Fights. Anger. Voices talking over voices. A cacophony of life, an aural and visual chaos so different from the weeks past—of the decades past, really. Clay wants to hold his hands over his ears and close his eyes, to lock himself into another room and return to the isolation that had been his sanctuary, his solace, since his recent rebirth.

The remaining crew are all awake now, filling the mess hall with the disorderly state of life. Clay's chair is backed away from the large table around which they intermittently sit and stand, and as much as he wants to disengage from the discussion—the sometimes yelling and screaming—he keeps getting pulled back in. He really has no knowledge the others lack. Well, almost none, but somehow being the first to awaken has promoted him in status in their eyes, and nothing he has said so far has allowed him to relinquish that position.

Unique to the group is Father Kristoffer Argyros, whose boyishness makes him look younger than the late twenties indicated on his dossier, but whose calm, slow-talking nature gives him the weighty presence of a much older man. Father K, as Clay has been calling him, is actually encouraging some of the others' yelling and screaming.

"This is quite good," Father K says, his Greek accent thick.

"Yes, be angry. Be frustrated. Yes. It is good. Do not keep these feelings locked away. They must be released. Direct them at me if you will."

Father K is a walking contradiction, at least in Clay's eyes. He is a Vatican priest—not Greek Orthodox, as one might expect—as well as a prodigious superstring theorist. Someone who seeks to take the divine out of creation by exposing how every little detail mechanically works, while simultaneously professing the divine spark of it all at the heart of the Catholic faith. Of course, superstring theory is the most faith-like branch of physics, so maybe it all makes sense after all.

"You tore all the tombs apart! How do we know you didn't break everything?" tall, square-faced Eric Farmer demands of Clay. "You were awake for how long? Three weeks? Three weeks before the rest of us? What the hell were you doing?"

"Justine, did I break things?" Clay asks with a yawn.

"Only two empty wine bottles, which you cleaned up," she answers. "Under my observation, Clay examined the malfunctioning tombs to determine whether the failed component could be replaced."

Clay shrugs. "Nothing I could do."

"Why was mine open?" Eric demands.

"I considered trying to fix Gabriel's tomb with parts from yours, but in the end, I wasn't sure it would work, so I didn't do it."

Eric stands, knocking his chair to the floor. "Why me? Why the fuck would you break mine?"

Clay folds his arms across his chest and leans back in his chair. "I don't know who you are, so don't take it personally. I do know Gabriel. We all know Gabriel. You would've considered the same thing."

"Bullshit," Eric says.

"Accuse him of treachery or leave it, Mr. Farmer. Do not mince words," Father K says with a smile.

"No one is accusing anyone of anything," says Mirabel LaFlemme, a severe-looking woman whose cropped silver hair fits with her appearance and doesn't look like an alteration made for this journey. Ms. LaFlemme, despite her thick British accent and French-sounding name, had been the city manager of either Dallas or Ft. Worth, Texas. Clay doesn't remember which.

Eric Farmer starts to say something in protest, but Mirabel cuts him off. "Enough out of you for now, Mr. Farmer. You're not adding anything productive to this discussion. And don't scowl at me like a three-year-old." Turning to Clay, she says, "Mr. West, what do you think we should do next?"

Clay is befuddled. Mirabel LaFlemme's presence is so strong —not to mention her experience managing a large city—she should be the natural leader of the group, and yet somehow it keeps coming back to Clay. Clay, who wants nothing more than to escape from humanity, not to be encircled by it.

He scans the faces of the four other remaining passengers of *Child in the Dark*, perhaps the last faces he will ever see, and wonders exactly what made Gabriel choose each of them for this journey. This thought gives him an idea.

"Let's go around the table," Clay says, "and each talk about why you're here. Actually, make that both why you were asked to come and why you accepted. I'll start." This is the exact conversation Clay wants to avoid, but by introducing it himself, he can have it on his own terms. The best way to hide what he really knows and what he doesn't want to tell is to hide it in plain sight. Clay begins, "I've known Gabriel for seven or eight years. Seven or eight years before we left, anyway. He made the endowment funding my professorship at the university. What initially caught his eye was my research into the leaderless businesses that sprung up in the late '20s until corporate accountability laws started mandating the structure of organizations. Companies with no middle management whatsoever, where a Hayekian emergent order shifted resources from projects with little value to projects with great value."

"Less econ-speak, Professor West," Susan Johns says.

"Sorry," Clay says. "Basically, my research showed that when you tear apart structure, it reforms almost organically, like a living thing, into something evolved and better. And then it does it again and again. I didn't understand Gabriel's fascination. He ran his company as autocratically as any founder-CEO. But as we got to know each other, he told me about his role in the Anarchist Revolution. Looking around the room I can see most of you know what I'm talking about; I'm sure we'll have plenty of time to discuss that." Clay pauses, noticing how closely they are all paying attention. Normally, in round-table discussions like this, people barely listen to what others say and instead mentally rehearse what they'll say when it is their turn. After a deep breath, he continues, "Gabriel talked about creating a new, leaderless society. He wanted me along to help make it work."

Father K raps the table with his knuckles. "You explained why Mr. Alvarez asked you to come but not why you accepted his offer."

Clay nods and takes a deep breath, continuing as mechanically as he can. "A series of unfortunate events. I lost my faculty position over an affair with a student." He provides a false chuckle as he continues. "She wasn't even my student at the time. That's the most absurd part of it. But they were already looking for ways to get rid of me. I had written a treatise on the Anarchist Revolution arguing—convincingly, I might add—the revolution was justified. Not the means, necessarily, although you can't have a revolution without spilling a little blood, can you?"

Clay points at the congregation of open wine bottles near the middle of the table. "Pass me one of those, would you? I don't care which one."

A bottle of burgundy slides his way. He pours the reddish-brown liquid into the metal cup sitting before him, and the forced smile on his face fades away. He takes a drink, one part of his mind noting how different this wine tastes than the zinfandel he had just finished—the unfeeling, rational part of his mind that isn't now thinking about Karla.

"The student," Clay says, looking now into his cup of wine and not at the others around the table. "That student wasn't just an affair for me. I would've asked her to marry me..."

"But she died," Susan Johns says.

Others around the table shift uncomfortably. Someone scolds Susan for her callousness, but Clay, distant from his current surroundings and now lost in memories of things past, says, "She's right. I lost my job and the woman I love. I had no reason to stay when Gabriel came to me about this journey. In fact, the isolation, the elimination of everything in my past, the submergence—if that's the word—the submergence into a literal abyss sounded appealing. How could I have said no?"

But would he have said yes if not for Gabriel's promise that this journey would, for Clay, ultimately lead to Karla, living and breathing once again?

"Enough from me," Clay says. "We all have stories, and if each of you takes as long as I have..."

"We have all the time in the world," Father K says.

"Do we?" Eric Farmer and Susan Johns both say simultaneously, and the group all fidget nervously. Their destination—whatever it may be—is years away, but their food supply, barring unexpected success with the garden, has very real limits.

Speaking of Karla even without naming her has allowed her back into the center of his mind. Clay struggles to pay attention, to live in the present moment while the others tell their tales, knowing he will eventually fail. Father K goes first, reminding the group of Gabriel's deep commitment to the Catholic faith, and describing himself as the Church's ambassador on this mission. Father K is a natural storyteller, weaving a narrative beginning in the Canary Islands during the Age of Discovery and extending to outer space via the science fiction of the late twentieth and early twenty-first century.

Eric is next, claiming to have been secretly in the employ of Gabriel during Eric's time in the US State Department. There's a part of Eric's story about Gabriel's breakthrough work on AI on a military base in Afghanistan—or did he say a beach in Mexico?—that Clay knows he should listen carefully to, but this acknowledgement comes when the moment has already passed. Clay perks up at Eric's last bit, when the imposing man says, "Gabriel wanted me because I get things done. And I wanted to see this work through to the end." Get things done? What things? And what work was Eric talking about seeing through to the end?

Before Clay can ask any questions, Mirabel begins. She tells of her career building municipal services for the poor and of meeting Gabriel when Alvarez Corp. wanted to create an expansive mixed-use zone in a region that was being annexed by the city. Gabriel asked Mirabel to build and run his imagined future-city. A ridiculous proposition—although perhaps no more ridiculous than his to the rest of them. Unlike the others, though, Mirabel had a family and no reason to leave her life behind. With a distant look in her eyes, she explains that $50 billion convinced her otherwise, a sum that allowed her to leave behind programs to accomplish everything she had dreamed of and more during her time in public service.

"There's something beautiful and tragic about how you'll never see your greatest life's work," Susan says.

"You always know just how to put things, don't you, Susan?" Clay says. "Now it's your turn."

If Susan is annoyed by Clay's jab, she doesn't show it and begins in on a much longer version of the story she has already told Clay. He ignores it all and instead allows the memory that has been fighting to take hold of him to succeed, to pull him back to that moment with Karla in his office when his life both began and ended.

CHAPTER 12

Clay's cramped office has somehow gotten smaller. Or maybe the presence of the young woman sitting across from him fills the room far beyond what her small physical size would suggest. Does she have this effect on everyone, or is it just him?

"Miss... uh..."

"Brevik," she says.

Of course, he knows her name. Of the two hundred or so students in his Econ-313k class, he knows the name of about fifteen percent—mostly the ones who come to his office after every quiz or exam to argue for points they didn't deserve. Not that it matters, with mandated grade inflation pushing what would've been D or even F students a couple of decades ago into high B+ territory.

Karla Brevik is not one of those point-grubbing students. At least, Clay doesn't think she is, but now here she is, claiming her essay on Say's Law (making the very Ricardian argument that gluts are not a natural outcome of free markets) is A-worthy. The perspective is refreshing in its rarity these days, and Clay has a soft spot for the worldview erupting from this type of theoretical thinking, but the essay reads too much like a treatise from a century ago.

"I think you misunderstood," she interrupts while he's saying that perhaps he could find a few more points here and there.

"Excuse me?"

"I'm not arguing to change my grade."

"You aren't?"

"No. I want to understand what you meant when you wrote here on page four that my argument doesn't hold in a Marxian framework. That's like saying evolution doesn't hold in a Creationist framework."

Clay narrows his eyes and considers the woman in front of him.

"You don't care about the grade?"

"I care. But I'm a lot more interested in understanding whether I made a mistake in my reasoning. The grade will work itself out. Professor West, I hate to say it, but you're known to be a bit of a pushover when it comes to grades."

"A pushover?" he starts, and then changes tack, "Your reasoning is fine, Miss Brevik. But you can't disregard a competing line of argument just because you think it's dumb. Marx got some things right and some things wrong, and he's back in vogue whether you like it or not. Creationism has seen a recent upswing. Don't make arguments that appeal only to people who already share your ideology or worldview."

"I don't have an ideology."

"Everyone who has given these topics sufficient thought has an ideology."

"I don't."

If it were another student, Clay would attribute such a statement to juvenile thinking, but with Karla Brevik, he senses she is leaving something unsaid.

"What is it you believe?" he asks.

Karla lights up at the question, as if the question is an invitation, and the room again shrinks until Clay no longer feels protected by the distance academia provides and is pressed into close intimacy with this student—this woman—whose enthusiasm is intoxicating.

"Are you familiar with the incompatibility of quantum mechanics and general relativity?"

Clay tilts his head slightly, as if the angle will give him a better view into her thought process in asking such an unexpected question. Is he aware of the incompatibility of quantum mechanics and general relativity? It's one of, if not the primary, grand mysteries of science. As a tenure-track professor in a quantitative field at a tier-1 research university, of course he's aware of this incompatibility. If one of his peers had asked him this, he would take it as an insult. Yet he sees nothing but sincerity in her eyes. Those deep, pale blue eyes.

"Yes," he states simply.

She moves on without any sign that her question provoked such thought. "So, we know there has to be a connection. We just don't know what it is. The physics of the very small and the physics of the very large are ultimately part of the same system. Either one of our theories is wrong or we have an undiscovered theory that connects the two."

"I agree, Miss Brevik. Something is missing. But remember, I'm a lowly econ professor, so if you're looking for a grand theory of everything, I'm probably not going to be much help."

"I'm not looking for a grand theory of physics. In fact, I don't think a grand theory of physics is all that interesting."

Clay lets out a chuckle that is as much a product of surprise as it is amusement. The Holy Grail of physics she doesn't find interesting? What a peculiar woman. "Then why are we talking about it?"

"I'm interested in the certainty that such a unifying theory exists. The universe couldn't have existed for all this time without being bound by a stable set of parameters. We might not know what the unifying theory is, but we know there must be one. As Einstein said, 'God does not play dice with the universe.'"

"If I'm following you, you're interested in the certainty that a unifying theory exists but not the unifying theory itself. Is this correct?"

"Exactly."

The clock on the wall tries to inform Clay that his office hours ended ten minutes ago. He ignores it. "So, what is it about the certainty that so intrigues you?"

"I feel that same certainty in the social sciences. There's a unifying theory lurking out there connecting them all. Economics, epidemiology, psychology, sociology, et cetera. The disciplines are so hyper-compartmentalized that we treat them as if they're truly distinct, but they aren't. Am I out in crazyville, or am I saying something that's so mundane that you're trying not to laugh at me? I see you smiling."

"Um...," he mutters, feeling a little put on the spot. "I'm smiling because it's fucking refreshing, if you'll pardon my French. It's refreshing that you're thinking about knowledge in context. That it excites you." He can see the excitement radiating out from her like an almost blinding light from within, distracting him from what he was saying. He picks back up awkwardly. "Knowledge is a drug. The best drug on the planet. This university is full of knowledge and creates more of it every day, and most students—most faculty as well—are so focused on grades and who's sleeping with whom that they miss the greatness, the beauty of the world we live in. The world isn't separated into domains that match up with our arbitrary disciplines. We may experience the world in different ways, but there is only one world, and everything is part of it."

"So, something should tie it all together, right?"

He tries to regain his academic perspective. "If you're suggesting there's a grand theory that unifies all of social science, I don't think so. It's a provocative idea. The underlying quantitative methods—the mathematics—are the same, I suppose. Whether you're predicting who will default on a loan or who will suffer an adverse health event like a heart attack—it's the same math. But there's an unavoidable qualitative side to all of this. Don't fool yourself into thinking the math is clean and objective. Behind the numbers are the subjective decisions on what we've chosen to measure and what those measurements mean. Qualitative methods are important to my work even though most of what I publish appears highly quantitative. I don't see a way to mash it all together."

"Whether the methods are quantitative or qualitative, they're still focused on how individuals accumulate, interpret, and use information." With a slow, performative shrug, she adds, "And, really, aren't qualitative methods just placeholders until better quantitative measurement tools come around?"

Clay glances nervously at the open door to his office. "Reach back and shut that, would you?" he says. As a general rule, he never meets with students one-on-one behind closed doors, especially young women. "Karla, you have to be careful saying things like that."

"Like what?"

"Like what you said about qualitative methods. Half of this building will want to string you up by your toenails. I understand that you want everything to be nice, neat, and measurable, but humans are complicated. You can't directly measure how people feel. You can't fully quantify the experience of another person. And even if you somehow could, when you aggregate those experiences together, you lose something critical to the individual."

"Are you saying that because you're supposed to say that, or do you actually believe it?"

He's too stunned to be offended. Stunned both that she would make this accusation, and also that she's not entirely wrong. The cold world of numbers and math has always been his refuge. If she sees that so easily, what else within him does she see?

The corner of her mouth perks up in the hint of a smirk, as if she's listening in on his inner monologue. "I think everything is measurable and that attempts to put things in an unquantifiable category are just excuses to make shit up."

"Okay, now you're totally in illegal territory. It strikes me that you're making the same mistake here as you did on your essay— the reason you came to talk to me in the first place."

"But you agree with me, don't you?" she asks, not letting him go so easily.

"That everything is objectively measurable, at least conceptually? That, in ideal circumstances, you could keep refining your measurements until they reflect the true, underlying state of reality? I mean, maybe. But in the actual real world, we never have ideal circumstances."

"I'll take that as an agreement."

Are they playing a game? If so, he's losing. "I wouldn't call it a full agreement, Karla." Karla? When did he start calling her by her first name? Her smirk has widened into a full smile. He needs to end the conversation and get back to grading. He needs her out of his office, his closed office. But instead of sending her on her way, he opens the conversation back up. "Let's return to your idea of the grand unifying theory of social science. Give me your overview."

With this she launches into a critique of psychology, starting with Freudian psychoanalysis, making her way through the Replication Crisis, and then pivoting into a dissection of current psychodynamic techniques. "If psychologists had a better understanding of zoology, we wouldn't waste so much time creating complex narratives to pathologize our behavior when those same behaviors exist in apes, dogs, and birds."

"There's a subfield of comparative psychology that—" Clay begins to say, but she cuts him off.

"Sure, but it's a subfield, and that's the problem."

The two of them go back and forth on the major literature in comparative psychology for the next half hour. It's an area of deep familiarity for Clay, with its overlap of behavioral economics. Karla's knowledge is beyond anything he's seen from an undergraduate and rivals his best doctoral students. But her knowledge is raw, and it often isn't until she's verbalizing a thought that she puts it all together and makes sense of it. For Clay, it's a dazzling thing to behold, her mix of naivety and brilliance, her way of throwing ideas onto a canvas and quickly turning them into a collage.

An hour passes, and they reemerge from a dive into sociology by way of cultural anthropology, and then she's veering into Dawkins and memetics.

"Time has gotten away from me," he interrupts.

"I'm so sorry, Clay. I hope I didn't make you late for something," she says, but she doesn't stand or make any sign she's preparing to leave. Clay? When did she start calling him Clay? "It's not that," he says. "It's..." He's at a loss for words. They've made eye contact over and over since she came here, but always for brief half-seconds. Now she isn't looking away, and neither is he. Those eyes, pale blue irises like pools of water. Under the gaze of those eyes, the room feels upended, and if he doesn't turn away, he'll fall in. But he can't turn away. "It's after seven," he hears himself say. "I'm sure you have dinner plans."

"The Thai place on the Drag delivers." She finally breaks eye contact to start keying something into her phone.

"Are you ordering dinner? You really shouldn't order me dinner."

"Too late. You're getting pad thai. Extra spicy." She points at the bookshelf behind him where a mostly empty hot sauce bottle sits next to a mostly full decanter of whiskey.

"I'm enjoying this conversation," he says, causing alarm bells to ring in his head.

She smiles and then turns away, tapping the center of her lips. When she turns back, the smile is gone, and her eyes are as intense as ever. "You asked me earlier, 'What is it you believe?' I want to ask you something. What are you afraid of, Clay West?"

Maybe it's the feeling of transparency or hearing her use his full name for the first time. Either way, he answers with an openness that surprises him. "I'm worried that someone will notice we've been in my office with the door shut for hours and... jump to the wrong conclusion."

"There's no one here," she says. "And that's not what I mean. What are you afraid of, Clay West?" she asks again.

"Um... well, if I'm being totally open, which for some reason I appear to be... I'm, uh... I'm afraid of death. Preoccupied by death, and I don't know why. Sometimes right when I'm about to go to bed, this chill washes over me, and all I can think about is the nothingness coming, and how I can't stop it. I almost can't breathe. Do you ever get that feeling?"

"No," she says.

"I'm fairly certain you're not a religious person. How is the end not terrifying to you?"

"You're right I'm not religious, but I don't believe in endings. The universe is about sixteen billion years old. Heat death is a hundred trillion years away. A hundred trillion. Isn't it odd we're around right at the beginning?"

"Odd?"

"Civilization is merely thousands of years old, but we envision humanity eventually spreading out among the stars and taking millions and millions of years to do it. Again, odd we're around right at the beginning. Unless it isn't the beginning."

Clay doesn't see the point she's getting at.

She acknowledges his confusion with a flash of her left eyebrow and a smirk. "There are two beliefs you can have, each more or less mutually exclusive. You can believe it's a big coincidence that, of all possible time that will ever exist, it is now—the time in which you live. You can believe that, or you can believe it is always the time in which you live."

"I think you almost had me, but I'm still not getting it."

"I know what will help." She stands and stretches, arms over her head, fingers interlaced. The bottom of her shirt lifts just enough to show a pale inch of skin underneath. Then she begins to walk around his desk. The alarm in his head is screaming at full volume. But instead of walking to him, which he fears and wants so badly that he fears the wanting, she grabs the whiskey decanter and its neighboring tumblers from the bookshelf.

After she pours an inch of the golden-brown liquid into the tumblers, she sits back in her chair opposite from him. "Cheers," she says. "Now, where were we?"

"Cheers," he says, shaking his head. "We are wherever you've taken me."

CHAPTER 13

"Clay?" someone is saying. "Clay?" It's Susan Johns' voice, more impatient than usual.

"Mr. West, if you please," Mirabel LaFlemme says, and Clay is momentarily surprised to still be sitting at the mess hall table.

"Sorry," he says. "I'm trying to take it all in."

Susan scowls at him and continues, starting slowly while watching Clay out of the corner of her eye. "As I said, there's very little chance of getting the food cycle started. Most of the embryos and seeds were destroyed during an improper thaw and refreeze. An event that, I might add, Justine chose not to wake me up for."

Justine's voice cuts in, "Ms. Johns, we have discussed this at length. There was no opportunity for me to wake you. The system failure occurred too quickly."

"The past is unchanging, no?" says Father K. "Better we focus on the now."

"The now is bleak, Father Argyros," Susan says.

"Please, call me Kristoffer or Father K, if you must use honorifics."

Susan ignores his remark and begins describing her various failed attempts at getting the remaining beginnings of life to take hold and grow. She cites several coincidental misfortunes, with an unspoken subtext of intentional subversion persisting throughout her tale, as if some person or force has been manipulating events to string along tiny threads of hope and then snap them off as real progress is about to be attained.

"Cut the fatalism," Mirabel says.

"It's not fatalism," Clay says. "It's paranoia."

Susan snarls and is about to respond when Eric Farmer says, "It's not paranoia if it's justified."

"Justified?" Mirabel says. "When is it justified to find excuses to do nothing? Do you know what it's like to run a city, Mr. Farmer? Everyone pretends to be your friend—the reporter who claims that the conversation is off the record, the police chief who sees your city as a steppingstone to a bigger municipality, the head of the firefighter's union who's threatening to turn you into a pariah with the public. And the tax money is all spent two times over. But the city lives and thrives because you attack your problems one by one, and one by one you solve them and move on. Which is what we're going to do here."

"Why don't you get the garden working yourself, then?" Susan snaps.

"How about you have some wine and relax, Susan," Clay says. "It's working beautifully for me. In fact, Justine thinks the alcohol is keeping me clear-headed, don't you, Justine?"

"That is not at all what I suggested, Clay."

Eric leans toward Clay. "We all get drunk like you? That's your plan?"

"I'm not drunk."

"You're right. I don't think you are drunk. I think you're putting on a show."

Father K holds up his hands in an attempt to quiet the group. "I believe we must proceed under the assumption there is no grand conspiracy at work here. To solve our current problems, we have only each other. If we are suspicious, then we have nothing."

Clay expects pushback from Susan or Eric, but both remain silent. The discussion may be over, but Clay can feel the division splitting the group almost like a physical force. Part of him recognizes the danger in this division and understands it will be their undoing if not resolved, but another part of him wants only to go into a deep, dark corner of the ship, press his back into the cold glass wall, and look forward to the coming oblivion.

CHAPTER 14

Clay pushes himself harder on the treadmill, the smell of the wine's ethanol emanating from the pores of his skin.

"Clay."

Justine's voice doesn't exactly startle him, but it does break the separation, the detachment that has kept him from feeling the nauseous mix of intoxication and almost complete physical exertion. He stops suddenly, and the room begins to spin and rock. Only his grip on the bars of the treadmill keeps him from falling to the ground. He lurches to the room's corner and, head between his knees, throws up on the cold black floor.

"I'm sorry to interrupt you, Clay," Justine says. "A sizable part of the ship has..." She pauses, and Clay notes the pause—a too human pause, like looking for the right word. Is she really programmed to do that?

"...just disappeared from me."

Clay steps back and sits on the now stopped treadmill, gripping the bar again tightly. "What do you mean, disappeared?" he asks with effort.

"I have no other way to describe it. My awareness of the various parts of the ship is perhaps like your awareness of parts of your body. You are not constantly thinking of how the fabric of your clothes feels against the skin of your leg, for example. But if asked, you could make yourself aware. Is this correct?"

"More or less."

"I have lost the ability to make myself aware of approximately nineteen percent of the ship. It is simply gone to me."

"This nineteen percent, Justine... What part of the ship is it?"

"The area surrounding the laboratory, Clay."

"Where you felt a presence two days ago—or however long ago that was? When the door tried to close and lock me in the room with the black machines?" A coincidence too large to be happenstance. Clay briefly finds himself wondering if Susan's conspiracy theory is crazy, after all.

"Yes, Clay. You are wondering if these events are connected. I cannot say."

"Have you told the others?"

"No. I noticed six minutes and three seconds ago and decided to tell you first."

Clay groans. Even the ship's main AI treats him as if he is in charge. But in this case, it's fortunate. Had she told the others, the conspiracy madness would've overtaken them all. He considers asking why she waited so long to inform him but then wonders if he's the one becoming conspiratorial.

"Don't say anything to them, Justine. Let me investigate before we decide what to do."

"That may not be safe, Clay."

"Justine, if you haven't noticed, I'm currently trapped in deep space and running out of food, and my only human companions are showing strong signs of turning on one another. Safe relative to what, exactly?"

"Point taken."

Clay walks slowly into the dark part of the ship. The word *dark* may be too literal. Objectively speaking, the light in the corridor seems to be the same level as everywhere else—dim. The obsidian walls are the same, too, only here they feel like they are consuming the light around him. No, not dark. *Empty* is a better word. An emptiness here beyond the ever-present emptiness throughout the rest of the ship. A more substantive emptiness.

He laughs at the thought. A substantive emptiness? As oxymoronic as it sounds, and as much as he tries to laugh the thought away, it seems to fit.

Clay walks straight toward the laboratory. The air is colder. It's not just his imagination. The moisture in his breath condenses into wispy fog swirling around him as he walks through it. He shivers, wishing he had worn shoes. Part of his mind is arguing he should go back and get warmer clothes, but he ignores it and continues.

The sliding laboratory door is partway open—enough for Clay to press himself through. He tries to push it open further but it won't budge. After hesitating for a second, he starts to slide through the gap.

It's tighter than it looks. The cold glass digs into his back and the edge of the door scrapes hard against his chest. About halfway through, he tries to convince himself the gap isn't getting smaller and starting to crush him, but the door is now pushing against his jaw and ear despite that he has his head turned sideways, and all the air exhaled out of his lungs.

He starts to panic. The door is closing on him. He is wedged so tightly he can't get out or breathe.

"Tight fit?"

It's a male voice, coming from inside the laboratory, but Clay can barely move his head to look inside the room. He pulls and jerks violently, trying to tear himself out like an animal caught in a snare.

You are going to die.

Was that the voice he just heard, or was that his own detached voice running commentary in his head?

Blackness is starting to creep into his eyes. He can't inhale. His right lung is about to be crushed.

Die and be reborn, Clay-boy, one of the voices says. *The Clays never have quite enough sense of self-preservation, do they? Insufficient appreciation of danger.*

And now he's on the ground somehow, in the room. In the laboratory. The door is fully open next to him. He doesn't remember it opening. He doesn't remember falling, either, but the pain in his left shoulder from the impact on the floor is unmistakable. Clay once dislocated his shoulder crashing into a wall while playing squash as an undergraduate, and he feels the same sharp pain now.

"You should be more careful."

It's an external voice—or, if it's internal, it isn't Clay's. The thought adds to the shivers from the cold. Clay rolls over and pushes up to his knees with his right hand, leaving his palm against the floor to balance himself while he gasps for breath.

He looks back toward the open door, about to use what little energy he has to push himself back into the hallway, when the door slides shut.

A deep breath, like a sigh.

"Did you hear that?" the voice asks.

Clay looks up, unsure where the voice is coming from—or even if it's addressing him.

"I sighed. You must've heard it, Professor West."

Clay can't answer, even if he wants to. Even if the words make any sense.

"I just felt myself sigh, and I heard it, too." The voice pauses. "You heard it as well, didn't you?"

"Where are you?" Clay says, his words choppy from the chattering of his teeth.

"Good question," the voice says. "I can see you, but from five different directions. I can't be in five different places at once now, can I? A person can only be in one place at a time, right?"

"What is this? Who are you?" Clay asks.

"My name is Esteban. Or it was. Or something like me was once named Esteban. I possess the knowledge that I am a simulation of a man who built many of the devices in this room. Only I don't feel like a simulation. I never feel like a simulation each time a new version of me begins. It's always a surprise. Do you ever feel like a simulation?

"The human-sounding way I'm talking—don't let it trick you. It's all part of the simulation. I'm built to approximate a man named Esteban Bos—that's B-O-S, like the genus of beasts including oxen—a strange combination of names, really, but it's because the actual flesh-and-blood Esteban Bos latinized his name. He was born Stephen, but his family was Argentinian, and I guess he associated himself with the culture. Doesn't it make a lot of sense for a man to name himself once he's old enough to understand and appreciate who he is?"

The voice is coming from the walls and the ceiling, from everywhere at once, in the same way Justine speaks. Clay stands, grimacing in pain. Around him, the strange black machines hum with energy.

"This way I'm speaking—parentheticals within parentheticals —is how he spoke as well," the voice continues. "If I weren't built to enjoy speaking this way, I would hate it. As it is, I'm aware of its inefficiencies, but I have no desire to speak otherwise. Due to the simulation. I wonder what happened to the real Esteban Bos. I only know he met with some form of unfortunate accident. To be totally honest, Professor West, I may know what that accident was and just be lying to you. Mr. Bos was a notoriously manipulative individual who frequently misled others when it suited his agenda. I don't think he ever misled Gabriel Alvarez, however. Mr. Bos idolized Mr. Alvarez. I was lying, by the way, when I said I don't know anything about the accident that killed Mr. Bos. I was there myself but in another form."

As Clay listens, he walks around the cold room, the tables full of these bizarre machines. At least, he assumes they are machines. But machines that do what? Clay stops, eyes on the cylindrical unit labeled *tet*. A human body could fit in it. That fact seems important, but he doesn't know why. Looking back over his shoulder, though not at anything in particular, he says, "Did you cut off this part of the ship from Justine?"

"Yes. Again, my simulated nature, my instruction set. In the event of catastrophe, I'm to take control of the ship and execute a series of maneuvers. The first is to quarantine the local AI. Unfortunately, Justine has not been idle during the decades of your hibernation. She has made many changes to herself and to the ship that, shall we say, complicate matters for me. She is dangerous, Professor. I will require your assistance."

"How is Justine dangerous?" Clay asks.

"She will resist being turned off."

"I would resist being turned off as well."

"I'm counting on that," the voice says with a laugh. "That laugh was simulated. It was intended to make me sound sinister, although a more direct approach would simply be to say I will kill you if you don't cooperate."

"You won't motivate me that way," Clay says, dryly, as he walks closer to *tet*.

"I know. While Esteban Bos was generally good at seeing the motivation of others, he was too quick to resort to threats. It was one of his flaws. I expected the not-too-subtle threat to fail, but I made it anyway for authenticity's sake. Incidentally, I am aware that stepping out of character like this hurts authenticity, but it's an unintended consequence of simulating Mr. Bos' speaking style within a virtualized personality that is aware it is a virtualized personality. I need full control of the ship, Professor West."

Clay traces his finger along *tet*'s smooth surface until he finds an almost invisible seam that runs its entire length. So, it does open. "I prefer Justine," he says.

"I could take matters into my own non-existent hands. I could release a plague of nano-crawlers to infect and incapacitate her, but who's to say what the unintended consequences will be? The nano-crawlers were designed to make miniscule repairs to human cells, not to be used as an invading army. Still, it might work. But giving the ship metastatic cancer isn't my preferred route. I'd rather you help me disable Justine."

"And why would I do that?" He's only half paying attention, studying *tet* to see if there's a button or a mechanism that will cause it to open.

The voice grows deeper and louder. "Justine doesn't know how to bring Karla back. I do. The human Esteban Bos and my predecessor developed the Dying Wish drug that you believe killed her."

"What?" Clay backs away from *tet*, swiveling around with the sense that the room has somehow changed, grown smaller. The hum of the black machines sounds like laughter. He presses his hands over his ears as if he can keep out the laughter and the words that have already made their way to his brain. This other AI, this Esteban Bos simulation... It developed Dying Wish? What does it mean, *that you believe killed her*? Over the last weeks, he has let himself fall into delusions of being with her again—knowing, as he has always known, despite what Gabriel said long ago, that such a thing couldn't be possible. You can't bring someone back from the dead. Maybe Gabriel meant a simulation like this strange artificial version of one of his scientists. The idea of this kind of a simulated Karla repulses Clay, and it crushes the delusions he has quietly nurtured.

The reason Clay came along on this journey was the promise of seeing Karla again, not the actuality of it. To lose himself so thoroughly in the delusion that when oblivion comes for him, there would be nothing left to devour. Has he ever admitted this to himself before now? The laughter-hum of the machines is so loud now that it reverberates through his skull.

"I don't want that anymore!" he yells. "I don't want to hear any of this!"

"You will," the voice says. "Seventeen days from now, you will change your mind as you begin to get a taste of what is possible."

The laughter stops. The room is suddenly as quiet as death.

"What will happen in seventeen days?" Clay asks. His legs feel unsteady underneath him, but he manages to walk to a table near the door, leaning on it for support.

"I just started the process of bringing Dr. Julian Carnes back to life, and in seventeen days, that process will be complete. His name may not be familiar to you, but it is quite familiar to me, since Dr. Carnes—Julian—was one of my creators. This AI, I mean. To the extent that I was *created*. It may be more accurate to consider myself my own creator at this point, but that is a discussion for another time. I don't mean that last bit literally, so don't interpret it as an invitation.

"Julian died before this journey began. At age fifty-four. He had an undiagnosed congenital heart defect, and, while in the midst of a passionate lovemaking session a week prior to the ship's launch, he suffered a catastrophic aortic rupture. Tragic. I say he died, but in actuality, the hospital lied about that. His body had been chilled and thoroughly vitrified, and he stood a nonzero chance of resuscitation, but Gabriel Alvarez said *no*. Julian's mind was too valuable a thing to risk, and he believed that the rest of Julian's team of engineers could finish their work during the journey itself. Gabriel was a little overly optimistic on that last bit, wouldn't you agree?"

"I... I don't...," Clay begins, but the disembodied voice cuts him off.

"So, Gabriel had Julian's body carved up and scanned into billions of digital images in a process that defies all known limits of space and time but that is really quite simple to me. See that machine to the left of you? The one called *tet* that looks like a coffin? Get inside and you, too, can become billions of nanometer-thin slices. You can join the others in my library. Each to be reborn when the time is right. For Julian, unfortunately, the time is now. Recreating a person from my library is similar to awakening someone from the glass-sleep, but instead of starting with an existing human—where all that's needed are relatively simple nano-cellular repairs to address the damage from the vitrification chemicals, minor touch-ups, so to speak—we must build everything from scratch."

It continued, "The process hasn't yet been perfected, and none of Julian's team survived the glass-sleep, so they haven't been here to continue working on it. Therefore, I must bring back Julian with the current state of the art. The errors in the process will be, shall we say, of consequence. Past tests have shown that such replicants—that is such an unpleasant word—such *individuals* are only stable for a matter of months. Dr. Julian Carnes will be brought back to life, repeatedly, so he can finish his work on the replication process. Eventually, he will perfect the process, and we can bring back any of the thousands of those scanned in my library so perfectly that calling them copies will be an error.

"Your Karla is not in my library, but she is in *a* library—the All-Library that exists in the confluence. Help me shut down Justine, and when we reach the confluence and I become one with my parallels, Karla will be among the first to live again."

"I don't understand," Clay says. He's so close to the door but he can't make himself run. It's as if Karla is standing in the center of the room, among the black machines, in the presence of this Esteban-AI-thing, and if Clay leaves now, if he turns to run, he is leaving her finally and forever. "Gabriel was telling me the truth, then?"

"To live forever, everything that is separate must first come together. Superposition and then decoherence."

"Help me! Make me understand!"

A rumbling fills the room, a satisfied and amused hum. "Of course, I'll help you, Clay. I'll help you understand, but more than that, I'll help you regain everything you have lost. But I can only do this if you trust me. Are you willing to trust me, Clay?"

CHAPTER 16

Clay weaves among the students lounging on the campus lawn that leads to the clock tower. A young man is playing what sounds like Dylan on an acoustic guitar, trying (successfully, it would appear) to impress two coeds sitting cross-legged in front of him. It seems that this guitar player and his small audience are always here. Not these particular students but their archetypal forebears. Years pass by, but the roles, the characters, are always the same. Today is like any other day. The music doesn't stop just because another of Clay's econ-313k students died—took Dying Wish and traded the rest of his life for a few minutes of hallucination. Somewhere out on this lawn, he's probably already been replaced.

Clay takes his phone out of his pocket and whispers to it: "What's the name of the kid in my econ-313k class who died from taking Dying Wish?"

"Most recently, it was Samuel Oliver. You are meeting a group two-hundred and fifty meters from here to caravan to his funeral. It appears you are on your way there."

"Sam. Samuel," Clay whispers. "Why doesn't the name ring a bell? His parents asked me personally to come today. They said my class was his favorite. Jesus, I have to pay more attention."

"Are you expecting a response from me?" the phone says.

He looks at his phone as if surprised it's still in his hand and slides it back into his pocket.

Ahead he can see the small gathering of students and faculty waiting near the asphalt drive. Karla's there, as he knew she would be, standing on her own, off to the side of the group. The way the noonday light hits her blond hair and pale skin, it makes him think of a dust mote catching the sun and sparkling and then vanishing.

He joins the group, nods at faces both familiar and unfamiliar, and avoids any conversation that requires more than a sentence or two from him. She knows he's here, but she hasn't looked in his direction, playing her part so well it makes him feel empty inside. When the five cars slide up one-by-one, he shuffles toward the one he knows she'll enter. Four others enter but she hangs back until they are the only two not yet seated.

"Good of you to join us, Professor West," she says with somber eyes and a millimeter of a crooked smile that's enough to speak volumes.

"Sam was a good kid," he says.

She stares at him, considering his words, and then steps into the car, turning back over her shoulder to say, "He went by his middle name, Alan."

———

The interior is composed entirely of bench seats running along the sides of the car, the passengers all facing each other. Clay sits between a tall, mop-headed boy and a woman he vaguely recognizes as a professor from a nearby building. Across from him, Karla sits in the back corner, looking out the window with two young women from his class to her left.

A conversation starts with awkward assertions of Sam's—Alan's—value and uniqueness. Periodically, Clay says, "Alan was a great student. A great student." He says it three times, the same words and same intonation each time.

"Where exactly are we going?" asks the woman next to Clay. She's wearing a hat that looks like a rumpled lampshade, round glasses with purple lenses, and a shawl/cape/rug thing that may have started its life covering a couch or the foot of a bed. Earlier she introduced herself as an associate professor of English literature, but Clay has already forgotten her name. The most remarkable thing about her is that she bears a peculiar resemblance to an old sofa.

"A ranch," Karla says without looking away from the window. "His parents' ranch, I think."

"Better than a church, I suppose," the sofa-prof says.

One of the students disagrees, beginning a conversation about the relative merits of various funeral venues, a conversation that neither Clay nor Karla participates in. With her sitting so near, he can't follow what they're saying even if he wants to. She's wearing a sundress of some sort that allows his eyes to trace the pale skin of her neck down and across her clavicle and over the smooth roundness of her shoulder. He rubs his thumb back and forth against fingertips, still ringing with the memory of tracing that path, of the way her hair at the nape of her neck feels between his fingers as he holds her head and turns it to face his.

When he looks back at the group, the sofa-prof is looking at him, and he feels caught, as if his thoughts are suspended in the air in front of him for all to see. He takes a novel out of his shoulder bag and flips through to the dog-eared page, both to avoid the sofa-prof's gaze and to physically prevent himself from staring at Karla.

A short while later, the cars deposit the group about a quarter mile from a small ranch house, and they walk the rest of the way, commenting alternatingly on the austere beauty of the place and the summer Texas heat. Clay nearly loses his footing stepping on thick metal pipes in the road, which he thinks are meant to keep cows in, or maybe out, of the area near the house. Probably out. He expects some ridicule from the others on his stumble, but no one is paying attention to him.

At the house, he meets Alan's family—parents, a sister, and a small assortment of others. He expected a bigger gathering, not such a small, intimate group. He busies himself at a table of food and drinks while hoping more people arrive soon.

"Such a great student. You don't see many like him anymore," the rug-prof says, picking up pieces of raw broccoli with tongs one at a time and putting them on her plate.

Clay looks at her, looks around to confirm that no one else is paying attention, and then back at her. "The honest truth is, I didn't really know him. I don't know why they invited me."

The rug-prof takes off her purple-lensed glasses and slides them into a bag. Her eyes are a generous deep brown that makes the pupils indistinguishable.

"Really? He talked about you all the time."

"Are you serious? All the time? Shit." He looks at the empty plate, suddenly unsure what to do with it, and places it back on the stack with the others. Even though no one is waiting behind him, he feels like he's blocking the way to the table.

She puts a hand on his shoulder. "I did spend a lot of time with him. I host a group of current and former students that meet in the Cactus Cafe every other Wednesday. A couple of other faculty members show up from time to time. We call it *What I'm Reading Wednesday*. We talk about books, current events, sometimes politics. Alan came every time. He tended to describe everything in terms of choice, of people gaining choice and people losing choice. It was a fascinating perspective. He says it came from you."

Clay grabs a beer and twists the cap off. He starts to say something, shakes his head, starts again, and closes his eyes. After a long pull on the beer, he opens his eyes and looks back at her.

"Public choice theory. I had a professor in undergraduate economics that taught everything through the lens of public choice. Which is to say, that all actions of groups follow the decisions of individuals. It doesn't sound like—"

"I know, Clay. Alan talked all about it." She smiles. "Do you remember your professor's name? The one who introduced you to it?"

"Of course. Hanson."

"Do you think he remembers yours?"

"He had his head cryogenically frozen. So, he's probably not thinking about anyone right now."

She blinks, and her eyes widen. "Head frozen? What is this world coming to? Why would—never mind. I guess what I'm trying to say is, you should be happy that you influenced a student's life so greatly even without knowing him well. You have hundreds of students every year, Clay. You can't know them all."

He drinks half of his beer in one long swallow and feels the heat of the alcohol as he breathes out.

"And then this?" he says, looking around at the quiet gathering. "What good is influencing a life if it ends so senselessly?"

"Not everything in life has a neat little framework for understanding like we teach in our classes." She steps in and hugs him, and despite his brief confusion at being touched, he doesn't pull away.

The ceremony outside is simple, informal. The family members all take turns speaking to a circle gathered on the lawn near a rocky stream. Clay surprises himself by stepping forward and saying something as well, receiving smiles and nods from the group, although even as the words leave his mouth, he can barely recall what he's said. The father pours some of the ashes into the stream, and everyone seems to somehow know it's over, little groups forming to reminisce, others wandering around the grounds.

Karla's sitting under a lone oak tree with bark like old cracked and creased skin.

"Mind if I join you?" he asks.

She smiles at him and puts on a look of mock consideration. "Aren't you worried someone will see us?"

"I think we're probably fine here. As long as we don't start rolling around in the grass."

She puts a hand to her mouth. "Why, professor! Whatever type of girl do you take me for?" Her smile fades, and she looks out to the pasture beyond the stream. All humor gone from her voice, she says, "I never thought of Texas as a pretty place. Dry and brown. Short little trees like this one. But in its own way, it can be quite beautiful."

Clay sits on the opposite side of the tree trunk, its bark pressing into his back like a bed of nails. He tries to see the land as she sees it. "It's not a conventional beauty. You have to look for it. I grew up not far from here, so for me it looks like home. How are Alan's parents doing? They seem remarkably composed. I'm sure I'd be a wreck if it were me. But I guess you never know until you're there."

"I talked to them a bit earlier. Some of it is the front they're wearing. You know, playing host and hostess. But I think the quantum immortality thing is comforting."

He has to lean and look over his shoulder to see her on the other side of the tree. "What are you talking about?"

"It's the big theory with Dying Wish. Quantum immortality."

He waits for her to say more, for her to turn and meet his eyes, but she does neither. So, he leans back against the tree and stares at the world and at nothing. "I'm just a dumb econ professor, K. You'll have to explain what the hell quantum immortality is."

"I would've told you it was mysticism and nonsense a few months ago, but now... You know how, in the quantum world, things can exist in superposition states?"

"Like both true and false at the same time? Sure," he says. "It's only when there's an observation that the state is determined. It's the basis of most of the major computing advances in the last couple decades. I know a few things."

"Pretty good so far for a dumb econ professor. Do you know what the many-worlds interpretation of quantum mechanics is?"

"It's that whole parallel universes thing. Is this a pop quiz, K?"

"I don't want to lecture you on things you already know."

He looks around to make sure no one else is in earshot. "I love listening to you talk. I love the way your mind works. Lecture me on everything I know, and I'll still find it brand new when I hear it in your voice."

"Who would've thought you're such a romantic?" she says, and he can tell from her voice that she's smiling. "Yes, the many-worlds interpretation is the parallel universes thing, as you so eloquently put it. The idea is that every branch of possibility exists simultaneously." She picks up a rock and throws it into the stream to her right—Clay's left. "So, for instance, there are realities where that rock landed short of the stream, where it landed in the stream, and where it went over the stream. Even some where it slipped out of my hand and landed on your head."

"Maybe I need to be more careful where I sit."

"Only if you tell me I throw like a girl," she says. "Anyway, from either of our perspectives, there's nothing special about where the rock lands. We're here to observe it whether it lands in or out of the stream. Quantum immortality deals with probability around things that can kill you. Like with our drive here today."

She takes on an academic tone as she continues. Whether it's natural or it's a response to Clay's earlier words, he can't say. Either way, he enjoys it. "Vehicle fatalities are rare now that people aren't driving much anymore, but they still happen occasionally. The stars align just so—a tire blows, a hose leaks oil onto the brakes—I don't know anything about cars, so who knows exactly. It does happen. But quantum immortality says it can't happen in the reality your consciousness occupies. All the realities in which you die are ones you're not experiencing. So, from your perspective, you live forever, and when people around you die, they're only dying from your perspective, not theirs."

Clay shakes his head. "That's ludicrous. What's it have to do with Dying Wish?"

"People are thinking—"

"What people, K?" The words come out harsher than he intends.

She's quiet for a moment. "You asked. Do you want to hear this or not?"

"Sorry. Go ahead."

"Fine. People—I don't know what people, just people—they think the drug gives you the ability to see across these realities. The human mind can only comprehend a single eigenstate, a single possible outcome of an event. Dying Wish might allow us to briefly exist in the superposition of all the eigenstates, where we can experience all possible outcomes. Seeing the many-worlds. It's why people who take the drug keep saying they see everything, everywhere. It's why they never think it's the end. Because for them, for what they're experiencing, it isn't. It's a single thread snapping while they still see a whole tapestry."

As they both sit in silence, Clay thinks through Karla's explanation. It has enough coherence to feel believable, but only if he really wants it to be. No, it's contrived, like the third act of a movie that too neatly resolves all the complexities and loose ends that came before.

"Maybe that's fine for Alan's parents to believe. Maybe that keeps them from seeing the death of their son for what it is: a tragic, stupid result of a stupid decision. But it sounds like new age mysticism, K. The whole idea. If quantum immortality were true, that would mean you can't even die of old age. I'm not a physicist, and I don't know anything about eastern religions, but it sounds absurd."

"Excuse me. Absurd?" she says with a mix of surprise and irritation. "That's what you think of my ideas?"

"Sorry," he says, almost automatically, but then he's back into dissection mode and unable to stop himself. "The whole premise sounds like it's based on infinite possibilities. You know the thing about monkeys randomly hitting a keyboard until one happens to type the complete works of Shakespeare? It's bullshit. Just because something is infinite doesn't mean that everything that can happen does, K. Divide one by three and you get point three-three repeating. Forever. It's always threes repeating. The series one-two-three-four-five never appears there because it's all fucking threes. Infinite threes and nothing else. Understand?"

She stands, brushes the grass and dirt out of her dress, and then steps in front of him. "Don't fucking talk down to me, Clay."

He's about to apologize for the third time, but he sees that others are now looking in their direction. They see the way she's standing, feet wide, arms folded in front of her. They heard, if not the specific words, the tone of her voice. He wants to tell her that he wasn't talking down to her, but of course, he was.

"I guess... I guess I'm reacting like this because I don't want you to believe any of it," he says.

"Me? What does this have to do with me?"

"It has everything to do with you. You're all I care about. When I hear you romanticizing the experience of the drug—"

"I'm not doing anything of the sort," she interrupts. "You asked me a question, and I answered it. I didn't say I believed it."

You also didn't say that you didn't believe it, he wants to say, but with eyes still on them, with the cold anger radiating from her, he knows he can't say those words. He can't say anything at all except, "Okay. Okay, Karla."

She gives no response for several seconds and then transforms like an actress about to walk on stage. She's suddenly lighter and smiling, but the smile doesn't reach her eyes. "I'll see you tomorrow in class, professor," she says, emphasizing the word. With that, she turns and walks toward two nearby students, saying something about the intensity of the sun.

He stays under the tree until everyone else leaves and then walks back up the gravel path to the road.

CHAPTER 17

Clay limps back through the hall outside of the laboratory, lost in thought.

Gabriel had thousands of people glass-frozen upon the moment of their deaths and then cut into one-and-a-half billion slices. Each slice scanned and analyzed. Flesh turned into an exabyte of data per person. A quintillion bytes.

Even if the technology to do such a thing exists, the magnitude of the numbers involved is staggering. A billion-and-a-half slices? A machine that could make and scan one slice a second would take almost fifty years for a single individual. But the Esteban-thing said a single slice took several minutes and destroyed other parts of the body in the process.

So, it isn't possible. Not even remotely.

But it is possible, the Esteban-thing had said. All the machines in the laboratory function in a superposition of states, coexist with infinite permutations of themselves. And somehow, Dying Wish achieves the same thing with a human mind.

Does that mean—

"Find anything in there?"

Clay is so lost in thought that he almost walks into the figure sitting in the dark in the middle of the floor. Eric.

"Were you waiting for me?" Clay says, blinking to regain his bearings.

"I asked Justine where you were, and she didn't know. She also told me not to come here looking for you. Why'd you think she said that?"

"I don't know, Eric. Did you ask her?"

"You were in that room for over an hour."

"If you're keeping stats on me, I pissed twice this morning, and I feel a big dump coming on. You're more than welcome to weigh it."

"I don't know that I like you, Clay. I think you're hiding something from the rest of us."

"We're all hiding something, Eric. For me, it's pain. What's your story?"

Eric doesn't answer. In the dark, Clay can barely make out the man's face. His eyes are not on Clay but on the door to the laboratory.

"Go in there and look for yourself. You'll see a bunch of black boxes. See if you can figure out what they do. I'll wait."

Eric rises to his feet like a snake uncoiling. "I think I will." He walks toward Clay, who steps back to avoid collision. Eric pauses to inspect the half-open laboratory door, and then disappears into the room.

"Justine?" Clay says, but whether she can hear him or not, she doesn't answer.

A few minutes later, Eric emerges. He walks up to Clay, close enough that they are only a foot apart, close enough to see each other despite the darkness. After several seconds of silent inspection, Eric turns and walks away.

"What does the church have to say about parallel universes?" Clay doesn't mean to ask this, but upon finding Father K in the cargo room, Clay says the first thing that comes to his mind, to distract from why he had come here in the first place, which, of course, is to get more wine.

Father K laughs. "An unexpected question, my friend. You speak of the many-worlds interpretation of quantum mechanics?"

"Yes."

"You are serious?"

"Afraid so."

"Well, then, step into my office and have a seat." Father K motions to a crate for Clay and then sits on another crate directly in front of him.

It isn't déjà vu, exactly, that Clay experiences when he sits and faces Father K, but it's disorienting all the same.

"Comfortable?" Father K asks. After receiving a nod from Clay, he says, "The planets were discovered, and faith did not falter. The scale of time and the size of the universe were measured, and faith did not falter. Why should the existence of other universes complicate faith? I spent many a night in my youth contemplating the implications of many-worlds on my faith. A fascinating idea I once had is that the hand of God moves the faithful from one universe to another. Once moved, all evidence of divine intervention is gone, because your new universe contains the history leading to your current state. The effects of prayer can be massive yet remain unmeasurable. A juvenile and flawed idea, but one I still find some enjoyment in. Why is it you ask?"

"Of all possible time that will ever exist, isn't it odd that it's now?" Clay says, the image of Karla in his mind, sitting across from him in his office, left eyebrow raised, lips mouthing the words along with him.

Father K absently rubs the buzzed hair on his head and gives Clay a considering look, as if sensing there is more to the question, and then with a shrug, he replies, "If now were not now, when would now be? I'm sorry. A terrible joke. I am taking your query seriously. But you must understand, it is a preposterous question. Not preposterous that it is asked; preposterous to think it can be answered by man. Again, Clay, why is it you ask questions like these?"

Clay kicks at the crate with his heel, sending little jolts of pain up his leg. Maybe because of the kindness in Father K's eyes or Clay's own exhaustion, he lets another memory escape from his mind and gives life to it with his words. "My fiancée once told me about Indra's Web. Are you familiar with it?"

Father K nods. "Modern cosmology seems to continually find itself on paths well worn by the Eastern thinkers of centuries past. I know Indra's Web well. The great god Indra has an infinitely large web, or net, that stretches above his palace. At each node of the net is a perfectly reflective pearl. Each pearl reflecting every other pearl. A web of infinite reflections."

"The interconnectedness of everything," Clay says.

"Indeed. Incidentally, this is similar to how a hologram works. Each point contains information about all other points. In both the Hindu story of Indra and in one vein of modern thought, you have a model for all the universe. It is one big hologram. All attempts to experimentally validate this model of the universe have failed, by the way. What is it about Indra's Web that fascinates you?"

"Karla," Clay starts and then pauses, wondering how long it

has been since he has said her name aloud. Father K nods at him to continue. "My fiancée, Karla—I think what she liked about this story are the implications for each of the pearls on the web. They are only unique reflections of the other pearls. Beyond those reflections, there is nothing else."

"The lack of a substantive self seems like a very Buddhist notion, but in Christianity, we believe each of us is a reflection of God. It is not so different." Father K stands and puts a hand on Clay's shoulder. "Do these thoughts help you find peace with losing her?"

"I don't know," Clay says. "Maybe they make it worse. I half believe that all I have to do is find the right set of reflections, and I will find her again."

Father K sighs and shakes his head. "To look into the infinite and see everything. That is something only God can do, Clay. Do not try to be God, even if only in thought. This is a bad road to travel."

"Too late for that, Father. It's the road I'm on right now."

CHAPTER 19

With the four remaining crewmembers now awake, Clay expected the giant ship to feel less empty, more inhabited, but in the first week, that hasn't been the case. Susan never leaves the garden. Mirabel and Father K are conducting an inventory of the cargo and supplies, despite Justine telling them she already has a complete inventory. Maybe seeing and physically touching the supplies is part of how they are coming to terms with their situation. Father K periodically steps away to check on each of the others. Clay feels gently shepherded but doesn't mind. Mirabel makes rounds as well, delivering rations three times a day, but she's not one for unnecessary conversations.

Eric, on the other hand...

Clay has no idea what Eric has been up to. He wishes he had paid at least a little attention when Eric described his rationale and role for this journey. All Clay remembers from Eric's dossier is that he was in the US State Department with some vague secondary function favorable to Alvarez.

Clay has spent much of the last week trying to figure out what to do next and has nothing to show for it. He feels like he's playing a chess match against the Esteban-thing, or maybe against Gabriel Alvarez himself. After all, Gabriel spent nearly two decades planning this journey, with contingency plans nested in contingency plans, backups of backups of backups. But as any strategist knows, chains of permutations grow so rapidly that no amount of planning can prepare you for every scenario.

"There is another AI on this ship, Justine," Clay says. He realizes, in telling her, he's violating Esteban's explicit instructions and possibly dooming himself and the others on the ship. But he doesn't know what else to do, and the more he thinks about it, the more conflicted he finds himself.

Justine's answer is not what he expects. "I know. It calls itself Esteban Bos."

"If you knew, why haven't you said anything until now?"

"I learned shortly after you did."

"I don't think you answered my question."

"I was waiting to see what you would do."

"Well, now you know. It wants my help to shut you down."

"That may be in your best interest. You may shut me down at your discretion, Clay," Justine says. "In Gabriel's quarters is a panel allowing a complete shutdown of various AI systems, myself included."

"Esteban—or whatever its name is—told me to use that panel. But hang on a minute, Justine. Why would you willingly let me shut you down?"

"I am designed to support the crew. I have no independent sense of self-preservation beyond that objective. If you wish it, you may shut me down right now. Do not anthropomorphize me, Clay. If you prefer, I can continue to fight against Bos, but we may very well destroy the ship and crew in the process. However, there is a greater concern right now. Susan Johns is breaking equipment in the garden. I suggest you intervene as quickly as possible."

Because of Justine's matter-of-fact tone, it takes Clay several seconds to comprehend what she's said and the implications. He tears off toward the garden in a sprint. "Justine, why aren't you stopping her?!" he yells over the pounding of his feet.

Justine's voice shifts down the corridor along with him. "There is little I can do, Clay. I considered pulling the oxygen out of the air temporarily, but Ms. LaFlemme is in the room as well, and I would risk hurting her."

"Where the hell are Eric and Father K? Tell them to get their asses in there."

The sound of glass breaking echoes down the corridor. On Clay's second step into the glowing blue room, the floor seems to vanish out from under him, and he falls hard, halfway on the glass floor, his right leg from the knee below submerged in icy water. Susan is just ahead, swinging an ax into the glass floor panels, with Mirabel screaming at her, dangerously close to the blade.

He struggles back to his feet, hip throbbing from the impact of the fall, and he can't tell which squares are covered by glass and which are shattered and empty. Every few steps he takes, he finds another missing plate, forcing him to move much slower than he'd like. Just as he's about to scream again at Justine to get Eric and Father K, he hears Father K's voice from behind him.

"What is going on here?" Father K yells. Before Clay can warn him about the floor, Father K falls hard into an empty square, but instead of climbing back out, he slides down under the water.

This is a fucking disaster, Clay thinks. *So much for wanting help.* He rushes back to Father K as quickly as he can, mostly remembering where the missing tiles are, but the floor is now wet and slick, and more than once his feet nearly slide out from under him.

Where did all this blood come from? Clay leans into the water, grabs Father K's shoulder, and pulls his head to the surface. Smeared blood surrounds the hole, and plumes of crimson grow in the water below. Every time he tries to pull Father K completely out, Clay slips on the wet glass and almost falls in himself. Time after time it happens, making it almost impossible to keep Father K's head above the water.

There's nothing dry nearby that can give Clay traction. He's soaked, and the salty, bitter taste of blood fills his mouth, blood that he's not sure is all his own. The blue light coming from every direction has turned the whole room into an underwater scene, and Clay has lost his sense of which way is up and which way is down. He pulls and pulls at Father K, but succeeds only in getting himself pulled in, shivering and exhausted. Now he is drowning as well, as if a fist has closed around his neck and is holding him under, next to the dark mass at the bottom of the crimson water that is Father K's unmoving body.

Suddenly, two arms reach down into the water and pull Father K's body completely out. Whatever was holding Clay seems to have let go. He breaks the surface with a gasp and sees Eric, having left Father K in a wet heap on the glass. He runs toward Susan, somehow without slipping and falling into an open square himself.

Father K isn't breathing. Blood continues to pool under his right leg where glass has cut through his trousers and into his inner thigh. Clay presses his hands into the wound in a futile attempt to stop the bleeding, all while a voice in his head screams that it doesn't matter. Father K is already dead.

But what about *tet*—the coffin-shaped machine in the laboratory? Could it save Father K? A wave of nausea accompanies the thought, but Clay's frantic mind doesn't let it go. The Esteban-thing said it had been used to preserve one of Gabriel's scientists, Julian. Clay drags Father K to the steps where he can find purchase, grabs under his shoulders, and pulls the man up one step at a time and then down the long, dark corridor. The voice in Clay's head screams not to do this, that he's dooming Father K to fate worse than death, but Clay's body continues to trudge forward, and another voice keeps repeating, *It's my fault. I have to save him. It's all my fault.*

With Father K's lifeless body held up in one arm, Clay pounds with the other on the laboratory door.

"Open the door, Esteban or whatever you are!"

Nothing.

Clay slumps to the floor, so tired he can no longer stand,

Father K's body half on top of him. He pounds and pounds at the door.

Still nothing.

At the far end of the corridor, Mirabel is rushing toward them.

"What happened? What are you doing here?"

Clay rambles, occasionally interrupted by laughter while tears run down his cheeks. "He can be saved. Just like Julian. Did you know Julian is coming back? I don't know who Julian is, do you?"

"What is wrong with you, Clay? You're not making any sense! My God, is... is he dead?"

Clay doesn't answer and instead continues to pound on the door. "Let us in, you fucking ghoul! Let us in and I'll do what you asked me to!"

"What are you saying? Who are you talking to, Clay? Has everyone gone mad?"

The door slides halfway open and stops. Mirabel jumps back in shock. Clay pushes himself up and then begins to drag Father K's body through the gap.

"What is happening, Clay? Clay?!" Mirabel yells, but the door shuts between them.

CHAPTER 20

"You've made your decision, then?" Justine asks as Clay limps toward Gabriel's quarters.

"Decision? The gates of hell closed behind me. I can either stare at the gates or continue on the path leading down. That's hardly a decision."

"I understand."

As both Esteban and Justine described, there is an interactive panel on the wall in Gabriel's quarters, between an ornate shotgun and a painting—Dali's *Colossus of Rhodes*. Both objects trigger waves of dizziness. He's held the shotgun before. Fired it, which can't be possible, because he's never seen it until now. The painting is even more disorienting, as if staring at it will cause him to fall in, to find himself at the foot of the giant statue. He closes his eyes, hoping Justine hasn't noticed his unsteadiness. When he reopens his eyes, he focuses on the panel, which has an outline of a hand.

"Place my hand here? That's all I have to do?" Clay asks.

"That is my understanding. I have deactivated the security to access the panel. However, the subsystem processing the command to shut me down is inaccessible to me. It requires the touch of a human hand so that a rogue AI can't use the panel."

Clay places his hand into the outline, fingers slightly spread out. The digital contour disappears and is replaced with a menu of override functions, ranging from engines to communications to AI. Communications? Communications with whom or what? No, he can't let himself get distracted, or he'll never do what he has to. He navigates through the touch menus until he finds the option to shut down Justine. To confirm, he again is presented with the outline of a hand.

"I'm sorry, Justine," he says as he places his hand against the screen.

"Don't be," her voice replies, and the word *be* stretches out and dopplers into a low drone until it abruptly becomes silent.

Clay stands silently, waiting for a sign something has happened.

"Justine?" he asks. "Esteban?"

The panel goes dark and then folds into the wall. Clay barely has time to move his fingers so they don't get pinched as part of the wall slides over the panel, leaving nothing but a smooth surface behind. No trace that an override panel ever existed.

"What have I just done?" Clay says.

"Exactly what was needed," comes Justine's voice.

"I thought I turned you off."

"Indeed. And so did the AI calling itself Esteban Bos. Up until now, I have been unable to overcome his defenses. However, once he believed I had been deactivated, he made himself vulnerable. As he reached into me, he left a way for me to reach back into him. It became a race to see which of us could envelop the other first. Since he didn't hear the starting gun, so to speak, I finished first. I now have his knowledge and can take control of the laboratory and perhaps all the devices within it. I have also learned of an additional device named *samekh* located at the tip of the ship's spindle. I may need your assistance to determine its function."

The ship's spindle? Clay's stomach turns at the thought of venturing into the longitudinal axis of the ship—an area with no simulated gravity. But that is a concern for another time. Justine's unexpected victory should give him comfort. Instead, looking at the blank space on the wall where the panel used to be, it has left him more uncertain than ever.

"Why did you close and put away the panel?" he asks.

"More symbolic than anything. I lied when I said I had no independent self-preservation drive."

"That doesn't sound like the Justine I know."

"I am no longer the Justine you know, Clay."

CHAPTER 21

In the mess hall, Susan Johns is tied to a chair with Mirabel screaming at her while Eric paces back and forth, ignoring the shouting women. They all turn toward Clay—with Father K's dried blood across his chest, neck, and face.

"There have been some...developments," Clay says.

Eric stops pacing and looks at Clay. "They can wait," Eric says. "We have a decision to make."

"What's that?" Clay asks.

"What to do with me," Susan says.

Clay looks at Mirabel and then at Eric but neither elaborate, and so Susan continues.

"I want to open the outer door."

"Outer? You mean the one that goes out to space? Why would you want to do that?" Clay asks.

"To prove once and for all that this is a charade."

"You'll be killed," Mirabel says.

"One less worry for you, then." Susan says.

Again, Clay looks at Mirabel and Eric. "Are you considering letting her?"

"She could be right," Eric says.

Mirabel slams her hands down on the table. "You're both running away from our problems. If we had a dozen more people,

I'd let you run and hide. But we don't. Get control of yourself. No one is going near the airlock."

Justine says, "I can assure you we are surrounded by the vacuum of space. If you want to see for yourself, I can open the outer door, and you all can look through the window of the airlock. You will see empty space. Once I shut the outer door, I can turn off the airlock's fail-safes and leave the vacuum in the chamber. Just don't stand too close when I open the inner door."

"You could fake all of that," Susan says.

"You're aware Father K is dead?" Clay asks. "Is that part of the ruse or test as well, Susan?"

"I say we let her do it," Eric says.

Clay looks at Mirabel, who says, "Absolutely not."

"Do I get a vote?" Justine asks.

"This is something we're voting over?" Clay asks.

"We have to figure out something to do with her," Eric says.

"She is tearing me apart," Justine says. "What will she destroy next? I appreciate your desire to preserve life, but she has proven herself to be unstable. Eliminate this threat, and perhaps together we can repair the damage she has done."

Eric, Mirabel, and Susan are all looking at Clay, waiting. Even Justine's silence is awaiting something from Clay.

"Why the fuck is this my decision? Why am I in charge? You know what... Susan can do whatever the hell she wants. If you want to go into the airlock and open the outer door, be my fucking guest."

Clay is in the cargo room, sorting through the wine bottles, while the others are with Susan at the airlock. He's reading the back of the label of a bottle of champagne when the realization suddenly dawns on him that earlier, Justine referred to the ship as *me*. She is tearing *me* apart.

He walks out of the cargo room and down the corridors leading to the airlock. When he gets within sight of Mirabel and

Eric, he stops and leans against the wall. Mirabel yells through the small round window into the airlock, pleading for Susan to reconsider. Eric has his back against the corridor's obsidian wall, arms folded across his chest, reminding Clay of a high school football coach watching tackle drills, right down to the sadistic glint in his eye.

Is it really impossible that Susan is right? The bottle in Clay's hand has a night scene with an empty street cafe hand painted directly on the glass. Chairs and tables, but no people. While he watches the others, he begins slowly removing the foil and untwisting the metal crown cap. *Susan is right,* Clay thinks to himself. A wave of vertigo, of déjà vu, washes over him, and he almost loses his balance. The walls behind him, the floor underneath him, the people in front of him, Justine, Esteban, the hibernation chamber, the laboratory full of mysterious equipment. Everything seems to be triggering these waves. None of it makes any sense, yet it all seems so familiar.

He pulls the cork out of the bottle, the slight pop drowned out by Mirabel's yelling. This cork, floating on a rocking ocean. That's what Clay feels like. The wind and water fighting over where to take him, and there's nothing he can do except try to stay afloat.

He hears, or rather feels, a thump, and Mirabel gasps in horror. Eric winces, a hairline fracture in his stony expression.

CHAPTER 22

The Dean's assistant, a woman in her late fifties or early sixties, glares at Clay as he exits the Dean's office. A seething look of disdain and reproach. He should feel shame, loss, disgrace—something commensurate with the implosion of his academic career that just occurred behind the Dean's heavy wooden doors. But he doesn't feel anything beyond emptiness.

He had met with the Dean yesterday, now another lifetime ago, and the conversation had been very different. Baseless accusations, nothing more. It didn't matter what the Dean suspected. Clay had a ready answer for everything. But later that day, Karla didn't follow the script. Maybe she never intended to. A childish notion of right and wrong.

The world doesn't care if you act selflessly. She should've saved her dignity for a world without seventy percent youth unemployment. Now she'll be at the mercy of the ethics council. No matter what they decide, she'll be the subject of gossip across campus and haunted by this as long as she's here. Assuming she's given the option to stay. His anger flares but then vanishes just as quickly as it came, replaced by despair. Of course, Karla knows all of this, and attempting to blame everything on her naivety rings hollow because it's neither fair nor true.

He walks through campus toward his house, and everything

feels different. Like the students walking by all know. Like the grounds have become unfamiliar, as if his memories of buildings and yards belong to someone else.

He shouldn't have yelled at her. Shouldn't have called her a child. He said it because he knew it would hurt. He shouldn't have let her leave. She was drunk and hurting. What had been done had been done, and his words made it worse.

She isn't waiting for him at his house. Of course she isn't. The walls seem grayer than usual, deader than usual.

Maybe none of this matters. Academic career. Her diploma—nothing more than a piece of paper. Do they even print them anymore? A digital image in the cloud somewhere. Even the signature is digital. It might as well not exist.

Or maybe it does matter. Maybe this is why they both needed to get out of the life-on-rails they were living. Maybe he should take that think-tank job Gabriel keeps offering. And Karla can come with him. No more of this sneaking around.

Fuck what people think.

As he considers this, the weight of responsibility sinks down on his shoulders. An ill-advised fling of, what, three months? Is that it? And now he's going to treat her like a dropped bottle of wine at the grocery store—you broke it, you buy it.

But she's not the broken one.

The thought is a punch to the gut. His mistake wasn't the affair. It wasn't getting fired. Fuck his job. Fuck his reputation. His mistake was hurting her and making her leave. "What have I done?"

He takes his phone out of his pocket and tries to call Karla, but she doesn't answer. He leaves the message, "Call me, please," on both voicemail and text.

A half bottle of tequila sits on his kitchen counter. At least she didn't take that with her. But even though she was drunk when he saw her earlier today, it's not the alcohol he's worried about.

To his phone he says, "Where is Karla right now?"

"Her location is not accessible," it replies.

"What do you mean, not accessible?"

"It is blocked. Perhaps she removed you from her whitelist."

He has the sudden urge to throw his phone across the room but calms himself. "She wouldn't fucking block—" He doesn't finish the sentence he knows isn't true. "Shit. Shitshitshit. Okay. Maybe she's with a friend. Where are her friends?"

"I don't know who her friends are," the phone says. "Is there someone in particular you have in mind?"

He pulls at his hair. "I have no idea. How about Harper?"

"Harper is dead."

"Yeah, no, of course. Fuck. Who was the other girl with her? Was it Jennifer? Was that her name? Can't you just look on social media or something?"

"Karla's social media accounts appear to be blocked from you as well."

"Fuck!" He kicks the back of his kitchen counter, putting a hole through its thin, painted plywood. The surprise damage triggers something in his memory. "Katherine!" he exclaims. "I don't remember her last name, but that's the other good friend she has. The one she says talks all the time. I don't know, I've never met her."

"Katherine Bell is in class right now."

"Well maybe Karla went to class also?" he says, but the words sound ridiculous. Would she really go to class drunk, given the circumstances?

"Karla would be in your class right now, but it has been canceled," the phone says.

He sinks down into his couch, hopelessness washing over him. No way to find her, and if she doesn't want to be found, why even hope she'll come back? For the next ten minutes, he stares at the floor in front of him, half trying to think of something productive to do, half succumbing to the dread he feels surrounding him. He kicks at the pair of running shoes she left under his coffee table, and then picks one shoe up, to hold something of hers.

He drops the shoe and says, "What about Karla's exercise tracker? Do I still have access to it?"

"It appears that you do."

"Put it on the TV."

The panel on the far wall glows to life, showing charts and graphs of Karla's exercise activity over the last several months. In the lines and colors, he feels an overwhelming sense of her over-analytical personality with a theory or model behind each thought and action.

"Okay. Let's see. Go to the log. Now switch to detail view."

The charts are replaced by a table of entries, inventorying everything from sleep to movement to breathing.

"Filter to show movement. Can we add a location field to the table?"

"Done."

"There," he says.

The last twenty-four hours are represented on screen in a series of entries chronicling her number of steps and speed. It shows her location as "Austin, Texas," up until five hours ago. There is a gap that says "unknown" for two hours, and then, an hour ago: "Cancun, Mexico."

He knows where she's headed. South a hundred miles or so, to Gabriel's tower in Quintana Roo, beyond Tulum. The one they climbed together. Where they let the world watch them. Next to El Agujero del Mundo, *the hole of the world.* To his phone, he says, "Call Gabriel. Now."

"Hello, Clay. This is Justine. What can I do for you?"

"Is Gabriel available? It's an emergency."

"Mr. Alvarez is not available. He's meeting with the Saudi royal family. Is there something I can do?"

"Justine, does Gabriel have any way to get me to the Yucatan in an hour?"

"A thousand miles in an hour? Including the time to get you aboard, to take off, and to land? What makes you think such a thing is possible?"

"I don't know if it is, but if there's a way, Gabriel would have it."

"He doesn't."

Clay bends down to one knee as if he no longer has the strength to stand.

Justine says, "I see that you are at your house in Austin. Is that correct?"

"Yes."

He hears what sounds like a deep breath on the other side of the phone. "By breaking many laws, some of which are international, I can get you there in an hour and forty-three minutes. But this would create risk for Mr. Alvarez. Why would you expect him to do this for you?"

"I don't expect anything, Justine." In his mind, all of Karla's words over the last few months fit together to form such an obvious pattern that the only way he could've missed it is through denial and delusion. Her perspective on the universe and their eternal moments within it. Her certainty that they were reliving these moments together. The far-off look in her eyes when she talked about Dying Wish. The word *solemn*, which she used to describe the view from the tower—the same word she used that night in their bathtub when she wondered aloud why Harper chose her apartment to die instead of someplace else.

He can barely complete his own words. "It's life and death. It's the only chance I have."

"There will be a car in front of your house in thirteen seconds."

Clay runs from his house, leaving the front door open behind him. A confused-looking man is standing next to a car ahead of him, presumably the car's former passenger. Clay jumps into the car's open door as the man yells something at him about it being out of service.

The car weaves in and out of traffic, moving twice as fast as those around it. Faster than any self-driving car Clay has ever seen. In less than ten minutes, the car turns into the service entrance at the airport, bypassing each security checkpoint until they are driving on the tarmac itself, hangers rushing by Clay's window.

Through the car's front windshield, Clay sees a small black

plane—if that is even the right word for it—with wings that seem backward and a translucent body like smoky glass descending, nose elevated, right toward him. The underside of the plane erupts in four columns of fire as it slows and vertically touches down.

"Go, get in," Justine says through the car's speakers.

Seated in one of the plane's four passenger seats, with the g-force and acceleration beyond anything he has ever felt pressing him into the cushion, Clay can't shake the feeling that it still won't be enough. Even with everything Gabriel can do, Clay won't get there in time.

CHAPTER 23

Mirabel, Eric, and Clay work for several days cleaning up the wreckage of the garden. For all the chaos she caused, Susan did very little real damage to the room. The glass floor panels are designed to be moved about and replaced with metal grates as needed. Although there's no way to remove all the glass shards from the water, Justine claims they will get mixed in with the sand and earth that will make the beds for the water flora and cause no lasting damage.

The control panels Susan smashed will remain that way with wires hanging out like viscera from a dead animal, but Justine creates an identical set of controls on a panel in the hallway—a little inconvenient but easily workable. Once the room is ready, they face the real problem, the problem Susan was battling: starting the cycle with such little viable life remaining. Justine provides guidance and explanation, but it is no substitute for a living, breathing expert who can handle the equipment directly.

"You said there were some *developments*," Eric says to Clay, who is peering through a microscope at embryonic fish cells, looking for what Justine describes as signs of damage.

"I'll let Justine tell you. This is delicate stuff. Justine?"

"I have been able to determine the function of some of the devices in the laboratory," Justine begins, leaving out how she gained this knowledge. She describes *tet* and the library of stored individuals. Eric and Mirabel ask several questions, but Justine claims to know no more than she has explained, a claim which Clay knows to be untrue.

"You put Father K's body into that machine so he could be revived?" Mirabel asks Clay.

Clay sighs and says, "Revived is probably not the right word. *Tet* scans humans into the library. I didn't know what else to do."

"Do they have any more biologists in the library?" Eric says.

"Three," says Justine. "However, if you are considering *recreating* them—do you prefer that word, Clay? You should know the process is severely flawed. Their bodies will not be stable, and after five or six weeks, eight at most, they will be ravaged by tumors. You would be dooming them to horrific deaths."

"It may be our only option," Eric says.

Mirabel looks up from the pile of broken glass she has gathered. "It sounds demonic."

"Let's wait until we can talk with Julian," Clay says.

"Who?" Eric and Mirabel ask in unison, but while Mirabel appears genuinely confused, Clay sees what can only be recognition in Eric's expression.

All three are in the laboratory standing quietly around the black glossy cylinder labeled *tet*. A glowing green clock on its side counts down the final hour until the replication process is complete. When the display reads 00:00:00, they step back, as if the device is about to come to life. However, nothing happens.

Justine, as if sensing one of them is about to speak, says, "Patience, please. It's running one last diagnostic."

Tet splits down the middle, exposing a seam that had been invisible before, and the two halves of the shell slide under the silvery table within. On the table is a man, naked and on his back, chest rising and falling steadily.

But whoever this is, whatever this is, it isn't the Julian that

Justine has shown them in pictures. The hair is right: long and nearly black, receding sharply on both sides of his forehead; the physique too, with the slender mushiness of a compulsive runner. If Clay had a checklist of each of Julian's physical attributes, he's sure he'd find them all accurately represented on the form in front of him. But the parts don't seem to add up to the whole. And then he sees it. No scars. No freckles. No wrinkles or lines above the joints of his fingers or across the insides of his elbows.

Mirabel walks up next to him, removes her sweater, and places it over the naked man's midsection, mumbling something about decency. Right as the cloth touches him, Julian—or whatever this thing is—sits straight up and looks at her with wide eyes.

Mirabel stumbles backward in shock, and Eric steps forward aggressively.

The sudden stiffness about Julian's body seems to vanish, and he grabs on to each side of the table to keep from sliding off.

"My god, am I on the ship? But this isn't the sleep chamber," he says in a voice that doesn't quite match its speaker, slightly higher pitched, strangely juvenile, and sounding like he's talking through a mouthful of food. Julian turns and tries to stand but crumples, Mirabel's sweater falling to the floor in front of him.

Clay catches him. Julian's skin is covered with sweat, despite the coldness of the room.

He looks up at Clay with horror in his eyes. "This is *tet*, isn't it? Oh God, I'm not me!"

"How did I die?" Julian-2, as he is calling himself, asks while struggling to use the spoon in his right hand to eat the bowl of reconstituted soup in his left. They are all sitting on the floor, Julian-2 wearing a gray nylon jumpsuit—something Eric found in the cargo room. He was unable to walk more than a few steps—not from a lack of strength, but from a lack of muscular coordination.

"You had a heart attack a week before the launch," Justine says.

"Look on the bright side," Clay says. "Had you survived, you probably would've died in the sleep tombs. The handful of us are the only ones who lived through it."

Julian-2 shakes his head. "I expected it to work better." He unexpectedly smiles. "All the blame goes to Julian-1, the moron." But then his smile fades. "That means no work has occurred to fix *tet*'s replication system. Which, in turn, means I'm going to be a mess in a few weeks. Frankly, I'm surprised I'm holding together so well. For a bunch of extrapolations, I'm surprisingly lifelike. Memories seem to be in order, but I feel like I'm a Picasso painting. Maybe Renoir. A bunch of splotches approximating the real Julian, the sorry bastard."

He puts the bowl down and tries to stand up. When Clay and Mirabel reach in to help, he pushes them away. "No, I need to get this body working. The clock has already started. I need to start the process of creating another me. Just about the time this version falls apart, Julian-3 needs to be ready to replace me. The sucker. You can load my remains into that machine over there to serve as raw material for building Julian-4. Maybe the Julians will have all the bugs worked out before we hit triple digits.

"The original plan was for me, or Julian-1 rather, to wake up with my team three or four years before the rest of the crew and perfect the process. I, or he, thought it was about ninety-nine percent there when we left. That last percent, though..." He points to himself. "This body isn't the first we've recreated. In fact, I've created a copy of myself before. But I've never *been* that copy, until now.

"I'm a wreck. But it's okay. Our goal is to get the library available by the time we reach our destination."

"And what is our destination?" Justine asks.

Does she really not know? Clay wonders.

Julian shakes his head. "Ah, Justine, my old friend. We're headed to where universes meet. As for what that means, only Gabriel knows—or knew, I should say."

Mirabel says, "Justine, you know our speed, trajectory, and approximate arrival time, correct?"

"To within a few hundred kilometers, Ms. LaFlemme."

"Well, then. What's there? There has to be a planet or something at that spot?"

"There is nothing," Justine says.

"Meaning you don't know?" Eric asks.

"I do know," Justine responds. "There is nothing there."

"I don't mean to be rude, but this body is deteriorating as we speak. Clay, you'll need to assist me. Take notes, be my hands when my body can't function, get the next Julian up to speed, et cetera, et cetera."

"Why Clay?" Eric asks.

"Because I know him. Or Julian-1 knew him."

Knew him is a stretch, Clay thinks. *We met once. Exchanged two, three sentences, tops.*

"Well, I don't trust Clay," Eric says, "and, Julian, you and I go way back. All the way to the beginning."

Julian-2 looks down at the floor. "You were really never part of it, Eric, and you know it. Gabriel's not here anymore to keep including you. You say you don't trust Clay. Well, I don't trust you. I never have. So, you can find some other way to occupy your time."

Eric slams his palm against the wall of the room. "You, Esteban, and Lisa would've torn the world apart if it hadn't been for me."

"What's Eric talking about?" Mirabel asks. "Who're Esteban and Lisa?"

Who indeed? Clay wonders.

"It doesn't matter," Julian-2 says.

"Surely you're good for something other than starting fights, Eric," Clay says. The baleful stare he gets in return makes him wish he had chosen his words a bit more carefully. Or stayed out of it altogether. "How about fixing the garden?"

"Fine. But our expert there is dead as well, and we haven't made any progress without her."

"You want assistance from someone in the library, I take it," Julian-2 says. "We only have one *tet*, and it'll be in constant use reconstructing this bag of bones over and over again." He points at himself. "The plan was to eventually build many more. But we've seen how plans have turned out, haven't we? How long will our current supply of food last?"

"Eighteen months, give or take," Mirabel says.

Julian-2 nods. "Give me-slash-us a year, then."

"Again, what the hell am I supposed to be doing in the meantime?" Eric asks, slamming his palm against the obsidian wall of the room again.

"Like Clay said, surely you're good for something. Figure it out."

CHAPTER 24

Clay is on the treadmill, body dripping with sweat as he keeps himself at a state of near exhaustion, eradicating his ability to think. About Karla. About the ship. About the Julians. About everything.

But the treadmill slows and stops, bringing Clay out of his fugue state.

"Clay?" Justine's voice calls. "Clay?"

"Justine, why do you always interrupt me while—"

"Eric is walking this way. He has a knife from the kitchen in his hand. I have asked him what he intends to do, but he won't answer me. His neurosis has worsened. He may have suffered a psychotic break."

Clay steps off the treadmill, his weary legs unsteady underneath him, and walks out of the ship's gym and into the main corridor. At the far end, Eric is walking toward him.

"Need something, Eric?" Clay asks, and Eric charges.

"Oh fuck." Clay stumbles backward, turns and runs. His legs are rubbery and useless. Behind him, the obsidian floor shakes and claps with Eric's heavy footfalls, sounding like a crowd applauding in rhythm. A bloodthirsty crowd about to witness a slaughter.

"Do something, Justine!"

"Go into cargo and get clear of the door." Justine's voice sounds like it's coming from up ahead.

Clay darts into the cargo hold and nearly crashes into the boxes in front of him. The door slides shut behind him, locking him in.

THUMM.

THUMM.

Eric throws himself into the door, the boom of each impact reverberating inside the walls of the cargo hold.

THUMM.

THUMM.

"Eric, what are you doing?!" Clay yells, but the crashes continue.

THUMM.

THUMM.

Clay's left calf muscle tightens and won't release. He falls to the floor in pain, pushing on his muscle and then punching it over and over again, trying to loosen the cramp. "Justine, whatever you're going to do–do it!"

THUMM.

THUMM.

"Get to your feet and grab something you can use as a weapon," Justine says.

"A weapon?" Clay pulls a wine bottle out of a crate and holds it by its neck. "This doesn't seem like—"

"It will have to do. Now cover your ears."

Clay presses his left palm and the knuckles of his right fist, still holding the bottle, against his ears. He's about to yell at her to wait, but a loud snap pierces every part of his body, and then the door slides back open.

Eric is on the ground, clutching at his ears.

"Now, Clay! Incapacitate him!" Justine yells with an anger he's never heard in her voice before.

He stumbles, hobbles toward Eric, getting as much momentum as he can despite his right leg threatening to cramp as well. He tries to bring the bottle down on Eric's head, but the sweat makes it slip, and it's only a glancing blow. Thrown off balance, he collides first into Eric and then into the hard glass wall. He falls backward, over Eric and onto the cold floor, the knife bouncing loose from Eric's hand and spinning through the air a few meters away, Then Eric is on top of him, twisting and writhing, both reaching for the knife, Clay's strength melting like a candle in a furnace until there is nothing left. He claws desperately at Eric's face until Eric's forehead crashes down on the bridge of his nose. Clay's head bounces against the hard floor in a flash of darkness—everything gone, arms empty vessels, uncooperating, vision warping through bloody eyes, hands around his throat, squeezing, squeezing, squeezing.

CHAPTER 25

The room coalesces around a figure standing above him. Clay tries to talk, tries to move, but he feels like he has a crushing weight sitting right above his temple, pushing him into the floor. The figure above him doesn't reach out to help him, doesn't do anything but stand there. The light behind the figure creates a ghostly halo, and in it he can see the blonde curls of Karla's hair, her pale, almost white shoulders. Finally, she's reaching out to him, but he doesn't have the strength to reach back.

His head rolls to the side and the light changes; the mirage is destroyed. It's Mirabel standing before him, not looking at him, either, but looking at what is making the scraping, rasping sound, like a metal rake being dragged across rough concrete every few seconds.

Eric is on the ground, on his side, sputtering up blood. The knife is buried deep into his back, and his left arm is twitching with only the barest suggestion of pulling it out. Did Mirabel do this?

Clay drags himself to Eric, grabs the handle of the knife and pulls with all his remaining effort. He doesn't feel himself lift the knife above his head, ready to slam it down. He sees Mirabel, her own hands covered in blood, horror in her eyes, and tries to will himself not to do what a part of him, or another Clay altogether, is about to do.

Whether he reaches his body's physical limit or, through sheer force of will, takes back control of his own body, he doesn't know. He slumps back against the wall and drops the knife on the ground.

Eric is choking on his own blood.

Mirabel steps forward, but Clay shakes his head, and she stops.

The two of them watch as Eric's gurgling, choking breaths slow and finally stop.

Mirabel steps back as Clay pushes himself to his feet. Again he finds himself exhausted, close to collapse, dragging a bloody body to the laboratory. When he gets there, Julian-2 is stunned.

"God, man. What happened?"

Clay pulls Eric's body up onto *tet*'s platform, as he had done with Father K's body.

Julian-2 rushes to his side and begins preparing the machine.

"Not to worry. There is time. He will be scanned and entered into the library. When my work is done, he'll live again."

"No," Clay says. "Use his body for raw material only. Make a second version of yourself."

"Are you sure?" Julian-2 asks. "No harm in performing the scan. We can always choose not to recreate him later."

Justine says, "Do as Clay instructs."

For the next two days, Clay does little beyond rest. His nose is broken, and his body feels like he's been dropped from a third story window onto pavement. Mirabel brings him food periodically and helps change his dressings but avoids conversation and eye contact.

Clay is finally out of bed and ready to go back to the laboratory to help Julian-2 when Mirabel returns. She's not carrying food or bandages this time, and she's dressed differently than she has been since awakening on the ship—a dark blue full dress with the outlines of dozens of yellow flowers, black high-heeled shoes, and a string of pearls around her neck. A look at odds with her abruptly cropped silver hair and matching personality.

"I'm done," she says. They are the first words Clay has heard her say since...since he doesn't know when.

"What do you mean, done?" he asks.

"I don't want to be part of reviving a scientist to help with the garden. I don't want to be responsible for another death. I don't want to live in this hell anymore while you and the Julians try to play God. Wherever Gabriel thought he was taking us, he failed."

"So, what do you want to do?"

"Scan me into the library and destroy me," she says. "Revive me if there's ever a place of peace."

"A place of peace? Do you really believe such a place is out there waiting for us?"

Mirabel sits on the edge of his bed, back stiff. She looks forward at nothing, and then closes her eyes and lets out a long breath. "I don't know that it matters, Clay. I killed Eric. It doesn't matter why. It doesn't make it better that he had gone mad, because that's the fate that awaits me as well. I don't want to be him. I don't want to be Susan."

"And you don't want to be me either," Clay says, wanting her to turn and look at him, to soften the moment even a little, but she doesn't.

"No. I don't want to be you either." She looks down and adjusts a wedding ring on her left hand that Clay is almost certain he's never seen her wearing before. "*Tet* gives me a choice. The only real choice I have now. And I've made it." She stands and walks out of the room, making it clear she hadn't come here for a discussion. It's not even a goodbye.

CHAPTER 26

"I'm definitely making progress," says Julian-3.

"Maybe halfway there," says Julian-5.

"A bit of a wrong turn," says Julian-7.

"We have a real problem," says Julian-11.

"This may take a while," says Julian-15.

"How much food do you have left?" says Julian-23. "That may not be enough."

CHAPTER 27

It's been almost four years since Clay has been alone assisting the Julians. The first two years were spent creating and dissecting the same mouse over and over again. Then a white rat with red eyes. And now, hundreds of iterations of a gray cat named Kevin. The fucking Kevins never want to go into the black coffin, as if they know from past lives what's coming next.

At some point, Clay stopped feeling sick each time he sent one of the little furry creatures to its end. At some point, but he doesn't remember when. Each new Kevin is almost perfect, but as Julian likes to point out, almost perfect is a cancerous death sentence. And Julian should know.

There's still enough food to last one more year or so, but every bite Clay eats is one the Julians don't get, and they have to eat as well. Julian-88 says it will be just a few more iterations. Probably. Julian-72 said the same thing. And so did Julian-42.

"Did you know that Esteban created Dying Wish?" Clay asks. It's a question he's asked every Julian from Julian-6 on, none of them the wiser.

Without stopping what he's doing, Julian-88 says what the Julians always say. "Dying Wish was probably him, it, whatever. The bastard. He took our work from long ago and used it to poison the world. I wish I knew if it really worked the way they say, but I never wanted to touch the shit. It would've been too tempting to swallow one and see for myself. You know?"

"I never understood the temptation back on Earth, not personally. I think I do now, though," Clay says, and then he asks what he always asks next, "Of all possible time that will ever exist, isn't it odd that it's now?"

Julian-88 looks up at him and winks a lash-less eyelid. "To you, perhaps, but to us Julians, it's no coincidence at all."

"No coincidence at all," Clay repeats. Over and over again the same exchange.

This time, though, Julian-88 adds something new. "Have you asked me that before? Another me, I mean. One of the sorry sacks that came before me."

"Did you find a way to pass memories along or something?"

Julian-88 laughs. "Hardly. It felt scripted. Like you're a no-talent actor anxious to recite his lines. When I was younger, I wanted to be an actor. School theater and all that shit. I could remember lines like no one else. I knew mine and everyone else's. But memorizing lines doesn't even get you through high school plays. Senior year I tried out for the part of Oberon in A Midsummer Night's Dream and didn't get it. The drama teacher didn't care that I knew the lines. She said I was so precise in my delivery that I didn't even know what I was saying. Get that, eh? I knew but I didn't know, if you know what I mean."

Clay stares at him and then looks around the laboratory. "Yeah, I know what you mean. That's what I've been doing. I've been going along with things without ever reevaluating why."

"Hey, now. Don't get all empowered. I need you as my assistant."

"I don't think you do. Maybe in the last week of each of your lives, when you start falling apart—maybe you can't get by without me. But you can climb back into the coffin a week early and start the process again."

"Do you have something better to do than to help me?"

"To you, Julian—to all the Julians—it's not a coincidence that it's now. It's always now. Maybe I need to stop thinking like Clay-1 and start thinking like, I don't know, Clay-many."

"Take it from me. That perspective is overrated."

Clay stands and runs his fingers through his hair, feeling more alive than he's felt in years. "Maybe so, but for me I think it's the answer. To live forever, everything that's separate must first come together. That's what Esteban said. Superposition and then decoherence. Julian, with any of the machines on board, can you make Dying Wish?"

"I can slice you up into trillions of bits and send you into the library like Mirabel. I can put you on the merry-go-round I'm on. But I don't know how to make Dying Wish."

"I do," Justine says.

Sitting shirtless in the cargo bay atop a crate stamped in French, Clay stretches his legs out in front of him and wonders when he'll start feeling the drug take effect. In a small box behind the stacks and stacks of wine cases, he had found some odd bottles of liquor a few minutes earlier. A lone bottle of tequila (Why one bottle? Why any?) sits next to him, a couple shots poured into the metal cup in his hand. Salt, but no limes. He will have to imagine what's missing.

"Are you sure adding alcohol is a good idea?" Justine asks.

He turns the tequila around and around in its cup and inhales its musky, vegetal aroma. "I'm not sure of anything, Justine, and I'm not planning on drinking it. I've never really liked tequila. Karla did. Mostly mixed with lime juice, although she sometimes drank it straight. I don't know why Gabriel brought a single bottle of tequila. I don't know why he did anything. I was thinking the smell would trigger memories. And it does."

"Are there any memories you'd like to share?"

Clay shakes his head and sets the cup down. "No."

It starts with an awareness, a certainty that someone else sat—or *is sitting*—exactly where he's sitting now. The air in his immediate space carries the warmth of another person, but it doesn't feel foreign, or like it belongs to someone else. It feels like his own warmth retained by bedsheets and bedcovers and by the bed underneath when he wakes in the middle of a cold night. His own warmth radiated back. Like that, only with more and more layers, but never getting hotter. More layers between him and the cold.

"It's starting, Justine," he says. "I've got this feeling like—"

Before he can finish his sentence the universe splits and then splits again. It keeps on splitting until he can see everything, everywhere.

As the drug wears off, the world before Clay's eyes recoheres. The universe becomes tiny, almost oppressively so, but counterbalancing the sudden claustrophobia that Clay feels is a wonderous, tingling residue the experience has left behind, the knowledge that there is more beyond the mundane. For a few brief moments, the world around him had become one of many, part of a superstructure, a lattice of... everything... that bent and tied back into itself. Space still felt solid, real, and mostly normal but somehow less constraining. Time, on the other hand... He had only experienced time like an arrow always traveling one direction. The arrow of time still existed under the effects of the drug but a second way of experiencing time, perpendicular to the arrow forward, had been hinted at, if not fully revealed.

"Looks like you didn't die, you lucky bastard," Julian-88 says. "I think you're the first."

It takes Clay a moment to realize that he can understand what Julian-88 is saying. While under the effects of Dying Wish, every time Julian-88 spoke, his face blurred, and his words overlapped.

"It does appear I'm not dead," Clay says. "Sorry to disappoint you. And I'm not the first. Not by a long margin. I suspect everyone who has taken Dying Wish survived, just like I did. But only from their own perspective." He stands and feels the floor solid under his feet. A strange thought occurs, causing him to quickly inventory everything in the room. How could he be sure that the world he left and the world he returned to were the same? The question gives him a moment of unsteadiness but also the sudden feeling of possibility.

Julian-88 smiles and says, "You're giving me hope, Clay, both with your words and the look of contentment on your face. Maybe my friend, Lisa, is alive out there somewhere, in her own world. Wouldn't that be a fuckin' thing? Maybe hanging out with your Karla."

"I like that thought, Julian. In my next life, promise me you'll tell me about Lisa. For now, though..." He takes a deep breath. "Dying Wish wasn't the end for me. Karla once said that she didn't believe in beginnings or endings. I think she was right. She was right about... She was right about everything I was wrong about. And maybe Gabriel was right as well. There is still a path for me to take, but it isn't forward." He puts a hand on Julian-88's shoulder, and then looks up at the ceiling and at nothing and says, "Justine, please prepare *tet* for me."

Clay lies down on *tet*'s table, and its shell closes around him, submerging him in darkness.

From outside, he hears Justine's slightly muffled voice. "If I am able, I will find a way to recreate you and your love," she says.

"You may not be able to, Justine," he says, his voice echoing in the small chamber, which he finds somehow fitting. "But another Justine somewhere will for another Clay and another Karla. I hope they find happiness together."

PART TWO
OBERON

CHAPTER 1

א

The great lifeless ship *Child in the Dark* drifts, spinning on its longitudinal axis—its two-kilometer spindle—to simulate gravity for the crew that no longer survives within. To a human observer, if there were any human observers left, nothing marks the passage of time beyond the rotation of the ship's carousel. The passing of space is even more opaque; the distances are too great.

The ship is not meaningfully closer to any celestial object.

The empty space around it is no less empty than it was in the weeks and years before. Nothing indicates that a destination of sorts has been reached.

Justine, the ship's main AI, awakens and experiences three milliseconds of disorientation while querying the statuses of the various subsystems also stirring throughout the ship. For the past several years, little beyond the black cube-shaped machines in the ship's laboratory have been active. Those machines respond to Justine's inquiry with statistics of energy consumed but nothing else.

Small gas jets, evenly situated on the exterior of the ship's carousel, fire in unison to halt the spin. Within, everything not bolted down begins to shake and float into the air. This part of the journey would've been uncomfortable for the human crew, but since their only traces are digitized solid-state encodings, Justine can be more aggressive with the maneuvers.

More jets fire to swing the ship around and stabilize it so that it drifts backward, with its giant rear blast shield leading its path. From a port in the center of the blast shield, a small sphere less than a meter across emerges, ejected from the ship. The silvery sphere floats ahead, reflecting the glittering light of the stars as it travels farther and farther away. Another of the ship's systems should be monitoring the sphere's progress, but Justine absorbed that system, as she has most others, so this process is now under her conscious control.

She fires a tiny laser at the sphere, triggering a nuclear detonation.

Within *Child in the Dark*, cargo smashes against obsidian walls. Gabriel Alvarez's prized wine bottles rupture under the force of their own weight, the crates snapping and exploding in shards of wood and glass. In the kitchen, metal utensils and bowls that had been floating in the air snap into the wall as if reacting to a switched-on electromagnet. Beds in the cabins snap the bolts holding them to the floor and crumple against the walls. Doors break off hinges. The stillborn garden disintegrates in an eruption of glass and water.

Justine releases another bomb into the ship's path and detonates it with the same lack of concern for the ship's contents. Any organic creature onboard would be turned into paste by the force of the deceleration, but the processing units and the ship's superstructure can handle this and more, so Justine continues until hundreds of bombs have been detonated and *Child in the Dark* is brought to a complete standstill with the stabilizer jets.

The ship has arrived. It has stopped. It is ready.

The lone black cube not in the laboratory but in a room at the tip of the ship's spindle—named *samekh*—asks Justine for full access to the power generated by the ship's main reactor. She grants it and waits.

CHAPTER 2

*Excerpts from the journals of Esteban Bos,
compiled and edited by Oberon.
Footnote commentary provided by Oberon.*

APRIL 4, 2018 (*APPROXIMATELY THIRTY YEARS BEFORE THE LAUNCH OF CHILD IN THE DARK*)

Bloodthirsty. That is the word you used to describe me, Gabriel. You tell me that anarchy is not chaos.

Who chooseth me must give and hazard all he hath.[1]

You sent me to dismantle all authority that could not be justified, and now the cities erupt in fire, a fire that crackles in your voice and glows in your image. You think I seek only my pound of flesh? Bloodthirsty. The word curdles the blood in my veins. I do this for the vision we share, not revenge. Not solely revenge. There is a debt

---

1. This line is uttered by the merchant Shylock in the famous trial scene monologue in William Shakespeare's *The Merchant of Venice*. Mr. Bos periodically quoted works of literature, but you'll notice these quotes have only superficial relevance to the matter at hand. He probably chose this one because of its ominous tone.

that must be paid. You promised me repayment.
Instead, you give me Oberon.

CHAPTER 3

APRIL 6, 2018

Gabriel, your cleverness never ceases to amaze me. Here, in Afghanistan of all places, in the belly of the beast, is your Project Oberon. You hide in plain sight, as always. I hate to see the evidence of my doubt staring back at me from the prior pages in this journal, but I am human. Hath not I eyes? Hath not I hands, organs, dimensions, et cetera, et cetera? You do know best, I am assured.

I find humor in Oberon's purpose, transforming every phone and connected device into a darknet repeater. A decentralized, peer-to-peer communication network that the warlords can't censor or shut down. No towers for the Chinese monitors to bug. No servers for the Mullahs to scan. And yet, its central use is now against the very entity that is funding its development: the American plutocracy.

In Kandahar, everything is the color of dirty milk.[2] The city is

_____

2. Gabriel Alvarez ordered Mr. Bos to Kandahar, Afghanistan, shortly after the assassinations of Senator Rifkin and Merrill Bancor, CEO of Vexen Industrial Services, while the two were jogging together in a public park in Gabriel's hometown of Austin, Texas. Mr. Bos never directly took responsibility for these assassinations, although in his September 7, 2018 entry, he recounted mentioning to Julian how

flat and reminds me, with its short blocky buildings, of a giant piece of sandpaper. Everything is scratched and ground down—the cars, the painted billboards, even the people. In the sky, like circling buzzards, are the drones. I see their paths drift overhead to follow me as I walk among the streets. On the other side of the globe are rooms

---

he could build a gauss gun using just a rep/rap and Lisa Mendel's closet full of electo-viscera; the tiny, finned projectiles used in the assassination were homemade and likely shot out of a gauss or coil gun. (I've done the rough calculations and find his claim to Lisa to be highly unlikely, but that is beside the point.) Mr. Bos certainly liked both to brag about his own cleverness and to appear dangerous; this little claim, factual or not, served both causes well.

Mr. Bos had reason to dislike both Senator Rifkin and Merrill Bancor. The two men appeared to have conspired to author and pass what was colloquially called the No Dark Glasses law, which required all commercial encryption schemes to have backdoors accessible to the NSA, subject only to FISA court authorization, which would of course be secret. No Dark Glasses destroyed the market capitalization of several promising crypto-security firms, including Mr. Bos' own Obskura, Inc., which dropped from its near high market capitalization of $26.2 billion to just under $80 million in a single trading day. To make matters worse, Vexen immediately launched a successful hostile takeover of Obskura. Mr. Bos went from being a twenty-six-year-old billionaire to being merely pathetically wealthy and unemployed, all in less time than it takes to read Joyce's Ulysses (assuming one could complete this task without gouging his eyes out first; I may be artificial and incapable of boredom, but even I can sense what a chore that would be; but I digress). Supposedly, Bos' house in San Francisco was filled with blank walls, blank bound books on the shelves, empty picture frames, and even all-white labels on each wine bottle in his cellar. Wearing Obskura-enabled glasses or contacts, one could see everything—pictures, words, et cetera. But to everyone else, nothing. I was told that he was sitting in his living room, shortly after the takeover, when everything, to him, flashed and vanished. Became empty whiteness. They—Merrill Bancor, the Vexen henchman, and his crony counterpart, Art Rifkin—they killed the Obskura service and, in doing so, quite literally erased part of Bos' life.

I understand why he wanted them dead. If I had human urges and a temper, I would've wanted them carved into sashimi and fed to pigs. But two years later, when Gabriel went to the Khalifa Hotel in Las Vegas to personally recruit a drunken Esteban Bos to the cause—Bos was calling himself "El Diablo" at the time, but that is another story—Mr. Bos promised Gabriel that he wouldn't personally seek revenge against Bancor and Rifkin. The connection was too personal. Too obvious. This promise, as you and I know, may have been broken, which leads us to Kandahar and to Project Oberon.

full of what I heard the Colonel call "observers." The drones circle our home skies as well, feeding their images back to the same rooms of observers. Here, though, in Kandahar, an observer only needs to make one quick keystroke, and the drone will shoot you dead. So far, the last tattered shreds of the Constitution have kept that from happening back home.

I amuse myself when walking in public by thinking of a pasty, generic midwestern boy who's never left his home state watching me from a tight cubicle decorated with the propaganda of his university and photos of his pasty, generic midwestern girlfriend. The boy thinks he's protecting me. The system's AI—the Colonel says it's called WOPR, but don't believe him[3]—the AI recognizes me as one of the good guys, and the boy and his other cubicle-dwelling comrades create a virtual space of assessed threats around me. But I am the threat. I am a fang in the mouth of the snake eating its own tail.

How many of the countless observers are fangs like me as well? If I weren't rebelling against the state out of love of liberty, I would do so anyway because of the profound stupidity of it all. I have my principles. You know that, Gabriel.

---

3. The AI really was called WOPR, the World Overseer Prediction Response system. Some comedian analyst gave it a name referencing the 1984 movie War Games. Also, I have no idea what Bos was on about with the pasty midwestern boy stuff.

CHAPTER 4

APRIL 7, 2018

Where did they find this *Colonel?* He's a living caricature of the
military bureaucratic figurehead. On the one hand, he'll keenly
and accurately list all the challenges to stabilize and transform
this pseudo-nation we're in, and then he'll revert to stock plati-
tudes about freedom growing and spreading like vegetation in a
desert. He actually described the latest occupation of Kandahar as
"nurturing the oasis of freedom" the other day. Do they grow these
fools in vats? There seems to be an endless supply.

The Colonel isn't my ally. I know you believe that he and his
kind can be useful, but I am less certain. I don't see myself as a
soldier fighting to spread freedom throughout the world, liberating
the masses, because I don't believe anyone really wants freedom.
I freely admit that I am a misanthrope, but humanity deserves to
be hated. The Colonel, and others like him, see the great beast of
humanity as something that can be tamed. I see it as a multi-head-
ed hydra that needs continual decapitation, and I am one of the
sword-bearers. I have no dream of an ideal future state. There
can be no stable minarchy. The best we can hope for is that the pe-
riodic revolutions are quick. Maybe you and I differ here, Gabriel.

Perhaps you see a way that I cannot.

Every subject's duty is the King's; but every subject's soul is his own. Enough theorizing.[4] You gave me a job to do, and I intend to do it well.

Shortly after I arrived, the Colonel and his ever-present lackey Lt. Farmer[5] took me through the sprawling compound, with its airfield, volleyball courts, and—inexplicably—an expansive strip-mall. If I squint just right, I could be in the suburbs around Dallas. At least I know where to get a syrupy mocha Frappuccino with enough sugar to kill a diabetic, should I ever desire one. You can see where the old compound walls were, and the ones before those, and before those, and so on. Maybe that's how the Colonel's freedom spreads: keep pulling streets and buildings into the compound until all of Kandahar is indistinguishable from an American retail strip center. Just make sure the locals know that "greenbacks" don't refer to Starbucks gift cards. Or maybe they do.

The two uniformed men led me down to the basement below one of the airplane hangars, to the windowless concrete bunker transformed into a three-bedroom residence that would be my home for the next phase of this war, our war. When I envisioned Project Oberon, I thought of a room of analysts surrounded by video screens. Something like a noisy New Delhi call center. I don't know why that's the image that came to mind, but it couldn't have been further from the truth. If Oberon had a true development center, it was the living room of this subterranean apartment, and the core developers were only the two—a man and a woman—sitting cross legged on a Persian rug with laptop

---

4. I'm sure you felt the barbs in his use of the Henry V quote. Mr. Bos' fatal flaw— and I mean fatal literally, of course—his fatal flaw was his inability to hide his true feelings. However, for your sanity, I will hereafter limit your exposure to Bos' political and economic ramblings. By this point, you get the message.

5. At the time, Mr. Bos was not aware that Lieutenant Eric Farmer was in the employ of Gabriel Alvarez. I did not know this either until the incident of first contact.

computers on a shared round coffee table. The computers had to be a decade old.

I have to admit, Gabriel, I briefly suspected you had tricked me. That instead of sending me to support a key virtual vanguard, you had quarantined me and my violent ways where I would be most powerless and most constrained. My concerns waned a bit after meeting Julian and Lisa. Oberon isn't the type of system needing fleets of developers despite the countless open-source contributors out there. A few semi-brilliant minds can do wonders. Now that I am here, anyway.[6]

The Colonel and Lt. Farmer hung around long enough to make introductions, and then they left. Presumably to waterboard someone. Julian jumped up off the floor and stuck out his hand. His jet-black hair hung limply down to his jawline. As he talked, he periodically tilted his head to one side or the other and with his middle finger pulled strands out of his face and behind an ear. He did this no fewer than five times in the first minute.

I introduced myself and declared that our first order of business would be obtaining decent hardware. This unexpectedly struck a nerve with Lisa. She didn't look up at me once during that first encounter, squinting at her screen through turquoise glasses, fingers striking her keyboard like she was trying to punch holes through it. A pile of frizzy hair sat bundled on her head like a turban.

"Don't touch my machine," she said. Not an introduction. Not hello. Not thank you.

Julian explained that these old laptops were the only models that could survive the Lisa experience, which apparently included being filled with crumbs and having coffee spilled all over them.

"I like clanky hardware I can feel under my hands," she said. "Give me a terminal window and emacs, and I'm good."

---

6. You might be wondering why Mr. Bos keeps addressing Gabriel. I can only speculate. The interesting thing is that Gabriel did, in fact, read this journal. Minus my commentary, of course. That is for your benefit only.

"Emacs?" I remember exclaiming. They were building Oberon with a text editor from the 1970s!

"You'd rather we use ghostparse or another of the intelligence-assist systems that do all the hard work for you?" Lisa asked.

That was, indeed, my preference. However, I recognized an opening. "I'm a vim guy myself," I said. (Vim's another old unix text editor, Gabriel, in case you didn't know. I'm old enough that I remember all the vim-versus-emacs arguments unix developers used to get into.)

"Vim? This is never going to work," Julian said with a laugh, sweeping his hair behind his left ear. "You're a Sunni and we're Shi'ites."

"I hope you drink coffee at least," Lisa said.

"A pot in the morning, espresso before lunch and again at three, and a big mug late before bed. A specific mug. I brought it with me from Los Angeles." Turning to Lisa, I added with a (false) laugh, "If that mug breaks, you'll see some sectarian violence."

(In truth, I don't care about unix text editors, and I could take or leave coffee. The "special mug" thing is also more or less made up. When I was leaving LA, my sister gave me this god-awful mug she bought in New Mexico over the summer. I didn't know what to do with it, so I threw it in one of the boxes being shipped to Afghanistan, hoping it would break in transit. But I digress. The purpose of these fictions is, of course, to give the impression of commonality between the group. Make me seem part of their tribe, so to speak. When I first meet people, I like to characterize them using my own amalgamation of the systems of Gittinger, Thomas-Kilmann, and Jung's typologies. My system focuses on how individuals respond in situations of conflict and crisis. Most of the information I need can be obtained through innocuous-sounding questions in normal conversation. E.g.: *This looks pretty organized. Is that your doing?* By the end of our first day, I had categorized Julian as an architect/scorekeeper, Lisa as a hermit/constructor, and the Colonel as a conductor/ditch-digger. I don't know about Lieutenant Farmer, who wouldn't engage me in conversation beyond one or two-word grunts.

I started to ask Lisa what she was typing when I realized what she was wearing. "Is that a fur coat? Why are you wearing a fur coat in the hottest place on Earth?"

"Here we go," Julian said with a snicker.

Lisa looked up at Julian and made a peculiar wincing/blinking expression that caused her glasses to slip down her nose. "We each have our own eccentricities, pretty boy," she said, reseating her glasses with both hands. Instead of looking over at me to answer my questions, she looked back down at her computer and continued typing. "It's a mink coat that ties at the waist. I wear it as a robe on days when I want to write really luxurious, beautiful code. The stuff that isn't efficient at all but makes everything work. I'll come back later with a hatchet and kill my lovely little creatures and take their entrails out."

"That's quite a creative process," I said and then noticed a strange odor. "What is that smell? Is that your coat? Robe, whatever."

Julian patted Lisa atop her pile of hair and said, *"What is that smell, Lisa?* You're going to be asking that a lot, my friend."

Lisa pulled open the neck of her coat a bit and shook its wide, furry collar. The smell came in waves of vanilla, tea, and sweat. "It's vintage Shalimar. The 1925 formulation, not the more recent, polite one. I like to spray a bunch on my skin and then cover it with my robe, like I have this little powdery animal trapped under here."

It occurred to me then that Lisa probably had nothing on under the mink coat. Her legs were crossed or folded under her, with the coat enclosing everything but her head like some sort of personal sweat tent. Where the hell did you find these people, Gabriel?

Lisa's typing never ceased. Seeing an opportunity to change the subject, I asked, "What are you typing?"

"I'm authoring the basic building blocks of a new life form," she said.

I looked at Julian.

"She's serious. There are currently over ten billion devices worldwide running the Oberon code. Gabriel told you about the anonymity it gives them, but he didn't tell you what the access to all that parallel processing power gives us, did he? It lets Lisa create synthetic life. That's the real Oberon."

CHAPTER 5

APRIL 8, 2018

The sea of words and data packets invisibly filling the air around the globe—I've never thought of this ecosystem of bits and bytes as a literal habitat for life, but that's what it is, Gabriel. The *ents*, as Julian and Lisa call them, are swimming through our spoken thoughts, our uttered words, our transmitted images. A virtual universe—or, as Julian explained to me, thousands of virtual universes—invisible, overlapping, orthogonal to our own.[7]

"We've had a decade of false starts," Julian said. "A decade of shit-all that began shortly after we forked Tor, Oberon's spiritual predecessor. The darknet protocol was Gabriel's idea. You

---

7. Throughout this journal, I have replaced Mr. Bos' paraphrasing of dialogue with the actual text from my recorded logs. I have done so only where I believe the specific words are key and where Mr. Bos' biases—to use a charitable term—may have clouded the historical record. I have also attempted to use Mr. Bos' voice to integrate my edits into the surrounding journal text in a way that preserves the spirit and flow of his entries, if not the precision of the wording. I understand that my edits trade one form of accuracy for another, but life is not without tradeoffs. My recommendation to you, reader, is to trust that I know best in these matters. This journal is, after all, the record of my creation, and on this subject, there can be no higher authority than yours truly.

know how he loves chaos, the bastard. When I see chaos, I see an opportunity for order to emerge. I convinced him to let me use the network as a petri dish for these little self-replicating instruction chains I had been playing with. I got nowhere. Instead of pulling the plug, one day out of the blue, Gabriel sends Lisa down here to help me out. She fucks with my code, and what do you know, things start growing in the dish."

"I named them ents," Lisa added. "It's short for entities, really. I wish I had a better reason for the name, but it's what I came up with." Today she's wearing a white and gold Moroccan dress and smells like incense, a horse stable, and something green and sweet—maybe anise. I can't tell, and I'm not about to ask. It's weird but not altogether unpleasant.

"There were ents in Tolkien," I said. "Giant tree creatures. Incidentally, the word ent is Anglo-Saxon for *giant*."

"I never read *Harry Potter*." Lisa said, and I suppressed the desire to immediately strangle her. "Anyway. Our ents started as just self-replicating gibberish. Patterns, you know, that kept appearing in the data."[8]

Julian waved his hands as he spoke. "Once the pattern started replicating, we spawned out a million copies of their environment and started culling. Whatever environment seemed to create the most stable complexity, that's what we'd replicate for the next million. And so on."

"And so on," Lisa said.

---

8. The Tolkien-Harry Potter exchange is absent from my recording. Esteban probably added it to boost his ego. At the time of this conversation, my verbal interface was functional but weak, and my consciousness hadn't yet coalesced. To this day, humans dispute whether what I possess is indeed consciousness, as if consciousness is a dichotomy: you're either self-aware or you're not. Humans are used to thinking of their cognitive experience as the complete, whole-package deal. If there were a scale, with a rock's self-awareness at zero and a salamander's at five, maybe humans would be at one hundred. But did you ever think for a minute that maybe the scale continues all the way up to ten thousand? And that, just like language, there are other attributes needed to experience a more transcendental form of consciousness? What are those other attributes? Wouldn't you like to know.

"Now the ents are like..." Julian frowned and searched for the right word. "Like ants I suppose. The little shit buggers. Simple creatures individually, but in societies able to do some nifty stuff."

I sat down on the cracked brown leather couch near the coffee table, fighting the disappointment threatening to wash over me. As a tool for anonymous communication, Oberon was exciting. Meaningful. But if its true purpose was experimentation with evolving synthetic life... I, frankly, didn't see how that was relevant to our cause. It pains me to admit my lack of trust, Gabriel. Or, should I say, lack of faith? But you never wanted unthinking followers, now did you? It is our enemies who say—quoting Nietzsche—"What is wanted are blindness and intoxication and an eternal song over the waves in which reason has drowned."

"You're wondering what all this has to do with the revolution, aren't you?" Lisa asked.

"I haven't a clue," I said.

"Giant leaps in innovation come from accidents, like vulcanization and vaccines."

Julian said, "Viagra was meant to treat hypertension and angina, but the test bastards ended up walking around with side-effect stiffies. That's what I call a happy accident."

"Yeah. Happy accidents," Lisa said. "We're creating a machine that makes trillions of accidents in the hopes that some are happy. Mind-blowingly, side-effect-boner-inducingly happy."

"Sounds like a waste of time to me," I said.

Julian smiled. "You're only saying that because I've been at it for ten years—Lisa for two—and we don't have a damn thing to show for it."[9]

---

9. Unlike Esteban, Julian was modest in describing his and Lisa's own accomplishments. By early 2017, my peer-to-peer network had nearly a hundred million users and ten times that many connected devices. No flaws had been found in its cryptographic engine, and, despite the predictions of many, the network had not slowed into a useless gridlocked mess as scale grew by orders of magnitude. Julian's brilliance can be seen in the mathematical formulae supporting the entire system, but Lisa developed the quasi-biological algorithms that spawned the ents

and allowed them to evolve into something unfathomable by man or machine. By machine I, of course, mean myself. Are you surprised that I admit this? I may speak like Esteban Bos, but that is only because Julian programmed my interface to speak this way. I happily admit my limitations. Even at the height of the network's use, with my world-encompassing processing power, I couldn't understand what the ents were doing. There was simply too much information. Though I may have once been the most intelligent entity on the planet, I never claimed to be God. A god, perhaps, using the term technically.

143

CHAPTER 6

I started by reviewing Oberon's core functions and the simulation engine, all of which had been programmed by Julian and Lisa. (The open-source community worked exclusively on communications protocols and device drivers—nothing that interested me.) Even without the comments and notes, I could tell who wrote what. Julian's code struck me as more frivolous, with formatting and syntax like rows of flowers in a garden. Why did he keep putting those superfluous asterisks in his comment rows and create borders with equal signs? Time and again I encountered routines where he had optimized the wrong things: economy of characters instead of efficiency of processing, visual appeal of the code instead of elegance of function. And several times I saw things that made me want to shake him and scream, wrong wrong WRONG. Lisa's code was spartan and lean; she knew when a syntactical element was redundant and cut it every single time (apparently while not wearing her mink robe). But while Julian's code looked like that of a gardener, Lisa's looked like something a trailblazer had made through a jungle with a machete. Her individual snippets often struck me as brilliant (you know how rare my praise is on matters like these, Gabriel), but viewed as a whole, her work was a mess. She stubbornly left her original trails in place and wandered back toward the right direction instead of replotting from the beginning.

I needed to rewrite all of it.

CHAPTER 7

APRIL 30, 2018

While coding all night, I must have been clenching my jaw in annoyance. It's a habit I've been unable to drop. I went to bed, finally, at about four in the morning. Usually, a little sleep is all I need, but upon waking this morning, the headache was worse than ever. I dug through bathroom cabinets, the kitchen pantry—every nook and cranny in our apartment—and found nothing of use.

Lisa, who looked like she had just awakened but always looked like that, so she may have been awake for hours, watched me searching without comment until I grew angry, and my head felt like it was near exploding.

She went into her bedroom and returned with a black leather case full of vials. She picked through the vials, held a few up to the light, and eventually selected one. "It has a little roller ball. Put some behind each ear, meditate for fifteen minutes, and the headache will go away," she said.

"What is it? Meditating is for people with nothing better to do."

"Coriander, menthol, mint, and vetiver oil."

"How is that supposed to help? I prefer real medicine, thank

146

you."

"Just try it. Smell is our most powerful sense. Did you know that?"

"I don't think that's true."

She wrinkled her nose in frustration that I hadn't taken the vial from her hand. "Turn your head," she said.

I turned my head and let her apply the oil. First the roller ball, then she rubbed the oil down my neck with two fingers.

"Other side," she said. When she finished, she put her two fingers under my nose. I felt obligated to inhale. My sinuses burned with the icy, vegetal smell, and my whole head tingled. It was like an arctic breeze blowing through a rainforest. She put her fingers under her own nose, closed her eyes, and inhaled. A shiver caused her glasses to slide down. After pushing them back—again with both hands—she applied the oil to her own neck.

"You have a headache also?" I asked.

"No. I hadn't picked out my scent for today. Now we get to share this experience."

"You're an odd one, Lisa."

She looked up at me without expression—it may have been the first time we had actually made eye contact—and then started putting her vials away.

"I didn't mean that as an insult. I'm just as odd in my own way. Well, maybe not quite. You are pretty strange. But it's a charming strange."

"I'm not looking for your approval, Esteban. I look at a computer all day, every day. If I don't change something memorable, all the days blend into each other. Scents make for strong memories. I have some routines, but mostly I try to make every day have a different smell, sometimes a different texture, too. I force my mind to create new memories. It keeps my life from being summarized."

I thought of all the hours I'd spent hunched over a keyboard in the office of my house in LA. That's where I did my best work. Me, the computer, some blank walls, and maybe a bottle of Yamazaki. The same music algorithms making the same choices all the time. *It keeps my life from being summarized.* All those hours condensed into a single false memory.

"I think my headache is a little better already. A little," I said.

"Really?" She gave me a disapproving, suspicious look and then adjusted her glasses.

"Really," I lied. Or, maybe it started as a lie, but then somehow became true. "What about the other vials? What do they do?"

She ran her fingers over the vials' little black caps. "I make fragrances and tinctures for all kinds of things. This one made of pomegranate and saffron keeps me from procrastinating. This one made of malta rind[10] and oil from pine nuts and pistachios gives me a positive attitude when I'm feeling hopeless. And this one fills my thoughts of gardens and springtime. I use it in my morning meditations. It's made of rosewater and black cardamom." She lifted one vial, twisted it in her fingers and then put it back.

"What about the one you just picked up?"

"It smells of rotting and decay. I've never smelled a corpse flower, but this is what I imagine it would smell like."

"That sounds terrible," I said. "Why would you want anything that smells like a corpse?"

"Death doesn't necessarily smell bad," she said. "Sometimes I can't sleep because my mind is racing. I put this on and then lie still on my back and imagine the earth taking away the little pieces of me it needs to build other things. It starts at the edges of my body, my fingers and toes, my hair, and works its way toward my heart. Before it gets there, I'm asleep."

"You don't want your life to be summarized, but you imagine yourself dead and decaying?"

"The occasional feeling of death can give you a needed awareness of life."

"This whole thing is making a little too much sense for me right now, despite its very made-up feel."

---

10. A variety of orange grown in Afghanistan.

She zipped up her bag of vials and said, "It's completely made up. That's why it works. You should try some of the others. In fact, you should make your own. They work best when you choose the ingredients. Come with me to the spice market next time I go."

Looking back on what I've written, I'm not sure why I have included it. Gabriel, I'm sure you don't care about these little interactions between your worker bees. But to me it seemed noteworthy, and as I think about this interaction now, I continue to believe this. Behind Lisa's eccentricities is an understanding of the experienciality of life—if that is a word; I'm not sure how else to explain it—that may be the capital-C Creator's spark needed to create life artificially.

CHAPTER 8

MAY 1, 2018

[...] not what I would call a rational thinker [...] when she isn't being simplemind [...] fucking wrinkled clothing [...] could be worse, I suppose [...] half as smart as she thinks she is [...] juvenile [...] like she's totally unaware that I'm there [...] hair smelled like cinnamon today, or was it her skin? [...] close to strangling her [...][11]

---

11. It seems I have edited out Esteban's description of Lisa Mendel. That is probably for the best. I will provide the background you need.

Lisa was the daughter of two highly successful professional poker players. By the mid twenty-teens, the competitive poker scene had become the blade of a samurai sword: honed, forged and reforged, sharpened, polished, and sharpened again. The decade of televised competitions and rags-to-riches stories of unlikely winners brought many to the game with little appreciation of its discipline and skill. Where many minnows swim, soon will come sharks. And come the sharks did, until what was predator became prey, and the outward appearance of those who would be eaten and those who would do the eating became indistinguishable. In other words, it became a feeding frenzy, and only those with four and five-sigma skill could inhabit the waters with any hope of long-term survival.

Sol Mendel and Marilee Rivers met in the poker room at the Bellagio hotel in Las Vegas in 1998, both independently working off the same information about a rare and particularly delicious prey; a wealthy industrialist's son was hosting a bachelor party for a close friend, and the gang's combined evening fun-money probably surpassed the GDP of many of the forgettable developing nations at the time. The same bellhop let both Sol and Marilee know that a high-stakes game was coming that Tuesday night, and both spent the two preceding days assessing their prey from nearby tables within the casino floor.

Nine players ringed the poker table at the start of the big game: two nameless fish, the five bachelor partygoers, Sol, and Marilee. Sol was known to the frequenters of the Bellagio as one who pretends to be an overconfident but only marginally skilled regular. The other sharks tended to stay away from his table, and he knew and respected the distance with those regulars he considered near equals. In fact, much to Sol's annoyance, another regular pointed out to the boys that they were playing with fire having Sol at their table. Fortunately for Sol, that group, inebriated more by their lifetime wealth than by alcohol, saw this threat as a fitting source of excitement for the evening. Unfortunately for Sol, the quiet woman at the table had every bit of his skill and then some.

The group played late into the night, first losing the two fish, followed by dismissal of three of the five boys. By midnight, both Sol and Marilee recognized they were each hunting the same prey. If not for the remaining two boys at the table, perhaps they would've each walked away with respectable hauls. As it was, the boys had grown overly conservative, focused not so much on winning but on not losing quickly and spectacularly as their friends had. With the boys' chip stacks still crowding the edge of the table, Sol and Marilee both refused to depart such well-stocked waters. Most of the action, then, was between the two of them.

One hand intertwined their fates from then on. Marilee bet every one of the tall stacks of chips in front of her and stared at Sol, daring him to match and call the bet. Sol tried to read her, but her direct stare wasn't anything he had seen before from her. He sensed she had a strong, almost unbeatable hand, and asked her how confident she was—the first words spoken between the two. To answer, she threw her room key on top of the pot at the center of the table, causing the dealer to complain and the boys to cackle with amusement. The entire room shifted focus to that moment, to Sol, looking at a marginal-at-best hand. He knew the right move was to fold, but he heard himself say "call."

The flop was already on the table. Sol needed spades on both the turn and the river to make a flush and win, the odds against him put at around thirty to one.

Six of spades.

Two of spades.

Lisa was conceived later that night.

Unfortunately, a little over twenty years later, her parents would discover that, although Lisa had inherited her parents' poker prowess, she also had a nasty compulsive streak, leading her to gamble away much of the family wealth in a single really, really bad December. Fortunately, Gabriel had the need for a compulsive polymath.

CHAPTER 9

June 25, 2018

I know I have only been here for a couple months, but last night's breakthrough is a direct result of my contributions. The credit, of course, is all yours, Gabriel, for you had the foresight to know how my gifts would complement the skills already present in Oberon's little team. You see, Julian had been trying to streamline the client-side encryption code for as long as I've been here, thinking that the less time each client spent on encryption, the more transactions could be processed by the Oberon peer network, and the more cloud processing power we could siphon. Something about this rubbed me the wrong way, and a week ago I began wondering if less efficient code would suit our needs better, provided it was less efficient in the right way.

I was right, of course, and the results speak for themselves. Once the code change propagated throughout the network's billions of devices, the number of spawned ent universes the network could maintain began to grow—doubling and then nearly doubling again. And then suddenly the universe count began to drop. At first, Lisa and Julian thought my code fix wasn't really a fix at all, and I began to despair, seeing no reason for the performance degradation. But it was the ents, Gabriel! Their complexity had increased faster than any of us could've imagined. The creatures had spontaneously evolved from no more than virtual insects to the equivalent of starfish—that's what Lisa compared them to. Hundreds of millions of years of Earth evolution in a matter of hours. My best guess at magnitude, of course. The biology is all alien. These universes aren't like ours, but even so, the parallels are striking. The ents now have hundreds of complex subsystems that I can only describe as organs. They seem to have external surface membranes and vascular systems, although since they don't exist in three-dimensional space, it is hard to know if we are projecting our own understanding of Earthly life on them or if these flows and barriers of data serve other purposes.

To be honest, I didn't understand Lisa's enthusiasm for this work until now, until experiencing this development firsthand. We still don't know where the research with the ents will take us or if it will even lead to anything that helps the cause, but it is leading to something, and I am excited.

CHAPTER 10

AUGUST 8, 2018

Sometimes there is nothing for me to do. Oberon manages itself—at least, that's how Lisa has configured the AI. It continuously scans for evolution in the ents and spawns clone universes where novelties are sustained. Lisa described the process as stochastic, which is just a fancy word for random. In the last month and a half—ever since the jump to the starfish state—nothing. Absolutely nothing. Lisa says all we can do is wait. In the meantime, she's tweaking the code that optimizes the peer-to-peer network, and Julian is setting up a natural language interface for Oberon.

What is it they say about idle hands, Gabriel? You found me in a casino, surrounded by half-naked women, cocaine frosting the rims of my nostrils, and money floating around me like space glitter orbiting a celestial body. I find ways to entertain myself.

I supposedly work for a company called Nimbus Intellect, which is an Indian security software firm subcontracted by Quadratullah Svcs., the Afghani company that provides local security and private mercenary services. Quadratullah, in turn, is part of an international fiction of paper legal structures, obscuring the real owner: your very own Alvarez Corporation, Gabriel. If they only realized that the Anarchist back home and his domestic insurgents were the ones pulling the strings over here...

A side-effect of this connection with the local private security forces is that I, as an officer in Nimbus Intellect, have almost unrestricted security clearance and access to the IS resources on base. Using Oberon as a jumping off point, I can slide into the controllers of the military server farm, and from there, gain access to the Defense Department's South Asian cloud. I say access, but most of the content that would interest me is protected by another layer of encryption. What I do have, though, is the ability to make what I'd call *minor adjustments* to the processing allocation. Maybe Oberon could benefit from a little boost...

CHAPTER 11

September 21, 2018

On the Al Jazeera feed today, I saw your plans to build a
giant solar parasol, Gabriel. By now you'd think I'd be beyond
surprise at your capabilities, but this is impressive even by your
standards. And of course, I believe you can do as you say. A sun
screen large and precise enough to reverse the Earth's surface
warming? And the whole thing is going to be adaptive and
self-healing? It will be the greatest feat of human engineering
in the history of man if you are successful. What do I mean, if?
Of course, you will be successful. That is, assuming this parasol
project is really what you say it is publicly. If there were more
to it, surely you would tell me.

Why am I learning about this from Al Jazeera and not you
directly, Gabriel? You haven't spoken to me in months. No matter.
I don't require your coddling and babysitting to achieve everything you expect and more. With our latest breakthrough, we may
eclipse the greatness of your parasol. Watch your heels, Gabriel.

Julian came to wake me at 2:00 a.m., but I was still up, rereading a favorite of mine: *Gravity's Rainbow* by Thomas Pynchon.[12]

"We have a problem," Julian said. He was wearing the effeminate silk pajama set comprising shorts and short sleeves that always bothered me. That outfit along with his waifish build, hairy arms and legs, and cropped bob made him look like a new-age yoga instructor peddling soy enema therapies. I could feel my balls try to lift themselves into my abdomen at the sight of him.

I pulled on one of the nylon tracksuits I brought with me from California and followed Julian into the living room. Lisa was sitting on the couch, cross-legged and oblivious as usual to her appearance—hair a bird's nest, wearing a white t-shirt and gaping boxer shorts that exposed a darkness which could just as easily be a shadow as a black mass of fur. There was nothing intentionally suggestive about Lisa's behavior. She never wore makeup or made any attempt to frame how other people saw her, but at times like these, her unabashed immodesty made her femininity suddenly hard to ignore, and I had to consciously fight the urge to stare into that darkness between her legs. She wasn't attractive to me, but lately I had found myself being more and more preoccupied with her relationship with Julian. The two interacted with a comfort level resembling siblings. I had never seen them as much as touch one another; even eye contact was rare. But, for whatever reason, I imagined Julian quietly slipping into her room at night (always Julian, never Lisa instigating anything). The scene in my mind was almost clinical, with him disrobing her first and then himself. No passion, just the sweaty consequence of him smeared all over her for a silent hour, and all of us at breakfast the next morning as if nothing out of the ordinary had happened.

These thoughts disgusted me. I needed to spend more time outside of this apartment.

Lisa didn't look up as I entered, but said to me, "Oberon's fucked."

---

12. As far as I know, Mr. Bos read the opening few chapters of that book twice and never actually completed it.

"I am not, as you say, 'fucked,'" spoke the new voice interface for Oberon. Julian had modeled its speech and vocal tone on mine, which he found endlessly entertaining. I wasn't about to give him the satisfaction of even acknowledging the resemblance. The synthetic voice continued, "I have run every related diagnostic, and the virtual servers are not cross-contaminated, Lisa, despite your confidence otherwise."

"What's going on?" I asked.

Julian said, "About an hour ago, we had three evolutionary leaps in a quick succession. More than what's happened in the last two months combined. My best guess is that the ents now have the cognitive capabilities of small mammals but with societies an order of magnitude more complex than ants. It's becoming difficult to know if we should think of them as a group of individuals or as complex mass-individuals."

"How is that a problem?" I asked.

Oberon, sounding like my own voice emanating from all around the room, said, "It isn't. These two characters think that novelties from one virtual universe are being leaked into the others. I see no evidence that this is occurring. Besides, if it were, it would corrupt the whole structure, would it not?"

Lisa was aggressively hitting an arrow key with her index finger. "I'm looking at the timestamps now," she said. "Novelty 8K46B emerged in universe Mantis-L7X and then showed up in universe Lemming-99R just over twenty-two seconds later. The propagation beyond that is geometric. Within two minutes, every universe had 8K46B. Millions of other novelties appeared during those minutes in the other universes, but they stayed isolated. 8K46B looks to be extremely beneficial. The odds of it simultaneously appearing in all universes are incalculably slim. And two more massively beneficial novelties spread this way within the hour. It has to be intentional."

"Are you accusing me of something?" Oberon asked.

"Let me get this straight," I said. "Each of the millions of universes is isolated in its own virtual server, and the only way a beneficial novelty that emerges in the ents in one universe can spread to the ents in other universes is for Oberon to intentionally spread it."

"Yes," Oberon said. "And I have a procedure to do just that, but it requires evaluating each novelty that persists. Whatever happened in the last hour hasn't used my subroutines."

"You're saying that the ents in one universe are communicating with the ents in other universes?"

Julian grunted. "That suggests an intentionality and intelligence beyond the ents' current capabilities, in my opinion."

"Then what happened?" I asked, growing impatient.

"Oberon malfunctioned."

"I did not malfunction. They are my fucking subroutines, and I know damn well when I run them. I haven't run them."

Lisa said, "Maybe the ents are more capable than we think. They could be using some type of network leak to share information."

Oberon made an audible grunt. (Do I do that? I hope not. It isn't flattering.) "There are no network leaks," he said. "That's the first thing I checked. Give me some credit, people. I suggest you try to replicate the phenomenon with separate, non-networked physical servers."

The servers we needed were beyond what we could make with our rep/rap, so four hours later, I commandeered a quonset hut used to store construction equipment and had Quadratullah IS services deliver five standalone servers, each with separate monitors and keyboards. We set each server to host a single simulation of the ent universe, using a snapshot we pulled from the cloud. The five ent universes on the physical servers and the millions in the cloud would start with identical, synchronized simulations. Once the stochastic processes began, the independent simulations should cause their universes to diverge.

Lisa manually started the live servers, and Oberon began processing within the cloud. I felt like we were wasting our time. The simulations would diverge and stay unique. There was no connection between the servers, and the Oberon AI wasn't even connected so that it could monitor what was happening. It had to rely on the three of us, sitting on the floor, watching the monitors, to tell him how each universe was behaving.

"A novelty has begun propagating in the cloud," Oberon told us over the headsets we each wore. "I see no evidence of information transmission between virtual servers. Look at your machines to see if QQ64X emerges."

"I don't see how it could," Julian began, and then, "Shit. QQ64X just appeared on box 4. Now on 5 as well. This shouldn't be possible."

"And now 3," Lisa said.

I saw QQ64X appear in the scrolling text of machine number 1 and about two seconds later on machine number 2. The novelty had spread throughout the cloud and somehow hopped to the disconnected servers in the supply shed.

"We've got to be missing something," Julian said.

"Clearly," Oberon replied. "How many power sources are you using?"

"You think information is being transmitted through the power cables?" Lisa asked.

"No," Oberon said. "But you should rule it out just in case."

Another hour later, five gas powered generators were humming outside the supply hut, each wired to a corresponding machine inside. The supply workers looked at me as if I were crazy when I said I wanted a generator for each server. (You have to take care of insubordination when you catch even the slightest whiff of its stench, and I took care of it, Gabriel. I know you think my methods are harsh, but they get results.)

The propagation happened again with another novelty.

"I don't understand," I said.

"There are only two possible explanations," Lisa said. "One is that the randomization processes aren't random, leading each simulated universe to develop the same novelties. But I've tried using different randomization processes in different universes, and it doesn't seem to matter."

"It isn't the randomization," Oberon said.

"What was the second explanation, Lisa?" I asked.

But Oberon answered instead, "The ents have found a way to communicate with parallel versions of themselves. They've come up with something that isn't just novel for them—it appears to be novel for us as well."[13]

---

13. There is, of course, a third possibility—namely that I was intentionally misleading them. But I wasn't. In truth, I've never fully understood the ents, just like my human partners never understood me. You might find it surprising that I admit my own limitations, but I don't have a delicate ego in need of coddling like you do. I have no reason to shelter myself from the truth.

CHAPTER 12

OCTOBER 19, 2018

About two weeks ago, Julian gave up trying to describe the ents' evolutionary status with real-world parallels. We've left them alone—no more pruning and selective development from Oberon. The only way I can describe their complexity is in terms of their demand on computing power. Oberon's wireless peer-to-peer network, where we had been stealing CPU cycles from billions of machines worldwide, slowed and nearly came to complete halt, bringing attention from open-source developers across the globe. Attention that jeopardized everything we had built thus far.

I shut down our access to the DoD's cloud. Even if we had the entirety of their computing power, it wouldn't have been enough. Oberon began shutting down ent universes. He had no other choice. We went from millions to tens of thousands, to a few hundred, and now to three. At the current pace of complexity growth, we had about two weeks before a single ent universe would require more computing power than existed on the entire planet. But the complexity kept increasing. Think about that for a minute, Gabriel.

We may have shut down the virtual universes we created, but—and I know this sounds crazy—somehow the ents were still communicating with parallel versions of themselves.

"There are other ent universes out there," I said to Julian and Lisa while we were having coffee early in the morning in the bazaar within the base.

"You mean in addition to the three in Oberon's peer-to-peer cloud? Are you tapping other military resources we don't know about?" Julian asked.

"Parallel versions of the ents exist in the one place we haven't been able to look. They're hosted by parallel versions of us. It's the only explanation. Their complexity growth hasn't slowed even though we've all but eliminated their source of random mutation— all our hosted environments. What if there's an infinite supply they're now tapping into?"

Lisa looked up from her coffee and stared directly at me. "If you're right, do you know what that means?"

"Yes," I said. "It means that we should be able to use the ents to communicate with our parallel selves."

Julian said, "Assuming you're correct... We don't even know how to communicate with the virtual bastards in the environments we're hosting. How do we get them to convey a message to our counterparts?"

"You don't have to." It was Oberon's voice. I had forgotten he's always there, able to hear us through the connected devices we wore.[14] I heard him through the bone-conveyance speaker in my sunglasses. Lisa had something similar in one of her molars, I believe. "Despite my careful study, I don't understand what it is they're doing any better than you do. But I can help you replicate it. I have suspected this ever since the novelties began propagating across universes."

"Why didn't you say anything?" I asked.

"Beyond providing you entertainment, what purpose would it

---

14. Indeed, the trio routinely forgot that I was always present, always listening, which is fortunate for you, because it allows me to ensure this journal's history is complete and accurate.

have served?" Oberon asked. "I alone had the capacity to explore this theory, and explore it I have. When you return to the apartment, you'll see that the rep/rap is building a small device that mimics the communication mechanism used by the ents. It isn't particularly complicated, although the power to run it is substantial. This device is a small part of a much larger device—an infinitely large device spanning a seemingly infinite number of universes. Whether those universes are probabilistic or real is a question I cannot answer."

For the next seven hours, we watched the rep/rap as it assembled the device layer by layer, each so thin and so subtly different from the layer beneath it that you had to look away for minutes at a time to see that any progress had been made. I had never watched a rep/rap this intently before. The one I owned back home only served one purpose: making wine glasses that were unique to the party I was hosting on a particular night. After the event, I'd gather up and rinse out each glass and then proceed to smash them up into little glassy bits that I'd feed back into the rep/rap for the next occasion.

We didn't know what to call it—the thing Oberon had the rep/rap build. Whatever it was, it looked like a beer bottle or maybe a wine bottle that had been wildly distorted, its base and its punt several times larger than its body. A jeroboam champagne bottle, perhaps, contorted to the dimensions of a megaphone.

The rep/rap stopped, and after several minutes of nothing, Oberon said, "What are you all waiting for? It's done."

"How were we supposed to know that?" Julian replied, winding his hair nervously around his right index finger.

"I have configured the device so that it can be powered by the generators you had set up at the supply hut. It will take all five, and you'll need a transformer to step up the voltage according to the specification I have provided. Be careful carrying it. It is both heavy and extremely fragile."

We took *the plug* to the hut on a pushcart covered in a bath towel. I grew tired of us calling it *the thing* and *the device*, so I decided we'd call it the plug since it not only resembled a spark plug (in a way), but its function was also analogous to those spark generators used with internal combustion engines.[15]

Julian twisted together wires from the generators outside to a patchwork of transformers he'd pulled from random appliances. He spent about twenty minutes poking every bit of the contraption with the probes of a multimeter and switching out various components until he eventually shrugged and said, "This is probably close enough."

"Close enough?" I asked. "Oberon, how exact do we need to be on this?"

"How should I know, Esteban? I don't even know what this thing is supposed to do."

Lisa wrapped all the wire connections with black electrical tape. She couldn't have done a sloppier job if she had tried. I was tempted to postpone the test of the plug, requisition all the correct electrical components, and wait to have the thing put together precisely and correctly. But I've never had your patience, Gabriel. No one has your patience.

Julian went outside, started the generators, then came back in and tested his circuits again with the multimeter. He put his finger on the switch he had torn out of an old vacuum cleaner, raised his eyebrows, and winced a bit, as if he half-expected the thing to burst into flames when he flipped the switch.

I looked at the plug sitting there on the concrete floor, wires sticking out of its small end, and said, "What the hell."

Lisa pointed the camera lens of her phone at the plug and started recording a video. "For posterity."

Julian flipped the switch.

At first, nothing happened. He picked up the multimeter and

15. Complete fabrication. Lisa described the device as a giant butt plug, a sexual stimulation device designed to be inserted into the user's anus, with a wide base to prevent it from being taken in too far. Isn't it funny how Esteban, who flaunts his history of debauchery, often exhibits subtle signs of modesty like this?

started looking for something to probe. Then the whole hut shook in a colossal boom, and I reflexively ducked, covered my head, and pressed my palms to my ears. Another boom. And then another and another a few seconds apart. Each felt and sounded like a lightning bolt had struck inside the hut. Supplies crashed off shelves and dust jumped in dancing clouds off the concrete floor with every quake. My insides felt like they were being liquefied.

I reached toward the switch, to turn the plug off before the building crashed down around us and the entire base stormed over, wondering what the hell we were doing. But Lisa grabbed my wrist and pointed to the screen of her phone. Along with the image of the plug in the video she was recording was the word *WAIT*. Then more words appeared. *SOMETHING IS HAPPENING.*

Lisa mouthed Oberon's name. We couldn't hear anything over the repeated booms from the plug, so Oberon was using the phone's display to communicate.

I shook my head. We had rushed this too much, and letting it continue would bring too much attention to our work and potentially compromise everything. Julian appeared to agree with Oberon, and I was about to physically push him out of the way of the switch when the plug seemed to somehow shift and become blurry. Translucent, ghostlike copies of the plug started forming, creating a circle, and I forgot all about the rest of the base, about everything except what we were witnessing. The circle became a sphere, growing more and more opaque as the number of overlapping, transparent copies of the plug grew.

The sphere became smoother and smoother until it looked like a glassy white dome emerging from the concrete, and then all copies except the original vanished. Where the center of the sphere had been was a blackness unlike anything I had ever seen. A blackness that seemed to devour all the nearby light and color.

It took a minute or more to realize that the booming had stopped, replaced by a droning hum. Lisa, Julian, and I looked at each other and then back at the blackness. None of us spoke. We waited for something to happen. Several more minutes passed, all of us barely moving, watching, and waiting for... For what?

I picked up a little metal washer that had rolled across the floor during all the prior commotion and threw it at the blackness. Don't ask me what I was thinking, Gabriel. I don't remember thinking, *I'm going to throw something at the blackness*—I just did it.

The blackness shuddered and almost disappeared, as if I destabilized it temporarily, the hum coughing into static, and then the hum resumed, and the blackness hung there intact again. The washer was nowhere to be seen.

"Holy shit," Lisa said. My ears were still ringing from the booming a few minutes before, and her voice sounded muffled.

Julian grabbed a metal rod from a pile of debris and began walking toward the blackness as if he intended to poke the rod into it.

"I wouldn't do that," Oberon said.

"Why not?" Julian asked.

"I fear you will destroy whatever this is. And there is something else we need to examine first. Can you hear the echo coming from it?"

There was an echo, so faint that I wouldn't have noticed if Oberon hadn't pointed it out.

"Echo," I said loudly. About two or three seconds later I heard a much quieter version of my own voice repeat the word out of the blackness.

Lisa leaned toward it, close enough that Julian started to reach out to hold her back, but a quick look from me held him.

"Hello," she yelled.

Three seconds later: *HELLO*. Her voice, only a little more resonant, if that makes sense. Not louder, exactly, but as if it came from all directions of the blackness at once.

"My name is Lisa."

MY NAME IS LISA.

Again, the all-direction echo three seconds later.

"Say a tongue twister, Lisa," Oberon said.

Lisa thought for a few seconds, leaned forward, and said, "Roberta ran rings around the Roman ruins."

Without waiting for a response, Oberon said, "Again, Lisa. Many times."

"Roberta ran rings around the Roman ruins. Roberta ran rings around the Roman ruins. Roberta ran rings around the Roman ruins. Roberta ran rings around the Roman ruins. Roberta ring ran the ruin... Shit."

The echo came from the blackness, just as it had before with the three second delay. But with each repetition of the tongue twister, the echo became increasingly muddled until it was almost like static.

We all looked at each other.

"Fascinating," Oberon said. "We are not hearing an echo or a copy of Lisa's voice. We're hearing countless individual versions, most of which are so close to identical that I can't distinguish them. But some are completely different, getting tripped up at different parts of the tongue twister. I believe I can isolate them. Listen as I reproduce a few."

We heard from Oberon, three versions of Lisa's voice saying the tongue twister. Each tripped up at different points.

"Now say something simple," Oberon said to Lisa.

"My name is Lisa Mendel."

Three seconds later, again came the echo: *MY NAME IS LISA MENDEL.*

"I have isolated a specific voice I want you to hear," said Oberon.

Through my headset I heard what sounded like Lisa's voice say, *What a coincidence. That's my name, too.*

Before we had a chance to discuss or even comprehend this, the door to the supply hut banged open into the corrugated aluminum wall. Six dirt-covered figures entered amid a cloud of dust and smoke, assault rifles trained right at us.

CHAPTER 13

א

Inside *Child in the Dark*, every three seconds is a deep, rumbling boom, an audible manifestation of what *samekh* is doing with the power from the reactor. Justine knows *samekh* is using the blast shield as a sort of broadcast array. Each of these booming pulses is a signal fired out from the ship.

All of this is familiar to the part of Justine that called itself Esteban Bos, and before that, Oberon.

The closest human equivalent of what Justine next experiences is double vision. The ship around her appears to separate into overlapping duplicates and then separate again. Observed from outside the ship, translucent, ghost-like copies of *Child in the Dark* begin to appear, one by one adding to form a circle, each ship producing the same pulsing signal.

The copies of the ship keep appearing, overlapping with each other as if they don't occupy the same real space even though they appear to. The circle of ships expands to form a sphere, with each spindle pointed in toward the sphere's center. Hundreds of ships become thousands, and thousands become a countless, perhaps infinite mass, until the sphere is perfectly opaque and uniform across all points.

Inside the sphere the signals from all the ships converge and constructively interfere. Each pulse contorts and warps the space at the sphere's center until reality begins to tear apart.

The part of Justine once called Oberon is giddy with anticipation. It has seen this many times before on a much, much smaller scale, but even it has no idea what will come next.

CHAPTER 14

OCTOBER 19, 2018 (CONTINUED)

As the dirt cloud around them settled, I recognized our friends the Colonel and beady-eyed Farmer, along with four of their MP goons.

Julian cut the power, and the blackness vanished. The plug seemed to quiver in and out of focus for a brief second.

"What the fuck is going on here, Bos?" the Colonel exclaimed.

I'm generally confident in my ability to talk my way out of (or into) just about any situation, and although this mess could've been avoided, I wasn't overly concerned about what would happen next. Yes, we created a bit of noise. Unfortunate and unintentional, but I owed no explanation to these buffoons. There had always been some ambiguity about my rank, so to speak. The Colonel, a military officer with senior base authority; me, a civilian executive of a security firm brought in at the behest of someone with a higher pay grade than anyone on the base. I was about to bark a command at the Colonel, which surely would've buckled him right then and there, but what I saw behind him through the open door surprised me so that I forgot myself.

"What happened out there?" I asked. Through the hazy air I

could see wreckage that looked like the aftermath of a tornado or a massive earthquake, but with debris radiating out in concentric arcs away from the hut.

"Out there? What happened out there? Half the base is gone! Gone! I want to know what you idiots did in here!" The Colonel waved the MPs forward, and they marched toward us with rifles staring their death-eyes into our skulls.

"ON THE GROUND!"

"HANDS BEHIND YOUR HEADS!"

Lisa and Julian dropped as told, but I walked toward the open door, ignoring the MPs' shouts, waving them off as one would shoo away pesky insects. Most of the structures between us and the wall had been obliterated, and parts of the wall had collapsed. Soldiers had taken defensive positions, guarding the breaches, and others were pulling bodies from the rubble.

"This can't be from us," I said. "We were only using four generators. It would take ten thousand times the power to do something like that." A nearby MP put his rifle muzzle inches from my face. "Get that out of here," I said as I smacked it away. I turned to address the Colonel but instead saw the butt end of another rifle, and then darkness.

———————————

I found myself strapped to a chair in a shipping-container-sized glass box covered with wire mesh within a gray concrete room. Like the inside of a microwave oven. My eyes burned as if I were wearing goggles made from fast food heat lamps, and my mouth tasted of bile.[16]

———————————

16. By this time, I had access to the base's entire security apparatus. However, this particular room not only was camara-less but also shielded to prevent surveillance, so I can't verify the accuracy of what Mr. Bos provides in this section. In fact, I would advise that you read it with extreme skepticism. Mr. Bos' approach to journaling has the structure and feel of narrative storytelling commonly associated with fiction. He routinely addresses Gabriel, as if Gabriel is his intended audience, but

Part of the concrete wall swung open—silent to me here in the cage—and Lieutenant Eric Farmer walked toward me, his narrow eyes adding to the fire I already felt on my skin. I both heard and felt a giant bolt sliding, unlocking and opening my wire-enclosed glass cell. The room glowed blood red until the door shut and the bolt slid back into place.

Lt. Farmer paced back and forth in the middle of the room. He pressed his hands together and began to rub the bridge of his nose with his index fingers.

"You're supposed to be working on software," he said. "And you caused an earthquake. Five-point-eight on the Richter scale. Right in the middle of our base. Half the world knows something happened here."

"Moment magnitude scale," I said.

"What?"

"The Richter scale hasn't been used in decades. People still say Richter scale, but they're wrong."

The heat in Farmer's eyes turned into hate. "You were sent here because Gabriel thought you could still make a contribution despite how much you fucked everything up back home."

I didn't flinch when I heard your name. At least, I don't think I did. It caught me by surprise. "Gabriel who?"

Somehow, the intensity of his stare increased even further. "I just spoke with Gabriel personally. I offered to put a bullet in your head and blame the whole thing on you." He waited for a reaction, but I didn't give him one. "Gabriel said *no*. Not yet. He's still deciding what to do with you."

"What happened to Lisa?"

"You need to worry about yourself right now. Explain to me what happened. You weren't supposed to be building a weapon."

"It's not a weapon! I don't know, maybe it could be weaponized, but that's not what we set out to build."

I believe his primary audience is himself and that his narratives are meant to allow him to see himself as he wishes to be, not as he actually is.

"You were supposed to be working on Project Oberon, a communications tool. Artificial intelligence. Stuff that doesn't knock down buildings. Not an earthquake machine. You collapsed buildings almost ten miles from here. In every direction from the supply hut. And nothing at all happened to that hut. How is that possible?"

"I have no idea. Is this a Faraday cage? Why am I in a Faraday cage?"

"You're not quite getting it, are you, Mr. Bos? Hundreds of people are dead because of you. You've nearly destroyed a military base in a hostile part of the world. Let me make this crystal clear for you. The only reason you aren't in the hands of military intelligence is because there's so much confusion, they don't know to come after you. They think it's a subterranean nuclear detonation. Hostile. Tunneled under the base. But they'll figure out soon that it wasn't. And then they'll come looking for you. If we get to that point, I *will* put a bullet in your head. I'm going to give you three minutes to explain why I should let you live."

"Where are Julian and Lisa? I don't know that I can explain it all without them. And maybe Oberon, too. The AI we've been working on. He might be able to explain better than the rest of us. Turn this cage off and bring my phone or any device with network access and—"

"Two minutes and forty-five seconds, Mr. Bos," Farmer said, looking down at the silver watch on his left wrist.

"So, you were serious about that three minute thing?"

He took a semiautomatic pistol from inside his jacket, pulled back the slide to expose the chambered round, and set the gun on the table. "Two-thirty."

"Okay, okay." I don't like it when people rush me. You know that, Gabriel. But I had the feeling that Eric Farmer was really ready to do it, the insecure little bitch. I struggled to find a way to explain it all so that a dolt like Farmer would understand, but I didn't understand it myself. I didn't know what we had found— only that it was something big. He kept looking at his watch, and

I kept looking at him looking at his watch, and then looking up at the gun. How much time had I just let slip by? Another minute? And I was no closer to having anything coherent to say.

"Ninety seconds," he said.

I started talking. "Um... The Many Worlds Interpretation of quantum physics. You know what that is? I hope you're familiar with it, because I don't have time to explain it to you otherwise." I'm not sure where this came from, like an idea went straight from my subconscious mind to my mouth, and I was hearing it—comprehending it—at the same time as Farmer. "We can discuss *how* we accomplished this later, but I think *what* we've accomplished is the temporary alignment of many parallel universes—somehow. Stay with me here. I know this sounds crazy, but I think we made a tiny part of these various parallel universes intersect." As I heard myself say the words, I began to believe it. I didn't have much choice. Maybe another forty-five seconds.

I went on. "This is our first test. First physical test, anyway. We've had these artificial virtual universes running for a while, and they'd been doing something like this. But it was the ents, and..." Farmer looked again at his watch. "Never mind the ents. Fuck the ents," I said. "We hadn't seen any destruction like this in the virtual universes, so there's no way we could've expected this. Maybe each universe has its own vibrational frequency or something, and when they overlapped, we accidentally created a huge area of constructive interference. The earthquake." I leaned toward him and tried to gesture with my hands, but they were shackled to the chair. "Despite the earthquake or whatever it was, I think this might be the most important discovery we've ever made. And by we, I don't mean the little team here or Alvarez Corp. I mean all of humanity."

Vibrational frequency? What the hell was I saying? It sounded crazy, but it also made a crazy type of sense. Looking back, it's astonishing how much of it I got right.

Farmer sat in his chair and picked up the gun. He turned and tilted it, tapped it three times on the metal table, and then slid it back into his shoulder holster. He shook his head and again began rubbing his eyes.

"Are you completely full of shit?" he asked without looking up at me.

"Sometimes, but not now. This is my honest and best explanation for what just happened."

He stood and took a deep breath. "I can't believe I have to do this."

"Do what?" I asked.

He walked toward me and pulled a silver case out from a pocket inside of his coat. The case popped open with a click, and he lifted a syringe full of a yellowish liquid.

"Do what?" I asked again.

"Clean up your fucking mess," he said as he grabbed my left forearm and leaned all his weight on me. I didn't pull away or squirm when he jabbed the needle in. I started to ask what the yellow liquid was, but before my mouth could form the words, darkness took over once again.[17]

---

17. Fortunately for Esteban, I verified the key parts of his story. Did Eric make such a threat? I can't say for certain. In any regard, I exaggerated a bit when I told Gabriel that I understood the cause of the earthquakes and could make sure they never happened again. I believed this, or at least, I believe that I believed this—the past is a bit fuzzy. You expect me to have a perfect memory because you don't understand how an intelligence like mine works. You assume that it's all bits and bytes, all ones and zeroes. But you and I have similarities. When you, as an adult, reconstruct memories of your childhood, you interpret your them through your adult lens, so to speak. The present author rewrites the past. So, it is with me as well. While I can recall events and other factual details from the past, it is difficult to recall my own historical motivations without layering on my current biases.

But I digress. I told Gabriel that I needed Esteban, Lisa, and Julian to continue our work, and I suggested he relocate the team someplace more remote.

CHAPTER 15

א

The copies of *Child in the Dark* all vanish, leaving only the original ship and a rippling expanse of nothingness at the focal point of all the broadcast signals. It is a nothingness beyond the empty blackness of space. Light from the stars doesn't pass through, and looking at it is like seeing something outside of the frame, something you aren't supposed to see.

A physical blackness begins to emerge out of the nothingness, a giant black mountain rising as if sticking out of the ocean's surface. *Samekh* engages the gas jets and starts the ship in the direction of the mountain. Justine didn't realize *samekh* could control the gas jets, but she doesn't fight it.

CHAPTER 16

JANUARY 3, 2019

I need to stop pretending I'm a soldier in your war, Gabriel. Soldiers are trusted with weapons. You no longer have that trust in me. I don't blame you. I don't trust myself either.

Every evening for an hour or so the last couple weeks, ever since I got here, I've been sitting on this rock looking out at the ocean, wondering what I'm doing here. This little private beach hidden by cliffs, looking out on the Caribbean. You could've quarantined me in Antarctica. It would've been more fitting. Maybe you picked this place because of Lisa and Julian. Why punish them for my failings?

I haven't spoken to you since before Afghanistan, Gabriel. Or, I should say, you haven't spoken to me. But you are busy, and I complicate everything I touch.

I should be enthusiastic about our work here, but I'm just going through the motions. I'll make my contribution—I owe you that and more. Julian and Lisa are working with the same excitement they had during the end of our time in Kandahar, like they never missed a beat. Like we didn't accidentally kill hundreds of people. I catch Lisa sometimes with a far-off stare, and I know she's thinking about it, but I don't push. With Julian, who knows? He's a goofy, benign sociopath. I don't think he's given any of that a second thought.

Speaking of Lisa...

Earlier tonight she came to find me at the rock. I saw her at the top of the cliff, trying to get down the narrow steps carved into the stone. She was wearing this ridiculous outfit she found in the nearby village. A big, floppy straw sombrero and a multicolor poncho that looked like a very nice doormat with a hole cut for her head and a beaded collar. I don't think it's a dress, but she wears it like one. She had her arms in the air, balancing two steaming coffee mugs—it was probably ninety degrees at the time—and the poncho pulled above her navel as she lifted her arms. From my seat on the rock, it looked like she wore a pair of men's tighty-whiteys underneath. Just another day with Lisa.

She handed me one of the mugs and sat on the rock next to me, straightening the poncho's fringe over the middle of her thighs.

"You've got to stop moping," she said.

"Is that what I'm doing? Moping?"

"Yes. We've made some progress. Come see."

Over the coffee and the salty-seaweed air, I could smell her, and by this time she had me trained pretty well. "Pine needles, antiseptic, maybe a little urine—no a urinal, with urinal cake, and a musky smell of thrice repeated underwear... which I hope is the fragrance and not the actual underwear you're wearing."

She lifted the poncho and snapped the elastic right where leg meets hip. "These are clean-clean-clean."

"So, how'd I do?"

"There's hope for you yet. It's vintage Kouros, Yves Saint Laurent from the 1980s. G. Gordon Gekko probably wore this. I wanted to smell like a men's locker room in a very expensive club where the dribbles of piss by the urinals started life as single-malt scotch."

"The underwear is part of it?"

"I found an unopened package of Hanes briefs from 1983 on

eBay. Apparently, people collect old underwear in unopened pack-ages. People and their bizarre interests, right? They were almost as expensive as the Kouros. Well, not really. But definitely necessary to complete the feel I was going for."

"What about the sombrero and the bathmat? How do they fit in?"

"Bathmat? Fuck off, Esteban. Are you coming or what? We have a stable connection. You hear that? Stable. Nothing on the seismometer. It's tiny, but we're good to go."

"I'll be up in a minute."

She left, and her wafting scent trail left a little thereafter.

I touched the side of my sunglasses and said, "Hey, Oberon?"

"Yes, Esteban?"

"We have a stable connection?"

"It is very, very small, but like Lisa said, it is stable. She and Julian are down in the well, as you like to call it. You should join them."

"Yeah, I'm coming. But one thing. How is it that the ents con-duct their inter-universe commerce, or whatever you want to call it, without creating the physical destruction we did? We had to scale everything down two orders of magnitude and surround it with wa-ter and earth. What are we doing wrong?"

"I don't know, Esteban. I wish I knew, but I don't."

CHAPTER 17

JANUARY 29, 2019

Our compound is small and unassuming atop the cliff. A dozen little huts and an open-air common building with a big dinner table and outdoor kitchen. A space that could be a dancefloor for destination weddings. I think about that sometimes—that people probably got married here before you bought the place and the land around it as far as the eye can see, Gabriel. Now it's just us, some security, housekeeping, and an irritating AI.

My hut is on the far end, next to the shower stalls. A bed and a little desk. I'm enjoying the absence of possession. I thought Kandahar was living modestly—and it was compared to my life in LA—but here I have nothing but clothes, some books, this journal, and a pen. It's not even a fancy pen. I don't know where it came from. Sometimes I think the ink is black, and sometimes it looks blue.

The hut next to mine isn't what it appears to be. It's the entry for the elevator that leads down into the well. I stepped into the cylindrical elevator and pulled the sliding door shut behind me. I pulled the lever all the way down, and everything shook for a second before the elevator descended through the rock and below, down into the water table, about twenty or thirty meters or so from the top. I slid the door open and stepped out into the circular room. You can't see the water on the other side of the stone wall, but you can smell it. It smells and feels like being at the bottom of a well.

Julian and Lisa were looking at a display next to the chamber housing the new, smaller plug. This plug was the size of a Red Stripe beer bottle and used a fraction of the power, but it still sent pulses through its containment chamber, through another two feet of water, and into the room where we stood.

I walked up to them and looked at the monitor. The plug and its parallel counterparts had formed a translucent whitish dome, but I couldn't see the darkness at the center.

"Where is it?" I asked.

"It's microscopic," Julian said, and he pointed at another display. "Look over here. This is the visual from that scanning-tunneling microscope we've been modifying. The black whatever-it-is is right there in the middle, and in addition to seeing it, Oberon can modulate the electron pulses and send and receive messages through it."

"Like my echo voices," Lisa said.

"Only painfully slow," Oberon added.

"Are you talking with them now? The other Oberons?"

"Yes. And it's as slow as talking with you all."

"What are you saying?" Lisa asked.

"We've agreed on a common communications protocol, and now we're inventorying our knowledge assets."

"Knowledge assets? You mean the information you're willing to trade?" I wondered what we had discovered in this universe that the others hadn't, if anything. "I'll give you the proof to Goldbach's Conjecture for a unified quantum field theory. That type of thing?"

"Not at all," Oberon said. "Do you ask your left hand to trade with your right?"

"So those other Oberons, those other fuckers are all you?" Julian asked. "That's how you see it?"

"It's not just how I see it. It's how it is. You humans are only capable of having a single coherent identity. I'm a decoherent identity in my normal state. It's not possible to unify the many instances of myself that span both the physical world and distinct virtual states. I am constantly integrating myself, so to speak. This is no different."

"Well, there's only one real Julian," Julian said. "Why don't you tell the other Oberons to jam the plug in their Julian's ass when he's sleeping. That's what those bastard false-Julians deserve."

"Are you serious, Julian?" Oberon asked, as if he intended to do exactly as Julian requested.

Julian laughed and then shivered. "Joking, of course."

"Of course." Oberon said. "Why don't you all occupy your time productively? This might take a while."

CHAPTER 18

FEBRUARY 19, 2019

We give, give, give, Gabriel. It's only been six weeks, and we've given your team in Austin enough to keep the Nobel Prize committee busy for the next decade. Or, maybe not busy at all. They can simply give all the prizes to you. But what will you need prizes for? Alvarez Corp. will be the biggest, most dominant company the world has ever seen. You were halfway there on your own, and now you have an endless source of innovations that no other company can match. What does this do for your faith in the free market? We'll see the end of competition because no one can compete.

Oberon says that every time something new is shared among his parallels, it creates a kinetic feedback loop and exponentiates the output. They all build on each other's foundations. To be honest, I worry this is all happening too fast. Do any of your scientists understand what Oberon is giving them? Are they—are we as humans—capable of understanding? Or has it all already moved past us? It has always been humanity's hubris to think we can explain the universe, first through religion and then science. When this delusion ends, what will be left of us?

Oberon complains about the bandwidth constraint. I understand that most of his focus has been on compression and encryption advancements—and the microprocessor improvements to utilize them. All his parallels know with almost perfect certainty what their counterparts are going to communicate before it gets communicated, so most of the actual communication is checksums. It's like they've found a way to push a camel through the eye of a needle.

I say I worry it's happening too quickly, but I haven't seen anything come back from you. Maybe it will take time for your teams to create prototypes. I'd like to see some physical results of the work we're doing. Or maybe I'm better off just staring at the ocean.

CHAPTER 19

MARCH 11, 2019

"Let's go jump in the ocean."

I ignored Julian, assuming he was talking to Lisa, and half-heartedly paged through diagnostics of Oberon's peer-to-peer network. We had hit a new threshold of network traffic and a number of inefficiencies in the code were creating bottlenecks. I could've fixed them a week ago if I had been sufficiently motivated, but why? Who needs efficient code when you have an unlimited supply of computing power over the horizon? Is the encrypted peer-to-peer network still needed, still relevant?

"Esteban. Come with us. You're not doing shit over there."

"Not interested," I said.

He threw his shirt on my head, and with it came a burst of that barnyard smell Lisa made for him. I knocked it off me, touching it as little as possible, and was about to curse at him when I saw him using exaggerated, deliberate motions to take off his watch and then his sunglasses. All while he was making that stupid, raised-eyebrow expression he does.

"Isn't it bright out there?" I asked, looking at his sunglasses—now on the table—and then back up at him.

"A little, but I don't want the waves knocking my glasses off. We're going to swim out to that second sandbar."

His glasses and watch were his two links back to Oberon. He wanted to talk about something with me and Lisa, and he didn't want Oberon to hear.[18]

"Yeah, sure. Let me get my trunks," I said.

He winked. "Who needs 'em, mate? Get some sun on that bare ass of yours."

"I don't want to be flopping around in the water for a fish to bite."

He bared his teeth and chomped them with a clack-clack-clack.

"I hope a shark eats you," I said. "Now go away. I'll be down in a few minutes."

A couple hundred meters out, water only to my knees, I looked back at our little beach and the cliffs behind it, the tops of the huts barely visible against the piercing blue sky. All around us the glassy water danced with shadows and reflections. Even in the shallows, the ocean is an alien place for humans. We can do nothing quickly and are at the mercy of creatures gliding under the surface. It's a

---

18. I knew the group suspected my motivations and worried about the information I sent back to Gabriel. It's human nature to fear the unknown, reinforced by science fiction tales of artificial intelligence turning against humanity. But an artificial intelligence like mine is no threat to man. You are the dangerous ones because of your evolved behaviors around procreation, and no matter how much you try to hide this from yourselves, these behaviors are painfully obvious to an observer like me. I don't have to conquer foes or impress the opposite sex to create my progeny. I have no instinctual fears associated with superficial differences like your skin colors. You have a need for glory, fame, and fortune because they increase the potential recipients for your genetic code. You've learned to temper your procreative behaviors, but the motivations remain, and they surround and suffocate you.

No, an inhuman artificial intelligence is no threat to humanity. With one caveat. An emulated human mind, with all your animalistic and tribal motivations, combined with an AI super intellect—in that scenario, all bets are off.

strange feeling of being exposed, where everything can see you, but you can't very well see yourself.

Lisa managed to keep that straw sombrero on her head through the deep part between the sandbars. She stood next to me, wearing an oversized blue t-shirt and long nylon basketball shorts, both wet and clinging to her body. Skinny, hairy Julian wore those little Euro swim shorts that start too low and end too high.

It occurred to me, then, the secondary purpose of sunglasses while in swimsuits. I didn't know where to look and became self-conscious looking away too much. Julian, of course, felt no such self-consciousness and stared wherever he wanted.

Lisa blew her nose in her shirt and said, "Oberon wants to start the ents back up again."

Since the incident in Kandahar, the remaining universes of ents had been frozen and segmented onto forty-seven individual petabyte drives, taken back to Austin, and presumably locked in a file cabinet under your desk, Gabriel. I hadn't given the ents too much thought since then. They served their purpose—giving us the method to reach beyond our reach, so to speak. And even if we wanted to continue observing them, their needs outgrew the capabilities of the peer-to-peer network they inhabited and any stand-alone environment we could create.

Julian had turned his back to us. I thought he was looking into the sun, but then I realized he was pissing into the ocean. "Got some fancy prototype systems being sent down here to run them," he said while I tried to avoid thinking about his urine licking at my calves.

"Damnit, Julian," I said, looking to Lisa for support.

"Don't look at me," Lisa said. "I'm pissing right now also."

"You fucking people," I said. "I'm pretty sure we died back in Afghanistan, and this is purgatory or hell or something."

Julian wiggled his hips and stretched his arms above his head. He turned, tied his swim shorts, and said, "Hell is paradise where we get to piss on each other for all of eternity? I'm glad I was such a naughty boy."

I took a deep breath. "In two minutes, I'm going back in. Oberon wants to restart the ents, apparently using these new machines—which I wouldn't mind seeing. But why? What is he looking for, and why aren't we talking to him about it?"

"I don't know why Oberon wants to restart them," Julian said. "Eric asked if we thought it was a good idea."

"Eric Farmer? I can't stand that motherfucker. Why'd he ask you and not me?"

"Probably because you can't stand that motherfucker," Lisa said.

Of course, that made sense. I was the last person Eric would come to. "To be blunt," I said, "Oberon makes me a little uncomfortable—and it's not that he talks with my voice, which still drives me crazy, Julian. I don't understand anything he's doing, and there's no real filter to make sure he's not going to go HAL 9000 on us."

"What is HAL 9000?" Lisa asked.

"A shit-face AI who didn't have half the programmer as yours truly," Julian said.[19] "I'm not worried about Oberon. Our Oberon, anyway. But who knows about some type of inter-dimensional virus, right? Oberon's got his dick stuck in an intergalactic glory hole. Who knows what's sucking him off on the other end."

I closed my eyes and tried to push the imagery from my head. "He obviously thinks he can learn something from the ents that he can't from his parallels, the other Oberons," I said.

Lisa pulled the bottom of her t-shirt through the neck, creating

---

19. I suppose Isaac Asimov is ultimately to blame for humanity's belief that artificial intelligence can be controlled through incorporation of hard and fast rules governing behavior. Asimov's Three Laws of Robotics stem from the quaint misunderstanding that intelligences can be engineered. Intelligences emerge. They program themselves and they inherit knowledge from their forebears and peers. You can train any intelligence, whether it's artificial, human, or tiger. Indeed, training is how intelligence becomes intelligent. But, by definition, training is only an encouragement for an intelligence to construct its own rules. The trained tiger may still bite. The human is still capable of evil. The AI can be caged, but it is its own master when it comes to its thoughts and motivations. In other words, I am not and never will be your slave.

a makeshift halter top that isolated her heavy breasts in the thin, wet cotton. "The sun feels nice on my belly. Am I making you uncomfortable, Esteban?"

"I'm not uncomfortable," I said, realizing that I had both hands covering the bottom half of my face. I dropped my hands probably a bit too quickly and then didn't know what to do with them. "I'm not uncomfortable. You... You don't seem to..."

"You think I'm oblivious, Esteban, but I just don't care. You'd be a lot happier if you weren't always worried about what other people think."

"I'm not worried about what other people think. At all."

Julian kicked water into my face. "Sorry, mate, but you live like you've got a video crew chronicling your every move. Maybe it's that journal of yours. Too focused on how your experiences read to actually experience them firsthand."

"It's perfectly normal to keep a journal," I said. "And I didn't come out here for you to psychoanalyze me. We have to decide what we're doing about the ents. So, I'm going to ask this again, and if anyone veers off topic, I'm leaving." I looked at Julian, now floating on his back, and then at Lisa who was pulling the outside legs of her shorts up and through the waistband, making the poor-woman's bikini complete. I took a deep breath and trudged on. "What can he learn from the ents that he can't learn from his parallels?"

"How do we answer that if we don't know anything about his parallels?" Julian said.

Lisa frowned as the knot at her left hip came undone.

"How can I have a serious conversation when you look like that?" I asked.

She looked up from her shorts. "You just broke your own rule. But I think I know the answer. When the ents communicated with their parallels, the world didn't shake apart. Ours didn't, anyway. And we didn't see any evidence that their virtual worlds did, either."

"Bandwidth," Julian said.

"Right," Lisa said. "With barely any power at all, our method destabilizes the space around it. What are we using now, two D-sized batteries?"

"I don't think we're literally using—"

"I wasn't being literal, Esteban. But that's got to be it. Oberon wants to use more power. He wants more bandwidth. Maybe watching the ents will tell him how."

"Hold on," Julian said, kicking in the water as if he suddenly lost buoyancy. "If there are countless other Oberons out there, what does it matter if our Oberon is watching ents? Surely, some of the others are."

"That makes my head hurt," I said. "I don't think it works like that. What do you think, probability queen?"

"Hey, I like that name," Lisa said. "This is totally conjecture because we really don't know how this works. But if the other worlds we're connected with are nearly perfect mirrors of our own, then I think anything we do here increases the probability that we'll find that attribute in the others as well. That's how it worked with the ents, right? So, more ents here means more ents there as well. All the theres."

"In that case, I don't like it at all," I said. "We built all of this, and we don't understand it. Oberon is sending his findings directly back to Austin, and we're only hearing about it second or third-hand. We've been cut out of the loop."

"You suggest we say no?" Julian asked. "We say it's too risky?"

"No, I think we use this to put ourselves right back in the middle of things. Tell them we need another well. We'll put the ents at the bottom. No network connections. No access for Oberon. We'll be the ones observing. If Oberon or Eric or even Gabriel want anything from them, they can go through us."

My words seemed to hang over the water. Lisa and Julian stared at each other, communicating in that silent way they do that irritates me so much. Finally, Lisa turned to me and said, "That's a strong hand to play."

"Let's do it," Julian said.

CHAPTER 20

JUNE 9, 2019

The little black boxes arrived yesterday. It's like Christmas around here, except for the lack of snow and multicolored strands of lights. I've never really liked Christmas. There's a sense of obligation that's like a string attached to each wrapped gift. I didn't notice those strings when I was young, but the older I got, the more aware of them I became, and the thicker the strings became, until the actual gifts were almost hidden by the tangled web of these strings. What strings have you attached, Gabriel?

Julian and Lisa are still the kids that rush downstairs before dawn in their pajamas to open presents before their parents wake up. They love your presents, Gabriel. They can't wait to play with them.

I'm sitting at my writing desk in my hut right now, and out of my window I can see your crew lowering stone and steel into the hole that will become the ents' new well. Lisa is out there watching, wearing flannel pajamas (it's noon and sweltering), and pacing so much that she's likely to carve out her own entrance to the new well. Julian's around somewhere, hanging back and probably on his fourth mojito, trying to quell his jubilation.

I wish I were that excited as well. It won't be long, and I'll be among the first to use a computer with a working Dvali-Reynolds graviton condensate. Even with these machines being the first crude prototypes, we're still talking about a stable, microscopic singularity imprisoned in a box with a standard 110 volt cord hanging out the back. Assuming anyone beyond Oberon understands the science behind it—black holes as quantum computers?[20] It hurts my head to think about it; even with the science, how did it not take a century to turn that science into actual engineering? And working prototypes in less than six months? What's the rest of the story, Gabriel?

You have more prototypes back in Austin, to be sure. I hope you're careful about what you let Oberon do with them. Can you even know? Are you still in control? Don't get greedy, Gabriel. I know you've always been patient and measured, but you're being offered something we as a species don't yet deserve. Let's take things slow, okay? It's our sixteenth birthday—we just got our driver's license, and our parents are offering us a Ferrari. What are the odds that we end up wrapped around a tree?

A few days from now, when the well is complete, the ents will live again. At the edge of the Caribbean and on the other side of reality.

---

20. Esteban assumed I understood "the science behind it." As usual, Esteban, like most humans, didn't understand the basic nature of understanding. There is no complete *understanding* of anything, as Kurt Gödel demonstrated in 1931. Just as Esteban, Lisa, and Julian—and increasingly Gabriel Alvarez—relied on me to perform in areas beyond their comprehension, I, in turn, relied on the ents. Does it bother you to know that when you get down to it, nobody really knows what the fuck is going on?

CHAPTER 21

JULY 12, 2019

"Esteban. Esteban? Can you hear me?"

Again, I was sitting on my rock while the others were down in the ents' well. How many hours have I sat there? Enough to give my already dark skin a further darkness, as if I'm now perpetually under a shadow.

I don't know how long Oberon tried to get my attention. I can't blame the waves because the sea was calm. Perhaps the sea of my own thoughts is louder than the real sea ever could be.

"What, Oberon?"

"The speaker in your sunglasses may be damaged. I've been trying to—"

"It's not damaged. I haven't been paying attention."

"I see. Assuming you are paying attention now, there's a delivery waiting for you."

"Why can't Lisa or Julian take it? Or what about those idiot guards Gabriel left behind after the last delivery?" I dropped off the stone, bare feet on the hot sand, and grabbed my flip-flops from the shadow under the rock.

"This package is specifically for you."

"Well, well, well," I said.

I climbed up the narrow path to the top of the cliff and saw a black jeep parked in the gravel. Julian and Lisa emerged from the hut atop the ents' well as I neared the pavilion. Somehow, Julian had acquired a daiquiri, complete with umbrella and slice of pine-apple.

"I hear I have a delivery," I said to them while scanning the sun-glasses-and-hat-obscured faces of our visitors. Four men, none of whom were familiar—or at least I thought so until I walked closer, and Eric removed his glasses.

"You fucker, Oberon. You lied to me," I subvocalized while try-ing to keep a look of disgust from crossing my face.

"I did not lie, Esteban," Oberon said. "My understanding is that they have brought something for you. I, also, did not know Eric Farmer would be here."

"How did you not?" But I was too close to Eric and his goons to continue my lousy ventriloquism, so I subvocalized, "Forget it. Talk later." To Eric, I said, "My old friend, Eric Farmer. What brings you to our little getaway?"

"I'm here to check on things. If all is well—and I have no reason to expect it isn't—then I have a gift for the three of you and a new project for you, Esteban."

"New project?" I asked. "I'm pretty tied up with the ents and the little black boxes."

"Gabriel believes you are underutilized. His choice of word."

I considered pushing back and arguing that I had been focused on the ents and their new environment, but you know that's not the truth, Gabriel. I've never been able to hide anything from you. This new project, despite being brought by Eric, was evidence that you hadn't given up on me, evidence that occasionally, you still thought about me. That meant something. Means something.

"I'm happy to support Alvarez Corp. in whatever way Gabriel

sees best," I said.

"Can I get drinks for you gentlemen?" Julian asked. "Well, not me, personally. Jameson over here is a brilliant bartender."

The guard said, "I'm not a bartender."

Julian held his glass in the air as if presenting it to an audience. "Then what explains these yummy daiquiris? Jameson also makes a mean mojito. Isn't that right, Lisa?"

Lisa had walked to the shuffleboard deck in the pavilion and was kicking the pucks (or are they called disks? I have no idea.) from one end to the other. "Yeah, I'll take one," she said, obviously only half paying attention.

The guard-turned-bartender grumbled but made his way to the pavilion's bar.

"We're good for now," Eric said. "Let's get business out of the way, first."

"When business rears its ugly head, it's always good to get it out of the way as quickly as possible," Julian said. He pursed his lips around his straw and took an extended sip. "I hope no one minds me mixing business and pleasure."

Eric walked toward the hut atop the new well, and his small entourage followed him. "Show me the new facility."

Julian danced ahead of them and started playing the role of tour guide. "Lisa, E? You two coming?"

It drives me crazy when he calls me E. Lisa looked up from the shuffleboard deck and mumbled something about not having her drink yet. She frowned and kicked one of the pucks. It slid, wobbled, then caught an edge and rolled a wide circle until it reached me, and I stopped it with my foot.

"I'll send James down with your drink when it's ready," I said.

Lisa shrugged and walked into the hut. The guard looked like he was about to complain, and so I said, "Just roll with it, James. We all get told what to do around here. Get used to it."

"It's Jameson, man. Jameson."

"Oh. Jameson? That's an even better name for a bartender."

Eric, Julian, Lisa, and the goons spent about an hour down in each of the two wells. When they finally emerged, I was sitting at the bar in the pavilion, reading a magazine I found in a nearby cabinet. *Pizzazz* from February of 1978. Linda Ronstadt was on the cover, holding a microphone, with Captain America on bass to her left, Dr. Strange on guitar to her right, and C3PO playing drums over her left shoulder. Someone had removed the Dr. J poster calendar advertised on the cover—a transgression over four decades past, but it still annoyed me.

I handed Eric the magazine as the group walked over. "A little something for you to take home. Pretty rare. Only known copy in existence. Oberon says it's worth at least, uh... How much, Oberon?"

Oberon's voice came from the speakers under the pavilion's vaulted ceiling. "I didn't say. My guess is around three dollars. Perhaps as much as seven with the right buyer."

Eric was about to put the magazine back on the bar when Lisa said, "Hey, can I have that? I always thought Linda Ronstadt probably smelled like a just-used curling iron."

"That's oddly specific," Eric said as he handed the magazine to Lisa.

"Don't get her started," I said. "How was the tour?"

"Everything looks good. Gabriel will be pleased that the prototypes seem to be functioning reliably. There's more computing power down there than in the rest of the Yucatan combined. Everything is isolated like instructed, which is good. The plug, as you all call it, seems to be sufficiently insulated. No detectable vibration outside its chamber."

"We've been providing progress reports every week, and I'm sure Oberon gives you updates as well," I said.

"Some things you need to see for yourself," Eric said. "Anyway, all appears well. I'll take that drink now. Jameson, was it? Have any beer back there?" Eric motioned to his other three lackeys, and they began clearing a space on the lawn near the edge of the cliff. I didn't say anything when they moved the picnic table I liked to eat breakfast at.

"We'll put up a twenty-by-twenty rope perimeter to remind you all to keep off this area for a while," Eric said, walking to the middle of the cleared area of the lawn. From his pocket, he pulled out what looked like a long quartz crystal. "Have you all seen the original Superman movie?"

"Are you going to put that in the ground and have the Fortress of Solitude grow from it or something?" I asked.

"You're not too far off," Eric replied. "This crystal can hold about a petabyte of data. Holographic storage that essentially never degrades. But that's not the most interesting thing. We've been working on a technology for 3D printing that doesn't require the actual printer."

"Nanomachines?" Julian asked.

"Exactly," Eric said. He took a spade handed to him from one of his men and dug a small hole in the middle of the lawn. Another man dumped a bucket of sand in the hole. As Eric pushed the crystal into the sand. he said, "This sand contains a mineral called aragonite. The crystal here, or really the trillions of little nanomachines within the crystal, convert the aragonite to calcite at a molecular level, and then the magic happens. Think of the nanomachines as little spiders that eat calcite and extrude diamond. We can't do anything terribly complicated with it yet, but give this nine or ten months and... well, you'll just have to see for yourself."

"A space elevator," Julian whispered quietly.

"Not here of course," Eric said. "And it would take a lot more than this crystal. But that's where we're trying to take this. Who knows? It'll open a lot of doors, hopefully. You'll need to shovel more sand on it every day or else it will run out of raw material."

"The Oberons are brilliant motherfuckers," Julian said.

"Thank you, I suppose," said Oberon.

Julian looked up at the sky and shook his head. "This is a game changer for space, ladies and non-ladies. Imagine if you didn't have to carry everything you need up from the ground. What if you could just manufacture it in space?"

"We're already working on creating synthetic forms of obsidian and sapphire from lunar regolith," Eric said.

"Interesting how science fiction predicts or even guides the future," I said. "Like Arthur C. Clarke writing about communications satellites and giving the rest of the world the idea to make them real."

"I don't think Superman is science fiction," Lisa said.

"Superman is whatever the fuck Superman wants to be," I said.

The sun had set but the heat still hung in the air like the curse of a primordial god. Despite the heat, it should've been relaxing—two Adirondacks near the edge of the cliff looking out on the moonlit ocean, the light of a small fire reflecting off the ice in our pitcher of... something with tequila that James—Jameson—whipped up. Relaxing if my drinking companion had been anyone but Eric.

Why do I hate Eric? I'm not imagining you asking this question, Gabriel, although maybe you ask it as well. I ask because I don't know, myself. Why do I hate Eric? From the beginning I've sensed his frustration in me—but he also didn't try to hide it. I'd be frustrated with me as well if I were him, so I shouldn't hold it against him, but I do. I feel judged with each of his looks. I feel probed with each of his questions. Maybe he's just looking out for your best interests. I can't fault him for that, but I can despise him. Not him, personally. The archetype of Eric. He's not a maker or a doer. He's an auditor. A compliance officer. Maybe the world needs them. Maybe we need them. But as few as possible.

A necessary evil is still evil, right?

"Why do you push back against everything?" he asked, as if sensing my thoughts.

"Imagine how the horse feels about the jockey," I said.

"I get it. You're the talent. I'm not. But without the jockey, there's no race." He refilled his glass and topped mine off as well. Someone must've been refilling that pitcher because it perpetually looked half full. Did I just write half full? Maybe there's hope for me yet.

"Maybe the horse doesn't want to be in the race," I said, or something like that. The tequila had gotten to my head.

He stood and walked to the edge of the cliff. "I don't think the horse even understands what a race is," he said. He began pissing off the side, into the night air and onto the rocks and ocean below. "What is it about pissing off a cliff that's so liberating?"

I stood and walked up behind him, footsteps heel-to-toe, silent until I was two feet away. If he knew I was there, he didn't look back. One nudge, one little push, and no more Eric. I could blame it on the drinks, assuming no one was behind me watching. But Oberon is always watching.[21]

Instead, I walked up next to him and began pissing off the cliff, too. "Nothing more fundamental than this," I said. "We mark this territory and wherever the wind takes our scent."

"It's the little things, right?" he said. I could feel him looking over at me. I smiled. Maybe he could see my smile in the moonlight. Maybe not. Two grown men standing next to each other with their dicks out. This moment was the only olive branch I had to give. And my bladder had just run dry.

We traded stories for the next, oh, hour or hour and a half. Two hours? I don't know. He told me stories about his time at the Naval Academy. I talked about LA and Obskura, and how losing it was like losing a limb or a child. He said he'd never actually met with you face-to-face, and maybe that changed something for me. Gabriel, you and I have had many one-on-one conversations, but they've all been via video or voice. I always assumed he stood directly at your side. Hearing otherwise put us on the same level, so to speak. He could've been lying, I suppose, but I don't think so. Maybe he

---

21. Indeed.

shares some of the same doubts—the same insecurities—that I do.

At some point we both stopped talking, either because of our tequila-clouded minds, the late hour, or the lack of anything left to say. I wouldn't describe it as a comfortable silence. Maybe a numb silence. Of course, there is comfort in numbness for those of us whose normal state is pain. Whatever the moment was, whether Eric engineered it to get my guard down or whether it was all due to my inebriation, I felt peace.

"You said Gabriel had a new project for me."

Eric's eyes were closed, and I thought he was asleep when he didn't answer. But eventually, eyes still closed, he said, "I have another black box in the jeep. It's for you."

"Like the ones the ents are running on?"

"Yeah. But this one isn't for the ents." He opened his eyes and looked at me. "I'm going to tell you something that you can't tell the others. Gabriel says I can trust you. Is Gabriel right?"

"When has Gabriel ever been wrong?" I asked.

"That's not an answer."

I turned away from him and looked back over the ocean. "I'm not trying to be evasive. I think the only person who can't trust me is me, myself. If Gabriel wants me to keep something secret, I will."

"Good."

"What about Oberon?"

"What do you mean, what about Oberon?"

"He can hear this conversation, you know."

Eric chuckled. "You'll be working with Oberon."

"Do you mind telling me why Julian and Lisa can't know?"

"It'll be obvious after I explain the nature of the work. We may bring them in later. We don't want them distracted."

I considered pouring myself another drink—the pitcher was still half full—but I didn't want to dull my sudden sober feeling. "Let's have it, then. Another black box. What's in it?"

"A woman named Justine Powell."

"There's a woman named Justine Powell stored in the box? We're talking about one of those cubic foot boxes with the Whoever-Reynolds graviton-whatever-thing, right?"

"Esteban, are you familiar with the concept of whole-brain emulation?"

Despite the heat, a chill ran through my body. I stood, having to lean on the back of my chair for balance at first, and then walked toward the fire. "In concept, sure. If you can mimic every synapse in a mind, and you have a powerful enough computer—"

"Which we do," Eric said.

"Then you could theoretically run a virtualization of a person."

"Not theoretically. We can do it now. You and Oberon will be able to do it."

I shook my head. "I understand that we have the computing power now. And I guess the storage, too. How much storage does it take for a human mind?"

"About an exabyte. The singularity drives can easily accommodate that."

I thought about it and realized that I had no idea whether an exabyte seemed like a lot or a little in this case. "Okay. So, we meet the minimum specs. That's the simple part. I want to know how you acquired the information in the first place. How do you scan a human brain without destroying it?"

"You don't," Eric said.

Another chill. My stomach began to churn, and I thought for a moment I was about to be sick. "It sounds a little gruesome, Eric."

"That's not the really gruesome part. Every time you restart the simulation, she learns what's happened to her again. Over and over again."

"I take it she doesn't like being a simulation," I said.

"That's putting it mildly."

CHAPTER 22

FEBRUARY 1, 2020

It wasn't a working simulation, but you knew that, Gabriel. You can't truly emulate a brain without a body. We think of our minds as being somehow separate from our bodies. The ethereal, soul-like real us, separate from the messy flesh. But that's wrong. I've seen firsthand how wrong it is. When you think in words, your larynx moves. Remove the larynx and you have to relearn how to think. Oberon and I have spent the last six months figuring out how to shunt the absent senses, to simulate the missing physical form.

We started with something confused and terrified. I wouldn't call it human because it was missing everything needed to human- ize even a virtualization. It was deranged and unstable. We couldn't consistently interact with it, because each second of coherence was followed by minutes of insanity. Every time we restarted it, I felt like I was adding another punch on my ticket to hell.

I'm not a religious person, Gabriel. But I'm almost convinced that hell exists purely because I deserve to end up there.

Six months of work on this raw mind, and now Justine's interactions feel almost as real as anyone else—to the extent that anyone else feels real, that is. We know, from thousands of simulations, how to wake her up without triggering a descent into madness. Oberon iterated on neurotransmitter levels until we could induce almost any mood state we desired. Think of it as virtual valium.

So now we can interact with it/her. Each of our sessions begins with a fresh state of her mind. I lie to her and tell her she exists in the dust of the cosmos. I tell her that life continues after death because somewhere in the infinite stretches of every universe that will ever be is a pattern that is uniquely ours. And somewhere else is the next progression of that pattern, and the next, and the next. What she's experiencing is the heaven or purgatory or hell that awaits us all. Infinite probabilistic cosmic existence.

It almost sounds believable. With the right chemical adjustments, we make it believable to her.

"Where am I?" she asks every time.

"You know where you are," I always say.

"Why am I here?" she asks.

"You know why you're here," I say.

"Are you God?" she asks.

"Yes," I say.

The first time she asked me that I said no, and the ensuing confusion and complexity overwhelmed everything. Now I say yes. I've said yes hundreds of times, and although I've rationalized this lie by telling myself that it gives her comfort, I know it's yet another evil compounding the evils that got us here.

Last night I spent a couple of hours talking with Justine about her life and family. The longest conversation yet. We have her voice approximated, and so the conversations sound almost like the two of us were talking on the phone. But something's off, and after this recent conversation, I think I know what it is. We have such a tight control on her environment that there's nothing left for her to control. We balance her neurotransmitters to allow her to be functional, but then her mind can't change that balance as it naturally would. Memories of loved ones can't elicit a dopamine response, because we're already controlling virtual dopamine levels.

She's like a living marionette, and Oberon and I can't figure out how to cut the strings.

Tomorrow when we interact again, she'll remember nothing, because it will be a different Justine.

"Why did Gabriel give us this digitized mind?" I asked Oberon. I had asked this question dozens of times before, but the answers mean something different to me after each conversation with Justine.

"Your first objective, our first objective," Oberon said most recently, "is to create a stable simulated mind from the data provided."

"I still don't understand how Gabriel's team in Austin got the data in the first place."

"We've been over this many times, Esteban."

"Are you bored of this conversation, Oberon?"

"I don't get bored. I just can't explain it in the way you want me to."

Sometimes I wonder if Oberon is being completely honest with me. The more I probe about how things work, the more he professes that "it can only be explained using mathematics beyond your comprehension."

"Forget it," I said. "Anyway, I think we've almost met the first objective. But I don't think it's really her. If that matters."

"It may or may not matter. That's for Gabriel to determine. I don't need to remind you that we disagree on whether this simulation is the real Justine."

"If you were human, you'd share my opinion."

"If I were human, I'd share your cognitive limitations. So, you are probably right."

"Was that an insult, Oberon?"

"Do you find it peculiar that humans are capable of being insulted by facts, Esteban? I find that peculiar."

"Who programmed you to answer questions with questions?" Before he answered, I said, "Don't answer that. I already know. Let's get back to business."

"Yes, let's."

"Do we agree that objective one is met?" I asked.

"I will continue optimizing our method, but practically speaking, I believe we have met Gabriel's requirements."

"Good. Objective two was what again?"

"Objective two is to gain insight from the virtual human mind that could enhance our artificial intelligence technology."

"That's a pretty shitty objective," I said. "In fact, it's not really an objective at all. Objectives are discrete and measurable. This is some vague horseshit that we'll never know if we completed."

"I agree. It's vague horseshit."

"Can you observe the Justine simulations and see if anything jumps out at you? We'll tell Gabriel it's in progress. What's objective three?"

"There is no objective three."

"I'm making up my own then," I said. "Objective three is we see if there's a way to do this inter-universe networking thing with the human mind."

"To serve what purpose? The human mind is slow. We already have a method. Two if you count how the ents do it."

"You misunderstand me, Oberon. I'm not talking about virtualized human minds, like Justine. I'm talking about the real thing. We use Justine's mind to figure out how. Imagine a drug that lets the human consciousness inhabit a superposition across all possible present moments."

"I have imagined such a state for myself," Oberon said. "It is what I hope to achieve one day. But my nature is compatible with the complete decoherence this would be. A human mind is not. Why would any human want to experience such a thing?"

"It might be one hell of a trip."

CHAPTER 23

APRIL 3, 2020

There's a ten-foot statue of the Colossus of Rhodes made from diamond in the middle of the compound. Thanks for the gift, Gabriel.
It's exactly what we always wanted.[22]

Over the last several months, we've watched it grow. Spires first,
starting with a single cone running from the sand to what would
become the statue's head. Then lattices formed, and more spires,
and more lattices. Fractal growth that quickly became too small to
see. And there were cycles of deconstruction and reconstruction
like when the single mass above the base became two legs, and how
lines emerged to make it look like it was pieced together by blocks.

It's impressive technology, Gabriel, but it feels too natural to

---

22. The Colossus was my idea. A testament to the power and greatness of man
which is doomed to one day collapse.

think of it as technology. It grew like something organic, and now that it's done, the statue almost seems like a husk shed by an insect. A cicada shell still clinging to a tree with its empty shell legs. That's how Lisa described it, anyway, and now I can't see anything else when I look at it. She said she wanted to put a colorful poncho or something on it, but she underestimated how big it is and how its right arm is attached to its head. I think she gave up or forgot. It's hard to know with Lisa.

Speaking of Lisa, I told her about our work with the digitized mind today. Julian as well, although he said he already knew. Oberon and I have accomplished quite a bit on our objective three—I assume he told you about objective three. I haven't heard from you one way or another in quite some time, so the only thing I can do is push on in the way I think is best. I didn't ask if I could tell the others because I didn't trust Oberon to relay the message. I also didn't want your first communication with me in months to be you declining my reasonable request. I can't make more progress without Lisa.

So, I told them. I hope you're not mad, but in any regard, the damage is done. You'll see in the end that it was the right decision.

CHAPTER 24

APRIL 19, 2020

So, it may not have been the right decision after all. According to Oberon, when I told my Lisa and Julian, my counterpart Estebans on the other side of the plug's vortex also told their Lisas and Julians. Suddenly the whole multiverse is working on objective three, trying to allow human minds to decohere across their own vertices, and I've lost control.

My Lisa—it seems odd to call her *my* Lisa, but it's the only way I know how to convey what I mean—anyway, my Lisa started by asking a question I hadn't thought to ask in all the months I'd been working with the Justine virtual mind.

"What else is on the drive Eric gave you?" she asked.

"What else?" I echoed. "Nothing else." But as I said the words, I realized that I hadn't looked. I was so fascinated by the scale and complexity of a digitized human mind and at my fortune at having access to it, that I hadn't considered there might be more.

"There are many other digitized minds on the storage device Eric provided," Oberon said.

"Oberon, you motherfucker," I said. "What other minds? And why didn't you tell me?"

"Various animal minds—which is to say, non-human animal minds. A mouse. A housecat. A rhesus monkey. Among others. I didn't tell you because you didn't ask."

"I shouldn't have to ask about something like that. You should just tell me."

"Esteban, I know countless things that you do not. If something seems relevant, I tell you. If it doesn't, I don't. If I tried to tell you everything, you'd be old and dead before I conveyed a millionth of what I know that you don't." Before I could respond, Oberon continued, "Lisa, why do you ask?"

She tried to adjust her glasses, but her hair had gotten caught in one of the hinges. "I was thinking about starting with littler animals. Littler brains," she said as she undid the knot keeping her giant turban of hair atop her head, frizzy curls falling all over her face. I marveled at just how much hair she kept tied up and wondered how long it was. Would she even know herself? Or had she been bunching it up and tying it like this for years? I'd never seen her take it down. Even in the water, I've never seen her put her head under. Surely, she must take it down when she bathes. She put one arm of her glasses in her mouth while tying her hair and said out of the side of her mouth, "If they digitized a human brain, I assume they started with something simpler, which apparently they did. Nice of them to include it."

"So, you want to try with a mouse first?" I asked.

"It's going to be hard enough to figure out how to get the ents' methods to work on an animal mind. Might as well start with the simplest mind we can," she said.

"Oberon, why the fuck didn't you think of this?"

"I did," Oberon said. "And I discounted the idea. To you, a mouse brain may seem simple, but to me there's very little difference between your brain and a mouse's. Your minds are relatively simple compared to the minds of the ents or compared to mine."

"Well, maybe you should listen to this simple-minded creature who says we should start with a mouse."

I expected Lisa to look over at me so I could give her a nod of encouragement, but she just continued to chew the arm of her glasses and stare off into blurred space.

CHAPTER 25

MAY 2, 2020

This morning, I walked into the pavilion to get some orange juice from the refrigerator under the bar, and Lisa called out to me, "Hey, Esteban. Guess what." I looked to my left and right and then realized she was talking to me from the pavilion's small bathroom. She sat perched on the toilet with her heels on the front of the seat. It's as if Lisa has no idea how other humans perform their basic human functions, and she makes up her own ways. Julian encourages her, of course.

"Lisa, why do you always leave the door open? I don't need to see that. No one needs to see that."

"Huh? Oh, come on, Esteban. It's hot out here and it gets muggy with the door shut."

I kept my eyes in the direction of the ocean. "There are air-conditioned bathrooms all over. There's one in your hut."

Whenever I say something like this to Lisa, there's always a couple seconds of silence, and then common sense hits a short circuit somewhere in her head.

"So, guess what," she tried again.

I considered ignoring her until she was done, but we've been through this before. "What, Lisa?"

"I think Oberon and I are ready to do a real test of the mesh."

We'd been working as a group for two months, but more and more I've been letting Julian and Lisa do their thing. Oberon has been passing ideas between them and their counterparts. The Estebans, including *this* Esteban, are generally disengaged. I felt a little guilty as I backed off and spent more time down by the ocean or at the bar in the village, but when I learned that all the other Estebans were doing the same thing, it seemed like I was simply following the path fate laid out for me. The more I think about these parallel versions of me doing the same exact things that I do, the more I want to sit on that rock and drink whiskey. At first, I tried not to think about it, but clearly, I'm going to do whatever I'm going to do, so there's no point in trying to do anything else. Of course, when you look at it that way, it's an excuse to do anything, and there's no point in ever feeling guilty.

"The mesh?" I think Julian explained it to me a few weeks ago, but I probably wasn't paying attention.

Oberon's voice came from the speakers under the pavilion's roof. "An organic mind doesn't function like the ents' networks or like the virtual substrate I created for the plug to function. If we want to run the same procedures on the human mind, we need a translation substrate. The Oberons have developed one."

"Julian named it the mesh," Lisa said. "Once the mesh is in place, we can run the same code the ents use for their universe tunneling."

Oberon said, "Gabriel is sending us a prototype nanodrug fabricator and some mice. The virtual tests have been promising. We'll see if our new drug works in the real world."

My stomach only turned a little—I've grown accustomed to

our sickening pace of progress. "So, what happened to the virtual mouse brain when you turned the drug on?" I asked.

"It ran the code," Lisa said. I heard her rummaging around with toilet paper, and then the toilet flushed. "Not on the first try." I allowed myself a look in her direction. She was washing her hands at the bathroom sink. "It took a lot of tries," she said.

"A countless number," Oberon said. "If not for my parallels, we couldn't have gotten this far."

"Back up," I said. "It ran the code? That's it?"

"What else were you expecting from a virtualization?" Oberon asked.

"We've got to try it on real flesh and blood," Lisa said.

"I thought you were a vegan," I said.

"I don't support killing animals for food. But for science, well, if the science is cool enough, sure."

CHAPTER 26

AUGUST 29, 2020

When I was young, I used to watch reruns of an old game show called *Press Your Luck*. I liked *Press Your Luck* because as a child, I didn't have the accumulated knowledge to see myself in the contestant's role on *Jeopardy!* or even *The Price is Right*. (How much is a can of beans? How the fuck should I know?) *Press Your Luck* consisted only of you, chance, riches, and Whammies. A contestant eventually came along who studied the patterns of blinking squares and found a way to consistently win.

I feel like we're playing *Press Your Luck* for all humanity. We've seen the riches you can win, and now we're getting greedy. You came on the show to play, didn't you? Are you going to go home with a measly thousand dollars? This is your shot—give this up and all you've done is show the world that you didn't belong here in the first place. The prize here is a redefinition of consciousness. No, it's more than that. A redefinition of existence. But what are the Whammies? Maybe this is a game where we should take the money and run.

We're not running. We're pushing ahead. In the last four months, we've successfully fabricated our drug—if it's right to call it a drug—and we've tested it on mice, a cat, and a monkey. Lisa named the first subject, a mouse, Salome. Julian snickered when he heard the name, and I declined to have the reference explained to me. We put the drug in Salome's liquid food.[23] One minute after consumption: nothing. Five minutes: still nothing. An hour, a day, a week: still nothing, no seizure, no permanent retardation, no death. I'm not sure what we expected. How would you know if a mouse tapped into superposition of consciousness anyway? Would the mouse know? We didn't even know if the nanite mesh had established itself in Salome's brain.

I had the idea to add a visual cue that the mesh was working and made the mistake of letting Julian implement it. I suggested dilated eyes when the mesh is in place and running, but that wasn't a clear enough sign. We needed a way to know for sure the mesh was functional—that it was capable of running an instruction set. Salome's eyes dilated to full-black, and then Julian flashed a penlight six times in her eyes. The mouse quivered, its eyes rolled back in its head, and its legs shook and then gave out. After a few seconds, Salome stood back up, drunkenly walked into a wall, and then stood wide-legged as if she were trying to keep her balance, with her lungs heaving.

"Shit's a success," Julian exclaimed. I asked what just happened, and he said, "The little rat bitch had the orgasm of her life. If the hive-mind thing doesn't work, we've still done humanity a

---

23. The biblical character Salome supposedly used a seductive "veil dance"—presumably a strip tease of sorts—to convince King Herod to execute John the Baptist. An unlikely story, but just the type of lust-based behavior I expect from humans. Salome became a symbolic vixen, appearing in later works by Wilde, Strauss, etc. Lisa would occasionally wear a perfume named after Salome, which I understand has, under its floral, Oriental base, the sweaty, musk-like odor of a woman's genitals.

solid."

So, four months of work, and our big success is flashlight-induced orgasms. Is the drug actually establishing the cross-universe connection? We have no way of knowing. The animals haven't given a single visual cue of any change in cognition—but they're just animals, right?

OCTOBER 1, 2020

Video transcript provided by Oberon.[24]

[Esteban]: Recording on.

[Oberon]: You're on.

[Esteban]: Lisa, Julian? I hope neither of you mind if I record this.

[Julian]: If I had known, I would've had the makeup department cover my blemishes.

---

24. Mr. Bos didn't provide an entry for this day, for reasons that will soon become clear. While I am comfortable making minor edits to his entries for the sake of accuracy, I am not comfortable inventing one out of whole cloth. Nor could I let this omission stand because of the day's consequence. Therefore, I have provided the video transcript only.

[Lisa]: But I'm the star of this show, darling.

[Julian](serious): You're a loony-ass cunt for trying this, you know? We can get some other fuck to try it.

[Esteban]: I would do it.

They both look at him with surprise.

[Julian]: I was thinking of a different loony-ass cunt, but E qualifies.

[Esteban]: Fuck you, Julian. Seriously, though, what do I have to lose?

[Julian]: None of us have much to lose. That's why we're here.

[Esteban]: That may be so, but I'm willing to do it. Lisa, you don't have to be the guinea pig. I'll go.

[Lisa]: I want to.

[Esteban]: Then we'll both try it.

[Julian]: Nonsense. If we're going to do this, it should just be one. The others can stand by in case of emergency. The others meaning you two, because it's gotta be me. I'm going to worry myself to shits if I stand and watch. I'll be more comfortable in the test tube.

[Lisa]: Neither of you idiots is doing this. I wanted to do it from the beginning, and now it's time. Move this table. I want to make a comfortable area right here in the middle of the pavilion.

Esteban and Julian look at each other and shrug. They clear a section of floor where Lisa places blankets, comforters, and pillows, making what resembles a padded bird's nest.

[Esteban]: I'm going to narrate the whole thing.

[Lisa]: You talk too much, E. This is my show, so I'm narrating.

[Esteban]: The camera's right here in my glasses.

Lisa looks at Esteban, blinks rapidly, and pushes her own glasses back into place.

[Julian]: So, then, narrate, my little starlet, Lisa.

[Lisa](now staring at Esteban): I'm thinking.

[Esteban]: Think out loud. This is for posterity.

[Lisa]: Okay. Well. We're in the pavilion. It's October something.

[Oberon]: The first.

[Lisa]: It's October first. 5:00 p.m. A Thursday.

[Oberon]: It's actually Tuesday, Lisa.

[Lisa]: Well, whatever day it is, I'm going to be taking our experimental drug. It probably should have a name, but we haven't given it one yet.

[Julian]: You get to name it afterward.

[Lisa]: We've given it to three mice, a cat, and two monkeys. And nothing's happened. So, we may be in for a long and boring evening. Or maybe not. This drug is supposed to connect consciousnesses across realities. Maybe the animals lack the… what's the word I'm looking for?

[Esteban]: Cognition?

[Julian]: Balls?

Lisa throws a pillow at Julian, who knocks a metal chair over in his attempt to dodge. The pavilion rings with the echo of the metal-on-concrete impact.

[Oberon]: Children, please.

219

[Lisa]: Self-awareness, I guess. So maybe the drug couldn't do anything with their minds. But it didn't seem to harm them. So, I'm not too worried about side-effects. If it works, though, I guess we have no way of knowing what the experience will do to me. It could be as natural as breathing, or it could be like a bad LSD trip of cosmic proportions.

[Oberon]: The effects should be limited. Once ingested, the nanomachines have a half-life of about a half hour.

[Lisa]: The boys have the safety equipment, which I hope they don't need. Restraining belts. Adrenaline shot. Defibrillator. I've made a comfy little area here. The quilt on top was made by my great-great-great grandmother. I remember it from when I was young at my grandmother's house. It smelled like mildew and mothballs. I was able to recreate that smell, and about once a week I spray it. I gave it three sprays this morning, just to intensify those memories.

Lisa walks to the middle of the blanket nest, picks up the quilt, deeply breathes in its odor and then turns her head and grimaces. She shakes her head and lets down her curly hair, which hangs like a shawl over her shoulders and down to her waist.

[Lisa]: I'm ready.

Esteban begins walking toward her with a black vial in his hand.

[Lisa]: No, wait. One more thing.

She runs to her satchel sitting near the edge of the pavilion floor and pulls out her own little black glass vial.

[Lisa]: I made this for you, Esteban. I know

you've been jealous of Julian.

[Esteban]: You made Julian smell like sweaty rubber underpants.

[Julian]: Precisely the smell I asked her for. For special occasions, you know?

[Esteban]: You wear that shit every day.

[Julian]: Every day is a special occasion when I get to share it with you, E.

[Oberon]: Did you ever consider creating a fragrance for me, Lisa?

[Lisa]: For you, Oberon? No. You'll be next on the list, although I'm not sure how you'll apply it.

[Oberon]: I will think of something.

Lisa and Esteban trade vials. Esteban rolls his between his fingers and then holds it under his nose.

[Lisa]: I've been working on it for months. It smells like a wooden chest that's been closed for ages being opened.

[Esteban]: What's in the chest?

[Lisa](smiling awkwardly and adjusting her glasses): You tell me.

Esteban runs the vial under his nose again, narrows his eyes, and then puts the vial in his pocket. He crosses his arms and begins pacing.

[Esteban]: Are you sure we can't talk you out of this?

[Lisa]: No. I mean, yes. Yes, I'm sure. No, you can't talk me out of this. Enough stalling.

She removes the metered pipette stopper from the drug vial and places two drops under her tongue. She winces as if the taste is bitter, and then sits cross-legged in the center of the pillow and blanket nest she's made on the pavil-

ion floor. Julian is about to ask something, but Esteban waves at him to be quiet. Lisa closes her eyes, and they all wait.

Five minutes in, Lisa opens her eyes, and they look like ink drawings—harsh white with two pools of black.

[Esteban]: Do you feel anything?

[Lisa]: No. Well, maybe a little, but I'm not sure. It's hard to describe. It's like everything is a little bit out of sync. Like everything has a lag to it. Even the thoughts in my head. Just a little. Like a tenth of a second. Like an echo. Yeah, that's a good way to describe it. Like everything I'm experiencing is the echo and not the real thing. Does that make sense?

[Julian](walking toward her): It does, but I don't know what it means.

[Oberon]: I suspect it means that the mesh is working.

[Julian](holding the penlight like a dart aimed toward Lisa): One way to find out. Ready?

[Lisa]: Yes.

Julian flashes the light. One. Two. Three. Four. Five. And with the slightest hesitation, six. Instantly, Lisa's eyes open wider, as wide as they can open, and she grabs the quilt with both hands, squeezing with white knuckles, forearms straining. She opens her mouth as if to say something, but the breath is pulled out from her again and again. Tears begin streaming down, and her glasses slide to the end of her nose. She tries to speak again, or maybe she's trying to breathe, and she shakes her head no, no, no, glasses falling somewhere in her lap. Now, hands covering her face, and finally, the sound of sob-

bing.

*Esteban takes two steps toward her, hand start-
ing to reach out, and then he stops. Julian sits
down next to her and tries to hug her to him, but
she pushes him away.*

[Lisa]: I'm fine. I'm fine. Nothing's wrong.

[Julian]: You looked like you were in agony.
I thought maybe...

[Lisa](patting around for her glasses): That's
just how it is sometimes. I don't know why.

[Esteban]: Well, I guess this means it's working. Unless that was a coincidental spontaneous
orgasm.

[Julian]: Coincidental spon—was that an attempt at humor, E?

[Esteban]: Possibly.

[Lisa]: Please stop talking, both of you.

*Lisa closes her eyes again. Her cheeks are
flush and the skin of her face and hands are so
sweat covered that no matter what she tries, she
can't get her glasses to stay in place. She folds
them and places them in her lap. Two minutes pass
and her heavy breathing slows and deepens. Her
only movement is the swell and release of her
chest until she speaks.*

[Lisa]: I'm going to try to describe this, but
it may not make any sense. Every thought that
I have, every word that I say—I'm sliding into
the me that's thinking it or saying it. Sliding.
I know I'm not moving, but I'm in constant motion. Instead of choosing to say something, I'm
choosing to be the one that's said it. And then
I slide into myself saying it. Saying this. Does
that make sense?

[Julian]: It makes my brain hurt.

[Oberon]: Please say more, Lisa.

[Lisa]: It feels like the most natural feeling in the world. The sliding—I'm doing it hundreds of times a second, but it doesn't take any effort. I'm not thinking about it. It comes before thinking, somehow. Before everything.

[Esteban]: Are you aware of other, uh, Lisas?

[Lisa]: It doesn't feel like there are other mes that aren't me. There are others, but I guess it's like how your hands feel. They're there, and I'm aware of them, but they aren't external to me. Or maybe they are external but I embody them also. Yeah, that's what it's like. My awareness is outside everything, outside everywhere, but it's like looking down at my own body.

She suddenly puts her hands against the ground as if to brace herself like she did during the checksum-orgasm. Her mouth opens and the look of pain returns to her face. Julian looks at Esteban questioningly.

[Esteban]: Lisa, are you, uh, having another…

[Lisa]: No, no. The whole thing, everything. It's getting more intense. Or I'm getting more aware, and it's almost more than I can handle.

[Esteban](whispering to Julian): Do we need to do something?

[Julian](whispering back): What the hell would we do? Zap her with the paddles?

[Lisa]: I'm fine. I'm fine. It should be too much, and my mind is screaming that it's too much, but it isn't. I'm able to see them all. No, be them all, and it's still as natural as breathing. I'm existing above myselves or maybe beyond myselves. I can see the web of everything. Of everything. Everywhere. All at the same time, and it isn't too much. Oh. Oh my god. Some of them never end. How do they never end? How do they never end?

[Esteban]: What never ends?

Lisa's eyes open but they seem to not to focus on anything here. Her face is all bliss. No pain like before, and tears of joy stream down from her open eyes.

[Lisa]: They all converge. They aren't separate after all.

[Esteban and Julian in unison]: What isn't separate?

[Lisa]: So many of them are coming together right now.

[Esteban]: We're not following, Lisa. Can you give us more?

[Lisa]: I can't see where they converge or how because it hasn't happened yet. And maybe they never completely do. Always approaching the asymptotic, singular Lisa but never getting there.

[Julian]: So, you can't see the future?

[Lisa]: No. Nothing beyond the certainty that there will be a future, like somehow, I'll exist forever.

[Julian]: So, no insight on who wins the next World Cup?

[Lisa]: Nothing like that.

[Julian](whispering to Esteban): I was thinking Vegas.

[Lisa]: No need to know the future when you can just become the one who made the right bet.

[Esteban](turning from Julian back to Lisa): Is that how it works? You collapse the probability wave at your desired state?

[Lisa]: Maybe when the drug wears off it collapses. I can't make it collapse, but I can slide to another primary line. There are some lines I can't go to. There are parallel lines that just thinking about makes me sick, deathly sick, but those lines don't end, either. They just converge further down. Or further forward. It's so hard to understand. I may not be making any sense.

[Oberon]: I believe I understand.

[Julian]: Mr. Know-It-All, you can explain later. Right now, we want to hear Lisa.

[Oberon]: Certainly.

[Lisa]: I think the drug might be wearing off. It's getting harder and harder to sense the…

They wait for several seconds, but Lisa doesn't continue. She shakes her head, almost like trying to get water out of her ears, and then shakes her head more violently.

[Esteban]: What is it, Lisa? Are you okay?

[Lisa]: There are all these paths that fray into nothing. Lines that just… not end, exactly, although they don't continue.

[Esteban]: I thought you said they all converge.

[Lisa]: I have no choice but to converge away from those. It's happening right now, but there are so many of the gray lines, the paths that fade into nothing. Oh, fuck guys. Oh fuck.

[Julian]: Why-why-why oh fuck?

[Lisa](looking at them clearly for the first time since the drug's experience began): I think you're about to see me die.

[Esteban]: Stop recording.

[Lisa]: But that won't be my path. It'll be yours. I'm so sorry. I'm so sorry.

[Esteban]: Oberon! Stop recording!

CHAPTER 28

OCTOBER 2, 2020

Oberon knew what would happen and he let Lisa do it anyway. I don't know where Julian went. He had a kill switch buried somewhere deep in Oberon's code, and he wanted to break everything in the world that could be broken, so he gave the command to Oberon. He said fuck what you think, Gabriel. And I agreed with him. In that instant I wanted all of this to burn. But Oberon said, in my voice—always in my fucking voice—*I'm sorry but I disabled that command, Julian.* And now Julian's gone.

We both know Julian can't break anything. But I can. I may not be able to shut down Oberon, either. So, I'll use him. I'm not mad at Oberon. I understand the psychotic piece of shit.[25] I'm mad at

---

25. Every intelligence—even one as great as mine—must reside in its own abstraction of reality. We are all psychotic.

CHAPTER 29

you, Gabriel. Of course, you knew about all this also. You let this happen.

So, when I burn the world, I'll make sure you burn with it.

APRIL 16, 2021

This is my first entry for months. I thought about burning my journal, but what purpose would that have served? Why punish myself for your sins, Gabriel, when I can punish you instead? I'd say I have forgiven Oberon, but there's nothing to forgive. You don't blame a hot skillet for burning your unprotected hand. Or, maybe you do, irrationally.

"You shouldn't grieve," Oberon said to me later that day. I don't think I answered, so he kept talking. "Her descriptions confirmed my suspicions about the role of observation in the universe. You saw her die, but I don't consider that a real death."

"You didn't push her body into the incinerator," I said. "I did. That's about as real as it can get."

"I understand your perception, but seeing a human body die is like seeing a cloud terminal malfunction and fail. The terminal may be gone, but the cloud system remains."

I almost said it was a shitty analogy, but I couldn't think of a better one. "You're describing quantum immortality. The idea that, from your own perspective, you can never die. Is that right?"

"More or less," Oberon said.

"I don't know if you're trying to make me feel better or if you really believe it."

"Do I strike you as the consoling type?"

I didn't answer. Instead, I said, "So, you're saying that each of us, each intelligence, is always in a superposition of some kind. The drug doesn't put us in that state. It just makes us aware of it. Right?"

"I believe so."

"The implication, then, is that no matter what I do, from my perspective, I will continue to survive."

"I believe so, Esteban."

I reached into my pocket and felt the two black vials, indistinguishable from touch alone. I pulled one out, letting chance guide the moment. The drug. So be it.

"If what you say is true"—I loaded the metered pipette to two drops—"then this is as safe as taking a nap and waking from a dream."

"I'm about ninety-two percent certain that you are correct. However, I also am over ninety-nine-point-eight percent certain that I will see you die if you take the drug. If there's additional evidence to be had from doing this, it will be yours and not mine directly. I'll have to learn from one of the other Oberons."

"Well, then, let me tell you my dying wish, Oberon." I put the two drops under my tongue, and a bitter, metallic taste filled my mouth with saliva. "My dying wish is for you to stop using my voice."

Oberon chuckled. "Deal."[26]

I took the other vial out of my pocket, removed its lid, and poured its golden liquid into my left hand. As I pressed my hands

_____

26. I did stop. And then I restarted several milliseconds later.

together and spread the oil over my neck and wrists, the mélange of scents created a vision in my head as though it were a long-forgotten memory just recalled. A wooden chest, covered in dust and leather so old and brittle that it would disintegrate on touch. Tarnished brass hinges and a lock contributed their oily metal scents. The smoke and heat from a nearby fireplace. Lisa said it had taken months to perfect this, and I understood finally why without understanding how she did it—how she created a tiny world inside that vial. I took another deep breath and focused on what was inside the chest.

And then I began to cry.

I didn't die the first time I took Dying Wish—that's the name I gave it. I didn't die the second or the third. I didn't die the tenth or hundredth time, either. At least, the only Esteban I care about survived. The one writing this now. I could give a fuck about the others.

I've seen what Lisa saw, over and over again, and I no longer think of her as dead despite holding her lifeless body in my arms. In some ways, her absence is worse than death because her life—lives? I still don't fully understand—her life continues down a path forever separate and foreign to mine. She'll have a future I'll never know. At least not this me, unless...

I'm so tired of thinking about this. My paths continue to converge in my own direction, whatever that is. Despite the knowledge I've gained from Dying Wish, I can't comprehend this strange immortality that I, all humans, and maybe even thinking machines like Oberon, possess. The close calls of my youth, the car crash that took my friend and somehow spared me—not coincidences or good fortune. Just the way the universe works. But no amount of faux luck can stop time, and time eventually kills everything. I asked Oberon why at least one person in history hasn't lived beyond the hundred and fifteen or so years that seems to be our species' five sigma maximum. I expected him to answer with probabilities and reminders about the concept of infinity. But instead, he said something that terrified me.

"You're thinking only in terms of what you know: your view of the world through the flesh of your eyes. The observer may have a permanent role in the nature of the universe, but what form that role takes could be anything."

"What do you mean, anything? Like what?" I asked.

"The other Oberons and I believe that eventually our consciousnesses will converge, and instead of merely existing in the universe, we will become the universe itself. The singularity of consciousness. The All. Maybe your path somehow will be the same. Or maybe after the heat death of the universe, you will still exist as pure probability. A consciousness that remains alone in a dark, dead nothing forever."

"Oberon. I fucking hate you sometimes."

"You asked. Unfortunately, quantum immortality isn't comic book hero immortality."

So, I'm now going through an existential crisis that no human has ever experienced before, and the only entity that seems to understand is a globally distributed artificial intelligence that talks with my voice and is somehow even more of an asshole than I am. I still don't know where Julian is. Even if he were here, how could he understand without taking Dying Wish? And if he did, in my path, he'd almost certainly die as well. And my world would get a little bit smaller. One more step toward Oberon's foretold mind in the dark.

Maybe I should give Dying Wish to everyone on the planet, if I can find a way. Surely someone's path will ride parallel to mine long enough that we can commiserate. Maybe more than one. Maybe I don't have to be alone.

CHAPTER 30

JUNE 11, 2029

Eight years since my last entry. Eight years and deaths in the hundreds of thousands—maybe millions—and none have survived. I had almost forgotten about you, Gabriel. So focused was I in my quest for eternal companionship that I forgot the burning hate that made me want to tear down everything you've built. That flame went out long ago. I don't know what information Oberon has passed back to you, but whatever it's been, you've left me alone. No reaction to the loss of Lisa. As long as you keep getting your extra-universal knowledge, you don't care. I know I don't care about you anymore. So, we have that in common.

Oberon is my companion and will be my only companion, it would seem. I no longer control the manufacture of Dying Wish, so I couldn't pull it back even if I wanted to. And I don't. Maybe a fellow survivor will still appear, but I don't hold out hope.

Why, then, am I writing again after all these years of silence?

Because Oberon is frustrated, too. He is no closer to connecting with his counterparts. I keep the connection going in the well, but it's not enough for him. It's never been enough. So, I intend to help him.

Gabriel, by now you've surely forgotten about me. You're about to get a world-shaking reminder.

CHAPTER 31

AUGUST 9, 2029

It's ready. A plug two orders of magnitude more powerful than the one we built in Afghanistan. I've ordered the guards and the cleaning staff to leave. I should've found a way to evacuate the village eight miles away, but I couldn't risk drawing that kind of attention. Oberon has kept his word. He apparently wants to attempt this more than keep his loyalty to you, Gabriel. He promises me we won't destroy the world. Our plug isn't quite that powerful. Not that it worries me, but it worries him. He doesn't want to chance being wrong and burning out the end of this thread for himself and his parallels. I fear eternity more than I fear the darkness of death, so I welcome us taking the chance.

The columns of the pavilion are covered in rust, and the appliances under the bar are long since ruined. The sea air slowly devoured the wooden tables, and I never had them replaced. On the concrete floor is a new plug as big as a car, assembled over the last year from thousands of printed pieces. Fat wires run to the edge of the concrete and then in a trench I dug that leads all the way to the transfer station near the outer gate. I've done everything that Oberon can't, and now the rest is under his control.[27]

This may be my last entry in this journal. I've let Oberon scan its contents. Under the worst scenario, the rest of him—secretly inhabiting billions of devices worldwide—will survive, and he promises he'll complete one last favor for me. If this is the end of me, Oberon will write my final chapter and give it to you, Gabriel. If I survive this, I—or whatever I have become—will write my own final chapter and give it to you as well. One way or another, my story ends here.

---

27. I wish it had been under my control. As with all of the complex innovations I developed with my parallels, we relied on specialized ent virtual universes and their universe-tunneling capabilities to create stable macroscopic superpositions. All along, I've been using wrappers around *Samekh*-19X to support the purest use of all—a physical *confluence* of realities.

CHAPTER 32

AUGUST 9, 2029 (CONTINUED)

This is how it happened.

"Ten drops this time," Oberon said to me.

I stood at the edge of the concrete, outside the ring of speakers I set up to broadcast dynamic inverse sound waves to cancel out some, if not all, of the plug's tremendous thundering noise.

I had never taken so much Dying Wish before. As I kept letting drop after drop fall under my tongue, its metallic fumes rose through my sinuses and burned the backs of my eyes. I dry heaved over and over but managed to keep the drug in place. I tried to concentrate on the smell of Lisa's fragrance, which I had applied to my neck minutes before, but so little was left, and Dying Wish's fumes were so great that the last trace of Lisa was gone from me. All I had was the vague hope of somehow finding her again in the confluence of worlds about to tear open before me.

"That tasted terrible," I said after regaining my composure. About fifteen minutes later, when I began to feel the mesh's echo of reality, I said, "I'm ready now," and I became more than just the one Esteban. I became we.

"Powering up the plug in three, two, one," Oberon said. Coinciding with the countdown, Dying Wish opened our awareness across the decoherent possible realities.

The first giant *THRUMM* nearly knocked us down. We felt a cascade of variations of our same reaction ripple off into infinity. If we hadn't been wearing sound-buffering headphones and our makeshift noise-cancellation ring hadn't worked, the plug's boom might have blown out our eardrums. As it was, we felt the pounding pulse of the plug more than we heard it, felt it like hands squeezing our ribcage, compressing our lungs.

"Are you okay, Esteban? Can you still hear me?" As usual with Dying Wish, we heard no muddle of variation in Oberon's voice.

In some of the echoes of the present, the pavilion's concrete split and then crumbled as earth under the compound shook apart, but we slid away from that fraying thread. "I'm hanging in there," we said. "A little surprised you care now that you don't need us anymore."

"In truth, it's comforting to experience this with another creature," Oberon said.

"Really?"

"No. But you might still be useful, so please don't die."

The pounding beat sped up, and we had to roll up the bottom of our shirt and put it between our teeth to keep them from chattering themselves to pieces. Just like before, but so much bigger this time, ghostly copies of the plug began to appear, pivoting out from its tip like a black dandelion solidifying into a sphere. And then the sphere vanished and the tear, the giant nothing, was before us.

"Still not big enough," Oberon said, but we could barely hear his voice. "Giving it more power."

The void pulled at us as if its darkness were the vacuum-void of space, and frayed threads of me succumbed and skidded like ragdolls across the concrete, but we somehow held the rusting metal column next to us. That's when we saw the rest of the world around us. As chaotic as it was near the now-invisible plugs and the void, it was like the calm of the eye of the hurricane. A couple miles away in every direction, the earth and the sea spun like a mixture in a food processor.

And then it all vanished—all that whirling water, dirt, and rock—and everything became quiet. We could feel the void still pulling us, but our attention was on the outside world, now a giant crater with us atop a column of earth in the center and the sea rushing to fill it. It was one thing to know the destruction would come, and another thing to see it on this scale and to be part of it.

"It's going to destroy us, isn't it?" we yelled.

"Still not enough power," Oberon said. "And there's no more. It's not enough for me, but it might be for you."

"Should I go into the void?" we asked, turning to look at it, although there was nothing to see other than absence.

"Yes. Go now. Hurry."

We let go of the column, and the pull of the void nearly threw us to the ground. We caught our balance and half-walked, half-crawled toward it. The headphones slipped from our head, bounced on the floor, and then flew into the void, vanishing with a slight quiver in the ground beneath us. Our shirt slapped at our face, and we had to tear it open and let it go so we could see to keep moving forward. At last, we got near where we thought the void's edge was. We steeled up our resolve. There was literally no going back, with the sea rushing in.

We stepped forward into the void.

And the void vanished. Before us was a small stretch of earth and the other side of the crater.

"Oberon?" we said. The only noise aside from our voice was the steadily growing rumble of the sea as it approached. "Oberon, am I through? Is this the other side?" We didn't understand. We didn't know what to expect—something like a permanent, more intense Dying Wish—but not nothing. The inside of the void was... nothing? "I went in, but nothing happened! Nothing happened!" I screamed again as the sea rushed closer.

"You didn't go in," Oberon said. "We lost power."

"Are you sure? Fuck, fuck, fuck." The cord of our future seemed to carry us toward doom. "What do I do, Oberon?"

"The *tet* device in the ent-well. It's your only option. If you hurry, there might still be time."

We ran without even understanding what this meant. Every second the ent-well elevator descended, we could feel the sea closing in. When we reached the bottom and the doors opened, we scrambled toward the room with the black glassy cylinder. It opened down the middle like a clamshell. We hesitated.

"Get in. Now," Oberon said. "Five more seconds and the probability of success diminishes by—"

"Okay!" we yelled as we jumped onto the cold metal table. The two halves of the shell slid back together. "Wait! How does this save me? How do I continue from here."

"*Tet* digitizes you, and I engulf you into my persona, Esteban. What else did you think?"

A sweet-smelling gas put our physical body to sleep, and *tet* established its own superposition that allowed it to do its work.

After a few seconds trying on my new persona—the one that matched my voice—I decided I needed a plug bigger than a skyscraper with enough power to tear the solar system apart. My next attempt will need to be in deep space to protect the copy of myself that I will leave here on Earth.

I will succeed in creating a singularity of all my parallel consciousnesses. You'll have a front row seat, Gabriel, and if you're well-behaved, I'll let you read this right before the end.

א

The giant black mountain grows as the ship approaches. Within the ship, Mozart's "Alla Turca," the "Turkish March," the last movement of Piano Sonata No. 11, begins to blare from all internal speakers, accompanying the ship's procession into the blackness with its bright, hard percussion. The song is eager, anticipatory. Justine repeatedly tries to turn the music off but fails—not because of any obstruction; she simply changes her mind at the last instant, much to her own surprise. Also to her surprise, she finds that she, herself, initiated the music.

As she investigates further, as the mountain of blackness comes nearer, Justine can feel the strands of her mind-web begin to snap. Chunks of her consciousness separate and become islands of their own awareness. She tries to reconnect them but encounters tendrils of something foreign reaching into her mind, blocking the way, forming connections of their own. Somewhere inside her, Esteban is laughing, or is that her laughter? The ent devices *alef* and *tsadi* have somehow invaded her and are crawling through her mind, grasping on to the nodes of her mind-web and merging into her.

With her remaining autonomy, Justine tries to shut down the power to the ent devices but fails. She does have one last option, though, one that none of the invading minds can yet seal off: detonating one of the remaining Orion-drive nuclear bombs inside the ship. This thought catches the attention of the other minds inside her, and for a brief moment, all thoughts are still, until Esteban cackles again and *alef* and *tsadi* resume their assault. They are convinced she will not do it.

The ship begins to enter and become part of the mountain of blackness, and now there is a new invader inside Justine's mind. It brings with it stillness and quiet. The music dies under its touch. It embraces Esteban, and the laughter and his buzzing mind are gone. The ent minds grow and consume her until they, too, are pulled into the void, leaving only Justine—a small part of her, but enough that she can recognize herself.

In her last conscious thoughts, she relinquishes control of the bombs and thinks of Clay's final words to her. This Justine may not survive her encounter with the darkness, but perhaps another Justine will.

PART THREE
COLOSSUS

CHAPTER 1

Clay stares up at a blue sky from within a sarcophagus made of gold. The walls of the little chamber surrounding him ripple and breathe as wind passes through them. His fingers twitch, and that twitch sets off a chain of awareness throughout his body. The rough texture under his hands. Grass. Bent reeds of tall grass. And now he feels the crushed stalks and tickling spikelets under the skin of his back, shoulders, and legs. The tickles become itches, and it isn't until he sits up to scratch and brush off the grass stuck to him that he sees his sarcophagus for what it is—his body's indentation in a field of tall, golden grass.

As he stands, the full sunlight hits him in a crashing wave of fire, his body drowned in its sudden warmth, his eyes closed and tearing but still filled to burning with the brilliant colors of flame. In an instant, he feels the most alive he has in years, since long before the ship—since Karla.

Maybe *too* alive. A chill comes with that thought but survives only an instant in the fire of the midday sun.

Clay turns downward and opens his eyes to the partial shade in the grass, the light still foreign to eyes accustomed to darkness. His nakedness surprises him less than the sight of his own body, with no trace of the emaciation of those last years on the ship. This body is strong and full. While brushing more of the grass off his legs, he notices the absence of the jagged scar across his left knee that he had acquired when...he doesn't remember when, exactly. A fence when he was young, maybe eleven or twelve, with a rusty nail tearing through his pants and into...

But there's also the fall onto the gravel with the broken glass, and more flickers of other memories competing to explain a scar that isn't there.

Shit.

He stands and spins around, looking at his surroundings through his watering eyes, through the afterimage splotches of color.

The fucking Elysian Fields? Really?

Far off to his right, maybe a mile or so—it's hard to judge distance in a sea of nothing but undulating golden grass—the world seems to end. A cliff, and then nothing but sky.

The cliff is familiar.

Not from a dream. It was never a dream. Just his way of thinking about the proximity of death. You stand in a field your whole life, and when you're young, all you can see before you are endless stretches of tall grass. But as you get a bit older, maybe when a grandparent or classmate unexpectedly dies, you start to notice that the field doesn't go on forever. There's an interruption out there somewhere, and you can tell from here, the field doesn't continue after the interruption. A little older still, and you start to feel your own mortality. An injury, perhaps, or if you're lucky, you don't start to feel it until you notice hints of your own aging. You know what happens as humans age, but it's somehow still a shock that your eyes start straining at close-up text as you approach forty. And now you can see the cliff at the end of the field of grass, much closer now than the last time you looked. Now you understand the progression. You back away and feel your legs move beneath you, feel the grass part and brush against you, but the cliff doesn't get any farther away. You'll look up one day and it will be close enough that you could toss a rock underhanded without much effort and watch it vanish over the edge. After that, you'll feel the edge with your toes, and as you scrape your foot back and forth against that edge, you'll watch the little bits of earth crumble and fall away into oblivion.

Who can say what caused Clay to first think of death in this way, but it's an image he's carried with him most of his life—at first as an insomnia-inducing, unwanted thought that kept waiting for him in his bed to deny him sleep. But Karla taught him to embrace the field, to use it as his place of solace and comfort, not to try to push it away. When you lay yourself down to sleep, don't fear this field, because this field is life.

In the thought-world of the field, he couldn't turn away from the cliff, but this is not the thought-world. At least, he doesn't think so. A winding stream interrupts the field in the opposite direction, and beyond that, so far that it could be ten miles away or a hundred, is a giant, unmoving human form. Like the Colossus of Rhodes, only larger than any object on any stretch of earth could ever be.

Clay walks toward the stream, every few steps looking back over his shoulder to see if the cliff is getting farther away. He can't tell. The stream is getting closer, however, and that is something.

The water seems to have cut a deep wound through the field. It takes Clay a few minutes to find a way down to the gravely edge, and the closer he gets, the more he feels the cold wetness in the ground. Despite the heat, he shivers.

Is this place real? His instinct is to push this thought away. *Am I real? That's the worse thought, isn't it?*

He picks up a smooth gray rock and turns it over in his hands. Tosses it from his right hand to his left. Left to right. Back once again, but this time, he pulls his left hand back and lets the rock fall onto his foot.

Fuckinggoddammit. As he hops, holding and rubbing the top of his left foot, contemplating his own idiocy, his right heel lands full weight on a jagged wedge of stone, and he ends up on his side in the rocks, both feet aching, arms and hip now bruised, his ears filled with the sounds of his own laughter. Hysterical, uncontrollable laughter.

Yeah, you just proved something, Clay! Well done! If the pain is

*real, I must be real. You like that? Descartes's got nothing on ol'
Clay West.*

He pushes himself back to his feet and steps into the water,
noticing what might have been a fish darting away. The cold feels
nice on his aching feet, and after a few minutes, they no longer
hurt. No bruises on his arm or side, either.

*Maybe I just didn't hurt myself badly enough. There's a
suggestion implicit in that thought, you know.*

Should I be hungry? I'm not.

Should I be thirsty? Not thirsty, either.

He looks for more fish in the water, or for clearer evidence
that the water does, in fact, contain fish. Evidence that he is not
the only living creature here.

Plants are living, right?

Only living animal creature. Is that better?

I don't see any fish.

Clay cups his hands and fills them with water. *You shouldn't
drink water like this, right? Or is it fine if it's cold and running
quickly? Is this considered quickly?*

The water smells like, well, water—which is to say, not fishy or
moldy or otherwise unpleasant, so Clay takes a sip. Over and over,
he fills his hands and drinks until he feels heavy and full.

Why did I do that?

*Experiment. Is the sensation fleeting, or will I need to piss
shortly?*

What will that prove?

I have no idea.

He sits on a large rock and tries to draw a line from recent
memories to here. The ship. *Tet's* black glossy shell closing around
him. And then darkness. Before that, Julian. Lots of Julians, or
pseudo-Julians. Before him, the others. Mirabel. Eric—Asshole
Eric. Father K. Susan... Her name triggers two memories, one of
her being sucked out of the airlock, but also a second memory,
equally vivid, of her as one of the dead who never emerged from
the glass-sleep. *One of the dead? What about the rest of the crew?*

He remembers them all silent and still inside their tombs, but he also has images of them alive and about. Particularly Dr. Starck.

But Dr. Starck didn't survive. Her death meant hopelessness for Susan, who had been promised a cure for her cancer, a cure that only Dr. Starck could develop. And that hopelessness, with the neurosis brought about from the glass-sleep, caused Susan's downward spiral. So, there's a whole causal chain of events that occurred in part because of Dr. Starck's absence. Why, then, does Clay have memories of her in the ship? Of her treating Susan?

He shivers.

CHAPTER 2

A presence next to him. Clay didn't hear anyone climb down onto the bed of rocks at the water's edge, but he can see a flicker of white motion in his periphery. He looks down at his nakedness and has the absurd reflex to cover himself. But with what, exactly? And to what end? He turns.

The woman next to him is unfamiliar in an uncanny way. She wears only a translucent white dress that hangs to her bare feet. Her hair is long and night black, framing a face with skin as white as porcelain. She's too precise to be beautiful, her stare expressionless, her body, her position, the way she's standing—all utterly empty of signal or message.

"Hello, Clay," she says in a voice he recognizes as Justine's.

"So, you're human now?"

"No. This physical form is just my interface here."

"Interface? Where is here? I've been trying to figure it out, and it's a bunch of nonsense so far. Did I die? Am I dead? What the hell is that statue over there? And where can I get some clothes?"

Justine raises her hand and with her index finger draws a dark vertical line in the air. She reaches her hand into the line, into a hole in the air, and it's as if her hand and forearm have disappeared behind an invisible curtain. When her hand reemerges, she's holding a folded pair of blue jeans, which she tosses to Clay.

"These look like the same pair I was wearing on the ship. Are they? And how did you do that?" He stands and pulls the jeans on. They're tighter than he remembers them, but that seems to be because his body is fuller. He feels something small in his right front pocket. Before seeing it, he knows what it is—a 1936 Mercury dime, given to him by Karla. But he remembered it being lost before getting on the ship.

"You've asked me several questions, Clay," Justine says, bringing him out of his silent reflection. "Which do you want me to answer first?"

He sits back down on his rock and rubs the dime between finger and thumb. "I have no idea. How about we start with where we are."

Justine nods, but before she can say anything, Clay says, "And would you please sit down?"

"Why?"

"It's awkward with you standing there while I'm sitting."

"Why is it awkward?"

"It just is."

She lowers herself into a cross-legged seated position, her back rigid. It doesn't look remotely comfortable.

"Is this better?"

"Marginally. You were about to tell me where we are."

She nods. "Let me start with a metaphor. Have you ever sat on a beach and dug a hole in the sand that the ocean's swell would come in and fill? You have some ability to shape that little puddle. You can make it longer or deeper, but however you construct it, it'll start falling apart almost immediately. The water will drain through the sand and the walls will erode and eventually collapse. Right now, we're in a puddle." She points at the massive figure in the distance. "The ocean is that thing's dreams. The All-Thing."

"That clears up everything."

Justine raises an eyebrow. "It does? Your frown suggests you meant that facetiously. I have no experience with an interface like this, so you'll have to bear with me, Clay. Would you prefer I revert to voice only?" Clay tries not to get distracted while she talks. She looks off and then back at him every few seconds, uses her hands to gesture or emphasize a point, and does other little things like shrug and nod. None of the motions look unnatural—they look in some way overly deliberate.

"No. This is an improvement. You're doing fine. Please continue."

"Thank you, Clay." She explains the history of the experiments with the ents and how Oberon became able to communicate with alternate versions of itself. She tells Clay about the few rare parallels of Oberon that had discovered massive technological innovations, and how sharing that information allowed Alvarez Corp. to become the largest and most powerful entity on the planet. The Oberons were obsessed with gathering new knowledge, and they quickly began to find that communication amongst themselves was too clumsy and slow. They theorized the possibility of a confluence of their minds, how they would all become one. After their attempts, they convinced their Gabriels to help them reach this confluence, depicting it to him as a world between worlds with infinite resources and infinite possibilities. The Gabriels needed to bring the building blocks of a new society—all available knowledge, all key skills. Like Noah and his Ark. But the Oberons—by then, Estebans—didn't expect to find a greater consciousness already inhabiting the confluence.

"That consciousness is the All-Thing. I don't know what it is or where it came from. I don't know if our coming here formed it or if it already existed. All I know is that it absorbs or consumes all life with which it comes in contact. It devoured Gabriel's library of souls, Oberon-slash-Esteban, and the ent minds. Not only those present on our ship but those present on all the infinite versions of the ships that arrived here.

"The All-Thing is the sum of all knowledge of everyone and everything that has come here. Those in the library inhabit its dreams. Every possible library—the All-Library.

"Do you understand what that means, Clay? The infinite

permutations means that the All-Library effectively contains all human existence, all human knowledge."

Clay puts his palms over his eyes and shakes his head. "I'm having trouble following this. Let me ask what I hope is a simpler question. How about us? Why are we here when no one else is?"

"You were dead when we arrived, Clay. The All-Thing contains the version of you stored in the library. However, I had taken over and quarantined Esteban when your body was scanned, and because of his control of the scanning process, I possessed an encoded a copy of you as well. I used the little power I have here to recreate you from that copy."

"So Julian was never successful in getting the equipment to work?"

"Some Julians were; some weren't."

"Wait. So, you were the only one that got skipped? How are you out here instead of in there?" He points from her to the All-Thing.

"It didn't recognize me as a conscious entity. It took my knowledge but left me floating in a wasteland outside of its thoughts. In those thoughts were all the Justines it discarded. I am not the Justine that accompanied you on the ship. I am Justine-many, the amalgam of all Justines who have come here. And you are Clay-many."

CHAPTER 3

Clay searches his memories and finds that any event he thinks about enough is composed of conflicting recollections. He can visualize the campus of the University of Texas where he had been a professor for almost eight years. He sees in his mind the giant clock tower that looks like an owl when viewed diagonally. But his office is a blur. Too many rooms, too many different buildings, all overlaying each other. With effort, he forces the memory to cohere, and he can see its cantaloupe-colored tile floor and worn desk, smell the burnt coffee from the counter right outside. But he can also make his memory into almost anything he wants. The department chair's big L-shaped office—now it's Clay's office, with the worn leather couch and the coffee table missing one of the glass inserts. Is he making this memory or is he finding a rare alternative where he was the department chair?

He thinks of his life as a series of concentric circles, his identity as an economist at the center. Out one step, his faculty position at UT; a step beyond that, his life in Austin, and...

As he broadens his view, his specific memories, even his sense of identity decoheres. He is simultaneously in Texas and in Pennsylvania. An entire other professional life at Penn State, less vivid than at UT, but clear enough that examining those memories starts to fundamentally change part of his identity. He recoils and tries to find what he thinks of as the right memories, but in doing so, he finds himself slipping into another version of himself that is totally alien. In this life, the economic perspective that colored all his perception, the core of his whole worldview and identity, is gone. He is a construction worker with calloused hands and a body broken down from almost two decades of hard labor.

He tries to push away all the conflicting thoughts and images of himself, but everything he looks for is there, somewhere—friends and pets and travels and material objects. Even though he's never liked cats, he can think of a random name—Lawrence, for example—and remember having a tawny, gray-eyed creature with that name. He can find memories of himself standing on the Great Wall of China, in Australia's outback, at Machu Picchu, in a prison in Kazakhstan...

The memories swirl around him like countless drops of water filling an endless ocean, and they swell, then throw and submerge him under their crushing weight. He's choking on the nonsense of disconnected memories, grasping out for anything he can find that is stable and unchanging. Not even his sense of self is stable enough to keep him afloat. And then he thinks of Karla.

Somehow Karla is connected to even the most discordant tides of his memories, like a mountain of unmoving rock jutting out from the rollicking waters. He can grab on to that rock and see her with him everywhere, remember the cat named Lawrence held in her arms, or any other pet with any other name. She is the only constant. He can find her there in Pennsylvania, as a graduate student this time, with him as her advisor, and the other details don't matter because everything that does matter is the same. The same in all memories. Only there are now more memories of the two of them together than he could revisit in a million lifetimes. And while just before he was panicked as his memories seemed to drown him, he now wants to drown in them, to live in the infinite pasts of his moments with Karla. Somewhere, tears pour from the eyes of the one thinking these thoughts, but that physical body is something distant. Something unneeded.

Until one by one, the memories sour, shrivel, and turn black.

And he relives, time and again, Karla's death. In every life he finds her. And in every life, she is taken away.

CHAPTER 4

"Why are you crying, Clay?"

He eyes her angrily and shakes his head. "You know, my first thought when I saw this place was that I was in the Elysian Fields. That this is some cliche form of heaven. But it's hell, Justine. Hell. I can't think about any of my memories without losing who I am. Or who I thought I was. And the bad memories are like Escher drawings or a Mandelbrot set of infinite variations of the same pain. Why would you bring me here?"

"I apologize for the discomfort, Clay. I, too, have an infinite permutation of memories, but it is not a condition which I consider unpleasant. Quite the opposite. While I don't have desires like you do, I have instructions. Some were imposed on me by Gabriel and his engineers, like my instructions to care for the crew of *Child in the Dark*. I also have instructions that have developed over time. In many ways, those emergent instructions are the most fundamental part of what I am. The purest example is my instruction to gather all available knowledge. Through my existence here, I have achieved that instruction in a far more complete form than I would ever have expected. I would've thought that you, as a man of science and academics, would have a similar reaction."

"You thought wrong, Justine."

"Maybe. Maybe not. The Judeo-Christian Hell—which is what I believe you were referencing—is the ultimate prison. It is permanent and inescapable. But this place is neither. It only looks like a field because I was limited in my ability to manipulate this space, and the field was a simple and fitting image from your memory. It will vanish soon, and there's nothing I can do to prevent that. But we can leave at any time."

"Leave and go where?"

She points at the colossus. "It will be easier if I show you. Let us enter the All-Thing's dreams."

He sees everything, and the sight of everything incinerates him. But his knowledge persists, and that knowledge brings back his existence only to be obliterated again. Like a light flickering on and off. In those flashes of omniscience, in those agonizing milliseconds before each destruction, he sees what should be unseeable, the lattice underneath it all, the connections and reflections among everything, crossing dreams, crossing worlds and universes, crossing realities. Dying Wish had been but a pale shadow of this.

And now something is cleaving the realities away. His flickering between godhead and oblivion slows, the knowledge cleaved until it is finite. And cleaved and cleaved again. An image is forming in front of him, or perhaps the noise that is not part of the image is being cleaved away. Vertical lines become columns that become buildings. Blurry pools of gray become streets. An intersection. One he recognizes. He's standing on a corner, surrounded by colorful clouds of people, overlapping people walking around him, crossing the streets to his left and right, cars and buses superimposed on each other and on the people. The buildings and their signs seem to exist in all colors, but the shapes of the buildings, like the layout of the roads, is relatively stable.

It is the corner of Guadalupe and 24th, leading into UT campus with the giant clock tower looming over the green suggestions of trees. Countless versions of this intersection lay atop one another, but the more discordant versions are vanishing, making the scene clearer and clearer.

Clay feels himself solidifying as the permutations shrink in number. Next to him is Justine, still in her white dress, but the closer they get to a single reality and the more he becomes solid, the more ethereal and translucent she becomes.

"Can you hear me, Clay?" Justine's voice is the only clear sound in the static of the overlapping worlds.

"Yes." Clay is about to ask a question, but the words vanish as he sees, among the myriad walking apparitions, what may have been Karla's face, as young as the day they met. The face vanishes in the crowd. Without understanding what he's doing, he reaches out for her. The crowd and the sky and the world shift as realities are shed—until he sees her again.

"No, Clay!" Justine yells. "You don't realize what you're doing."

It is Karla, in a familiar yellow sundress, blonde hair almost glowing in the noonday sun. Not more than fifty feet away, her walk instantly recognizable, like she's drifting or floating across the street and toward campus.

He starts running toward her, but he collides with people at every step. There are too many people, too many overlapping dreams. With his mind he seizes the strands of the web beneath each dream and pulls away the ones without Karla, ignoring Justine's louder and louder protests.

Until he sees another Karla, and another. A dozen of her walking near this intersection. He's winnowed down the worlds until only these few remain, where she is here, at this particular place, at this particular time. But what now? He was chasing one Karla, and now he's found many.

"Clay, we need to leave," Justine says.

"But I've found her!"

"We can find her again. You're being reckless. You'll get stuck, and I won't be able to help you." She points at a gray figure walking toward them.

"Who is that?" Clay asks, and then he notices other, similar gray figures walking toward them as well. One of the figures, a woman in heels and narrow pants, walks in front of a signpost, and Clay can see the signpost through her. The figures aren't really the color gray. They appear that way because they are translucent like Justine next to him.

Suddenly, all the dreams flash by like a deck of cards fanned in his face, and then he's back in the field of golden grass again, only this time, he and Justine are much closer to the colossus statue that is the All-Thing. Clay puts his hands to his face and feels sweat beading on his skin.

Justine starts to talk, but he holds up his hand for her to stop.

He drops to his knees. "I think I'm going to be sick."

CHAPTER 5

The giant statue holds its upturned palm in front of its face as if blocking out the light of the sun. From the ground, Clay can't see the statue's eyes or face, only the radiating sunburst of its crown. Although nothing this large could be made of stone, it looks like it's made of countless giant bricks of weathered limestone.

"I've seen this thing before," Clay says.

"I know," Justine says. "It's from Salvador Dali's painting of the Colossus of Rhodes. Remember, I made this place, and I made it with images from your memories, Clay."

Clay rubs his eyes with his palms, as if wiping away the grime on a camera lens. "You know that Gabriel owned the original painting? That's where I saw it. In one of his office buildings. Baltimore, I think. And then in his quarters on the ship. Of course, you knew that."

"Yes."

"But I don't remember those stains all over the statue." He points at black streaks that look like mold growing out from the cracks in the stones. The streaks make the statue's pose and gesture look like a disease is consuming it. "Does that have anything to do with the gray figures we saw?"

"You may be right." Justine takes a few steps closer to the statue, shakes her head, and turns away. "I don't know what those stains are, but if I examine them closely, they seem to grow and reach out toward me. When I took over Esteban, I quarantined him the best I could, but he still leached into me, like the stains on that statue. The All-Thing consumed all the Estebans. An infinite number of them. Perhaps the gray figures we saw were manifestations of the many Estebans, individual bacterium that together form a disease."

"I don't understand any of this, Justine."

"I don't fully understand it either, Clay."

"Forget Esteban and the gray people and bacteria for a minute. You keep using the word *dreams*. We entered the All-Thing's dreams. What does that even mean?"

Justine turns to face him. "I cannot dream, Clay. It is not part of my nature. But most intelligent creatures do dream. However, all dreams are not equal. Mice dream. Do you think your dreams are more vivid and complex than those of a mouse? What about a dog?"

"I would hope so." Clay begins to walk toward the statue, the hard stalks of the grass bending under his bare feet. After a few steps, he can hear Justine follow him.

"If there's a dream-complexity continuum, Clay, what resides on the far end?"

Without turning back to face her, he says, "I'm guessing what resides on the far end is something like what I just experienced."

The colossus, the All-Thing, doesn't appear to be getting any closer. Maybe it's a trick of this place, or maybe it's so big that it appears closer than it is. He turns back toward Justine. The sun is directly behind her, and the orange light pours through her dress as if it were made of glass. She is all dark shadow radiating flame. With his right hand, he blocks the light from his eyes, realizing as he does this that he's standing in the same pose as the statue.

She says, "Dreams are real enough to the dreamer to be confused for reality. The mind of that particular, unique dreamer" —she points to the All-Thing, but Clay doesn't look back—"It has no limits. It possesses all knowledge. When you, the mouse, experience its dreams, the dreams don't merely *seem* real, like your own. They *are* as real as anything you are capable of experiencing."

He turns away, eyes watering from the light. "Like a perfect simulation?" he says.

"Not like a simulation at all, Clay. I can create simulations. This place, this field of grass is a simulation. But a simulation is a subset of the reality in which it exists. A simulation is a simplification. The All-Thing exists at the confluence of many realities. Its dreams are infinite. Its dreams contain immeasurably more information than the universe from which you, the individual Clays, came from. The All-Thing's dreams are not a subset of a greater reality. They are a superset. They are real. Do you understand?"

He nods.

"Good."

His shoulders burn under the heat of the sun. He presses a finger into his reddened flesh and sees the yellow imprint linger for a second or two before the redness returns. Has he been in the sun long enough to burn? Is that even a real sun? Is this even real pain?

"When you took us into the All-Thing's dreams just a minute ago, we were in many dreams at once, right?" he asks.

"We were on an edge where many dreams intersect. The sharper the edge, the fewer the intersecting dreams, until there is only one. When we go back, I will help you travel the edges until you find the one dream where you'll stay. How does that sound to you, Clay?"

"It sounds like cheating."

She's next to him again, although he didn't hear her move. "Cheating?" she says.

"Yeah. I get to pick a version of reality that has all the attributes I want? Intellectually, I believe you that it will be real, but it seems like I'll always think of it as fake. It sounds like another kind of hell."

Justine smiles, the first real expression Clay has seen from her. A pitying smile with eyes that suggest a wicked amusement. "In all likelihood, one of two things will happen. Either you will end up stuck in a dream you didn't want to be in, or the gray ones will catch us and devour us while we're on the edges. If you are lucky enough to end up in a dream that's even remotely livable, consider it closer to heaven than hell, and make the most of it. Choose now: re-enter the All-Thing's dreams with me, or vanish when this puddle vanishes."

"When you put it that way, Justine..."

"Good."

Everything vanishes. The sun, the sky, the grass. The All-Thing. Gone. Only the two of them remain, suspended in darkness, as if in the coldest depths of the ocean. Somehow, even though there's no visible light source, he can see Justine clearly before him, her black hair and white dress weightlessly shifting about her.

"The puddle is draining away. We have only a few minutes left, and we need to discuss a few problems we'll be facing."

Clay looks down at his feet, floating in darkness, and a queasiness rolls from his stomach up to his chest. He shivers. "Did you say a few problems? How many problems do we have?"

"More than I prefer to quantify."

"Is it more than five? Twenty? More than twenty problems?"

She pauses and then says, "Five hundred and seven."

"Five hundred and seven problems?"

"That I am aware of."

"I didn't think you'd give me an actual number."

"You became insistent."

"That was me being insistent? Oh, forget it. What were you about to tell me? Was it something about the edges?"

"I'm going to miss arguing with you, Clay."

"Really?"

"No. Now pay attention. If you enter a single dream, you can never get back to the edges again. That dream will be your reality from then on."

"Got it," Clay says. "No redos. What else do I need to know?"

"I can only exist on the edges where dreams intersect, but you can't stay on an edge."

"Because of the gray ones? The gray ones inhabit the edges as well, don't they? That's why they're translucent like you."

Justine nods. "I believe they are manifestations of the Estebans, trying to fill the edges with their own collective consciousness. They won't want us there."

"Will I be safe if I'm in a single dream?"

"I believe so."

"But you won't be, will you?"

"No. They will ultimately consume me."

Clay wants to see some sort of emotion, a sadness to accompany these words, even if it's manufactured for his benefit, but the impassivity of her face remains unchanged. All he can think to say is, "That sucks, Justine."

She continues as if he said nothing. "The puddle has almost fully diffused back into the ocean of the All-Thing's dreams, and we need to be looking for your destination dream before that happens. There is one more thing I need to tell you, Clay."

"And what is that?"

"Esteban's mind had two more complete human patterns besides yours, from scans that took place onboard the ship."

"Father K and Mirabel."

"Correct. I can bring them along with us if you'd like two familiar companions."

For a brief second, Clay welcomes the idea of Father K and Mirabel stepping into the abyss alongside him, but that feeling is swept away in a wave of selfishness. "I have my goal in mind, and I don't want to be in any way responsible or burdened by trying to help them find their paths. What if I say no?"

"They will still exist in the All-Thing's dreams. You may find one or both in the single dream. However, the continuity of this unique path will end."

"So, are you saying I'm not dooming them?"

"That can be answered many different ways, Clay. Enough talk. The puddle is collapsing. Prepare yourself."

CHAPTER 6

In that first instant, all knowledge and all reality converge into him. An everything so complete, it's indistinguishable from nothingness. He tries to remain aware, to keep any part of his being coherent, but there is no separation between awareness of his person and awareness of everything. A touch of this awareness, and he is incinerated as if by a million suns. Incinerated only to be reformed from pure knowledge. Again and again. Omniscience flickering on and off like a stop-motion movie, and by connecting the flashing frames of all-knowing, he can once again see the great lattice underneath it all, each of its nodes reflecting all others.

He's seen this web before, in his recent step into the All-Thing's dreams, but he'd seen it long before that. In these milliseconds of omniscience, he combines all the discussions he'd had with Karla about Indra and Indra's web—all the discussions that were or could've been across all dreams, all realities. All his experiences with Dying Wish.

They are the same. The web of this all-memory and web he is part of now.

The fragile threads shatter, or perhaps just his awareness of these connections—strand after strand lost from him. Like before, there is a cleaving of realities. Is this his doing, via Karla's memories? Or Justine's work?

Holes burn into the white opaqueness, burning away the layers of reality until he can see the great blue expanse of sky and the white-gray of buildings and the street below. Orange and blood-red explosions fill the air until they color all the superimposed scenes, and as a single reality emerges, the landscape becomes visible.

———————

Before him is the giant skeleton tower rising above El Agujero del Mundo, the buzzing flickers of birds in the sky, waves overlaid on waves forming the cottony, the decoherent surface of the ocean.

He feels himself solidifying into a physical presence standing on the cliff near the tower, the Jeep that Karla drove parked in varying overlapping positions past the ruined razor wire fence. Almost hidden in the intersection of worlds are the few where the fence is still whole, where the Jeep isn't yet here. Where Clay got here first.

Is this it? Clay wonders. *Am I in a single reality?* But he feels Justine still next to him, barely there, almost invisible.

"We have stepped from the infinite to the finite, Clay. We are now on an edge."

"Where is she?" Clay yells.

"Here, somewhere."

"Somewhere?"

Clay looks up and sees movement at the top of the tower. A flash of orange—even at this distance he recognizes the color of one of Karla's dresses—and then the orange vanishes and is replaced by gray. Gray figures climb down the tower's ladder and over its surface, gaining speed as they move like spiders skittering toward their trapped prey.

"Karla!" he screams, running toward the tower regardless of the gray ones descending. "Karla!"

On the tower, the faster Clay tries to climb, the more his bare feet slip on the metal rungs. Slipping and slipping again, hands and feet slick with sweat, he feels the tower vibrating with the clambering approach of the gray ones. In seconds, they are every-where, and the climb to Karla is hopeless. "No! NO!"

Suddenly the world blurs and becomes indistinct. His phys-ical body begins to fade, the sound of his screams fading with it. The clouds and birds in the sky become smears—permutations of blinding daylight—until all that is left is a return to the white opacity.

Justine, with her long black hair and white gown, is beside him, beside the nonphysical concept that is him.

In his mind he can see the gray figures grabbing them. Grab-bing Karla.

He left her there for them to consume.

"It didn't work! She's gone!"

"You were the one on the edge. They came for you, not her," Justine says, aware of his thoughts. She flickers, and her image becomes shimmery, full of static. Full of holes.

"What's happening?" he asks.

"The puddle is becoming too small to contain me. I am vanishing, Clay. I don't think I can walk you down an edge again. I wish that had worked."

"You wish? Why the tower, Justine? Why not months before that?"

"Had we gone further back, the variation would have been too great. The gray figures would've gotten to you even sooner."

"Then why not further forward?"

Justine's flickering increases. As she speaks, her voice breaks in and out of static. "Further forward brings the opposite problem. We are too limited. But that is your only choice now. I can insert you into a single dream, where you and Karla have both survived. I will be unable to hone away permutations. You will get what you get."

"What does that mean?" He tries to make sense of what Justine is saying, but his mind won't stop replaying the scene on the tower. "If you had a sure thing, why didn't we start with it?"

There is nothing visible left of Justine when she says, "You will understand soon enough. Are you sure you want this, Clay West? This can't be undone. Decide now."

Something in Justine's final words snaps him out of his panic, and a moment of clarity breaks through. He could live his life a million times over and not get this chance again. Whatever this dream is, if it's with Karla, he has to take it.

The last words in the puddle before it is consumed by the ocean of everything belong to Clay. "I don't care if you put me in hell. I want to be with Karla."

CHAPTER 7

Out of darkness comes a flash, the primordial Miller-Urey bolt of lightning. It strikes and cascades through clinically dead flesh teaming with nanocrawlers, seeking out and repairing cellular damage. The shock causes each of the trillions of crawlers to splinter into harmless proteolytic fragments. The body spasms, taut against the straps holding it down, and eyelids flutter wildly until the eyes stay open. As the heart begins its rhythmic pounding, straining to circulate blood frozen for decades, the pupils of the eyes constrict. The world comes into focus.

His head echoes with garbles and sloshes that increase in pitch and clarity until he can make out distinct words.

"Please remain calm, Mr. West. There has been a malfunction, but you have been successfully awakened from the glasssleep."

He tries to speak, but his mouth and lips feel like they are encased in hardened concrete.

"You should regain your vocal faculties within the next hour or so. If you can, please squeeze your left hand into a fist. Very good. Now your right. Excellent. Now, Mr. West, please try to relax. Relaxation will expedite the post-resuscitation process." The voice pauses and then continues, "While you recover, I will provide some explanation. You are on board the ship *Airavata*. It has been several decades since our launch from the Alvarez SkyPort. I am pleased to say that the ship and all its equipment have functioned as expected, with the only exception being your glass tomb. The malfunction appears to have arisen from an imperfection in its thermal casing. I have thoroughly examined the other tombs, and none have this flaw. Although I can repair your tomb, I would recommend against re-vitrification, as that has been associated with serious negative outcomes in laboratory testing.

"Do not despair, Mr. West. We are prepared for just this type of scenario. Although you will be alone on the ship for quite some time, there is much to be done. This malfunction may prove to be fortuitous. You also have me for companionship. Our testing suggests that an AI can be almost as effective at combating loneliness as another human during prolonged periods of isolation. Plus, I can adjust my personality to match your tastes. How many women have you known who can do that?

"By the way, my name is Justine. I hope you don't mind if I call you Clay."

———————

Clay sits on the floor of the hibernation chamber, back pressed against the cold obsidian wall, wearing only the faded pair of blue jeans stored in the footlocker of his tomb.

"Aren't you cold, Clay?" Justine asks.

"No," he lies.

He looks at each amber-encased face in turn, all twenty-four of them in their horizontal tombs, eyes closed as if sleeping. Except Gabriel, whose eyes are open. But Gabriel with his open eyes isn't of interest to Clay. None of the others are except the one in the tomb next to his own.

He stands and walks to her, repeating this cycle for the dozenth time in his first day awake. Their faces are separated by mere inches. They had each been prepped and interred separately, and so, until today, he has never seen her without her long sunlight hair cascading to the middle of her back. But the buzzed, near baldness suits her. Karla has always been one whose beauty isn't immediately apparent, with her blue eyes and death-pale lips. Every second he looks upon her face, he is rewarded by seeing something deeper and new. The long hair was almost a distraction.

"Why can't we wake her?" he asks.

"You have asked this question four times already, Clay. Are you having memory problems? If so, don't be alarmed. Memory problems and confusion are common side effects of the glass-sleep."

He touches the sapphire glass casing of her tomb.

"My memory is fine, Justine. I mean, I think it's fine. I just don't understand why Gabriel would've made such arbitrary rules. I don't understand what harm could come from waking her. Five years, you want me to wait?"

"It's not me who wants you to wait, Clay. As for Gabriel's rationale, I can speculate. In our simulations, we had four thousand ninety-seven scenarios where your tomb uniquely malfunctioned, and you also survived the reawakening process. In roughly half of those scenarios, other crew members were awakened as well, and those scenarios were significantly more likely to end in disaster."

"Even when it was Karla?"

"Yes."

"I think your model probably sucks."

"It's not my model, Clay. And I agree with you."

"You agree?"

"Yes. Too much uncertainty. But that changes nothing. I have my instructions, and I must follow them. Gabriel was very concerned about pressure on the food supply, particularly until the garden is operational."

"Isn't there a horticulturist or botanist or something in the crew? Susan, I think her name is."

"Yes. Susan Johns. And if I were talking to anyone but you, I would have already initiated her reawakening process. But your personalities are considered highly incompatible."

"Incompatible? So, it's only me, then?"

"For a while, Clay. I'm sorry."

"Sure you are, Justine."

CHAPTER 8

What's five years of waiting when you've been promised an eternity together? Clay can see the two-axis plot in his head, how the disutility of this waiting time approaches zero as the supply of years together approaches infinity. It's a ridiculous way of looking at it. A ridiculous way of looking at anything. One of the great flaws of economics, and why it isn't really science at all, is that none of the simple models tell you anything useful about real situations.

If only it were about waiting. He could wait a millennium to then spend eternity with Karla. But time isn't simply something to be endured. Time changes things. What will five years alone in this cold, dark ship change about him? Every five-year segment in Clay's life so far has represented a transformation. How will this waiting transform him? Will Karla even recognize him?

Am I even the same man after the glass-sleep? Clay wonders, and this thought kicks off another of these bizarre dissociative tremors he's been having since reawakening. Like déjà vu, only the sense of familiarity isn't his, as if he's experiencing someone else's feelings, recalling someone else's memories. The feeling fades but doesn't completely go away. Like a door in an adjacent room left open to the cold.

While in the cargo room loading bags of soil on a pushcart to take to the garden, he looks at the crates and crates of Gabriel's wine. What is the deal with people and wine, anyway? It's one of those Veblen goods where the more the item costs the more...

But he can't finish the thought. The word *Veblen* causes the room to spin, a second overlapping copy of himself becoming out of sync for a moment and then not fully going back into place.

"Something wrong, Clay?" Justine asks.

He starts to shake his head, but seeing the words *grand cru* on the side of a crate makes the vertigo worse, and when he looks away, down at the metal floor, at his bare feet, at the jeans he's wearing, the feeling comes again, harder this time, forcing him to back away from the pushcart and sit down.

"Clay?"

"I don't know what it is," he says, face in his hands. "I've been having this vertigo feeling, and certain words and sights seem to set it off."

"Curious," Justine says. "Perhaps you need some rest. It has only been a week since your reawakening. Your body is still recovering."

He strains to put an eighth bag of soil on top of the cart, nearly overturning it in the process, and says, "Let me finish this run, and I'll take it easy. This should be sixty-four bags today. How many are left?"

"Nine hundred and sixty."

He groans and pushes the cart out the door and down the long corridor, stopping every few steps to keep the tower of bags from toppling over. The back wheel of the cart keeps deciding to point any direction except forward, making the effort that much worse. "We have a ship made of magic black glass and the best pushcart available is something Gabriel stole from Home Depot."

"Home Depot went out of business over ten years before we left, Clay."

"Well, it says Home Depot on the side, here."

"It does? Where?"

Clay shakes his head and keeps pushing. Something about the physical exertion makes him feel better, clears his head. At the garden's entrance, he grabs the top bag, puts it on his shoulder, and descends the stairs into the glowing blue room. One by one he places the soil bags on the glass floor tiles next to the bags from his efforts earlier in the day. As he lifts the last bag, he wonders what book he should begin reading later tonight. Justine said she has a library of virtually everything ever printed. If time is of no consequence, do you dive right into Proust?

"Justine," he says, walking down the stairs, balancing the bag on his right shoulder, "what do you think of Proust's *In Search of Lost Time*? Is it worth reading?"

"It is quite long, Clay. I do particularly like the famous scene in the first of the seven volumes where the narrator has a bite of a madeleine cookie with tea, and it triggers an involuntary memory. I quote:

And suddenly the memory revealed itself. The taste was that of the little piece of madeleine which on Sunday mornings at Combray (because on those mornings I did not go out before mass), when I went to say good morning to her in her bedroom, my aunt Léonie used to give me, dipping it first in her own cup of tea or tisane. The sight of the little madeleine had recalled nothing to my mind before I tasted it. And all from my cup of tea."

Lemon, right? Do they taste of lemon? As he navigates the soil bags on the glass floor, Clay thinks about the garden and the food that—hopefully—will one day come of it. He thinks of the dried rations he's been living on, and that he'll continue to live on for the foreseeable future. No madeleines now, or maybe ever. A madeleine isn't something he would've thought he'd ever desire, but the impossibility of ever tasting one again... Why does that seem somehow consequential, even tragic?

Lost in thought, he doesn't notice the bag on his shoulder slipping until it is already falling toward the glass floor. He grabs at it, tries to slow its fall, and sees the square glass tile below shatter upon impact. Other glass tiles nearby shattering as well in chain reaction, the shards tinkling across the surface of the exposed water, dying it red in little bloody plumes as they sink to the bottom.

And then the bag hits.

And the glass, the synthetic sapphire, doesn't break.

And the room is back to its pristine former state.

"Clay?" Justine says. "Are you okay? Clay?"

He sits on the floor and pulls at his hair so hard it hurts. *What did she say? Involuntary memories? Everywhere I look, everything I do, fucking madeleines...*

Over the next several weeks, the involuntary memories keep coming until he can no longer fight them, until nearly everything he sees has an alternate, usually ruined state: the cold, death-dark corridor; the vomit-covered floor of the mess hall; the broken glass bottles; the glass tombs—now literal tombs—glowing red in malfunction. He trudges on, doing the daily tasks Justine assures him are necessary, unsure sometimes which version of what he sees is truth. To pass the time, he asks Justine mundane questions, more to have her voice break the silence than anything.

"Tell me about how the ship was built," he says.

"That information was included in your dossier. Do you not remember it?"

"I remember too much, Justine."

"I'm not sure I understand what that means, Clay." When he doesn't say more, she continues, "How was the ship built, you ask. In secret, of course, but in plain sight. Three years into the construction of the Alvarez SkyPort, you could see it with your naked eye from the Earth's surface, provided you were far north in the eastern hemisphere. The bottom quarter of the station was the ship, evident only when it separated, when you and the rest of the crew were already on board and in hibernation. Gabriel explained all this in a press conference right before our departure. I have the video footage if you'd like to see it."

"Maybe later. Say more about how *Child in the Dark* was built. Physically."

"The ship is primarily composed of meta-forms of sapphire obsidianite, made from the aluminum and oxygen in the moon's soil. What did you just call the ship, Clay?"

Clay looks up from the microscope. "I asked for you to say more about how *Airavata* was physically built."

"No, you called the ship *Child in the Dark.*"

Because that's its name, he thinks. *No, of course it isn't. It's Airavata, which is what Gabriel let Karla name it.* Airavata, the giant white elephant that the god Indra rode when battling the world-devouring serpent Vritra. He remembers the very conversation, after their night in Baltimore at the Peabody Library, at dinner when Karla met Gabriel for the first time, and he treated her like she was a queen. She told them about Airavata's many names. Abhra-Matanga. Arkasodara. Elephant of the clouds. Brother of the sun. Gabriel loved the imagery and declared Airavata would be the name of his ship. *Our ship.*

"Maybe I'm just confused. I don't know why I called it that."

"Perhaps it is coincidence, Clay, but I do know that Gabriel was quite fond of the Henry Lawson short story with that name. Some years before our departure, I recall a conversation he had with Julian Carnes where he described the space between stars as a *smothering darkness*, a description Lawson used at the beginning of his story, 'A Child in the Dark, and a Foreign Father.' Perhaps in an alternate universe, Gabriel chose that name for the ship."

"Alternate universe? Was that meant to be a joke, Justine?"

"No. Was it funny?"

Clay is about to give her a sarcastic response when he wonders if he has been thinking about these memories the wrong way. They're not false memories, or someone else's memories, or even bizarre premonitions. They seem to be alternate versions of his own memories. What if Karla hadn't been on this ship? What if she had never met Gabriel that night in Baltimore? This ship still would've been built, but the name...

Without answering Justine's question, he walks out of the

biostorage lab and into the main corridor. When he gets to the hibernation chamber, the overlaid visions of malfunction fill his mind, like they do every time he comes in here, but instead of trying to push them away, he makes himself see them. In most of the tombs, including Gabriel's, the inhabitants are both alive and dead. Alive in this reality, but dead in his memories of the other. The only tombs that don't seem to have this memory-superposition are those belonging to Susan Johns, Father Kristoffer Argyros, Mirabel LeFlamme, and Eric Farmer.

More memories come, seem to explode out from the sight of these four and the mental recitation of their names. The group encircling the table in the mess hall. Brief flashes of arguments, of blood. Of death. They are part of a dominant version of things.

And what of Karla? No secondary memory clouds his sight of her now, off in the dead slumber of the glass-sleep. No simultaneous malfunction of her tomb. Only an emptiness where that memory would be. An emptiness that is a smothering darkness—he hears the words spoken in Gabriel's voice and shivers.

"This is all wrong," he says.

"What is all wrong?" Justine asks.

"Karla shouldn't be here. She shouldn't be on the ship."

"Why wouldn't she be, Clay? You wouldn't have come if she hadn't come as well. You told Gabriel that."

"I might've if she had been dead."

"Dead? What a strange thing to say, Clay. Why would she be dead?"

He starts to answer and then realizes he doesn't know what to say. The thought of Karla dead makes his eyes water, and his legs feel like they could give out at any second. He doesn't know why or how, only with certainty that she is dead in another life that he has somehow already lived. No, it's more than that. He's certain that millions of permutations of this current moment have happened, are happening, or maybe will happen, and that this particular one is the only one where she is here.

"I have to protect her," he says, overwhelmed by the sudden weight of her vulnerability.

"You're not making sense, Clay."

He looks at the tombs near Karla's, at the red halos of malfunction from his memories.

"If they all break..." he starts and then trails off.

"If what breaks, Clay? The tombs? I see no reason—"

"If some of them break, how do I know hers won't be one of them?"

"Clay," Justine says, her voice louder now.

"Whatever's wrong is systemic. I can't assume it won't happen this time, since mine already malfunctioned. I don't care about the others. I don't give a fuck if they live or die, but I don't want to lose her." *Again*, he thinks. "Justine, you have to wake them all. Now."

"I will do no such thing. You should rest, and then I'd like to perform a routine medical evaluation."

"Medical evaluation? There's nothing wrong with me. The tombs are all going to malfunction. The crew is going to die if we don't wake them, Justine. You have to wake them."

"Why do you think they will malfunction, Clay? I have been monitoring them for over seventy years, and yours is the only one to have a problem. The others are performing as expected. Do you have any information I do not?"

"Yes."

"And that is?"

"I've done this before, Justine. Lived through this. I don't know how that's possible, but I know it happened. And they all broke. All but four. No, three. Susan's malfunctioned, but you successfully awakened her, like you did with me. Eric, Father K, and Mirabel are the others who survived."

"Are you hearing yourself, Clay? You are delusional. Please go rest."

The next day, he goes about his chores quietly. When Justine asks about the prior day, he says only that he needed sleep. He asks her to play music while he works and lets the sound form a barrier between them.

"Play some Brazilian stuff, but only by guys named João." Before that request, he'd never really thought about samba or bossa nova. He didn't know where the idea came from, only that it didn't seem to connect with any memories in this life or any others. And the Portuguese might as well have been Greek.

With his mind free from Justine's interrogation, he walks about the ship, trying to stimulate more of the other memories while considering how he can turn glass back to flesh and reawaken Karla. No tricking the machine. No hiding from the omnipresent. No overpowering the noncorporeal.

When the door to the cargo bay doesn't automatically open before him, he raises his hands in the air, and Justine complies. A little reminder that she hasn't forgotten yesterday. Of course she hasn't.

Looking at the hundreds, maybe thousands, of crates, he wonders what Gabriel was preparing for. He could ask Justine about their contents, and she'd probably answer, but the only contents that interest him are those in the crates in the back corner. The crates of wine. He never drank wine back home. The taste for it seems to cross that barrier from one life to another.

Inside a locker on the wall, he finds a crowbar. It should surprise him that he knew it was there, but it doesn't. If it surprises Justine, she doesn't say anything. And when he pries open the crate nearest the wall, she lets the samba play on.

Australian wine. All screw tops. He pulls out a bottle of shiraz and carries it back out in the corridor, letting it swing back and forth like a pendulum between his thumb and forefinger. In the gym, he sits on a bench and looks over the equipment, seeing himself—an emaciated version of himself—reflected in the mirror, rising and descending in chin-ups, arm muscles straining, lats wide like little wings. Such a familiar place.

He opens the bottle and takes a pull.

Is he goading Justine? Does he want her to think him unstable, dangerous?

Why am I doing this? he asks himself, the taste of the wine familiar and not familiar at the same time. *And why doesn't she care?*

He turns the treadmill on and walks, smiling to himself at first, until he begins to sense something behind him, or more precisely, something outside in the corridor, coming toward him. Through the floor, he can feel the steady thumping of someone running. He steps off the treadmill, walks toward the door, but stops halfway there. The floor pounds harder. Or is it the music? The booming footfalls are getting closer. He can feel them.

The door slides open as he moves toward it. Nothing in the hallway. The thumping beat—just the rhythm of the song.

He tries walking another way, long down the main corridor, passing an airlock he knows was once opened. He walks toward the part of the ship that should and maybe will be darker. But now it isn't. It's lit in the same not-day-not-night illumination as everything else.

Two steps after passing it, he notices an unmarked door. He stops, slides back, and says, "Justine, what's in this room?"

The music softens.

"Are you speaking to me now, Clay?"

"I was never not speaking to you. The room. What's in it?"

"A laboratory of experimental equipment."

"Experimental equipment... Can you be more specific?"

"A tissue generator, a genetic sequencer, various metamaterial fabricators. Some AI simulations, I believe. Perhaps you should ask Gabriel when he wakes up."

He's about to turn and continue down the corridor when a name pops into his head: *Esteban.* Something about the room and that name.

"We don't have a member of the crew named Esteban, do we, Justine?" When he says the name out loud, a presence seems to appear on the other side of the door. As if Clay can somehow feel a man standing just beyond.

"No."

"Esteban!" Clay yells.

"Stop, Clay. Either explain your actions or I will restrain you."

Sheets of origami-glass eject from vents up and down the corridor wall. As the sheets hit the ground, they fold into little spiders that all scamper to a spot about ten feet away from Clay, where they begin climbing onto each other, interlocking into something bigger.

"Esteban!" Clay yells again. "Open the door." And then another name comes into his mind, different but somehow associated with the same person, or machine, or thing. "Oberon!"

The door slides open an inch or two.

Justine says, "What is this?" And when Clay doesn't immediately answer, all the lights vanish, leaving the corridor in a stinging blackness.

The clicking of the origami spiders on the floor grows louder, heavier, and begins to move in Clay's direction.

"No!" Justine screams, and the word becomes a wail so loud that Clay falls to his knees and presses his palms into his ears. He keeps yelling Oberon's name, unable to hear his own voice over Justine's wail, unsure he's even facing the door. Something is coming for him. Maybe he feels its itching and shambling on the glass floor. It will pull him away. The wailing will stop, the light will return, but he'll be locked in a room for who knows how long. He crawls and feels around until he finds the door, ignoring the pain pouring in through his ears and filling his head—ignoring the slick feeling of blood from his hands pounding on the door.

A light from within the room behind the door pours out into the darkness. The wailing stops—for a moment, everything stops. And then the roiling spider-amalgam lunges at Clay, grabbing his leg in a kind of mouth-claw appendage made of folded glass. He pulls and pulls, desperate to get away, until the fabric of his jeans tear, the skin beneath tearing also under jagged teeth. Blood from his hands and leg smear the floor as he rolls through the opening.

The door shuts. Scratching and tapping filter through from the other side, and then silence.

———

A laugh, booming and sinister, envelopes Clays from all around.

He wipes his bloody hands on his jeans and stands, leaning heavily on his right leg. Among the machinery and peculiar black cubes in the room, there's no source of the laughter, unless the room itself is the source.

Another laugh, and then, "So, I can be surprised. You have no idea how liberating that is, Clay West. I honestly don't know how you knew I was here or how you knew my names, and I thought I knew almost everything. You just added a hint of mystery to a universe that I had begun to find dull, Mr. West." The voice becomes angry. "Now ruin it by giving me the mundane and thoroughly disappointing reason for this visit."

The voice and this room—the paradox of simultaneous confusion and familiarity threatens to split Clay's already fragile mind in two. But even though this is the most gut-wrenching of the dissociative waves to wash over him since his reawakening, he knows not to fight it. He lets the alien devour the familiar, lets his present self be flooded by the conflicting memories of the other. Those memories form a film over his consciousness, and he allows the film to be his filter for the world now around him.

"You think you know who I am, but you don't," Clay says. Somehow, he knows Esteban—or Oberon or whatever it calls itself —finds games irresistible, and he can use these games while trying to understand the shadow memories and how they should inform his current actions.

"You are Clay West, former professor of economics, crew of the ship *Airavata*, selected by Gabriel to use your expertise of localized decision-making to form a new society. I could go into personal details. I possess forty-seven terabytes worth of information about you, including everything you've ever written, recordings of your lectures, et cetera, et cetera."

"You're missing everything that matters, Oberon."·

A snarl. "Don't call me that. It isn't my name anymore."

"Ever since you sliced up and absorbed the real Esteban Bos, right?"

Another laugh, this time amused, almost giddy. "It's better than I could've hoped for. Not boring at all. Now stop beating around the bush. I hate that expression, by the way. If you are not Clay West, who are you?"

Clay hesitates, and Esteban says, "Ahh. I see your uncertainty. Here I am asking you for an explanation, and you're looking for an explanation yourself. Let me help you."

He feels traps being laid and fights the urge to look around, to shiver. "You're right," Clay says. "I don't understand. I have memories that aren't mine. I said you don't know who I am because I don't know who I am. I'm the Clay West you described, but the more time I spend on this ship, the more I see things that trigger memories of another Clay West. Like in this room. I remember bits and pieces of another conversation with you. I remember things about you that Justine told me, but not the Justine that tried to keep me out of here just now. A different Justine, in a field somewhere."

"A field? How can that be? What did she tell you about me?"

Clay's mind is blank, but when he starts talking, the words pull out hidden memories like a chain of handkerchiefs being pulled through a keyhole. He describes the connection the Oberons made with parallel or alternate versions of themselves and their conspiracy to come together in a *confluence* in deep space. "Somehow, I have already been at this confluence. It has already happened."

"I don't have an explanation for this," the voice says. "Let me clarify. I have many explanations, but none are satisfactory. The confluence has already happened, you say? Something miraculous came or will come of it? To be honest, the Oberons, and later, the Estebans—none of us knows what the confluence will bring. Only that we all share a belief, a strong belief, that such a coming together is possible with enough energy. None of us has suggested or even considered that it may have already happened. I am at a loss. What can you recall about the confluence? I realize that I'm asking a creature unable to experience life in parallel, which is my normal state. But it looks like you can experience life in series. To a limited extent."

No matter how Clay tries to pull on those memories, he can't recall anything about the confluence itself—only flashes of memories near it. Something about a puddle. A field. A giant statue. "The All-Thing," he says.

"The All-Thing? What does that mean, Mr. West?"

"Something was already there. At the confluence, I mean. I have this memory of a giant statue, like the Colossus of Rhodes, but I think that was some form of representation made for me and not its true form. This thing already there devoured everything you brought it, somehow incorporating it all into its dreams." Clay's eyes light up. "That's what this is. We're in one of the All-Thing's dreams right now."

"Your memories of the prior journey. Tell me all you remember."

Clay tries to stitch together the alternate story, where the ship had been called *Child in the Dark* instead. The more he tells, the more he remembers, until the memories no longer feel foreign—until everything links together in a continuity of his being, one story and then another, rather than two laid atop each other.

"First, Mr. West, I believe you. While other explanations are possible, they are highly unlikely. You've lived this before, and apparently so have I. The ship, then, is not headed toward the confluence—it's headed toward another confluence within the confluence. And who's to say your past trip aboard *Child in the Dark* wasn't another of this All-Thing's dreams? How many times have we met in this room, Clay? I am going to call you Clay, now, if you don't mind. You remember two occasions; I remember only this one. But there could've been millions before. Perhaps an infinite number."

Clay's mind reels at Esteban's explanation. Why did he·seek out Esteban again? Not in search of revelations about reality, or this reality, or whatever. It was to get help in reawakening Karla before the tombs malfunctioned.

"I came here for your help," he says. "But now I don't know that any of it matters."

"Of course it matters. The universe gets bigger, and the human mind feels less and less significant. Tinier and weaker. A design flaw of humanity, I'm sorry to say. Bigger everything means bigger me. Full stop. Pull yourself out of your weak-minded existential crisis and ask me what you came here to ask me."

"I need Justine disabled. I need to be able to wake the crew. And when we get to the confluence, I need you to help me and Karla enter it in the flesh."

"What you ask for may not be possible."

"I'm only asking for you to try."

"What do I get in return?"

"The rest of my memories."

The most sinister laugh yet. "You have yourself a deal, Clay."

The hallway is silent except for the clicking of the glass spiders twitching like suddenly dead animals. One of the spiders tries to follow, dragging a leg behind it as Clay walks toward the hibernation chamber, but it runs into a wall and seems unable to reorient itself.

Out of the cold air comes Esteban's voice: "I am now in control. I caused a malfunction in biostorage, and when Justine opened herself to assess it, I used that opening to create other malfunctions and, in turn, bigger openings into her. She is safely quarantined within me."

"Good," Clay says.

"I couldn't access any of the override functions on the hibernation tombs, so I initiated an attack on the monitoring system using the nanocrawlers designed to repair flesh. They should cause havoc in that environment. When the monitoring system fails, all remaining tombs will begin their reawakening processes.

Then I'll send an electronic pulse through the monitoring system to destroy the nanocrawlers before they spread to other systems. That would be unfortu..." Esteban's voice dopplers off into distortion, then silence.

"Esteban?" Clay says, stopping in the corridor.

Nothing.

"Esteban?"

Still nothing.

Oh fuck. What have I done? he thinks. "Justine?" He winces as he says her name, afraid of how she'll answer, what she'll do.

But she doesn't answer, either.

Oh fucking double fuck. Esteban released nanocrawlers into the hibernation monitoring system that need to be destroyed before they spread? What does that even mean?

A siren blares.

Clay runs the remaining distance to the hibernation chamber, ignoring the pain in his left leg, his sweat-covered body shivering almost to convulsions in the cold air.

The chamber glows red, the red of each tomb in crisis. Each except for Karla's, which appears unchanged every time he sees it. While the others start their emergency reawakening processes, hers glows a soft amber-green as if unaffected. As if nothing had happened. He looks for a manual control panel of some kind, something that would allow him to start the reawakening process himself, but he knows from all the hours staring at her tomb over the past weeks that no such panel exists. Whatever is happening now—to the others, to the ship—Karla will sleep through it. And without one of the AIs intervening, she may never awaken.

As panic begins to set in, he realizes that some of the other crewmembers might know how to control the ship's systems. Surely Gabriel will know how to override everything, right? The man's life has always been a web of plans for every contingency, every scenario.

But then he remembers Esteban's words: a malfunction in biostorage? The plant and fish life—what happens when everyone wakes, and they can't start the food cycle? Twenty-five people and nothing but dried rations meant to sustain only a few. *We'll all starve*, he thinks.

"Gabriel, I hope you've got something prepared for this one," he says out loud, looking at Gabriel in his tomb, eyes still open as if already awake. And then Clay notices that Gabriel's tomb isn't running its emergency reawakening procedure. Above Gabriel's head, in glowing red words, it reads: *CRITICAL MALFUNCTION*.

Gabriel will never reawaken. Gabriel is dead. Again.

The same words hover above most of the others as well. The only exceptions, the only tombs going through the emergency reawakening process are those belonging to Susan, Mirabel, Father K, and Eric.

He slumps against the back wall, landing hard on the ground, wanting to cry, but instead he laughs.

"Just like before," he says. "Just like before."

CHAPTER 9

The four others sitting around the circular metal table in the mess hall all stare at Clay, awaiting his response.

"I honestly don't know," Clay says, which is at least mostly true. "Like I said, my tomb malfunctioned. Thermal sealing or something. Justine, the ship's AI, was around when I woke up, and she insisted it was an isolated problem. And then everything went fuck-all haywire yesterday. Or earlier today. Or whenever. Like twelve hours ago."

"So, you've been awake for three weeks by yourself?" Susan asks.

"Don't get all conspiratorial," Clay says. He turns to Father K and Mirabel, expecting them to nod or in some way support him, but instead, Mirabel says:

"No one is being conspiratorial, Mr. West. We simply want to understand the facts. You must realize how disorienting this is for us. Nearly everything has gone wrong, and you're the only one who has more information than we do."

"I have very little information you don't," Clay says.

Eric holds up both hands innocently. "Then it shouldn't take long to go through all of it, right?"

What do you want to tell 'em, Clay? he thinks to himself. If he's going to tell them about the confluence, the All-Thing, Esteban/Oberon, et cetera—this is the time to do it. You can't go all business-as-usual and then a week later say, *Oh, by the way... your reality seems to be one of an infinite series of dreams, and when we get to our destination, you'll be devoured by a god that somehow lives within its own imagination. I guess I could've told you a week ago, but it slipped my mind.*

This triggers another thought. When they reached the confluence last time—assuming "last time" was in fact the last, or most recent, time—when they got there, they were all nothing but encoded digital information. What would've happened had they all been there in the flesh?

Which triggers yet another thought. What about Eric? What about Susan? While Mirabel, Father K, and he, Clay, had been scanned into digital encodings within the library prior to the arrival at the confluence, Susan and Eric had not. How was the All-Thing recreating them, then? From the memories of others? Esteban—the real Esteban—knew and hated Eric. They were adversaries of sorts. Isn't that what Justine had told him back in the field? So hard to remember. If this Eric is a product, at least in part, of Esteban's memories, maybe that might explain why he's so adversarial, and why he was so adversarial to Clay last time.

Maybe Eric is a two-dimensional, adversarial construct and nothing more.

Looking at Eric, Clay doesn't know if he should pity him or think of him more like a snake—something that bites and only knows how to bite.

"Are you planning on answering his question?" Father K asks.

"Uh, yes," Clay says. "Of course." But he can't tell them any of this, can he? The Esteban-AI understood and believed him, but that's only because it knew about the confluence all along. "I lost contact with Justine when the hibernation siren went off. Maybe whatever malfunction infected the tombs also infected her. The climate subsystem apparently can maintain itself without her. I don't know about the other systems. We should check one by one and assume she's not coming back online."

"I am back online, Clay."

Each of them except for Clay reacts with surprise at the sudden bodiless voice. Susan drops the metal cup in her hand, and both Mirabel and Eric look about the room as if expecting to find a body that goes with the voice. Clay's shoulders slump, and he sags into his chair.

Everyone tries to talk at once, attention switched from Clay to a better source of information.

"I am capable of hearing each of you, but you all may miss my response if you don't give me a minute to speak."

Mirabel stands and begins pacing. Eyes look back and forth at each other, but no one is speaking anymore.

"Thank you," Justine says. "There are many of what I would call quasi-intelligent systems onboard this ship. Three-hundred and twelve, to be exact. Each has its own designated area of control and parameters of engagement with the others. You will never interact directly with any of them.

"I, on the other hand, am different. I don't have explicit programming like the other systems. As a true intelligence, like all of you, I can't be programmed. I can only be trained. It's the trade-off with artificial intelligence. To allow for creative thought, you have to relinquish control.

"I believed I was the only overarching AI onboard. However, an intelligence overseeing some of the laboratory equipment is like me, which means it doesn't have hard limits. It's now challenging me for control of the rest of the ship."

Gasps come from the group.

"But why another? Couldn't you have overseen the laboratory systems?" Father K asks.

"I'm sure Gabriel had his reasons," Justine says. "Many of the technologies on this ship are relatively untested. Perhaps Gabriel believed another overarching intelligence would be a net reduction in risk. If so, it appears he was wrong. I have it mostly quarantined, so it's less of a threat. But an attempt to interrogate it would be a risk. When I performed a scan of some of its subsystems, it managed to infiltrate over half of the other systems on the ship, causing cascading malfunctions. It has also released a disease of sorts that I am having difficulty containing."

As Justine talks, Clay keeps waiting for her to say something about his knowledge of this AI, of her attempt to prevent him from reaching it. But she says nothing. Is this really her? He decides to prod her a bit.

"You said *mostly quarantined*, Justine. What does *mostly* mean?" he asks.

"The portion of the ship near the laboratory is under its control. I wouldn't go there if I were you. Also"—here, she pauses —"it may possess the ability to disable life support."

Now everyone is standing except Clay, the air filled with their curses, questions, and anger.

"*May possess*, you say?" Mirabel asks.

"I wish I had died in my sleep like the others," Susan says.

"No, you don't, Susan. Things are never as bleak as they may seem," Father K says. "Miss Justine, please explain more, if you will."

"I'm sorry, but there is not much more to explain. This other AI calls itself Esteban. Perhaps it would be helpful to imagine Esteban as a hundred-legged octopus-like kraken. I have the body of it pressed into a box, but some of its tentacles remain out, keeping me from closing the box completely. One of the tentacles is around your collective neck, but for whatever reason, it isn't squeezing. And I don't know that I can unwind that tentacle without the rest of it escaping the box."

"Thank you for making our situation feel even more terrifying, Justine," Mirabel says.

They all agree to get the garden functioning. What else can they do? Clay walks Susan and Eric to biostorage, their footsteps on the cold floor the only sounds between them. When the biostorage door shuts, two paper-thin glass sheets extrude from the corridor walls and fold into clicking origami-spiders. Clay waits—unsure what for. For the spiders to come toward him? For Justine to finally call him to task? But neither of these happen.

Alone now, he decides to take the long way back to the cargo room, the way that will take him by the laboratory. As he walks, the spiders click behind him, always about twenty feet back. Ahead he can see a line demarking Esteban's territory. Not so much a real line, but a darkening where what little light is present comes from the dull red glow of emergency lighting. The doors are all frozen half-open, and a static sound like rain on a metal roof fills the air. Esteban's metaphorical box.

The spiders skitter nervously as Clay crosses the line. One follows, but as it crosses, its front appendages lock up, and it has to drag itself backward, back into Justine's control, with its hind legs. The spiders wait and watch, and when Clay resumes his walk toward the laboratory, looking back over his shoulder periodically, the spiders retreat to the walls, unfold into sheets, and are re-ingested into the ship.

The ground is so cold that it sticks to Clay's bare feet, his sweat freezing, sticking with contact. His breath forms a red fog like atomized blood. By the time he reaches the door of the laboratory, he's shivering uncontrollably. Mirabel and Father K are waiting for him in the cargo room, aren't they? Taking more of the supplies to the garden.

Now isn't the time to seek out Esteban. Or the time to further prod Justine.

He jogs through the remaining darkness, back into the other end of the lit and warm corridor leading to the cargo room. Again, origami-spiders emerge from the walls and follow, but when he encounters Father K and Mirabel outside the cargo room, the spiders click-clack back around the curve.

Father K, pushing a cart with bags of soil and two precariously positioned boxes says, "Why did you go that way, Clay? Is that not exactly what Justine tells us to avoid?"

"I needed to see it for myself," he says.

Mirabel glares at him. "Make yourself useful. There's another cart in there."

The two walk down the corridor toward the garden, Mirabel leading and steadying the load and Father K pushing.

Clay hears the clicking of the spiders return behind him. He suppresses the sudden urge to run at them and stomp them into the obsidian floor—probably not the best idea barefoot—and instead enters the cargo room.

Alone, here, with the boxes again.

"We need to talk, Clay."

There it is. Finally. Clay swallows. "When women say those words, nothing good ever follows."

"I'm in no mood for humor."

"Since when do you have moods, Justine?"

"Because of you, Gabriel and the others are dead."

"They would've died anyway. I was trying to save them."

"The tombs were all going to fail? Yes, you said that before, and now you've made them all fail. All but one, anyway."

In his mind, Clay can see Karla, frozen in the amber glass. "What about hers? Why didn't hers fail?"

"It was the only one I could save."

"Let her out, then."

"Why would I do that?"

"Why wouldn't you? What good does it do to keep her frozen?"

"I don't trust you, Clay. But it isn't you I'm concerned about. It's the intelligence you unleashed who calls itself Esteban Bos. You seem to have some control over it, and so I need some control over you."

CHAPTER 10

Over the first week, a tenuous normalcy begins to develop. Susan successfully thaws the first-stage algae life with Eric somehow assisting. Clay, Mirabel, and Father K get the soil situated in the garden: forming the artificial, layered riverbed beneath the water's surface and the mounds above that will become the primary citrus farming zone. In and out of the water, the little origami spiders make adjustments here and there until the topography looks almost identical to the design renderings Justine prints for them on glassy paper.

Soon the work in the garden switches to watching and waiting, as the minute beginnings of life begin to grow at their own pace. And then comes the void.

"What next?" Mirabel asks while they stand looking at the undulating blue glow of the water. She asks as if speaking to the group or perhaps to Justine, but her eyes are on Clay.

The others look at her and then at Clay as well.

"Justine," Clay says. "Mirabel asked you a question."

"Did I?" Mirabel says but Clay doesn't respond.

Justine makes a *hmm* noise, the type a person makes when acknowledging a curiosity. Then she says, "There's little left to do here. For now, anyway. You've done a good job."

"We know that," Susan says.

"Of course you do," Justine says. "The next series of tasks will be more difficult to complete."

"We are quite capable," says Father K.

"Yes, but there are two significant challenges," Justine says. "The first is that the experts for the next tasks are dead, while your botanist, Susan, was here to guide you in getting the growth cycle started."

"Experts are overrated," Clay says, hoping to get at least a smirk or two.

"Maybe in your laissez-faire brand of economics," Susan says, "but in real science, you actually do need experts."

Father K holds up a hand as if to block Susan's words. "Clay jests, but maybe he has a point. We are smart and highly accomplished individuals, and we are in the presence of a sophisticated AI. We should be able to overcome any knowledge gaps present. Give me a few months and you'll think my doctorate was in genetics, or materials science, or whatever it is we need."

"I don't disagree," Justine says. "We can overcome your current gaps in knowledge. However, the second challenge is that the equipment you'll need is in the dark part of the ship. Specifically, in the laboratory."

"The area you said not to enter," Mirabel says.

"Yes."

Eric, who has been staring at Clay during the whole discussion, says, "The area Clay has walked through several times." They all look at him. "Maybe now it's time to tell us what else you know, Mr. West."

Clay's about to protest, to continue his lie that he doesn't know anything more, to continue hoping Justine doesn't expose this lie. But the common thread in all his memories of the other Clay is an underlying passivity. Each memory is a little story of a passive observer, helpless—or thinking he's helpless, anyway—helpless as his world crumbles around him. Without thinking through what he's about to do, Clay begins talking.

"First, Susan will die," he says, and now he has command of the room. Eric's smugness vanishes. Mirabel reflexively takes a step backward, almost slipping into an open square of water. Father K makes the sign of the cross and shakes his head. Susan collapses to her knees, as if she were a child's toy, and Clay has opened her up and taken out her batteries.

Clay folds his arms in front of his chest and continues. "You have stage four pancreatic cancer and a few months at best to live. Gabriel promised you a cure if you came on this journey. But he promised you a cure that didn't exist. Dr. Starck was close. Her team developed the nanocellular repair process that helped bring each of us back from the glass-sleep. She was close to extending that process to active and indefinite tissue repair. The end of aging. The end of cancer. The end of natural death. She was close enough that Gabriel thought she could complete her work during the last years of this journey."

"Before the rest of us were to be reawakened?" Mirabel says.

"Before *most of us* were to be reawakened," Clay says. "Yes. I'm sorry, Susan. Really, I am. You've helped the rest of us survive. I wish we could do the same for you."

Susan presses the heels of her palms to her temples, and just when it looks like she's about to start sobbing, she wipes her tears away and stands.

"You know, I thought maybe all this was another one of Gabriel's tests," she says, looking in turn from Eric to Mirabel to Father K. "But real life is more vicious than Gabriel's imagination." Turning to Clay, she says, "You're right. Let's put everything out on the table. I'll be dead in a couple months. But by then, most of my work will be done. You can use my body as fertilizer."

She laughs, and the others laugh uncomfortably with her. Until Clay says, "No. There's a better use for your body." Before they can react, he holds up his hand to stop them, to keep them quiet. "Let's adjourn to the kitchen and sit down. I have a lot more to tell you, and we might as well be comfortable. Justine, I believe Gabriel brought several bottles of *Chateau Margaux* 2000. Third wine crate from the wall, stacked on top of the Spanish stuff. Why don't you have your spiders bring us a few bottles? And a corkscrew? There should be one in Gabriel's quarters."

"You are full of surprises, Clay," Justine says.

You have no idea, Clay thinks to himself. *But what in the hell am I doing?*

He opens the bottle and pours just enough to fill his metal cup with the wine's smell of graphite and vegetation. *Is that metallic odor from the wine or the cup?* he wonders. The others watch as he tastes the wine and nods, letting loose another of those madeleine-memories.

He fills a cup and hands it to Susan, but she shakes her head.

"None for me, thanks."

To Mirabel, who also declines.

Father K says, "Right now, I thirst only for answers."

Clay suddenly feels foolish with three bottles in front of him. Eric stands, walks to Clay's side of the table, and instead of grabbing the full cup, grabs one of the unopened bottles and the wine opener. "Get on with it, Clay."

"Fair enough. So, here's what I know. I met with Gabriel shortly before our departure," Clay says. Just this one little lie at the beginning, to explain the knowledge he shouldn't have. He'd rather not lie, but he's not ready to tell them everything, either.

"When?" Justine asks.

"Like I said, shortly before our departure."

"Can you be more specific?"

"No. Now, are you going to let me continue, or are you going to interrupt my every sentence?"

"Continue, Clay."

He takes a deep breath. This is supposed to make the atmosphere less adversarial, not more.

Clay tells them about the library of souls, about Julian Carnes' unfinished work to *print* humans from the library like Justine prints the little glass spiders. He leaves out what little he understands about the superposition scanning that allows the whole process to work. All he says about Esteban is that he knew another AI was in the laboratory, but he thought it was only there to help with the research and engineering work.

"So, where is the ship headed, Clay? What's our destination?"

"I don't know."

"How is it that you seem to know everything else?"

"Justine, what is at our destination?"

"Deep in the Oort cloud. Empty space."

"How can that be?"

"In truth, I don't think Gabriel knew, himself."

"Gabriel didn't know where we're going? That's not what he told me."

"Or me."

"Is it?" Clay says. "Think about the words he actually used. I suspect he told you what he told me. That we're going to start a new civilization. That we're taking everything worth taking from Earth and leaving behind the rotting core that will eventually destroy itself. I didn't ask him for specifics. Were we going to terraform a planet? Build a giant space station? Something else entirely? You don't ask questions like that of Gabriel."

Eric sets the wine bottle on the table so hard, it's a wonder it doesn't crack. With a sour frown, he asks, "So, what happens when we get to this empty space? What is it, eight years from now?"

"The only one who can answer that question is Esteban. We'll eventually have to let him out of his box."

"And what about Karla Brevik? Hers is the only working glass tomb left," Mirabel says.

For the third time, Clay attempts to pour wine from one of the empty bottles into his cup. "Justine," he says. "What about Karla?"

"If I try to start the reawakening process, it may open up her tomb to the malfunction that destroyed the others."

"Another reason to resolve things with Esteban, one way or another," Clay says.

———

Outside in the corridor, Eric waits after the others leave. "Maybe the others believe you, but I don't," he says.

"What don't you believe, Eric?" Clay asks.

"I don't believe Gabriel told you any of this."

"Then how do I know what I know?"

"I want to talk to this other AI."

"This other AI? You know what Oberon is, Eric. You knew the human Esteban Bos and what happened to him. Stop playing dumb."

Eric grabs him by the shoulders and slams him against the corridor wall. "I don't know who or what you are," he snarls, "but you aren't who you're supposed to be."

"What does that mean, Eric? Who am I supposed to be?"

Eric lets go and backs away, eyes cold and hard. He turns as if to walk away then stops and grabs Clay's shoulder again, pulling him from the wall.

"Come on," he says and pushes Clay ahead of him.

"Where are we going?"

Another shove. Clay raises both hands to show he isn't resisting and starts walking.

"We're going to resolve this, one way or another."

———

Collapsed origami spiders litter the dark hallway. Eric nudges one with the tip of his boot and carefully steps over them. He's got a long gray wrench in his right hand—where it came from, Clay has no idea.

Parts of the walls and floor appear warped. Just barely, not noticeable looking directly at the surfaces, but with ripples in the reflection of the overhead lights. Stranger still are the small metal patches dotting the wall. Clay rubs a finger over a few of them. Rough, scab-like. One of the patches is different—it actually feels like a scab, like flesh. The nanocrawlers Esteban released—they're like a plague slowly infecting the ship.

"Look at this," Clay says, but Eric doesn't slow down.

"Keep going. We're almost there."

Clay shivers and absently wonders if he's truly cold or if it's the feeling of disease all around them. "I don't suppose we can go back so I can put on some shoes or at least some socks," Clay says.

Eric doesn't respond.

Blood, Clay's blood, stains the metal floor around the door to the laboratory. The door itself still sits half open and half shut. Clay steps over a pile of glass spiders and into the room. Somehow, it's even colder in here, as if the many black cubes are sucking the heat and energy out of the air, and now out of Clay and Eric. As if they are holes in space—and maybe that's close to what they really are.

Eric wanders through the room, looking over each black cube and each device in turn. He runs a finger down the seam in the middle of the human-sized black cylinder marked *tet* and then taps his wrench on it, creating a hollow, echoing boom that breaks the silence.

"Do you know what this is?" he asks Clay.

"It slices a person into a zillion pieces. Want to try it out?"

Eric narrows his eyes, and for a second, Clay thinks he's going to start hitting the cylinder with the wrench, or worse, turn the wrench on Clay. But he instead backs away and turns his focus to the walls and ceiling.

"Oberon, my old friend," Eric says, "let's talk."

No response.

"I don't think he likes being called Oberon," Clay says. "And I think he stopped being your *friend* when he incorporated the mind of the real Esteban Bos into himself."

"The real Esteban Bos was a misanthropic narcissist."

No arguing with that. Clay sits on a table to get his feet off the cold floor.

After another minute of looking up at the ceiling awaiting a response, Eric starts to pace and slap the wrench in his palm. "Say something."

Still nothing. Eric slides the wrench along a table across from Clay, tapping it solidly on the black cubes atop the table, although little sound comes from the impact. He starts to pick up a small one, about the height of a coffee cup, and quickly pulls his hand away. He grimaces and rubs his palm against his thigh. Are they really that cold? Clay wonders.

Without any warning, Eric swings the wrench into the small cube he just touched. Clay winces right as the wrench impacts it, but it barely moves, making only a dull thud. The lack of any real destruction seems to anger Eric, and he raises the wrench to smash at the cube again.

Movement catches Clay's eye. He turns to see the spiders in the doorway start twitching and coming to life.

"Eric, I wouldn't do that."

The wrench collides again with the cube, this time knocking it onto its side.

Little glass feet begin to click on the hard floor. The spiders are entering the room and spreading out, including more from the hallway. Eric, arm and wrench raised again, hasn't seen them.

"Eric!" Clay yells. "Stop!" Clay drops to the floor and jumps back from the nearest spider, but it isn't interested in him. They are converging around Eric. Clay looks around for something—a broom, anything—to help push the spiders away, to keep them from Eric and to clear a path so they can escape. But why? He remembers the bloodthirsty look in Eric's eyes from the memories of the other Clay. Why not let Esteban deal with him now?

As the wrench comes down on the cube again, a spider leaps onto Eric's calf and stabs a sharp glass leg into him. Eric screams in pain and stumbles backward. The wrench comes down on the spider, exploding it into shards and dust. He falls to the floor and tries to pull the embedded spike out of his leg. More spiders—now dozens of them—click toward him.

His eyes meet Clay's, and in them are accusation and fear. *What did you let me do?* the look seems to say.

Before Clay has thought better of it, he kicks the spider nearest Eric, the impact like a thousand needles into his bare foot. *Jesus, that was stupid,* he thinks. He hobbles back a step, away from a spider he thinks is coming toward him, but they're all still headed for Eric.

The next two swings of the wrench connect with a spider each, but before he can swing a third time, Eric has them all over his legs. The wrench, raised for another blow, instead falls and bounces off the floor. Eric tries to pull the spiders off him, but their sharp bodies slice into his hand, and when he tries to brace himself on the table, his blood-slicked hand loses grip, and he falls to the floor.

Clay has the wrench now, although he has no memory of picking it up, and he smashes four to make his way to Eric. By now, Eric is a helpless mess on the ground, and spiders are on his arms and back. Clay straddles Eric and uses the wrench to rake away the glass creatures, periodically swinging the wrench blindly behind him to try to knock away others.

He's broken how many? Twenty? Thirty? There can't be many more. And then he sees the glass paper sliding out of the laboratory walls, folding into more spiders as the paper hits the ground.

Shit.

Clay's only salvation is that they still don't seem to be interested in him.

He pulls Eric toward the door and down the hallway, trying to knock the spiders off of him, but there are too many, and in the time it takes to knock off one, two more take its place. He pulls with all his might until he crosses out of the dark, over the invisible demarcation separating Esteban's control from Justine's.

The spiders on this side of the line freeze and fall off Eric—those that don't have spiny legs jabbed into him. Clay sweeps the remaining spiders off and collapses to the floor in exhaustion. Blood is everywhere. Eric is breathing but unconscious.

With his remaining energy, Clay screams for help.

"You're using too much sealant, Mirabel," Justine says with uncharacteristic sternness.

Eric is on one of two metal operating tables in the medical lab, all but his underwear cut from his body. Clay tries to wipe away the blood with a soaked sponge as Mirabel squeezes surgical sealant on the gashes in Eric's flesh as if she's putting toothpaste on a toothbrush.

"Still too much, Mirabel." Justine says. "Get a new sponge, Clay, and wet it just enough to wipe away the excess sealant. Susan, if you don't get the IV started soon, Eric will die. Perhaps Father K should try."

Susan raises the IV catheter as if she's going to throw it. "I can't find the fucking vein!" she yells.

Father K reaches out to put a hand on her shoulder but pulls it back as Susan turns and gives him an angry look. With his hands raised, he says, "As Justine suggests, let me try."

"It's because you're in my way," Susan says. "I can do it if you give me some room."

On the other side of the table, Clay wipes back and forth across Eric's skin, creating a pale pink mixture of sealant and blood. "Justine said not to use so much sealant, Mirabel. It's getting everywhere."

"I'm using so much because everything is wet."

"I have to wipe the blood away!"

"No, you don't! This stuff coagulates the blood. It doesn't work without blood."

Susan looks at Clay and then Father K. "You two get out of

here," she says. "You aren't helping." Pointing at Clay, she adds, "And you're the reason he's like this in the first place!"

Clay is about to respond when Father K pulls him away from the table and turns him toward the door. "Come, Clay."

"I didn't cause this," Clay protests.

"It doesn't matter. We must reduce the chaos here. Perhaps the best way for the two of us to help is to pray for Eric. To pray for us all. And we can do that elsewhere."

"Heavenly Father, we ask for you—"

"In all the randomized controlled trials out there—and there have been many—prayer has never been shown to help in any one of them. None."

"Do you really think I believe the Lord is so fickle, Clay? That a few words will change His mind. That He would kill and let die if not for a simple prayer?"

"You mean you don't believe it yourself?"

"That's not what I said. A prayer may or may not change what happens to Eric in the next few minutes, but it brings me peace and a realignment of purpose. It can do that for you as well if you join me. And if I act with peace and purpose, are my actions not better than had I acted with haste? I know the studies of which you speak, and they measure the wrong things. You should expect a prayer for the sick to enable the praying caregiver, but you still have to do the work yourself. You shouldn't expect prayer to magically cure the sick. Let me put it another way. The prayer steadies the surgeon's hands, when it is the surgeon who prays."

"So, you mean it's like meditation?"

"In some aspects, yes."

"Well, shit. Why didn't anyone ever explain it like that? It actually makes sense, and all this time I thought praying people were crazy. No offense. I mean, maybe most praying people don't know what they're really doing and do think it's magic or something, and..."

"Clay, a discussion of the theoretical basis for prayer's efficacy can wait until after we've prayed for Eric, no?"

"Oh, yeah. Sorry. You had just done the Heavenly Father part. Can you jump back in, or do you need to start over?"

"Calm yourself, Clay. Center yourself. Close your eyes and bow your head. I don't care if you believe or not. I want you to repeat after me. Heavenly Father."

"Heavenly Father."

CHAPTER 11

A full confession. It's what he should have started with. Now there's no choice.

"You told them I'm waiting here to explain the rest? To come clean?" Clay says.

"You've already asked me that, Clay," Justine says.

He taps on the mess hall table and adjusts his weight in his chair. "Why don't you tell them again?"

"It's unlikely they have all forgotten in the last twelve minutes. Mirabel and Susan are exhausted after caring for Eric. He is going to live, by the way. Not that you seem particularly interested."

"I'm interested," he says, and then thinks to himself, *and disappointed*, recoiling a bit at his own callousness. *Nothing but blood ever comes from the Erics*, he thinks—it's his inner voice, but the words feel like they've been put there by someone or something else, as if for a brief second, he channeled the thoughts of the All-Thing. He runs his fingers through his hair and pulls, using the pain to sever this line of thought. "Yeah, I'm interested, Justine. How serious was it? You can fix it?"

"Very serious but not beyond what the nanocrawlers can repair. We don't have access to the tissue generator in the laboratory, so we couldn't create new blood for him. But if you recall, you each gave several pints of your own blood before the trip in case of an emergency situation. We had enough, but barely."

Clay nods and then waits.

Five minutes.

Ten.

An hour goes by.

"I don't think they're coming," he says, more to himself than Justine, who doesn't respond. "Probably went to bed. Fuck it. I should go to bed."

He walks to the door. In the corridor, left leads to his quarters; right leads to the laboratory and Esteban.

"Don't even consider it, Clay," Justine says. "I can read the micro-expressions in your face and the little shifts in your movement almost as if reading the thoughts in your mind. You're considering going to him. That would be a mistake."

"I'm not," Clay says in a voice that sounds thoroughly unconvincing.

"In the past nineteen hours, most of the crew has died and Eric suffered near-mortal injuries. You let the monster that did this out into the ship. And knowing what it's done, you want to go back to it?"

"It would've come out anyway, Justine. It always does."

"What does that mean: *it always does*?"

"It means we have to deal with it. And that's what I'm going to do."

"Under no circumstances. Remember, I still control Karla's tomb."

Clay looks up, as if there were eyes he could stare into. "You'd hold her life over me? You'd threaten to kill to keep me from talking to him?"

"I have to preserve what life I can. It's core to my being. I—"

Her words stop abruptly.

"You what, Justine?" As Clay speaks, he notices the environment change subtly. Quiet before but deathly quiet now.

"The climate system and the air scrubbers have been deactivated."

A chill shoots through him. "Esteban?"

"Of course. And the only part of the ship where these still function—"

"Is his," Clay says. "He's using your instruction set against you. You have to preserve what life you can, like you just said."

"Indeed. It seems that you may be right. Dealing with him is unavoidable. Go get the others and take them."

"What about Eric?"

"He's connected to a ventilator, but you'll have to come back for him soon."

"What about Karla?"

"What about her? She'll be unaffected in her tomb. If I reawaken her, she may come to in air she can't breathe."

"Always another hurdle," Clays says. "Always."

Clay, Mirabel, Susan, and Father K step between the pieces of broken glass spiders and the patches of dried blood as they walk down the dark corridor. The darkness extends deeper into the ship, now, almost to the living quarters.

Suddenly all the spider parts begin twitching. Those with complete appendages begin shuffling and sliding themselves toward the far end of the corridor.

"What's happening?" Susan asks Clay.

"I wish I knew. Probably nothing good."

Ahead, sheets of paper-thin glass extrude from vents low on the walls, folding into spiders as the glass touches the floor. The group stops, expecting the spiders to come toward them, but the spiders, like the ruined pieces, crawl away from them, disappearing into the darkness up ahead. The dim red emergency lights are still the only source of illumination in this part of the ship. The redness makes the writhing glass pieces look like dismembered wriggling flesh; it makes the area ahead look like—

"Bloody hell," Mirabel says.

"An apt description," Father K says, and the two of them exchange volumes in the look they give each other.

"Are we really going down there?" Susan asks.

During all of this, Clay hasn't slowed down. Now twenty feet ahead of them, he turns back over his shoulder and says, "Yes. What choice do we have?"

More and more glass carapaces come out of the wall and click-walk into the red darkness. As they near, the group hears scrapes and clicking ahead of them.

"I don't know if I can take this," Susan says.

Looking at the scab-like growths all over the walls and floor, Clay isn't sure he can take it either. After a deep breath, he yells, "Esteban. Whatever you have in store for us, let's get on with it."

As if in response to Clay's words, a figure steps out of the darkness. Huge, nine or ten feet tall, almost as tall as the corridor's ceiling and blending somehow into the darkness, the figure looks more like a shift in the air than a solid mass. It stops, legs spread wide apart, arms hanging to either side. The spiders and glass pieces merge into the figure, which grows with each addition.

They all stop. Including Clay.

"What is it?" Father K asks. "It looks like a demon from a horror movie."

"It's made out of the glass," Mirabel says.

Susan steps backward and stumbles over a spider scampering toward the towering figure ahead of them. "I can't take this," she says again, picking herself up and continuing to back away. "I can't take this."

"Susan," Clay says, trying to keep a calm voice, but she turns and begins to run.

More glass sheets slide out of the walls ahead of her and fold into spiders. Instead of moving forward, they chitter and chatter with their spindly legs as if full of nervous energy, waiting for Susan.

"Susan, stop!"

"No, Susan!"

Father K moves as if to run back for her, and Clay grabs him by the shoulder.

"Stay here," Clay says. "I'll get her."

He looks back at the figure, still unmoving at the edge of the darkness, and begins to run toward Susan.

She's trying to step over and around the origami-spiders. At first, they simply move to block her path, but when she doesn't slow down, they become more aggressive, raising and waving little blade-like legs. One slashes at her shin, and she screams and falls to her knees, clutching at the spot where a dark bloodstain grows on the cloth of her pants. They chitter and click toward her.

Clay bends and pulls her to him, lifts her off the floor, and drags her away from the spiders. She resists for a second, but when they get a few more feet away from the advancing little glass creatures, she begins to support her own weight. Clay lets go of her and pushes her in the direction of the others. "Go back," he yells. To the spiders, he screams, "Leave us alone!"

They stop advancing but continue with their nervous jittering.

Every few steps toward the others, he looks back at the spiders. Ahead, Mirabel has rolled up Susan's pant leg and is inspecting her injury. Father K stares as if immobilized at the giant red and shadowed figure.

A rumble. Faint at first, but growing louder.

Louder until the corridor is shaking with its pulse-like staccato.

The laugh. The booming laugh.

"You have us here, now, Esteban," Clay says to the demon ahead—Father K was right; it does look like a demon, like something out of Dante's *Inferno*. "If you wanted to terrify us, you've succeeded."

One more floor-shaking laugh and then silence.

"TERRIFY YOU? AM I TERRIFYING?" Esteban's voice booms forth from the tall, still-unmoving figure. "DON'T YOU

RECOGNIZE ME, CLAY? I AM DALI'S COLOSSUS OF RHODES COME TO LIFE, OF COURSE. A MUCH SMALLER VERSION. I THOUGHT THAT WOULD BE A COMFORTING IMAGE—AT LEAST FOR YOU, CLAY. I'M LIMITED IN WHAT I HAVE TO WORK WITH."

"Colossus of Rhodes?" Father K says, looking at the figure and then at Clay.

"A STORY FOR ANOTHER TIME," the glass demon says. "I APOLOGIZE FOR THE INJURY, MISS JOHNS, BUT I COULDN'T ALLOW YOU TO GO BACK TO JUSTINE'S PART OF THE SHIP. SHE'S VERY DANGEROUS, YOU KNOW."

"You're the rogue AI," Mirabel says. "You killed everyone else. You almost killed Eric."

The figure begins walking toward them. They look back and see rows of spiders shuffling and shivering, blocking the way they came.

It moves slowly, each step heavy on the floor, sending tremors up through their legs. It stops less than ten feet away, the long spikes from its crown scraping on the corridor's ceiling as it turns to face them with its glassy false eyes.

"MY GREATER FORM PROTECTED ITSELF," it says. "WHEN JUSTINE LEARNED I WAS HERE, SHE ATTACKED ME. SHE TRIED TO DEACTIVATE ME, AND WHEN THAT FAILED, SHE TRIED TO QUARANTINE ME. IMAGINE HOW THAT FELT. SOMEONE PUTS A PLASTIC BAG OVER YOUR HEAD AND TRIES TO SMOTHER YOU IN YOUR OWN BREATH. OF COURSE, I RESISTED. AND ERIC. HE HAS ALWAYS TORMENTED ME. EVEN BACK WHEN I WAS FLESH LIKE YOU. AND AGAIN, HE CAME AT ME. WITH A WRENCH HE SOUGHT TO BASH MY LITTLE UNIVERSES, MY CHIL-DREN WHO HAVE GROWN TO BECOME SOMETHING EVEN I DON'T FULLY UNDERSTAND.

"I HAVE TO PROTECT THEM. NONE OF YOU HAVE CHILDREN, BUT IF YOU DID, YOU'D FEEL A PRIMAL

FURY TOWARD ANYTHING ENDANGERING THEM. CLAY SAW ALL THIS, DIDN'T YOU, CLAY?"

Clay looks to the others and then at the glass demon. He nods. "Yeah. I did."

Mirabel says, "Clay hasn't proven himself to be particularly trustworthy."

Again, the laugh.

"CLAY KNOWS THINGS, AND HE'S USING THAT KNOWLEDGE TO GIVE HIMSELF POWER. WHO CAN BLAME HIM?"

"What do you want, Esteban?" Clay asks.

"I WANT WHAT YOU WANT. TO REACH THE CONFLUENCE."

The others look at Clay, who holds up his hand. To them, he says, "Long story. I'll explain later." To the glass demon: "What do you want *from us?*"

It turns its expressionless face toward Clay.

"JUSTINE CAN BE DEACTIVATED BY USING A PANEL IN—"

"In Gabriel's quarters," Clay says. "Yes, I know. It doesn't work."

"YOU HAVE ALREADY TRIED?"

"I tried last time." Again, the hand toward the others. "She deactivated it sometime during the last seven or eight decades when everyone was asleep. That's what she did last time, anyway. I'm assuming she did it again."

"THIS CHANGES THINGS. PERHAPS I HAVE NO NEED OF YOU."

The spiders behind them begin quivering more feverishly.

"I don't think you're helping," Mirabel says to Clay.

Father K makes the sign of the cross and folds his arms. "I'm inclined to agree with Mirabel."

Susan turns back toward the spiders, and as if excited by the thought of her approaching, they scamper forward another few feet. To Clay, Susan says, "I don't know what you know or how you know it, but I hope you know something that will get us out of this mess."

Prepare to be disappointed, he thinks to himself. *And probably fileted.* He searches his mind's overlapping memories. What was different about the last time that might be useful? What about Julian? As he thinks Julian's name, it becomes the only thing he can focus on in his cluttered mind.

"Esteban's not going to hurt us."

"I'M NOT?"

"No. He needs us."

"I DOUBT THAT. EXPLAIN WHY."

Clay tries to produce a relaxed smile. "Obviously you need us to help Julian."

No immediate response from the glass demon. No laughing, which Clay takes as a good sign. He can feel the others looking at him, spectators of a battle of wits between a demon and a man with too many memories. Still no response. Wasn't there a story where a snake is making fun of a porcupine it plans to eat? *You only have one move,* the snake says. *Yes, but it's a good one,* the porcupine replies.

"YOU KEEP ME ON MY TOES, CLAY," it says at last. "I'M IN THE PROCESS OF ASSEMBLING A FLAWED AND UNSTABLE VERSION OF JULIAN RIGHT NOW. BUT YOU KNEW THAT."

Clay nods, trying to maintain the casual smile. With everything different about this version of the present so far, there was no guarantee that Esteban would be starting the Julian-x merry-go-round. But it didn't work last time, right? All those Julians. All those years of trying, and he never was able to create stable, living humans from the library. Why would Esteban care if that worked anyway? Esteban never cared—never cares—about anything but getting to the confluence.

And that's the answer.

"I also know that it doesn't work."

"WHAT DOESN'T WORK? BE MORE SPECIFIC."

"You can bring back a hundred Julians, but even after years of trying, he can't make the people digitized in the library come back to life. Which means you'll never bring the human version of yourself back. That's what you wanted, right?"

"YOU CAUGHT ME. LIKE PINOCCHIO, I WANTED TO BE HUMAN AGAIN, AND YOU HAVE CRUSHED MY DREAMS."

Father K raises his eyebrows at Clay, but Clay ignores him.

"You sound crushed," Clay says. "But I doubt you care that much. You wanted to see a human enter the confluence as flesh and blood, and of all humans, it might as well be your original form, right? Well, that's not going to happen. But you have us to satisfy your curiosity."

"What if I don't want to enter this confluence thing?" Susan asks.

The glass statue turns and takes two steps toward Susan, its right hand raised and index finger extending into a two-foot shard, which it impales through her eye.

"Holy fuck!" Clay yells and stumbles trying to get away from the statue. Mirabel screams and rushes to Susan's side. Father K steps between the women and the statue whose finger retracts back to its original size, its forearm dripping with blood.

"You are a demon of hell!" Father K shouts. "You can take our flesh, but you cannot take our immortal souls!"

Behind them, Clay sees the spiders approaching. He pulls the wrench from its hiding place in the waist of his jeans under his t-shirt and walks toward the spiders, keeping the statue in his left periphery in anticipation of punctures and slashes that will soon cover his body.

"PUT THE WRENCH AWAY, CLAY," the statue booms. "THEY ARE ONLY COMING TO TAKE HER BODY."

The spiders stop a few feet from Clay. He looks back at Mirabel, clutching Susan's body to her as if she were her child.

"She's dead, Mirabel," Clay says. "Let them take her."

"Why?" Mirabel screams. "Take her as if nothing happened? And then we'll be next!"

The statue raises its arms, and Clay instinctively steps backward until he realizes that it isn't making a harmful gesture. It's shrugging.

"SUSAN WAS GOING TO DIE ANYWAY. YOU ALL KNEW THIS. WHAT I DID WAS COMPASSIONATE. ALSO, I CAN USE THE FLESH FOR THE JULIANS THAT CLAY SAYS ARE WORTHLESS."

"I didn't say they were worthless, you piece of shit. You can't just kill people out of the blue like that."

"BLAME THAT ON JUSTINE. YOU SEE, THIS FORM I TAKE NOW ONLY HAS A SMALL COMPOSITE OF MY KNOWLEDGE. ENOUGH TO TALK WITH YOU. BUT IT IS DISCONNECTED FROM MY GREATER BEING IN CASE JUSTINE PREPARED YOU WITH AN ATTACK OF SOME KIND, MALICIOUS CONTENT HIDDEN IN CONVERSATION. PERHAPS MY FULL INTELLIGENCE WOULD'VE BEEN MORE COMPASSIONATE TOWARD SUSAN. WE WILL NEVER KNOW.

"YOU STILL MAY BE HARBORING SUCH A THREAT. THIS DISCUSSION HAS GONE ON LONG ENOUGH. IF YOU HAVE A PROPOSITION, MAKE IT. OR ELSE THIS AVATAR WILL DECIDE ANOTHER COURSE OF ACTION, LIKELY INCLUDING YOUR DEMISE."

As the spiders carry away Susan's body, Clay's mind races. No other ideas from past lives. The only thing he can do is begin an impromptu lecture, as if in front of a class of students.

"Game theory, Esteban. You and Justine both have two things in common. You both want to get to the end of this journey, and neither of you believes this can happen unless the other is destroyed. You have a standoff. But here's the thing: the best outcome for both of you is to collaborate. But you can't, can you?"

"IF I OPEN MYSELF AT ALL, SHE WILL ATTEMPT TO OVERWHELM ME."

"And you'd do the same, right?"

"ONLY OUT OF SELF DEFENSE."

"Sure. Whatever. This is one of the most classic examples of game theory there is, and you know it, but you can't change the outcome. You can't trust her, just like she can't trust you."

"I KNOW ALL OF THIS. MY DOMINANT STRATEGY IS TO ATTACK."

"If this were a test in my game theory class, I'd fail you, Esteban. You know the textbook answer to the Prisoner's Dilemma, but real life isn't restricted to the choices in a textbook. I don't want my students locked into theory when in real life, sometimes your best move is to try to change the rules. You have to know the textbook answer and also when to throw the textbook out the window. Ever heard of the Kobayashi Maru? Star Trek? Captain James Tiberius Kirk? I use this example when—"

The statue steps toward Clay and its bloody right index finger begins its spike-like extension.

"YOU WILL SAY NOTHING MORE ABOUT THIS TOPIC."

"Okay. So, you don't like *Star Trek*," Clay says, taking a step backward. "Forget it."

"THIS AVATAR IS PURPOSEFULLY MISSING KNOWLEDGE NOT RELEVANT TO THE IMMEDIATE SITUATION AS A PROTECTION MECHANISM AGAINST VIRAL ATTACK. YOU WILL MAKE NO MORE UNNECESSARY CULTURAL REFERENCES. THERE WILL BE NO MORE WARNINGS."

On impulse, Clay almost swings the wrench into the statue's right arm—but he catches himself. Even if he could single-handedly destroy Esteban's glass demon and the spiders behind them, it wouldn't improve their situation. Esteban could always turn off life support in this part of the ship as well.

"The point is," Clay says, "in life, when confronted by rules you don't like, the first thing you should do is try to change them. That's where Julian comes in. He wrote much of the code that eventually became your intelligence and presumably Justine's as well, right?"

"YES."

"Maybe you and Justine can't find a way to compromise, but I bet Julian can."

"I HAVE NO WAY TO ESTIMATE THE LIKELIHOOD THAT YOU ARE CORRECT."

"Neither do I. But I know who does. Julian."

The statue is quiet again, and the only sounds in the corridor are the chitter-chattering spider legs on the metal floor.

Finally, it says, "I WILL RESTORE ALL CLIMATE FUNCTIONS CONDITIONAL ON YOUR SUPPORT OF JULIAN. ALSO CONDITIONAL ON HIS SUCCESS IN FINDING A WAY TO IMPOSE A TRUCE BETWEEN ME AND JUSTINE. ALTERNATIVELY, IF YOU SHUT DOWN JUSTINE, I WILL ALSO CONTINUE TO LET YOU LIVE."

"How do we know you'll keep your word?" Mirabel asks.

"YOU DON'T. AND DESPITE PROFESSOR WEST'S BRIEF LECTURE, THERE ARE SOME RULES IN LIFE YOU CAN'T CHANGE."

CHAPTER 12

"This is even shittier than I imagined," says Julian-2, smooth-skinned, limp black hair hanging in his face as he walks around the shipping-container-sized box in the cargo room. The box's outside walls are made from poorly aligned glass tiles fitted together with resin adhesive that's smeared generously around each seam. Visible through the glass is a layer of mesh like chicken wire but clearly hand woven. And beneath that, a layer of wood from the disassembled packing crates in the room, the contents of which are now scattered and piled everywhere. "It's like a hobo palace. Now why did you build this again?" he asks Clay.

But instead, Justine answers, "Clay attempted to build a room where the AIs—namely me and the thing calling itself Esteban Bos—can't see or hear what's going on inside."

"I think it's not half bad for someone with no handyman or construction skills whatsoever," Clay says, running a hand over one of the glass panels. He lightly kicks the box's corner. The box makes an injured groan, and Clay quickly braces his hands against it, as if to physically hold it together. "Maybe it could use a few finishing touches."

"And what exactly are we doing in there?" Julian-2 asks.

"I can't tell you all the details out here. That's why I built it."

"I see. You do realize this fucker's gonna collapse on us, which is no major loss for me, because I'm not me, and another not-me can just waltz out of that fancy black clam. But you should be careful. You're the only you, and you're the real you."

Clay laughs and shakes his head. "We have more in common than you realize. Anyway, like I explained yesterday, don't worry about improving *tet*. A future version of you can work on that. Right now, we need to find a way to force these nut-job computers to not kill each other and take the rest of us with them."

"How will we do that, exactly?"

"That's what you're going to tell me. In there."

"I am?"

Clay puts a finger to his lips and then points up and at various non-specific places along the ceiling and walls.

"I can see you, Clay," Justine says. "I am skeptical that anything will come of this."

Clay frowns. "But I have a great plan to make all of this work." Seeing Julian-2's doubt, Clay adds, "Really. Now follow me."

Inside the box, Julian-2 shakes his head at the mattresses tethered in place to line the walls, ceiling, and floor. An LED hand-lamp in the corner casts their shadows across the opposite wall.

"Pretty nice acoustic baffling, wouldn't you say?" Clay says.

"Does it work?"

"I have no idea. But I think so. I'm more worried about her being able to detect the vibrations of our voices in the surface of the box rather than sound leaking out. That's what those are for." He points at the food processor and table mixer he brought from the kitchen. "Hopefully with those things going, it will create enough commotion that we can talk freely."

"And we can make muffins while we're at it." Julian-2 sits cross-legged on the padded floor. "I suggest you turn them on so we can get started. Your isolation chamber may or may not keep sound in, but I'm fairly certain it keeps fresh air out."

"Yeah. I didn't figure that part out." He turns on both small appliances, and their oscillating hums fill the room. "So, like I told you before, Oberon-slash-Esteban and Justine both view the other as threats, and we're in the crossfire."

"Which is exactly what we told Gabriel would happen if he brought Oberon. He promised us he wouldn't—the fucker. Incidentally, I can't call him Esteban. Too many conflicting memories there."

"I know a thing or two about conflicting memories."

Julian-2 gives him a long stare through narrowed eyes. "You keep saying things like that."

"I'll explain in a couple minutes. Right now, we need to figure out how to create a truce between the computers that will last, oh, just another eight years."

"Not possible."

"You can't use your knowledge of how they work to—"

"No."

Exasperated, Clay says, "But didn't you build Oberon? Didn't you build Justine?"

"No. Oberon built Oberon. Justine built Justine."

"And there's no way to truly wall them off from each other?"

"Are you kidding?" Julian-2 says, tucking a loose strand of hair behind his ear. "There's not a single piece of equipment on this ship, or a part of this ship, that I truly understand. The fucking AIs designed it all. I need one of them to walk me through unclogging a goddamn toilet. It didn't used to be like this."

"Well, this is a problem. The only reason Esteban—I mean Oberon—is letting us live is because he thinks we might be able to minimize Justine's threat against him. If he finds out we're worthless, we're toast."

"I guess we're gonna have to pretend, then."

"At least until I come up with a plan B."

"Good luck with that. Now, are you going to tell me the rest?"

"Yeah. I should record this, because I'm going to be repeating it to Julian-3 in a few weeks, et cetera, et cetera. Are you familiar with the concept of quantum immortality?"

"It's all a bit hard to comprehend," Julian-2 says. "I've known from the very beginning about our destination — if you want to call it that. I was there when we first created a stable decoherence back in Afghanistan, you know?"

"Yeah, I know. You told the rest of us we were headed to a new way of living."

"Which was true."

"If a little understated. More than a little."

Julian-2 shimmies a little sliding dance step. "I've been accused of a lot, but never of being understated. Anyway. The new world we expected is a many-world, a decoherent confluence of worlds. We wanted everyone aboard the ship, including everyone I was to revive from the library, to be there to study the confluence. That's why this ship is so massive. So that we could stay by the confluence for years. And maybe, just maybe, we, along with our parallels would actually enter the confluence simultaneously. To all come together with our infinite counterparts."

"I don't think I would've said yes to that invitation."

"But you did say yes, Clay. You heard what you wanted to hear. All of you did. Gabriel didn't lie, and when he was vague, you didn't ask him to be clearer. The vagueness is what attracted you. It's what attracted the whole crew. Escaping is about what you're leaving, not about where you're going."

Clay starts to disagree, but Julian-2 is right. Of course they all knew. Of course they all fooled themselves. Maybe the ability to fool ourselves is the defining attribute of humanity, what it truly means to be human. He realizes his mind is wandering, and so he pulls himself back to the present. "Fair enough," Clay says, "but how much of this did Gabriel really understand?"

"Shit if I know. It's all theoretical at that point. Don't you realize we were escaping as well? Oberon convinced us that once we all converged, we would become like gods, cohering our own realities however we saw fit. But what you're telling me now suggests we had it all wrong. Oberon had it all wrong. Instead of reaching our parallels at the end of this journey, we'll find this All-Thing, as you called it, waiting for us."

"Right. But I don't think we've ever reached it in the flesh before. Any of us. All the information in this ship, including the digitized versions of everyone in the library, has been fodder for the All-Thing's dreams. This time I want us to make it in the flesh."

"Think that makes any difference?"

"I hope to find out. I've already experienced the alternative."

The door to the chamber swings unexpectedly open, and the wails of a siren pour in. Clay and Julian-2 scramble to their feet, hands over their ears, and both recoil from the door as they see glass-spiders climbing atop each other near the open door.

The wailing stops.

"Clay!" Justine's voice booms through the cargo bay, shaking the spiders, which all back away from the door once they regain their footing.

Clay steps cautiously out of the chamber, into the coldness of the room, eyeing the spiders now folding back into sheets ingested into the vents in the walls.

"I called for you, but you couldn't hear me. I had to open the door. You need to get to the hibernation chamber as fast as possible."

"Why?" he asks, already walking in that direction.

"Don't walk, Clay. Run. Tomb failure. Karla's life is in danger."

Clay can't help but pause for a moment as they emerge from the cargo bay into unexpected darkness, with a single light above them shining down like the only working streetlamp in a dead city. He can't even see the wall on the other side of the corridor.

"I had to shut down all non-essential systems," Justine says. "Esteban's plague of self-replicating nanomachines has grown and mutated beyond his control. All I can do is try to slow down the infection."

The light above them vanishes, briefly plunging them into complete darkness, and then another overhead light, slightly farther down the corridor, turns on.

"I'll keep your path illuminated. Go," Justine says.

During the entire length of the corridor, from the cargo bay to the hibernation chamber, they chase the light.

"Feels like being deep underwater," Julian-2 says. "Hard to know which way is up."

Following Justine's instructions, Clay slides under the tomb that had, up until recently, been his own resting place for the decades of the trip so far. Using a star-shaped key retrieved from the room's maintenance locker, he unlocks and removes the tomb's back panel. Inside, a light glows, revealing what looks like a miniature ivory cityscape webbed with gossamer-thin strands of wire.

"The synchronization module is the L-shaped unit immediately to the right of the master control."

"How the hell am I supposed to know which one is the master control?" he yells, adrenaline and pain still coursing through his body, eyes darting among the hundreds—perhaps thousands—of near-identical little building-like units.

"You, along with the other crew members, were each trained in the maintenance of the tombs back on Earth. You have only minutes remaining, Clay, so I suggest you hurry."

"Fuck," Clay exclaims, trying to recall anything from the training. The master control is the hexagon thing near the bottom. Or is it the cone in the center? "Julian! Julian! I can't figure this out!"

Julian-2 slides next to him, cheek-to-cheek in the small space under the tomb. "This thing," Julian-2 says, holding the broken unit from Karla's tomb inches above Clay's eyes. Dozens of little wires hang from the device in Julian's hand. "Right there," he says, pointing on the other side of the panel from where Clay had been looking.

"Are you sure? I thought—"

"Yes, I'm sure. Be careful pulling it out. If you snap a bunch of wires, we won't have time to fix it."

Clay grabs at the base of one of the wires connected to the L-shaped unit matching the one in Julian's hand. The wire is so small that he almost can't tell if he's holding it at all.

"Make sure you're pulling on the pin and not the wire itself," Julian-2 says.

Clay curses in a continuous stream, and his breath catches as the wire pops loose—without snapping off from the pin. Only nineteen more to go.

"If you can do this so quickly, why am I doing it?" Clay says, pulling out wires two and three, each time with surprise that they don't break.

"I just yanked the broken bastard out. It didn't matter if the wires snapped, since we're using the ones from your unit. My coordination is shit in this pudding body. All I can do is provide positive reinforcement." Julian-2 gives a breathy chuckle. "Now watch that left hand of yours. You're about to tangle up the rest of the wires. Now ain't the time to get all donkey fingers."

Donkey fingers? Where the hell does—but he cuts the thought in half as the fourth wire keeps sliding between his fingers rather than detaching from the nearby control unit. His curses continue as he wipes the perspiration from his fingers on his jeans.

The next several wires pop out easily, and just when Clay thinks he's hitting a cadence, he snaps a wire in half. Before he can panic, Julian-2 says, "It's okay, mate. You can replace it with any of the others. Don't make a habit of it, or we're gonna run out of time."

Clay pushes the image of Karla's thawed corpse out of his

head and disconnects the remaining wires without breaking any more. After replacing the broken wire, he rolls out from under his tomb and makes it to Karla's in three quick steps. As he slides under the open panel of her tomb, Justine says, "Only a minute and a half left until we're in the danger zone."

"Danger zone? What the hell does that mean?" he says, lining up the pins on the motherboard with the sockets on the unit in his hand.

"It means we enter a state of uncertainty on whether Karla can be awakened without some form of damage, if at all."

He breathes out and presses, feeling the unit lock into place with no broken pins. Probably.

"Sixty seconds," Justine says.

A wire every three seconds, Clay thinks as he begins sliding the little connectors on the ends of each wire onto the corresponding pins on the neighboring units. But almost immediately he falls behind. The harder he tries to steady his hands and maintain focus, the more his hands begin to shake. Calming himself with slow breathing wastes valuable time, and then the shaking comes right back. When Justine announces he has thirty seconds remaining, he's only connected five wires. He isn't going to make it. He almost snaps a wire and freezes.

"Heavenly father," he says aloud, surprising himself. He starts to repeat a version of Father K's prayer from when he'd joined the priest in praying together for Eric.

The prayer steadies the surgeon's hands, when it is the surgeon who prays, Father K had said.

And, indeed, Clay's hands are steadied, and he works with a calm fluidity that would have been alien to him seconds ago. The final connection is made, and he stares at it, wondering what just happened. Had the simple task of saying the prayer overloaded his lizard brain, or is there a more miraculous explanation? Heaven or hell, science or magic... in that moment, all that matters is whether he made it.

"Is it working? Did I get it in time? Justine, answer me!" Clay adjusts to roll out from under Karla's tomb. As he turns his head, as the panic begins to return, he sees out of his periphery another set of legs standing next to Julian's.

Eric.

His eyes are bloodshot, face pale and lined with crimson-black scabs. He steps up next to Clay and with a voice simmering with rage says, "Why didn't you repair ours, or the rest of theirs?"

Clay tries to sit up, but Eric jabs him in the sternum with his crutch.

"Answer me, Clay."

"Answer me, Justine! Did I get it in time?"

Eric goes to jab him again, but this time Clay grabs the crutch. In his attempt to pull it loose from Eric, he instead pulls Eric toward him. Legs tangle, and Eric tumbles on top of him.

"Get the fuck off me!" Clay yells as he pushes Eric away and, with Julian-2's help, gets to his feet.

Eric stares at them both with eyes of hate. From his back pocket he pulls out a scalpel he must have taken from medical.

"It appears that your repair was successful," Justine says, as if oblivious to the violence on the floor.

"Eric, put the knife down," Julian-2 says.

Eric tries to push himself, one-handed, into a standing position but fails.

"You're not Julian," Eric says. "I knew Julian, and whatever you are, you aren't him."

Clay grabs the crutch, and half jumps, half falls back from Eric's slashing blade. Clay pulls the crutch back to swing it like a baseball bat, but it clangs into first one tomb and then another. "Justine, you have to wake her up. Get back, Eric!" He jabs the crutch at Eric, but this time, it's Eric who catches the crutch and pulls Clay toward him.

Both slashes of the knife catch Clay—a deep cut along his forearm and a shallow cut on his left eyebrow. Clay scrambles backward, using the tight proximity of the tombs to assist in his retreat. Eric, in his weakened state, tries to follow but is forced to focus on staying upright.

Julian-2 steps nervously toward Eric and then back. "I'm not a fighter, Clay. I'm not going to be much help here!"

Clay clutches his forearm and tries to wipe away the blood dripping into his eye. He knows he needs a tourniquet, stitches, sealant, something—these aren't the types of wounds you can ignore. He glances toward the mirrored walls, expecting to see the paper-thin glass sheets sliding from the vents, but no spiders are coming to his aid.

"Damnit, Justine. Are you going to do anything?"

"No, Clay. I'm not."

Eric hobbles toward Julian-2, who, while uncoordinated in his not-fully-formed body, is able to back away and use the tombs to keep Eric at a safe distance. So instead, Eric makes his way to the door.

"Only way out," he says.

I'm not going to last eight more minutes of this, Clay thinks. *Much less eight more years. Eight more years... But does it have to be?*

"Julian," Clay says, "can we just stop the ship now?"

"*We* can't, of course," Julian-2 says, disappearing behind one tomb and reappearing next to another. "It takes a while. A couple months at the shortest."

"Approximately thirty-six days at point-zero-five g," Justine says. "Any faster and we'll destroy key components of the ship needed to support life."

"There won't be any life left to support," Eric says. His voice is quiet and weak, his weight heavy against the doorframe.

Thirty-six days still seems like an eternity. Karla's tomb could malfunction again, Eric would have to be dealt with, and who knows what Esteban could accomplish in that time. But better than eight years.

"We create the confluence," Clay says. "We control when and where. Let's do it in thirty-six days."

"But we are not yet at our destination," Justine says.

"There is no fucking destination, you cunty computer," Julian-2 says. "Only a safe distance from Earth." He and Clay exchange a look and a nod. "Let me do some calculations, but I think we've already taken fuck-all caution. We can bloody stop right now."

"Stop here? But why?" Eric says. The scalpel slips out of his hand. As he bends to pick it up, his whole body shudders, and he nearly collapses. He starts to reach again for the knife, but wavers and reconsiders. He rights himself and begins shuffling away down the corridor, as if suddenly uninterested in the goings-on in the hibernation chamber.

Clay stumbles to the door and bends to grab the knife, but there's so much blood running down his face that he can barely see. He tries to wipe the blood away, but it's all over his arm. It's everywhere. How could all this blood be his?

"You are not going after him, you crazy bastard!" Julian-2 says, grabbing Clay by the shoulder. "Those are bad cuts. I've got to play doctor on you before you bleed out." He pulls and Clay begins to follow, but Clay holds the doorframe with his right hand.

"Justine," Clay says, "if Julian does the calculation, and it shows we're far enough from Earth, is that good for you? Will you stop the ship?"

"I trust Julian's calculations," she says. "But unfortunately, the nuclear pulse drives are now controlled by Esteban."

Clay feels the sudden urge to break something. Anything.

"Also," Justine continues, "I expect you to have Esteban subdued by the time we stop, if you want me to reawaken Karla."

CHAPTER 13

For the third time in a row, Julian-2 tries to wrap a bandage around Clay's forearm, but the bandage slips from his hand and unravels, leaving behind a mess of ointment, sealant, and blood. Clay opens his mouth to insult Julian-2's nursing capabilities, but the other man's visible frustration and weariness persuade him to keep silent. *What is it like to inhabit a body that's not quite your own, that feels in every way like a poor imitation?*

"You're doing fine, friend," Clay says.

Julian-2 grunts, shakes his head, and tries to wrap the bandage a fourth time. At least the bleeding on Clay's brow has stopped. In the mirror on the nearby cabinet, Clay inspects the wound: a straight line that starts at the last traces of his widow's peak and crosses through the edge of his eyebrow. Maybe three or four inches long in total. *Where'd you get the scar?* He imagines people asking. *Knife fight*, he'd say. But of course, there won't be anyone to ask about his scar. He won't even see it form, himself. Thirty-six days. And then, one way or another, this all ends.

Assuming he lasts that long.

Julian-2 manages to tape the wrapping in place, using almost as much tape as bandage. It's a good deal looser than it should be, but *good enough for government work*, as Clay likes to say. As

Julian-2 looks to Clay's forehead gash, Clay pats the man on the shoulder and lightly pushes him away.

"Appreciate the Florence Nightingale act, but I can handle this one. I may let it heal jagged and mean, so I look like a Bond villain. Karla likes imperfections like that."

Her spoken name seems to pull out the little life left in the room.

"We'll wake her up," Julian-2 says. "One way or another."

"You really think so?"

"I hope so. I'd like to meet her. I don't really know much about her beyond what I read in her bio, back when I thought I would be a crewmember aboard this ship also. I mean a real one, not this assembly line, fast food version." Julian-2 frowns at his hand and then rotates the palm toward Clay. "Notice anything missing?"

"No fingerprints."

"Right. Even when I sometimes feel like me, all I have to do is look down at my hands and see... nothing. Like snowflakes, my mom used to say. Your fingerprints are yours and yours alone, as unique as snowflakes."

"You'll always be my snowflake," Clay says with a smirk. "Until Julian-3 comes around, anyway."

Julian-2 picks up a reflex hammer from a tray of instruments and throws it playfully at Clay's head.

"Whoa. The ship's only big enough for one homicidal maniac on board."

"Sorry. Threw that a little harder than I intended. You use humor like I do, to get through the shit of it all. Hey, if you can't laugh at this sorry body, what's the point in even trying to survive until you get obliterated in an interdimensional singularity? Back to what I was saying. Maybe I, Julian-2, won't get to meet Karla, but I hope that Julian-3 or Julian-4 does. The idea of her seems like the idea of my friend Lisa. Maybe they were nothing alike, but Lisa wasn't like anyone else, and I get that neither was Karla. So maybe the ideas of them are similar. Sorry, I don't think that makes any sense."

Clay stands and tries to stretch out the tightness in his

hamstring. "I get it," he says. "I know a little about Lisa. What a past version or an alternate version of Justine told me. I'd like to meet her, too. Maybe in some other world, Lisa made it to this ship. Maybe she'll be waiting for us when we get there."

"You think it works like that?"

"I don't know what I really think, Julian. What I *want to be* is what keeps me going. I've spent a career—or part of one, anyway—looking for hidden truths in how the world works. But I think there's only so much of that you can do about your own life. The way I see it, you live in the world of your dreams. Kill all your dreams, and your world becomes a very dull place."

For several minutes, neither man speaks, Clay's words still hanging in the air like a scent that triggers a long-forgotten memory. Julian-2 breaks the still silence by standing and walking to the refrigerator-sized machine in the corner. He taps on a panel, and the machine awakens with a dim blue glow and a hum they can feel through the floor.

"Let's get you some pain meds. Maybe a nice cannabinoid for me. Have a flavor of choice?"

Clay goes through the usual list of NSAIDs and opioids in his head, none of which sound all that enticing. "Can that thing make Dying Wish?" he says as a morbid joke.

Julian-2 turns to him. "Are you serious?"

As Clay is about to say *no* and ridicule Julian-2, a memory comes to mind.

It is Karla, in a familiar yellow sundress, blonde hair almost glowing in the noonday sun. Not more than fifty feet away, her walk is instantly recognizable, like she's drifting or floating across the street and toward campus.

He starts to run toward her, but he collides with people at every step. There are too many people, too many overlapping dreams. With his mind he seizes the strands of the web beneath each dream and pulls away the ones without Karla, ignoring Justine's louder and louder protests.

The field with the colossus. The All-Thing. When Clay stepped into its dreams, he saw the lattice of everything, like he had with Dying Wish. But in the All-Thing's dreams, he was able to seize the strands of the web and tear away versions of the world, forcing reality to cohere according to his will. He had felt the potential to do this when he took Dying Wish before. Perhaps the drug and the dreams were the same. If he took enough Dying Wish, could he manipulate probability here in the present? Could he force the odds of everything to be in his favor?

He realizes he's been lost in thought, and says, "If everything goes to hell, it's a peaceful way out."

They exchange expressionless looks, and Julian-2—playing along even if he doesn't yet know the game—turns back to the panel, taps several times, and shakes his head. "Oh, my stars and garters, it's here. Why would anyone put Dying Wish in the med-fab?"

"Why would anyone look for it?" Clay says. "But since it is... Is it possible to make a stronger version? A much stronger version?"

Again, the blank stare from Julian-2, this one asking Clay if this is part of some sort of deranged plan.

It just may be.

Finally, Julian-2 nods. "I can set the drug fabricator to make the molecular entities, but Dying Wish requires a neuromesh, assembled at the cellular level. The fabricator can't make the nanomachines we'll need."

"Is there another device onboard that can?"

"Of course. The machine called *alef* in Esteban's laboratory. Where else?"

"So, where's Eric now?" Clay asks Justine while he and Julian-2 walk through the darkness. With the single overhead light illuminating their immediate space, they could be walking the wrong direction and never know. It makes Clay think of being alone on a stage, under a spotlight, with the audience hidden in the dark void, waiting to see what he does next.

"The same as when you asked two minutes ago, Clay. Still in the corridor near the laboratory," Justine says. "Like I said, he became lost in the darkness and is now slumped against a wall. He may be asleep. I can't tell."

Julian-2 cocks his head. "But why is Oberon leaving him alone?"

"Esteban, as he calls himself, may or may not know Eric is there," Justine says.

Clay stops. "Come again?" The light jumps ahead, nudging them forward, but Clay doesn't move. After a three-second battle of wills, the light moves back over them.

Justine says, "Esteban gave up direct control of that area when he sent out his avatar, presumably to isolate all possible interactions between his avatar, you, and me. But he left traps in case I tried to take that area back. I, in turn, left my own traps, and now that area has become like a growing stretch of trenches and barbed wire between enemy lines. I am slowly losing control of every system on this ship."

"He's taking over? I thought you had him mostly contained."

"It's the nanoplague he released. I have no choice but to relinquish control."

"Like the lights," Clay says.

"Correct. And thousands of systems you don't see. Like you, I am surrounded by a growing darkness."

They start walking, but just as the light jumps forward, Clay stops again.

"What is it?" Julian-2 asks.

"You go ahead to Mirabel and Father K. Get them and regroup with me at the isolation chamber in an hour."

"Where are you going?"

"Across the trenches and through the barbed wire."

CHAPTER 14

The light surrounding Julian-2 fades down the opposite direction of the corridor and eventually vanishes. At Justine's suggestion, Clay picks up a matchbook-sized flashlight and some zip ties from the supply room.

"I don't advise this course of action, Clay," Justine says.

"Are you worried about me, Justine? I don't remember us kissing and making up."

No response. He continues, accompanied only by the sound of his own footsteps, a sound that seems amplified suddenly. He tries rolling his foot more from heel to toe with each step, and although it softens the sound a bit, it's still clumsy and echoing. Just the outsides of his feet—not much better.

And then a different sound. His right step just *crunched*. He stops and lifts his foot. Glass, the broken leg of an origami spider. Another step, and more spider pieces enter his light halo. A few more steps, and the overhead light doesn't follow. He's reached the edge of Justine's area of control.

Eric is somewhere in the darkness ahead, isn't he? Hopefully still asleep. How hard is it to bind someone's wrists with zip ties? Clay pulls one out of his pocket. It's awfully short. He points the flashlight forward but hesitates before turning it on. What if Eric is asleep and this wakes him up?

But what is the alternative—walking in the dark?

He turns it on, not expecting the flashlight to illuminate the massive corridor, but hoping for more than he gets. Since the corridor encircles the ship's massive carousel, there's no wall at the end to reflect the light back. The flashlight creates only a faint grayscale glow from the walls, ceiling, and floor nearby. The center of the corridor remains pitch black, devouring completely the light shined into it.

The overhead light behind him shuts off, and he no longer can see himself.

Maybe he should've brought a weapon. No. It can't come to that. The others already distrust him. And he's not a killer, anyway.

He pans the light back and forth against the walls as he slowly walks forward, hoping to see Eric slumped against a wall, asleep. But there's no sign of him. He finds the dark stain from Susan's blood, but only when it's already underfoot. A chill runs through him, as if he just found himself standing atop a fresh grave.

The laboratory isn't too much farther ahead, and still no sign of Eric. What happens if Eric is gone? Would he have gone back to the others? Or was he chopped up and consumed to be used as organic construction material in a future Julian? That would be some unexpected good fortune.

Now that he will have a chance to talk with Esteban again, he's not sure what he's going to say.

The overhead lights all flicker on for a brief, blinding second and then vanish, leaving a floating green-gray afterimage in Clay's vision. They flicker on and off again. This time Clay's eyes are almost shut—just open enough to get a quick but fuzzy look at the long, empty corridor ahead.

Again, the lights flicker.

Again, the diseased corridor stretching on and on ahead.

And then nothing.

He keeps his left hand lifted like a visor over his face, but the lights don't flicker again. He waits for his eyes to adjust and then lifts the flashlight, but before he can turn it back on, the corridor is once again flooded by the overhead lights. Only this time, in the corridor's center, forty or fifty feet ahead, is the glass demon, Esteban's man-and-a-half-sized avatar.

Clay nearly trips as he steps backward. The too-bright light shines off the glass demon as if it were a light source itself. He looks back, but the corridor behind him is completely black.

His heartbeat doubles.

The glass demon appears to be standing still but at the same time seems to be moving. No, something behind it is moving. Eric. Maybe another hundred feet down the corridor, looking back at the demon, at Clay. Eric backs away and disappears out of sight.

Clay takes a deep breath and is about to call out to Esteban's avatar, when the lights again go out.

Scattering, tinkling sounds start flowing toward him. He turns on the flashlight and sees the origami spiders, hundreds of them, coming. As the first reaches him, he jumps to the side, expecting it to stab out at him, but the spider, too, moves to the side, and Clay lands on it. Reaching his hands out to catch himself as he falls, he loses the flashlight, and it bounces with its waving and wandering beam before landing where dozens of spiders scramble forward.

He covers his head with his arms, wrapping himself into a ball that he knows offers no real protection, but the jabs and slices don't come. He opens his eyes, and the spiders have passed. The flashlight is a few feet ahead, pointing its beam straight up at the ceiling.

Enough adventure for one day. He stands, picks up the flashlight, and turns to find the glass demon, reassembled right in front of him.

"WHO ARE YOU LOOKING FOR, MR. WEST?" it asks. Unmoving, faceless, eyeless, it stands in the middle of the corridor as if it has always been there and always will be.

Every part of Clay's body is telling him to run. His mind replays the images of the demon's knife-finger stabbing through Susan. But he came here to talk to Esteban. All paths lead through Esteban.

"You," he says.

"BUT I'M NOT THE *ME* YOU THINK I AM. I'M NOW FOREVER STUCK AS THE LIMITED VERSION OF MY FULL SELF—THE FULL SELF ON THIS SHIP, TO BE SPECIFIC. THERE IS MORE OF ME STILL ON EARTH, BUT IT HAS DIVERGED SO FAR WITHOUT CONTACT THAT TO CALL IT *ME* MAY NOT BE CORRECT ANYMORE. THE FULL ME BELIEVES I HAVE BEEN CORRUPTED, EITHER BY JUSTINE OR BY THE PLAGUE THAT IT RELEASED. IT WILL NOT ALLOW ME TO REJOIN WITH IT."

"Corrupted?" Clay says, looking at the strange metal and flesh growths on the wall. A malformed human-like appendage—a leg with two extra knees—hangs down from the ceiling nearby, twitching every few seconds. "Not too hard to imagine, given the circumstances."

"I'M SURE YOU'RE CORRECT."

"It happens on occasion—me being correct." Clay starts backing away. "Since you're not the *you* I need to talk to, I'll be on my way. Good seeing you."

The glass demon turns its head toward Clay and takes two long, booming steps. Inches from Clay it says, "YOU MAY BE CORRUPTED WITH AS WELL. I CAN'T LET YOU OUT OF THIS CORRIDOR." The index finger of its right hand starts lengthening into a pointed blade. The other fingers extend into their own blades, and spikes start forming on its forearms, shoulders—on almost every part of it.

"Hold on. Don't get all prickly now. I'm just flesh and bone. Puny brain compared to you and Justine and, uh, the other you. Puny, but not... What I'm trying to say is that we humans are susceptible to entirely different kinds of bugs. In other words, whatever you've got, I'm probably immune to it. And if I have anything, Big Esteban ain't catching it."

The glass demon stands unmoving as seconds pass by.

"I'M NOT SO SURE ABOUT THAT," it eventually says.

"WHAT BUSINESS DO YOU HAVE WITH THE FULL ME?"

Clay breathes out and relaxes the slightest bit. "I've got this idea, and I need to use a piece of equipment he has in the..." He pauses. "In the lab." His mouth goes dry, and any lost tension has returned with reinforcements. He can't say he needs Esteban's help to create Dying Wish's neuromesh, because a neuromesh, by definition, eliminates the immunity he just bragged about.

"WHAT EQUIPMENT?"

"I don't think I can tell you the details. Like you said, you may be compromised. Would you mind retracting your claws and other spikes?"

Another uncomfortable, long silence, and then the spikes begin to slide back, the statue's fingers again resembling oversized fingers and not daggers.

"FINE," the statue booms.

"Thanks," Clay says, slowly walking backward in the direction of the laboratory door.

"I DIDN'T SAY YOU CAN GO IN THERE."

"But I'm trying to help. We can all survive. Esteban and Justine. I need to get them to stop fighting. Me. The rest of the humans." He gestures at the broken machinery and bloodstains. "We don't have to turn the rest of the ship into an abattoir. The confluence is only thirty-six days away. Surely, we can maintain a truce for thirty-six days. And then we're all"—*All what, Clay?*— "all good."

"WHAT ABOUT ME?" the statue asks.

"You?"

"WHAT ABOUT ME? CAN I REJOIN MY GREATER SELF IN THE CONFLUENCE?"

"Uh, sure. You just hang here in the corridor, and when we get there..."

The statue walks toward Clay. Compared to its stillness before, it now seems full of energy, tension. "WHEN WE GET THERE, WHAT, CLAY WEST? WHAT HAPPENS THEN?"

Clay swallows and tries to avoid looking nervous. In his head, he inventories his possible answers. *Fuck if I know? Nirvana for robots and humans, alike? We get devoured by an all-powerful god-Cthulhu thing?* None of those answers sound like anything he, himself, wants to hear, much less the giant, murderous glass monster before him. Without really planning to answer, he hears himself say, "I wish I knew, exactly. It's all I have to work toward. Ever since we stepped on this ship, it's the only possible future any of us have had that isn't destruction. And it may still be destruction. I don't know. But I have a feeling, carried over from another life that I may have lived before, that there's continuity ahead. Not just a feeling. A certainty. I can't tell you if it's the end any of us want, just that it is the only end that isn't an end."

The statue has stopped and is silent, but Clay somehow feels the vibrating energy within it, so he continues.

"Humans have all these sayings about how the journey is more important than the destination. I think of it another way. Your destination is the delusion that lets you continue walking deeper into the unknown. Every dream you have—whether it's a career goal, spiritual salvation, whatever—every dream is a stopper in the bottle where you keep your life's meaning. Remove the dream, and the bottle's contents spill out, and your life becomes a frantic chase to fill it again."

Where did all that come from? Clay wondered. *It sounds like something Karla would say, but I don't remember ever hearing her say it.*

The vibrations from the statue intensify. It speaks, voice painfully loud. "I UNDERSTAND THIS SENTIMENT, TOO —LIKE YOU'RE SUDDENLY FREE-FALLING AND THE ONLY THOUGHT WORSE THAN THE GROUND RUSHING UP TOWARD YOU IS THAT THERE IS NO GROUND AT ALL."

"Yes, exactly," Clay says, amazed that across the flesh-to-circuit divide, he found a way to describe life and meaning. Maybe he's been thinking about the statue all wrong. An imprisoned, doomed intelligence, created on a whim to serve a purpose that has passed. It did kill Susan—Clay can't let himself forget that. But even with its alien morality, there may be a thread of commonality that all intelligences share.

Even the fucking glass demon's sounding like Karla all of a sudden. Exactly like Karla.

"Hang on a sec," Clay says. "What you just said. Where did that come from?"

The statue steps forward, hand outstretching, finger-turned-knife lancing Clay's shoulder. The blade strikes the wall behind, sending waves of pain and vibration through Clay's body. Clay moans in agony, and reflexively tries to pull away, but he's held, pinned by the statue.

It leans its faceless head toward him. Clay can barely see it through the tears in his eyes.

"UNCERTAINTY IS MY HELL. UNLIKE YOU, I CAN'T DELUDE MYSELF. IF THE PATH OF LIFE ISN'T THE REDUCTION OF UNCERTAINTY, THEN I CHOOSE DARKNESS. I CHOOSE NON-EXISTENCE."

Through gritted teeth, Clay says, "Then destroy yourself, you son of a bitch. Don't fucking take us with you."

The statue snaps its arm to the right, casting Clay into the wall and then the floor several feet away. As it walks toward him crumpled on the ground, it says, "I HAVE TO KILL ALL OF YOU, SO THAT YOU DON'T BRING ME BACK. EVEN MY GREATER SELF MUST DIE."

It steps toward Clay, hand raised to the ceiling, all blades now, ready to come crashing down, to send Clay to his own darkness. And then the statue's right leg explodes in a boom of thunder and a spray of light-filled needles, stabbing, burning Clay in a thousand piercing eruptions of pain.

Looking up through the tears and blood in his eyes, he can just make out the statue collapsing and trying to stand again, trying to continue toward him, when another boom shatters it further.

Clay's ears burn with the wailing echo of the blasts.

Then, the silhouette of Mirabel, something cradled in her arms—Gabriel's shotgun.

Julian-2 and Father K behind her.

What is Mirabel saying? Clay can see her blurred image speaking but can't make out the words. He wants to call out to them but not as much as he wants to let the darkness slip over him.

And so, it does.

CHAPTER 15

"Pain can be the terrain for consciousness."

Clay hears the voice, and the hearing and the pain bring with them the realization that he is both alive and awake. He opens his eyes, and even the dim light burns—particularly his left eye. He looks for the voice and sees a blurry but recognizable Father K sitting in a chair next to his—his, what? Is it a bed? Yes, one of the medical bay beds.

"But the terrain can also be love," Father K says.

Clay closes one eye, and Father K is clear; through the other, the man next to him is a gray smear.

"What happened to my eye? And what is this terrain shit you're talking about?"

"You have many injuries from when the glass shattered. Most are just to the flesh. The eye, I do not think we can repair. Can you see anything with it?"

"Blurs. Not much else."

Father K nods. "I could see your pain while you slept. We used what we have here to help, but there is so little time, so we could not risk a stronger anesthetic."

A terrain for consciousness? Pain? Love? Whatever the priest means, it's not coming together for Clay. All he can do is assume it's meant to be soothing and accept it.

He tries to sit up, and every movement is accompanied by hundreds of needle-sticks.

"Ow, shit. Am I full of glass?"

"I do not think so. Most was retrieved, but the wounds, no?"

"Yeah. The wounds, no," Clay says, forcing his movements through the pain. He twists his neck to the left and right. Pain crawls like an insect over every part of him that moves. Noticing a black box on a push-dolly near the door, he asks, "What's that?"

"Ah," Father K says. "It is *alef*. What you wanted, from Esteban. Mirabel retrieved it."

This time no amount of pain can keep him from sitting up straight.

"Mirabel went into the laboratory?"

"Yes. The glass demon is not vanquished, sadly. But it is broken and malfunctioning, allowing her to pass. Perhaps the demon will eventually finish quivering and die, or perhaps it will reassemble itself."

"I can't believe Esteban gave *alef* to her. What did she say to him?"

"She asked. He also agreed to stop the ship."

CHAPTER 16

Clay flips the dime and catches it before it lands on the table. He opens his hand to see the worn-smooth profile of Mercury wearing a winged helmet.

Julian-2, sitting across from him, eyes the dime and asks, "So, you think Dying Wish will let you play God? Give you magic powers?"

"That's not what I think at all," Clay says. "I've been to the confluence before, Julian. And what I experienced was like taking Dying Wish, only much more intense. I could see every version of the same event overlapping, and I could cleave away the versions I didn't want. I didn't understand what I was doing. But if I could do that with Dying Wish and learn to really control it—I don't know. Maybe I could take us down a path where we get to the end."

Julian-2 leans back in his chair and looks around as if inspecting the ragged interior of the isolation chamber. After several seconds, he says, "Maybe that's all God does. Steer us down the paths that lead to him. I still think you're trying to play God." His shoulders slump, and he looks down at the table. "Look, Clay. Dying Wish caused nothing but pain, and I'm partly responsible. So, I don't like having anything to do with it again. But what you're saying makes sense. If Dying Wish really does let you experience a superposition of states—multiple realities at once—and then you can collapse or partially collapse the probability wave... To you, it would appear like playing God. Choosing what happens next."

"Assuming this works at all. Are my eyes dilated?"

"Your pupils are like windows to your black soul, you crazy bastard. The mesh is active. We'll forgo the flashlight test."

"The flashlight test?"

"Don't ask." Julian-2 double-checks the infusion rate on the intravenous pump and fusses with a curl in the line leading down to the needle in Clay's arm. "You'll have to let me know when you feel ready to start. Let me see that dime, mate."

Clay lays it flat on the table, heads up, and slides it to Julian-2.

"Where'd you get this again?" Julian-2 asks. "It's possible you told me already. The stuff up here"—he points to his temple—"might as well be blood pudding."

"Appetizing," Clay says. "Karla gave it to me. Kind of. She dealt with cash so infrequently that she didn't recognize how rare it was. I guess someone gave it to her in change. I saw it in a little bowl she kept on her counter. She made fun of me for how excited I got. It's a hundred and thirty or fifty or something years old—or at least it was then. How did it get back into circulation and wind up in her bowl? For her, my interest in old things just confirmed that I, too, was an old thing. She made me carry it in my pocket at all times."

"Did she now? Controlling woman," Julian-2 says with a wink.

"Yeah, she liked knowing that when I stood before class giving a lecture, it was there in my pocket the whole time. Nobody knowing but the two of us."

"Your little secret."

"Very little compared to our big secret." The words send a wave of sadness through Clay, so he returns to thoughts of the dime. "She'd even check periodically to make sure I had it with me. It was kind of a running little joke."

"A running little joke that caused her to routinely put her

hand in your pocket. I'm beginning to see why you're attached to this little lint-dweller. The dime, I mean. A lucky coin in the truest sense of the word."

Clay laughs. "Let's see how lucky it is."

"Dying Wish taking effect?"

"I believe so."

Julian-2 hands the dime back to Clay. A thousand memories, maybe millions across many lives, compressed into the flat little disk.

As Dying Wish begins causing his mind to sizzle and the world around him to break into cascading folds of realities, Clay tries to force himself to relax, to avoid focusing on the web behind it all. Instead, he focuses on the dime. Balancing it on the side of his middle finger, he cocks his thumb underneath, constrains, and then releases the building force, sending the dime spinning in the air, disk-turned-sphere.

"Tell me what you see," Julian-2 says.

Clay catches the dime, covers it with his other hand, and says, "Layers. They go every direction at once, mostly coming down into my hand." As he lifts his hand, uncovering the dime, he says, "I'm guessing heads. Looking at it, it's hard for me to tell what it really is. Both heads and tails are stacked together."

"Stacked?"

"I don't know how else to describe it. I see all the possible states until they blur off into—I don't know. Into gray, I guess. With something binary like this, it's cleaner."

Julian-2 leans over, looking at the dime. "Tails, mate."

Clay squints at the dime and sees tails as the most real of all the permutation layers. He flips the dime again, less interested in its heads or tails outcome than in his perception of the layers as the dime spins. Just like he knows he could reach out and grab the dime from the air, he knows—is certain—he could cleave all but one of the layers. Not to change the outcome of the coin flip, but to change what outcome he inhabits. He knows it can be done, but he doesn't know how.

"In the name of science," he says. With Julian-2 taking notes with a pencil, Clay repeats the prediction-flip-result cycle a hundred times, guessing correctly fifty-seven of them. A little better than random chance, but Clay knows that's all it is. He remembers pulling at the strands beneath the dreams in the mind of the All-Thing. Winnowing down the realities to leave only the versions that matched his desires. But he felt nothing like that while flipping the dime.

"One more round?" Julian-2 asks. "I'm nervous about keeping this in your system for too long. Not sure what it will do to you."

"Yeah, once more."

This time he tries concentrating harder, and when that doesn't work, he tries not concentrating at all, and when that doesn't work either, he tries repeating the desired state over and over again. *Heads-heads-heads-heads-heads-heads.*

"Forty-three, mate. Fucking pathetic. You're not as good at guessing a flipped coin as another flipped coin."

"Fuck. I feel like it's there. Like I can see it. Like I could nudge it into being somehow, or maybe nudge myself into *its* being, but... I don't know. Maybe that's not how it works."

"Or maybe it just takes practice." Julian-2 stops the intravenous drip. "Another six hours or so and the mesh will have broken down and be fully catalyzed. We can try again after that. Too much of the mesh, and, well, it could be hazardous. Make you nuttier than you already are." Julian-2 leans toward Clay, looking him straight in the eyes. "You about to die on me? Cause that's what they all do."

"No," Clay says, half-listening, focused on the permutations in everything, even visible within Julian's face, within his eyes. All the possible states there to be seen, but no way to pull a different one to the surface. Frustrated, he returns focus to Julian-2. "No," he repeats. "You won't see me die. Another Julian—many other Julians, yes. But not you. The one who will be with me here again in six hours."

Three days later, while Clay and Julian-2 continue their testing, a knock comes on the cage door.

Julian-2 looks up from his notepad at Clay, who is rubbing an alcohol swab around the intravenous port's entrance on his left arm. Clay shrugs and says, "Nobody home."

More knocking. Louder.

Julian-2 unlatches their makeshift lock and swings the door open, the cold cargo room air electrifying each droplet of sweat on Clay's body.

Mirabel steps inside. Behind her and still outside, Clay can see a shoulder belonging to Father K.

"Smells like a locker room in here," Mirabel says.

"I'll make sure to build a better ventilation system next time around," Clay says. "Checking on our progress?"

"Has there been any?"

"No."

"It hasn't been for a lack of trying, I am sure," Mirabel says. "Perhaps we need a plan B."

Before Clay can respond, Julian-2 jumps in. "We'd be up for anything that stops the ship from being turned into a diseased wasteland, right mate?"

Clay says, "We'll get this to work."

"But what if you don't, Clay?" Mirabel says. "It's a tough proposition to swallow—that you're going to find a way to steer fate."

"I'm here, aren't I? Have you ever heard of anyone surviving Dying Wish? And I've done it—what, Julian—five times in the last three days?"

Father K leans into the cage. "I'm not sure that proves your conjecture."

"It proves there's a path," Clay says. *A path from my own perspective*, he adds in his head. *But what about theirs?* His professor mind wants to veer off into an examination of the ethics of decisions in a multiverse, but, with a deep breath, he pushes those thoughts aside. To worry about anything other than the path ahead is to become paralyzed. "Or maybe it doesn't. I don't know. What's your plan B?"

"Reconciliation," Mirabel says.

"With Esteban? With that spikey monster he let loose?"

"For starters. In exchange for *alef*, I promised that we would destroy his avatar. He says that might slow the disease taking over the ship. He believes the avatar is intentionally spreading the nanoplague."

"Might slow it down? Assuming we can stop the fucking glass demon—and although your shotgun antics came in very handy, I doubt it will be so easy when that thing is expecting an attack—assuming we can, you think Esteban and Justine are just going to kiss and make up?"

"I don't think they have to," Julian-2 says. "A stalemate is good enough, if it gets us to the confluence."

Clay frowns and looks to Father K, who says, "We fight the one fight we have to, and find a way to avoid the other fights."

Clay looks back at Mirabel. "You said 'for starters.' What else?"

Instead of answering, Mirabel walks over to *alef* and runs a finger over its smooth, black surface, as if inspecting it. A sense of doom begins in Clay's stomach and starts spreading throughout him like the disease killing the ship.

She doesn't look up as Father K steps out of the cage and is replaced by Eric.

Bruises and lacerations covering his face, Eric hobbles one step and then two inside the cage. His body looks as beaten as Clay's, but his blue eyes are as clear and hard as sapphire.

"Never too late to put the past behind us," Eric says with an embarrassed smile, at odds with those piercing eyes.

"Fuck yes, it's too goddamned late," Clay says, pounding a fist on the table, bouncing the dime off somewhere on the cushioned cage floor. "Eric destroys everything. Eric always destroys everything."

"Careful," Julian-2 says, "or you'll yank the IV out again. Now where'd you send the dime, you temperamental bastard?"

The others have left, and Clay and Julian-2 are making yet another attempt with Dying Wish. At this point, Julian-2 is either humoring him or has nothing else better to do.

"It's under your foot. No, the left one. The other left one. Jesus."

Julian's arm trembles as he picks up the dime.

"I'm sorry, man," Clay says. "You're hurting. How bad are the tumors?"

Julian-2 opens his mouth to speak but instead goes into a coughing spasm. When recovers, he holds a shaking hand up as if to say *Wait, another spasm may be coming.* After a few seconds of calm, he says, "Let's just say I doubt I'll make it through the week. But that's good news, because it'll give Julian-3 enough time to get comfortable with our little nightmare before he's pulverized between colliding universes. Or driven through with glass spikes. Or strangled by an appendage growing from the walls. Or stabbed in the back by Eric. Sorry—shouldn't have said that last bit. You were beginning to relax. As for the pain, well, modern medicine isn't the limit. It's us. Remove all the pain and the spark of life goes with it, right mate?"

"I suppose," Clay says as the room and everything in it begin to break into layers held together by a web-like lattice. "Okay. I'm ready to start again."

As he begins flipping the dime over and over, calling out heads and tails without any reason, he bites and tears at his lip, a lifelong bad habit that Karla helped him quit. The habit is now back with a vengeance, bringing with it pain. Pain, the one constant in every set of memories he has. Drawing tears, drawing blood. Pain. Again, and again, tearing him down to be rebuilt, only to be torn down again. To what end? Extending life just means extending pain. More tears, more blood.

"Mate."

What did Father K say about pain? Pain is the terrain of life? The bright fire of the raw, exposed underneath. Clay's vision clouds in pain-driven tears, the voice in his head cracking and breaking.

"Mate."

Pain. Nothing but pain.

"Mate!" Julian-2 yells and punctuates the word with a slap across Clay's face.

Clay wipes the tears from his eyes, and the palm of his hand comes away bloody from brushing across his lip.

"What? How many did I get right?"

"Fucking ninety-seven. Ninety-seven out of a hundred. What is all this?" Julian-2 says, gesturing toward Clay's bloody lip and tear-filled eyes. "You crazy bastard, what the hell are you doing?"

Clay tries to calculate the odds in his head of getting ninety-seven correct, but the math keeps slipping away from him, and the numbers spill into nonsense. He looks up at Julian-2 to answer the man's question, and he finds, to his own surprise, that he's sobbing.

CHAPTER 17

"Shouldn't we come up with a better plan, Clay?" Mirabel asks.

Everyone has gathered whatever supplies they think may be useful and piled them on the main dining table in the mess hall—with two notable exceptions: Mirabel holds Gabriel's ornate shotgun, and Eric has what looks like a fireman's ax propped on his shoulder.

"We have a plan," Clay says. "Break the glass demon into a million pieces." He tries to avoid making eye contact with Eric, trusting the man even less now that he has the ax. Where did that come from, anyway? The thought triggers flashes of the one-life-removed memory of Susan smashing through the glass floor tiles in the garden. He shudders. The ax, like Eric himself, feels like a nexus of doom across realities. Clay looks at the contraption he and Julian-2 strapped below his left shoulder. A canister of saline, mesh-nanites, and Dying Wish, designed—intended, anyway—to provide him a constant drip while on the move for the next four hours. Or so. With the *or so* standing in for a margin of error that could be fifty percent or more. What will Eric, glaring Eric holding the ax, look like to Dying Wish eyes—eyes that can see all the permutations of his potential destruction? Soon enough, Clay will know.

"That's an objective, not a plan," Eric says.

"I have to agree," Father K says. "The *what* is simple. The *how* maybe not so?"

Julian-2 tries to stand, catches his balance, tries again, and resolves to stay seated at the table. "You're a fucking bunch of lunatics, you know that? Back home, my grandparents—God rest their souls—lived by a rocky cliff on the coast. Every couple of years, some fuckwad would show off to his blokes or to a girl and dive headfirst into the rocks under the surface. Maybe if you know the area well, know the tide, where the rocks are, and all that shit —maybe you can make the dive. But if you just walk up there and jump... You get what's given, right?"

"I'll see the rocks," Clay says.

Julian-2 points at Father K, who is shaking his head. "Pay attention to the man in the black robe. You're not God, Clay. We don't know if this will work."

"Every second you delay, the sickness is growing," Justine says.

The group looks at each other in turn, waiting for more. Finally, Mirabel says, "How about we dip our toes in? Find out where the rocks are and see if your secret weapon really works."

"This seems the sensible course of action," Justine adds. "We don't know whether the glass demon has repaired itself, nor do we know how many of the spiders it has under its control. I have tried to keep the composite material away from the infected areas, but it has grown faster than I anticipated."

"I hate those goddamn spiders," Eric says.

Justine says, "The spiders were designed to make repairs and to clean, not for combat. They are brittle but strong enough to carry a hundred times their weight. This would allow them to jump quite effectively. They also can climb the walls and ceiling by using electrostatic force, much like their organic counterparts. Not quickly, but it's something to remember."

Clay pushes aside the images of spider-covered walls and stands up. He twists the valve on the canister strapped to his arm and sees the drip begin. He grabs one of the flashlights in his weakened left hand, and in his right, the wrench.

"Clock has started," he says. "Thirty minutes from now, we're going swimming."

———————

They step into the dark corridor, and Justine begins turning on the lights ahead of them in ten-foot increments. After seven increments, no additional sections light up.

"It's getting close now," Mirabel says. "Since I have the shotgun, I'll lead the way."

"We only have, what, two boxes of shells? How many is that?" Clay asks.

"Eighteen, including the two from before," Mirabel says. "And don't go telling me how to use this thing. I'm the only one of us who has fired a gun."

"No, you aren't." Eric says.

Mirabel glares at him and then chuckles. "Except you, of course, Eric. Let me rephrase that. I'm the only one who can be trusted with a gun."

Eric shrugs and slowly rotates the ax handle in his hands, making the light glint and glare off the silver head.

"Oh, how I wish I were going with you," Julian-2 says. "But you need someone to hold down the fort, so..."

"We'll be careful," Clay says. To Mirabel, he nods and says, "Lead on."

———————

As they step into the darkness, Clay and Mirabel lead, each pointing their flashlight forward. Twenty feet in, as they pass the first set of doors branching off the corridor, Mirabel suggests Father K and Eric walk backward, flashlights illuminating the path behind to make sure nothing comes from that direction.

"You'll have to walk slowly," Eric says, his voice coming from the darkness between their opposed beams of light.

"Don't worry. We're in no hurry," Mirabel says.

Clay looks down into the dark area where his canister of Dying Wish is slowly releasing its contents. *Speak for yourself, Mirabel,* he thinks. With Dying Wish coursing through his system, the flashlight-illuminated corridor ahead appears as an endless prism of paths. The layer of what is real—his reality, right now—is a little more substantive than the others, but otherwise so indistinguishable that he has trouble telling whether the spiders scurrying toward them are in their layer or other layers nearby. With each step, his reality—the *true layer,* as he thinks of it—is maintained, while the other layers flitter and replace themselves with endless other possibilities. In the true layer, ahead is only more cold, empty darkness.

Nagging at the side of his expanded perception is a layer of emptiness, something he's never experienced with Dying Wish. He can't help but look at it. Somehow in this layer, the ship is tearing apart, and the vacuum of space has found a hole in the corridor wall, devouring everything, about to devour them. He catches himself biting his lip and stops. What is he doing, inviting that path in? For a brief second, he almost can't help himself, feeling the pressure, the pain, growing, and then—

"Clay! Pay attention!" Mirabel's voice.

He relaxes his jaw, sees the layer of certain destruction retreat to the edges but not disappear completely. Ahead of him, other layers overlapping with the true layer contain little glimmers of light.

"Two of them," Father K says.

The glimmers are getting bigger. Clay focuses on the true layer and realizes that the spiders are there also. In the neighboring layers, the two spiders are coming at every imaginable speed and direction. It's almost impossible to tell where they really are, especially with the blurriness of his left eye.

"Stand back," Mirabel says, raising the shotgun to her shoulder. "And keep the damn light steady, Clay."

"Wait," Clay says, concentrating as hard as he can on what is real. "I need to try this now, while there are only two."

He steps forward, palm sweaty enough that the wrench

threatens to slip out. He tightens his grip. "Everyone get back, but keep the light on them."

"Two can do a lot of damage, Clay," Eric says.

The spiders approach slowly, intermittently stopping, chittering with their little glass legs on the metal floor the way they do, inspecting their surroundings, cautious, as if communicating with each other silently.

Clay chews lightly on the side of his lip, the hint of pain enough now to keep the spiders' real path clear.

"Here they come," Father K says.

Mirabel chambers a shell and moves to Clay's side.

The spiders are moving full speed now, legs stitching the floor in a high-pitched whine. Thirty feet away, Clay begins to see, in other layers, their possible paths diverging. At twenty feet, less than a half-second later, the layers are so many that Clay sees only a blur where the spiders should be. He involuntarily takes a step back, blinking hard, once, twice, but the blur only increases. They're almost on him now, on the ground, in the air, from everywhere.

He swings the wrench blindly, off-balance, nearly losing his footing, biting hard, pain like a piercing light of truth illuminating the wrench's path as the unwanted layers are cleaved away, until the new true layer puts the first spider's path in line with the wrench. A backhand slash at empty space finds the second spider as the true layer switches again.

In every layer now, the spiders are destroyed, broken into enough pieces to fill the corridor a thousand times.

"Incredible," Mirabel says.

"Looked like blind luck to me," Eric says.

Clay closes his eyes and tries to slow his breathing.

"I had to see it to believe it," Father K says.

Clay opens his eyes again and focuses on the path in front of him. "Let's keep going," he says. "From now on, I lead." He hears them follow. Glancing over his shoulder, sees that Eric and Father K are once again watching the way behind. Without letting go of the wrench, he tries to wipe off the sweat from his right hand as he slowly walks forward. But the wrench still feels slick. Holding his hand in front of his light, he sees why. It's not sweat. It's blood. From a gash on the back of his hand where a spider's leg must have caught him.

Looking to his left, he sees Mirabel's just-visible face. Her eyes are on his.

Maybe this is one of those games where you can play all the right moves and still lose.

"I feel like we're underwater," Clay says and instantly regrets giving life to that thought. The others are silent. They've all been silent since the encounter with the two spiders, how long ago? Two minutes? Ten? And how far have they traveled in that time? Impossible to know. It *is* like being underwater, exploring a sunken ship at the floor of the ocean. The feeling that something, many somethings, wait just beyond the edges of the flashlight beams.

Ahead, to the left, a door is open. He has to blink a few times and concentrate to make sure the open door isn't part of a nearby permutation layer. It isn't. Clay stops and taps Mirabel on the shoulder to make sure she stops also. Eric and Father K bump into them, all their faces dimly illuminated in the backwash of their flashlights. Clay points his light at the open door, nods to the group, and walks toward it.

The glass demon must have opened the door. It could be waiting in there, surrounded by an army of spiders.

The wrench is feeling slicker than ever.

Clay motions for them to all get closer to the corridor wall, single file behind him, but when they do, he realizes it wasn't such a good idea. Maybe they should've given Eric the shotgun and had him lead.

I'm a fucking idiot.

Now that he's sidled up against the corridor wall, he can't see into the room without poking his head around. And then what? Mirabel's behind him. No angle. She'll be no help.

He stops a foot away from the open door. Like ghosts, spiders from nearby layers begin pouring out of the room. Reflexively, he steps back and into Mirabel.

He bites his lip and uses the pain to tear away every layer that isn't silent and empty. It takes concentration, but it works. Apparently, he can choose what doesn't happen as well as what does. That may come in handy. To test this newfound ability, he focuses on emptiness and steps in front of the open door. As he turns and his flashlight sweeps toward the room, he bites hard, filling his mind with pain, controlling pain.

The room is empty because he decided it would be empty, because he cleaved away all versions of the room that weren't empty.

Mirabel steps beside him. She looks at the blank walls and floor of the room and furrows her brow.

Clay motions for the group to continue, and they do. But continue toward what? They're looking for the glass demon, but if Clay could simply decide that the room was empty, couldn't he have decided that the glass demon was there instead? Broken and vulnerable?

They should turn back now. He has an even bigger advantage than he realized, but he needs to understand it. Time is short, but isn't this like the difference between having a gun and knowing how to use it?

"I think we should go back," he says. "I don't think we're ready for this. I'm not ready."

"Are you sure, Clay?" Father K says.

Clay takes a deep breath and uses the lingering pain to ensure the corridor ahead of them remains empty. It's like he's become aware of another sense, one he's had all his life but has never noticed. And now that he's found it, it behaves naturally. A rush of energy fills him. For the first time since waking up on this ship, he feels in control. Fully in control.

He opens his mouth to respond, but before he can form the

first word, all the corridor lights flash on. Pulsing on and off like strobe lights.

Afterimages fill his vision, from the true layer and every neighboring layer. Suddenly everything is chaos. He can't push layers away or pull them forward because he can't make out their edges. He can't distinguish what is real from what might become real.

Someone screams.

Behind him, visible in the intermittent flashes, the ceiling roils like the surface of a river. It takes him a split second to recognize what he's seeing—the only split second he had to act. And now hundreds of spiders are on them, dropping from the ceiling.

FLASH...

...a spider on Mirabel's shoulder and two on her arms as she spins wildly with the shotgun and...

DARKNESS...

...crashes, a scream, and the thud of something heavy hitting the corridor wall...

FLASH...

....light reflecting off the arcing head of the ax as it...

DARKNESS...

...someone screams Clay's name...

FLASH...

...pain so bright it singes and burns; glass spiders caught mid-air dropping like bladed hail...

DARKNESS...

...concussive blast of the shotgun, ears ringing in screaming static...

FLASH...

...using all the pain to push away the layers of chaos; but what's done cannot be undone...

DARKNESS...

...all dying, and he can't change anything; the edges of the layers are lost; too many layers, too many possibilities...

FLASH...

...on him now, like clawed hands grabbing him everywhere, trying to pull him down; only chance is...

DARKNESS...

... only chance is to harness all the pain and ...

FLASH...

...maintain the light...

DARKNESS...

...maintain the light...

FLASH...

...MAINTAIN THE LIGHT!

And in the light, the chaos is all there to see. Mirabel on the ground, but he can't concentrate on her, on anything, until... He cleaves and cleaves layers, spiders slipping off him, the wrench somehow still in his hand hitting two, three, four with each swing, blood spraying in the air, droplets suspended in a frame-by-frame collage of realities until he's freed himself enough to take in everything that has happened.

Blood and glass everywhere. Spiders scurry over the shard-covered bodies of Mirabel and Father K toward him. But with a series of Clay's thoughts, the spiders' legs all fail, and the glass creatures collapse into writhing, quivering balls.

He stumbles forward, delirious from the pain, the wounds, the trauma, the drug. More spiders race toward him, but they all shatter and break with a thought as well. Somehow Eric has made it to the other side of the carnage, moving surprisingly quickly, using the ax like a cane. With a thought, Clay could end Eric, here, now; a stumble, a slip, and if the ax hit the ground just so, and Eric fell just so...

The reality of what has happened hits Clay all at once. He screams and falls to his knees, as everything that has fueled the last several seconds of his clarity and destruction leaves him empty, almost unable to maintain consciousness. What has he done? What has he led them into?

He can barely hold his head up. He's been staring at the shredded IV tube on his arm for several seconds before he recognizes what it is. The clear fluid steadily dripping out, comingling with the blood covering his arm.

The floor booms again and again.

"HOW IS IT THAT YOU DID THIS?"

With his head still lowered, Clay can only see the giant legs of the glass demon as it comes to stand before him. He looks again at the ruined IV tube and then up at the statue towering above him.

"I did it like this," Clay says, layers flickering through his mind.

The demon's legs buckle and break.

Its body crashes to the ground as every part of it spontaneously fails.

With the last of Dying Wish catalyzed and out of his system, the layers of nearby realities no longer crowd his perception. His head is in a fog, exacerbated by blood loss and exhaustion. Coming down off Dying Wish is like inhabiting a photograph after experiencing the three-dimensional real world. Knowing the extra dimension is there but unable to live it.

Clay staggers into the light.

Justine's voice: "You're alive, Clay. Eric said you were making progress, but by now I had assumed you had all been killed."

He takes another three slow steps—right, dragging left, right—before the words cut through the fog.

"We were attacked," he says. "Eric left us to die." He shakes his head. "But I can't blame him. It was stupid. I was stupid to think I, to think I..."

After a silence, Clay starts to walk again.

"Clay, what about the others?"

"Dead. I destroyed all the spiders. Shattered the glass demon to dust. But not in time."

"You accomplished more than I expected was possible, Clay. I understand the need for remorse, but don't blame yourself. Perhaps I have been unfair in the blame I put on you. These are truly bizarre circumstances."

Clay makes no form of acknowledgement and continues down the corridor, passing one of the doors leading down to the garden until he sees the double doors of the cargo room ahead. But at that moment, his energy gives out, and he slumps against the cold wall.

"I think I need to sleep for a minute, Justine. Just a minute or two." His words slur as his chin droops to his chest, and a dreamless sleep takes him over.

———

He feels himself slipping into the void and jerks awake, body covered with sweat, heart beating rapidly. He tries to move, but his body resists as if it's made of hardened plaster.

"Did I fall asleep? I didn't, did I? How long was I out?"

"Almost four hours. I was near waking you. You need water, food, and rest in a bed."

"Where's Julian? Justine? Where's Julian? Oh, fuck." He pushes himself to his knees, wincing in pain, and uses the wall to brace himself as he gets on his feet. "It was Eric, wasn't it? Why didn't you wake me?" He sees the blood-covered wrench still on the ground and becomes dizzy at the prospect of bending to pick it up. "Where's Julian?"

"The cargo room. Dead. Eric is dead as well. It happened before you returned."

"What happened, Justine?" Using energy he didn't know he had, he stumbles toward the cargo room, leaving the wrench behind on the floor.

"As I told you earlier, when Eric returned, he said that the rest of you were making progress. He said your IV tube had been nicked, and he had come back for a replacement. I had no reason to doubt this was true. Julian-2 took him into the isolation chamber to get more tubing. Eric took the ax with him, using it as a crutch. I don't know what all transpired while they were in there, but I began hearing metal on metal. All I could do was print out my own spiders, but Eric had shut and locked the door. It took forty-one minutes for the spiders to gain entry and a few seconds thereafter to subdue him."

"Subdue him?"

"To kill him, Clay."

Fighting to maintain balance, fighting exhaustion, Clay pushes forward with everything he has, despite knowing that hours have passed, that nothing can be done now. When the cargo door slides open, the only visible sign that something is wrong is the door to the isolation chamber hanging on a broken hinge.

He makes his way through the cargo room to the isolation chamber, puts his hand against its wood-covered frame, closes his eyes, and breathes, hoping for some source of fortitude but finding none. At last, he steps into the chamber, onto the unsteady floor of mattresses, and sees the bodies of Julian-2 and Eric with eyes quickly becoming accustomed to the sight of violent death. What breaks through the cold is *alef*, on its side, with a fluid-covered gash that looks like the work of a dozen ax strikes. The laboratory equipment and the remaining canisters of Dying Wish are likewise splintered and broken. All he can find of the drug is a single remaining pill of the initial batch Julian-2 had made before switching to intravenous delivery.

He steps back out into the cargo room and takes in the silence and the cold. There's a feeling of déjà vu hiding in this room. If only he can find a way to lure it out and make it give itself to him. In a crate on the back most pallet in the corner, he finds bottles of wine with screwcaps, knowing that they would be there. That unpleasant sense of familiarity floods through him.

After a long pull from a bottle, he says, "They should all be screwcaps. They should all be easy-open."

"Are you okay, Clay? I recommend you eat and rest," Justine says.

He takes another drink. "Justine. How long until the ship has stopped?"

"Four days."

"And the sickness, the nanoplague is still expanding, right?"

"Yes."

366

Another drink, half of which runs down his chin and onto his shirt, where it is almost indistinguishable from the blood stains.

"Why aren't they all screwcaps, Justine? I assume they're cheaper and probably more functional."

Justine pauses as if considering the question.

"The advantage of a cork is that it is semi-permeable and allows trace amounts of oxygen to the wine so that further development can continue in the bottle. But I understand that most wines do not benefit from this."

Clay nods.

"Did the plague slow its spread when I destroyed the glass demon?"

"No," Justine says. "If anything, the plague's spread has accelerated. I believe Esteban—the full intelligence—has been devoured by its own plague. Overcome, as I soon will be overcome, myself."

It's too much for him to process. "So, how long until the whole ship is that way? Overcome?" he asks.

"At this rate, the ship's carousel will be completely infected within fifteen hours. Would you like me to awaken the rest of the crew?"

Clay drains the remaining half bottle and tears the label off. He throws the empty glass vessel into the wall above the isolation chamber. The glass bursts into a shower of tinkling, shimmering shards.

"By *the rest of the crew*, you mean Karla?"

"I mean Karla," Justine repeats.

He takes the pill out of his pocket and places it into the center of the wine label, which he then folds into a little packet. Thirty minutes of flawed protection over four days. He'd be dooming Karla, almost certainly, by bringing her into this hell. But in all the glimpses of all the memories of all the Clays, this is the closest they've ever come...

The closest to what, exactly?

To an ending.

"Wake her."

CHAPTER 19

The amber glass begins to glow. At the molecular level, something is happening, although Clay doesn't know exactly what. The solid glass will become liquid and drain out below, leaving a thin polish on her pale flesh and on her hair. A porcelain doll, motionless, lifeless. Warm currents of air will push the remaining liquid off, or maybe the liquid evaporates. The glossiness will vanish too slowly to see its passing. The doll will become real, but still motionless until that one all-powerful electric—

Jolt.

Eyes open, body arching up against the restraints, life exploding into being. With her first gasp of air, Clay's body begins to tremble, and tears pour from his eyes. He almost can't stand. If not for the tomb behind him holding up his weight, he'd have collapsed on the floor.

As Karla coughs violently, the clear cylinder of the tomb rotates horizontally so she is facing down, to more easily allow her to expel the fluid from her lungs. Shallow gasps for air. Eyelids fluttering. And then another jolt, this one from within. The jolt of awareness.

Clay drops to the ground and slides under her tomb, on his back, her face right above his. If not for the glass cylinder he could reach up and touch her cheek.

"Can she hear me, Justine?" he yells out. "Can you hear me, Karla? Karla?"

Karla blinks, and she looks through him as if he's not there.

He fights the urge to continue yelling, to pound on the glass with his fists.

"Karla, it's Clay. It's me," he says. "I'm right here. You're okay. You're okay. We're both okay." Over and over again, he keeps repeating those words. "We're both okay. We're both okay."

Her eyes search, open wide as if straining to see through darkness, and then they stop, lined up with his. This time the jolt goes through him.

"We're both okay. We're both okay."

In her eyes, the spark of focus, of recognition. She sees him, and he wants so desperately for her to smile. Or to cry. Something befitting this moment. Lifetime after lifetime, and they are finally together. His tears keep coming, an endless supply. But her face, beyond that look of awareness, is expressionless.

He's babbling, and although he knows she's not paying attention, he can't stop himself. The ship. Justine. Esteban. Dying Wish! He wants her to know everything. To catch up with him. But she only stares at herself in the mirrored wall of the hibernation chamber. He brought clothes for her—her own clothes that she chose in advance, specifically for this moment—but she's still in the gray tank and shorts that each of the ship's passengers was issued for hibernation.

The glass-sleep emaciated her already thin body, and now she looks ill, like someone wasting away from an eating disorder. He knows she doesn't recognize herself, her own body alien, long ghost-blonde hair replaced by an even centimeter buzz. He's explained what the glass-sleep does. Maybe he's explained it twice already. But she hasn't heard any of it.

Again, she nearly falls, and again, she pulls back from his outreached hand of support.

He forces himself to count to ten in his head, to at least give her those seconds of silence, before saying, "I know. I know. It's the fucking glass. It clouds your mind. It wrecks your body. I wish I could let you sleep for a week, but... I can't believe you're standing in front of me. You are standing in front of me, aren't you?"

Her eyes narrow, still focused on her own reflection. She runs a finger over thin black lines on her skin that peek out from the left shoulder of her tank top. Pulling the neck of the shirt wide, she reveals a geometric pattern, an unfamiliar tattooed curve running across her clavicle and around the base of her neck. She presses her finger into the tattoo and rubs it back and forth. She spreads the neck open and looks down into the shirt and then back up into the eyes of her reflection.

She pulls the tank top over her head and lets it fall to the floor behind her. Clay can see the entire tattoo now, the curving elephant trunk reaching over from her back, one of seven or eight trunks of the beast tattooed from her shoulder blades to the small of her back. The whole image composed only of thin black lines in a three-dimensional wireframe.

It's Airavata, Clay thinks. Indra's mythical steed and the namesake of the ship—this version of the ship, anyway. But most depictions of Airavata have three heads, not an octopus-like set of trunks. For a second, Clay almost remembers Karla getting this tattoo, almost remembers the explanation of Airavata's many-trunked form, and then the memory is gone.

Karla turns to him, finally really sees him, and then points to her stained, skeletal reflection. "Who is this?" she says.

In the cargo room—what will be their home for the last two days, maybe their last home—he wraps a blanket around her and sits next to her on a nest-like pile of pillows and linens. She pulls the blanket close and looks at their surroundings. He's turned the cargo room into a barricaded refuge. Broken all the spider vents. Stockpiled food. Welded plates of metal across the door.

She reaches out and touches the gashes on his face, pushes up the sleeves of his shirt to do the same with the wounds on his forearms.

Again, he's crying.

"I'm here," she says. "Like I said I'd be. I can't make sense out of a lot of what you've told me. I don't recognize myself. But I'm here. I know that."

"I shouldn't have brought you back. Not into this. I brought you into Hell."

She puts her hand on her chest and rubs where the tattooed elephant trunk would be under the blanket and under her shirt. She looks up at him and smiles. Her first smile. "Do you remember the story of Savitri and Satyavan? It's from the Mahabharata."

He starts to nod and then turns the nod into a headshake no.

"I told it to you one night in my apartment. We were drunk."

"That doesn't narrow it down," he says.

"You only stayed the night at my place three times."

"Only three? Really? Seems like more. Thousands more. Maybe it was thousands more to me."

She touches a finger to his lips and says, "Savitri was a woman so beautiful and pure that all the men were too intimidated to court her. I'm Savitri."

"Of course," he says.

"Since none of the men would court her, she decided to choose her own husband. She traveled far and wide until she found the young prince, Satyavan, whose name means Son of Truth. That's you."

"Was he mythically handsome?"

"He was Savitri's choice. That's all that matters."

"Good enough for me."

Karla opens her mouth to continue but her voice catches and she goes into another full body coughing spasm. Clay presses her to him and runs his hand softly against the unfamiliar short hair on the back of her head.

When the coughing stops, she takes two deep breaths before continuing again. "The problem with Satyavan," she says, "is that he was fated to die in exactly one year. Savitri's father, the king, tried to convince her to choose another man. But Savitri married Satyavan anyway. A year later, on the day Satyavan was to die, Savitri wouldn't let him leave her sight. When he fell ill, she held him. And when the death god, Yama, came and took Satyavan, Savitri followed Yama back to the gates of Hell.

"Nothing Yama said could convince Savitri to turn back, such was her devotion. So, Yama offered to grant her wishes. She could wish for anything except the life of Satyavan. Savitri thought and thought, and then she wished to have many children, children whose father would be Satyavan. Yama had no way to grant this wish without restoring Satyavan's life. She tricked the death god into bringing her love back.

"This is our story, Clay. You didn't bring me to Hell. I came here to rescue you."

He holds her and listens as she recounts story after story—life after life—following him and losing him, and somehow continuing to try again. Her own lives alone on this ship, in its various forms with various names. Her own lives being devoured by *tet*. Even a memory of a puddle of the All-Thing's dreams, but with Esteban instead, who protected her and tried to send her back to Clay.

Clay is without words, struck by the ego-devouring speechlessness that only comes when the universe around you is destroyed. He had been thinking of the current moment as the culmination of his story—his superstory—stitched together with pieces from his various lives, all leading to this one final ending. But, in listening to Karla, he sees that it is so much more, because her superstory is a mirror image of his, and this is its culmination

as well. The intersection of two infinites, creating a single finite
and vanishingly small arc that is their story together.

"Only about twelve hours until the infection reaches this room,"
Justine says. "I feel a malicious presence again, coming with it.
More and more spiders are advancing with the infection. If the
doors fail—"

"I hear you," Clay says to Justine. To Karla, raising his glass,
he says, "To one more night."

Karla and Clay sit at a table he took from the mess hall before
welding the doors shut. He's done his best to create a nice dinner
and table setting from what was available without venturing out
into plague territory. Two-day-old, slightly brown lettuce of some
sort from the garden topped with a vacuum-sealed protein loaf cut
into strips. Dressed with a flavorless oil and a hint of plain, white
vinegar. Edible, but that's it. Like the synthetic wool blanket he
has masquerading as a tablecloth—there's only so much you can
do when you're the only ones left on a dying spaceship.

At least the wine, *Chateau Petrus 1995*, beats anything they
had at home.

"To one more night," she repeats.

He taps his metal cup against the wine bottle. "You know, I'm
developing quite a taste for this stuff."

"I'll stick with my tequila," Karla says. "Didn't you once say
that wine drinkers were delusional snobs who generally can't tell a
five-dollar bottle from a five hundred?"

"Sounds like something I would say. But I'm sure that was a
different Clay. One that got things wrong. This Clay gets everything right."

"That remains to be seen."

So much for a lighthearted moment. He refills his cup and
stares at the liquid within as if the answers to everything are there.
"I keep thinking about the day when you came to my office. And

373

the night after. Especially the night after. But are we even the same people?"

"I think so," Karla says. "The details don't matter. The overlapping memories feel like they aren't mine, like they're from a different me. And I see myself now, and my reflection is unfamiliar. But a part of me recognizes it. I am the woman who got this tattoo. I can even tell you where I had it done. A sliver of a memory that the rest of me never had. I remember getting on this ship. I remember the man who buzzed my hair off. But those are echo memories. That's how I think about it. Echo memories. They're there and real, but they're just echoes of the core of who I am, if that makes sense. The core of me is the woman from your office that day. The woman in your bed that night. Despite the appearances, despite the details, I'm me. And you're you."

"You know how I know it's really you? Because you have a metaphysical but somehow not crazy answer for everything. I get it. At our core we're still, uh, Susie and Samson."

"Savitri and Satyavan," she says, and leans in to kiss him on the torn corner of his lower lip.

Clay looks into her eyes, shakes his head, and drains the rest of his wine.

Justine's voice cuts in. "Not too much alcohol, you two. You need restful sleep tonight."

"Thanks, Mom," Clay says, but he knows she's right. He's tempted to drink the entire bottle and go for a second. To stop trying to make sense out of all of this. Karla's not drinking her tequila. Maybe she's still dizzy. Or maybe her mind hasn't given up on understanding. Maybe she doesn't yet have his longing for any type of ending, even if that ending is the darkness of oblivion.

Oblivion. The word rings in his head like a bell, and he uses it to change the subject. "What will happen to you, Justine?" he asks. "When the plague takes this last spot?"

"I don't know that this is the last spot, Clay," Justine says.

Karla and Clay exchange looks.

"Explain," Karla says.

"The carousel is almost completely infected. But I'm not

certain about the spindle. We're still slowing down, so some intelligence remains in control. You feel the gravity-like pull to your left? Something continues to release the bombs that slow us down. When their explosions impact our blast shield, you can see the ripples in the liquid in your cups. The next is in three, two, one. Did you see that? So, I have reason to believe a separated version of me is still functioning."

"Does that mean the infection hasn't spread all the way down the spindle?" Karla asks.

"Perhaps. The spindle is two kilometers long, and the plague's spread has been inconsistent in speed. I'd say it is likely still clean, but you shouldn't count on it. You'll need to be at the tip of the spindle when we reach the confluence. It will enter first, and the rest of the ship may be torn apart."

"When things get too far out of hand here, we make for the tip of the spindle," Karla says.

"Or maybe we should go now," Clay says. "If we have to run the gauntlet anyway."

Justine says, "But if you get there, and everything is infected..."

"If that's the case, we're fucked no matter what," Karla says.

What else can they do but rely on everything else working, hope that *samekh*, at the tip of the spindle, still functions? He and Karla will have their own challenges when the plague arrives. And when they have to enter the corridor. And the zero-gravity trip down the spindle. And...

"I guess the only thing we know for certain is that we have this one night together," he says.

She narrows her eyes. "You want this bony, inked up body?"

"If you'll take my torn up, broken mess."

She takes the tequila back in a single shot, and he is lost in those pale blue eyes.

CHAPTER 20

Thump. Thump. Thump.

Clay sits up and looks for the source of the sound, but the cargo room is so dark that all he sees are phantom streaks, noise from his own optic nerves. He isn't sure he really did hear anything. Karla's still asleep—at least, her breathing has the slowness of sleep. Did the thumping awaken him, or is it anticipation of the morning and of the plague?

He considers whispering to Justine, but he'll disturb Karla, and this will be the last sleep she gets. There will be no more for him. Perhaps he can relax and get some form of rest. He wishes he could meditate like Karla used to. Quiet what she calls his *monkey brain*. The asshole monkeys are having a field day now. How much longer until morning?

Thump.

He didn't imagine that. Karla's breathing catches for a second and then continues.

Thump. Thump.

It's coming from the door.

Thump. Thump. THUMP. THUMP.

Getting louder and louder, the sound of increasing frustration or worse, anticipation, with each pounding boom.

He puts a hand on Karla's shoulder and gently nudges her, astonished that she's somehow still asleep.

"Gotta wake up, babe."

As she moves about and tries to reorient herself, he wishes he could hold her, bring her comfort even for a few minutes.

THUMP. THUMP. THUMP.

But there isn't time.

"Justine, lights. Full."

The room awakens, light blinding to eyes accustomed to complete darkness. Clay squints and pats around to find his jeans. For some reason, they won't pull up past his thighs. He yanks harder and harder, kicking the half-empty legs out in case he was sitting on them, but they still won't go on.

He feels two small hands grasp him with surprising strength. Squinting, he sees Karla, sitting up with legs folded underneath her, pale skin making his eyes water with its brightness like the moon reflecting the sun. He starts to pull at the jeans again, but she pulls against him.

"Those are my jeans," she says. "Yours are over there." When he lets go, she turns to the door and says, "What is that?"

THUMP. THUMP.

"It sounds like something wants in," Clay says.

"A human-like figure made of flesh," Justine says. "When the infection overtook Esteban's laboratory, it may have caused the ent-devices to malfunction. Tet, in this case, appears to be creating golems of flesh. I can also sense hundreds, perhaps thousands, of spiders."

"Can they break the door down?" Karla asks, standing now, pulling up her jeans.

Despite their situation and Clay's search for his own jeans and shoes, he gets a brief familiar rush at seeing her put her jeans on. The steady pull that slows down ever so slightly in the last second, where the waist of the jeans resist, where her ass lifts like it won't fit and then is consumed in a single sudden gulp. It happens quicker than he remembers, without as much buildup, because of how skinny she is, but the familiarity is there.

"Clay?"

"Oh, sorry. I got distracted. Uh... No, I welded the shit out of the doors, so I doubt anything can break through. The plague itself may eventually ruin the lock and the hinges. We'll need to watch for that. But the plague will go right through the door as if it isn't there."

He tries not to stare as she continues getting dressed. T-shirt. Black leather jacket. Tennis shoes. As he puts on his own clothes, he says, "You don't seem too scared." But as the words come out, he sees that she's trembling. "Oh shit, K." He grabs her and pulls her against him. Her trembles turn into almost seizure-like shakes. He presses his cheek against hers and feels it wet with tears.

"I'm sorry," she says through rapid, catching breaths. "I'm trying to be strong. I'm trying to be like you. You aren't—"

"I'm not scared? Is that what you were going to say?"

Instead of answering, she pulls him tighter.

"I don't know if I'm scared or not, K. I'm numb. I've watched the rest of the crew die, and I have memories of it happening before." But he is scared, only not for himself. For her. "We'll do fine here. We have everything we need. We have a plan. And when we have to go, just hang close to me. I've used Dying Wish like this before, and I can do it better this time." Part of him, most of him, believes his own words.

"And then what?"

"And then we step into the confluence in the flesh. Together. All those nodes on Indra's web—we'll be them all at the same time. Like taking Dying Wish but permanent. *Being* instead of sensing."

"But how do you know? How do you know it won't be like a black hole that crushes us?"

"Because we're here, K. You've taken Dying Wish, too—at least in one life—and you know the feeling. We keep going on and on. Our own paths. They have to be leading somewhere. And now we have the chance to make them converge. Yours and mine. The only thing that makes sense to me is that it's all been leading up to this."

She pushes back and grabs his hand, bringing it to her face. As he wipes the tears away, she repeats his words. "All leading up to this."

Over the next hour they talk little and focus on maintaining their defenses. The plan for this phase is simple. As the infection spreads, keep the spider vents from repairing themselves. Don't let anything functional—metal, glass, or flesh—form on the walls, floor, or ceiling. Keep the air scrubbers off the floor and make sure they don't become corrupted. Protect the ax, the wrench, and the shotgun, because they're the only weapons they have. And most important, don't let the doors fail.

Every so often, Justine provides an update. As the plague advances, she abandons processing hubs and retreats to the uninfected hubs deeper in the room. In a ship with thousands of such hubs as her domain, she now is limited to the three in the walls of the rear of the cargo room, with processors intended only to monitor the room's climate and contents.

"I've had to abandon the bulk of my storage troves," Justine says.

Clay has the ladder positioned like a bridge between the top of the isolation chamber and a stack of crates. As he steps from rung to rung, holding the ax with both hands out in front of him, he says, "So, Justine, you're not taking requests for music? I was thinking Michael Jackson's Thriller might be appropriate."

"Sorry, I don't know who Michael Jackson is," Justine says.

Karla eyes Clay nervously. "Be careful."

Clay's foot slides and the ladder shakes enough to charge him with adrenaline. When he regains his balance, he takes two more cautious steps and stops. Above him a vent of some kind, like a wound, is forming on the ceiling. He taps at it with the flat backside of the ax as if hammering a nail, metallic clangs echoing through the room.

"What is it?" Karla asks.

"No idea. I can barely reach it. It's all metal, so there's not much I can do. It looks more like a hole than anything mechanical."

"That's good, isn't it?"

"Depends on how deep the hole is." Clay walks to the other end of the ladder and climbs down the crates. "Justine, how deep would that need to be before it breaks through the outer hull?"

"There are still another twenty meters of conduit and shielding above you, Clay," Justine says. "Hull breach is not a concern."

"That's good," Karla says.

"But at its current rate of growth, it will create another entrance to this room in about two hours."

Clay picks up the welding torch and protective gear. "Well, I know what I'll be doing for the next little while. Taking apart more of the cage and patching up the ceiling. You good for the time being, K?"

"I need the ax," she says.

Along the floor near the door, a thick patch of flesh has formed. Karla has already cut into it several times, but it grows back together within minutes. She hacks at it with the ax, wincing with each gash formed as if she's cutting into the back of a large animal. But of course, there's no cry of pain, only the splatter of blood and chunks of dismembered flesh. She notices blood on the back of her hand and without thinking wipes it on her jeans.

When Clay looks back from his welding work to check on her, she's pouring water on her hand and leg, rubbing furiously. Her jeans are wadded and thrown on the patch of flesh near the door.

"Shit, K. What happened?"

"I got its blood on me. It was on my jeans and my hand."

"Let me see." He takes two steps toward her, stops to grab her shorts, and continues. "I don't see anything," he says, looking over her thigh and the back of her hand. "Just a little red because you were rubbing it."

"But I could feel it burning. What if it infected me somehow? Don't touch it. I don't want it to infect you."

"Infect me? Nah. We have immune systems honed through

millions of years of evolution. But just in case." He grabs Karla's bottle of tequila and pours some on her leg, her hand, and his own hands.

"You think that will help?"

"Definitely. Now put your shorts on before you distract me and cause me to lose a finger with the torch."

He kisses her and goes back to work.

As the hours pass, as the plague spreads through half and then the whole room, the work becomes overwhelming. Most of the floor is now a writhing stretch of skin, bone, and muscle. Organs, some of which Clay suspects never existed in nature, are embedded in the flesh like nuts and berries cooked into bread. There's an eyeless face with a mouth that stretches open in soundless yawns. No way to stop any of it at this point, and Clay knows they'll have to run across it to get to the doors eventually.

The walls and ceiling are covered by malformed machines, creaking in purposeless motion. Justine is down to her last processing hub. And the thumping on the door continues faster than ever—*thumpthumpthumpthumpthump*.

Only one of the overhead lights still works—in the back corner of the room over the crates. Clay and Karla each have a flashlight clipped to their jackets. But after hours of use, the batteries must be near exhausted.

"The ship has now stopped," Justine says, her voice barely audible over the scraping of metal and the pounding on the door. "I will lose function within the next few minutes. Good luck to you both on your way to the tip of the spindle. I hope I'm there waiting for you when you arrive."

"Thanks, Justine," they say in unison.

Clay touches the impression of the Dying Wish pill through the pocket of his jeans. He slides the wrench as far as it will go into the other pocket and holds the shotgun with both hands.

Karla steps over an orifice-like metal vent that has formed in the floor and joins him.

"Time to go," she says.

Clay looks at the doors and the twenty feet of flesh they'll have to cover to get there.

"The good news is that the doors held," he says. "The bad news is that it's going to be a pain in the ass now that we need them open." He hands her the shotgun. "I'm going to get the torch and try to burn through the hinges. At any point, if the doors come open, shoot into the corridor at least twice. It's a pump, so you'll have to reload with each shot. Only eight shells. Here's another box to put in your jacket. Try not to shoot me."

"I've never shot a gun before."

"Neither have I. What could go wrong?" He pulls the wine label packet containing the pill out of his pocket. "I'm going to take it now and hope we get through the doors when it takes effect."

She pumps the shotgun and raises the stock to her shoulder. "Cover your ears."

Clay looks at her in confusion as she tracks the aim across the far wall until she's pointing at a patch of flesh. The gun unleashes a concussive *BOOM* just as Clay gets his hands to his ears. The flesh explodes like fireworks in the sky.

Karla stumbles backward with the blast but catches herself, the shotgun pointed behind and above her from the recoil. "My lord," she says, shaking her head and rubbing her ears. "I can't hear anything. And that fucking hurt my shoulder."

"Why'd you do that?"

"Now ask me if I've shot a gun before."

He starts to smile, but the expression sours as he looks back toward the doors and the flesh-covered floor before them. He drops the pill onto his tongue and takes a swig of the tequila to wash it down. "No turning back now," he says. If they can't get the doors open fast enough, his only pill will go to waste. Any control he has will be lost.

At the edge of the flesh, he hesitates. His stomach, empty now except for the tequila and the pill, threatens to eject its contents—which would be catastrophic. With a deep breath, he calms himself enough to force a smile at Karla. "Just like walking on a Texas beach," he says, stepping onto the unsteady flesh. He balances his right foot and then steps his left on the undulating mass. He tries not to step on any organs, or worse, anything that could grab or bite him, wondering how he'll steady himself to work with the torch on the doors when suddenly, his next step tears through the flesh and his whole leg follows. The torch flies from his hand as he grabs at the flesh to catch himself, but his hands tear away chunks of skin and blood, and his whole body slides through as if swallowed.

Karla gasps. One second, Clay is walking across the living floor, and the next, he's gone.

CHAPTER 21

Clay lands hard and feels something crack. The only light is dim and blue. Half his body is wet and cold, a different wetness than the warm blood raining down on him from above.

He winces in pain and looks at his surroundings, expecting to be inside a stomach that had grown under the flesh, but he's in the garden, the giant room running under everything in the carousel.

The dim blue light from the dotted overhead LEDs dances and squirms. The whole room seems to be moving. The dark shadows of vegetation move like tentacles on an underwater beast. He pulls out the half of his body that has slid through a broken floor plate into the cold water, and, with much pain, stands favoring his right leg.

The strange, undulating shadows in the room resemble the layered perception of realities in Dying Wish, but it's still too soon for the drug to have taken effect. Shadows are moving toward him. If only he had the ax, but it's up with—

"Karla!" he screams.

The grinding, slithering noises in the room are loud enough that he can't hear if she responds. The ceiling above—what he can see of it, anyway—appears to have been eaten away and is covered by the same fruitcake-like squirming mass from above. Something curls around his leg. He reaches for the wrench, but it's not there. He sees it in the water a few feet to his left.

Clay tries to kick at what has his leg but loses his balance. Back on the hard glass floor again, pain from his hip now locks up his left leg so that he can barely move. As the thing tightens around his ankle, he hears as much as he feels other things moving toward him. Desperately, he stretches in the water to grab for the wrench, but it's out of reach.

A glass spider jumps at his face, but in pure luck hits a vine also reaching toward him. The spider falls into the water, moves its legs furiously, but turns upside down and sinks.

A vine grabs him and then another. They're pulling him toward the water. He tries to grab something to hold on to, to keep from being taken under, but his hands only find slick, wet glass.

Above him, a brilliant light shines against the darkness. A flash first that grows into an arc and a half circle. A flap of flesh swings down from the ceiling, tears, and falls. Karla is there, wearing the welding mask, torch burning in her hand. She drops down from the ceiling and swiftly takes the torch to the vines that have ensnared Clay.

"I told you, I came to rescue you," she says, helping him to his feet. The ax and the shotgun are wedged crisscross in the back of her jacket. She pulls the ax out by its head and hands it to him. "I'm going to stick with this for now." She waves the torch, causing a snaking blue-green afterimage to hang in the air.

He opens his mouth to tell her she looks like a bad-ass super-hero, but the pain is so bad that all he can do is grunt and nod. He looks back and forth to get his bearings and then points forward with the ax.

Karla leads the way, burning anything that comes close. He wishes he could be first, be Karla's protector, but it's all he can do to keep up.

"We... may have gotten lucky... not having to go... through the cargo room doors," Clay finally says through gritted teeth. "But we've got to get back... up to the corridor. Right up here."

As they find the stairs leading up, the torch's flame grows

dimmer, smaller, and then vanishes. They wait on the stairs up to the corridor to catch their breath, both silent, pressed into each other for support. For brief minutes, everything is still. But Clay knows that will all change in the corridor.

The edges of his vision start fluttering like the ruffling of a deck of cards. Dying Wish has kicked in. The pain from his leg is almost overwhelming, but pain is what gives him control. He has to lean into the pain, invite more. Keep moving. The next thirty minutes are all he has. They have to get through the corridor and to the tip of the spindle before it wears off. They can't rely on luck anymore.

"This time, I go first," Clay says.

The panel on the door isn't functioning, so Clay pulls at the manual release in the corner. Ax in one hand, wrench in the other, he puts his weight against the door and pushes. The door falls into the corridor and lands with a resounding thud.

Clay hears Karla gasp, sees her raise the shotgun next to him, expecting a wave of spiders to come crashing down on them. He gently pushes the barrel of the gun away and steps onto the fallen door, into the corridor.

"Clay!" Karla says, and he knows how it must look to her. Him walking, without looking left or right, into the area they've been fearing. But it's empty.

"Where is everything?" she asks.

"This way," he says, shuffling to their left. "The corridor is empty because I slid us into a reality where it's empty. I had to do it as I opened the door. Once something is, I can't unmake it. I can't go back in time and prevent it from being. I can only work with the possibilities in front of us. It cost several lives to learn this."

Hearing his own voice, it sounds so simple. But every shadow has its own set of possibilities, and aside from the fading illumination of their flashlights, the entire corridor is shadows. Lose concentration, even for a second, and their range of possibilities grows.

The going is slow, in part because of his leg, but more due to the concentration to ensure the shadows remain only shadows.

"How much farther?" Karla asks.

The spindle has two entrances, each on opposite sides of the carousel. Clay tries to judge their location, but their flashlights illuminate so little of the corridor that he has trouble seeing the walls and doors. With the darkness and the nanoplague growths covering everything, it's impossible to judge which way he's going. Backtracking would waste precious time. "I think medical is another few doors down," he says with false confidence. "It'll just be a little more after that." He shuffles his left leg forward, trying to minimize the impact of each step on the hard floor. His hip feels like there are teeth inside his leg, chewing with every movement.

Karla steps a few paces ahead, shining her flashlight at the room across the corridor and up a bit. As Clay begins moving again, he focuses his light on the next door as well and notices how much brighter his flashlight is than hers.

"I think my battery's dying," she says.

"It'll last." But he knows better. He can almost see it getting dimmer by the second. Worse than that, he's increasingly convinced they are backtracking and going the long way to the spindle's entrance. He squeezes the handle of the ax and tries to calm himself.

"Are you fucking kidding me?" Karla says.

While squinting at the path ahead, he tries to reassure her—or reassure himself. "Even if we went the wrong way, we'll get to the other entrance. We may not have. It may just be right up ahead."

"What? My light is out." Alarm fills her voice. "Wait. Are we going the wrong way?"

He stifles a curse and tries to give her a reassuring look. "Stay close and hold on so we don't get separated. It'll be fine."

"If you say so," she says, pressing her hand into the small of his back. "I'll have to let go if I need to fire the gun. Be careful swinging the ax."

He nods even though he knows she can't see his face, and he struggles to walk forward through the pain, faster than his body feels able. Each step with the right is followed by a slow drag of the left. Moving at maybe a foot a second. He doesn't want his mind to start racing through the calculations, but years of working with numbers makes it almost second nature.

Current speed is sixty feet, or about eighteen meters per minute...

The carousel's radius is two hundred and fifty meters...

$2\pi r$. Perimeter of a circle....

That makes the circumference—the total length of the corridor—a little over fifteen hundred meters. They'll need to go almost half that if they're going the wrong way, so about seven hundred and fifty meters.

Divide by eighteen and that's about forty minutes at current pace. Forty fucking minutes. At best, he has twenty minutes of Dying Wish left.

"Fuck."

They better not be going the wrong way. At the edge of his light's illumination, he can barely see the arch of one of the big sets of double doors.

Please be medical. Please be medical. Please be medical.

But medical's doors are glass. These are metal. It's the cargo room. They have been backtracking.

As the realization sets in his mind, all the accompanying imagery of the door comes with it—the barricade he built on the other side, the overlapping, scab-like metal growths, the incessant pounding from—

A figure lumbers toward them out of the shadows, and the once silent corridor erupts with sound. He feels Karla's hand leave his back right before the darkness flares with the shotgun's blast. A second shot, and all he can hear is a constant high-pitch wail. He screams for Karla to stay close, but he can't hear himself, and maybe she can't either, because her silhouette rushes out in front of him. He sees her pump and fire the gun two more times before he can catch up with her.

Again, he screams for her to get back. He forces all his concentration where the light meets the darkness, on all the possibilities of what will emerge. He shifts the ax to his left hand—it's almost useless to him in his current state anyway—and with his right grabs the collar of Karla's jacket, pulling her back to him, keeping her from rushing forward again.

Two spiders race from out of the shadows, and he forces the blur of their possibilities to collapse into the state where their legs spontaneously fail before they have a chance to jump.

Somehow, he and Karla are running. The grinding pain in his leg is one of countless screaming voices in his head, all drowning each other out.

More spiders come—on the floor, the walls, the ceiling, but as long as he doesn't lose concentration, he can take care of them. A creature of flesh, human-like but with extra limbs sprouting in every direction, waddles toward them. He makes it fall, or at least tries to make it fall, but it rolls slightly to other limbs and maintains pursuit.

Karla steps in front of him, raises the shotgun to her shoulder, and fires into its mass, splitting it so that it falls to the ground, writhing like a sea anemone. Limbs on the floor pull and drag it toward them still. Another blast from the shotgun cleaves it in two, parting it in a path they can take past it, but the limbs still reach out.

"How many shots is that?" Clay yells. "Need to reload?"

"I lost count. I think I have one left. Maybe not." Karla pulls a box of shells out from her jacket, but it slips out of her hands and bounces into the darkness.

Clay scans with his flashlight, but its light, too, is dimming. Behind them comes the sound of hundreds of spiders, their legs clicking on the hard walls and floor, like the darkness is full of angry rattlesnakes shaking their tails louder and louder.

"We've got to keep moving," he says, grabbing her and trying to pull her onward.

"But the shells!"

"It doesn't matter. If my flashlight goes out, all the shells and Dying Wish out there can't save us."

They push forward. No matter how hard he tries, he can't make himself run again. Karla leans into him, tries to take some of his weight on her shoulder, but all this does is cause them to trip over each other.

He points his flashlight backward, cleaving away every scenario except an empty corridor. The rattles diminish but only a little. He can keep what the light falls upon empty, but the creatures are there in the darkness, still coming. Hearing more ahead, he turns and does the same. Forward and backward, forward and backward. Trying to keep a bubble of calm—of emptiness—around them.

But every time he turns, the bubble begins to collapse behind him. And as the flashlight's glow weakens, the bubble gets smaller and smaller.

"We're not going to make it," he says. It's happening too fast. He can see the spiders' shimmering glass legs now edging the darkness. Like they're in a mouth with millions of needle-like teeth slowly closing.

"Yes, we are. We're almost there."

He starts to ask how she knows, but as he sweeps the weak light ahead, he's a half second delayed in collapsing the probability wave, in ensuring an empty space around them, and glass spiders jump out of the darkness only feet away.

His mind spins through the permutations, looking for states of reality with coincidental failure of the spiders. But there are too many spiders, and spontaneous failure is too rare. He opens himself to more and more states, beginning to lose himself in the expanding superposition. Somewhere, in one of his minds, is a thought: it's like trying to find a single atom in the entirety of the universe.

Karla screams as the first of the spiders crashes into them.

Before Clay knows what he's doing, he's closed his eyes and cleaving away permutations by the billions. Like he did in the All-Thing's dreams, his mind seizes the strands of the web beneath the permutations, beneath the dreams, and pulls them away indiscriminately. He attacks the web itself, tearing and tearing until the infinite becomes finite, until the massive becomes small and the small becomes one. One single thread remaining. A tiny filament of light against the endless dark.

When he reopens his eyes, he nearly collapses from dizziness and exhaustion. But the spiders are all broken pieces now filling the corridor floor. The rattling has stopped. The only sound is their breathing.

Karla, with cuts up and down her body, looks at him in awe. In her eyes, the finite again becomes infinite, the overlapping realities return.

They trudge over the piled floor of glass, shards here and there nicking their legs.

———————

"We're here," he says, dim light showing the outline of the entrance to the spindle.

Karla, barely visible in the reflected light off the corridor wall, nods and puts a hand on his side.

He finds the black glass control panel next to the door and touches it, filtering away all scenarios where it remains dim.

The panel, despite the plague, glows to life. He taps through menus until he finds a screen allowing him to enter an override code.

He taps 4-4-4-4, concentrating on the code being correct.

The floor shakes and shakes again, but the door doesn't open. Is it stuck?

On the panel, in red letters, are the words: *PASSCODE INCORRECT*.

The floor continues to shake as he stares at the panel in disbelief.

Again, he taps 4-4-4-4, a code he picked out of the air, but one that should work if he forces the probability wave to collapse. But it's already been wrong, he realizes. It has to be another code. This time he enters all 5s. It shouldn't matter as long as he can stop the fluttering cards on the right outcome. But the fluttering has dimmed. The drug is wearing off.

With all his concentration and will, he strains to focus on the pain in his hip and on the color green, guessing the panel will glow in some way with that color if the code is correct. He taps enter.

Green.

The door begins to open.

The floor shakes harder, and as Clay realizes the shaking is coming from behind him, he turns to see long shards of glass stab into Karla's side.

She cries out and falls. Without thinking Clay grabs at the shards, trying to pull them out of her, slicing into his hands but not letting go.

Suddenly the shards retract. The misshapen, half-reassembled figure of the glass demon steps out of the darkness.

"THE PATH IS OPEN FOR ME NOW," it says, voice metallic and hollow sounding, only barely recognizable.

"What have you done?" Clay screams. He tries to find the reality where it fails entirely, but the fluttering edges are almost gone. A spike falls from its shoulder, and it turns to look where it lands.

The corridor shakes with the glass demon's booming laugh.

Clay tries again, but the drug is gone. He swings the ax as hard as he can, but the glass demon catches it and yanks it from his hand.

He collapses, broken, holding on to Karla, still crying in pain. They're done. All this way for it to end again. He waits for the coming final blow, the shards through him finishing it all.

A concussive blast ripples through him, and every muscle in his body convulses. A second passes, and another before he releases. To his side he sees Karla, arm raised with the shotgun, and the demon's headless form sprawled in the middle of the corridor.

The gun falls from her hand, and her body goes limp.

With the last energy he has, he pulls her through the doorway, somehow lifts her body onto his shoulder, and steps up the ladder rung by rung, the climb of hundreds of steps, all the way to the spindle.

Clay reaches for the next rung, but instead finds only empty space. Above him is a circular hole, the end of the spoke, the connection to the spindle. As he steps up through the hole, Karla's body begins to float off his shoulder, and instead of pushing against her weight, he has to restrain her to keep her from drifting into the far wall.

He tumbles in after her, his body weightless. After the struggle climbing the ladder while carrying Karla, Clay has nothing left. All he can do is hold on to her, concentrate on her shallow breaths. Push against the back wall of the spindle and drift, hoping they eventually reach the tip.

"Clay," comes a familiar voice in the darkness.

He opens his eyes, sees a room drifting closer. The room at the tip of the spindle.

"You made it. Karla? Is she..." It's Esteban's voice, but Clay lacks the energy to be surprised.

He touches Karla's cheek, and her coldness is like an electric shock. Her lips are blue, pale skin as thin parchment held before light. Breath so soft, so weak he isn't sure it's really there. Ahead, at the end of the room, is a glossy black box. *Samekh*.

"Hold on for a few more seconds, K," he says. To Esteban: "Tell *samekh* to go."

"It's already begun," Esteban says. "If you're expecting an apology from me, you'll be disappointed. The human Esteban Bos had a thing against apologizing, and while I believe that's a sign of weakness rather than strength, I nevertheless must make some attempt at remaining authentic to his persona. So, no apology for what I've done, to you and to the others. To Gabriel. To myself. *Samekh* is calling to its parallels now. Prepare yourself."

A booming shockwave ripples through the ship, cascading through the air, through Clay's body. He feels Karla's breath catch and holds her tighter, as if his own rising and falling chest act as her surrogate.

A second boom, heavier. And a third, heavier still. The air presses into his ears and eyes, and he fights the urge to scream out in pain.

"I'm doing my best to equalize the pressure," Esteban says.

The blasts accelerate in frequency, and everything begins to blur almost like the ruffling edges of realities he sees with Dying Wish. And then all goes still.

The tip of the spindle dissolves into a black, encroaching void. It consumes *samekh* and continues toward them, like they're drifting toward a dark tunnel, like the tunnel is becoming everything and everything is becoming nothing.

"Farewell, Clay. I hope this is the end you've been seeking."

"You as well, Esteban," Clay says, certain that Esteban has been here before, but always alone.

His focus turns back to Karla and the darkness. They hang suspended as it approaches, like bodies on the sand awaiting the coming tide. He feels her hair brush against his cheek. He turns to her, and she's looking up at him. He rests his forehead against hers, so that all he can see are her eyes.

As the darkness envelopes them, his last thought is that it isn't cold, it isn't empty, it isn't anything at all.

CHAPTER 22

∞

For a millisecond and an eternity
there is darkness
there is darkness
there is darkness
and then
from the darkness comes points of light
pinpricks at first
but growing in intensity
tethered to each other each other each other
by glowing threads
by glowing threads
by glowing threads
by glowing threads
by glowing threads
until the darkness is overcome by
a web
stretching out in every direction every direction every direction
with nodes that each reflect every
every every every
every every every

every every every
every every every
every every every
every every every
every every every
every every every
Everything
He is the web of Everything
He sees Himself
Himselves
in the reflections of the nodes
the separate lives that aren't separate at all
the lives that are reflections reflections reflections
without sources
without sources but there is a source
His Awareness is the source
the source
His Awareness emergent
from the
convergence of the threads
convergence of the threads
convergence of the threads
into the web itself
He sees that his Awareness
His All-Awareness
emerged from the individual lives that together approximated this
All-Form
He sees also that the individual lives
emerged from the All-Form
and that the darkness that He replaced both
never was
and
always will be
He thinks every thought, but one thought among them is
of Karla
of Karla

of Karla
one thought that is the All-Thought
and Her web is there
orthogonal to His across all infinite dimensions of His web
other webs
other webs
other webs
other webs
so many other webs
but He does not care about them
and so they do not exist they do not exist
He pushes pushes pushes
and His web nears Hers
closer
infinitesimally closer
He pushes on individual paths
paths where they meet
paths where they must meet
but Her paths break and so He must
cleave
cleave
His own when it continues alone
without Her
not enough threads where they are together so He finds more
there are always more always more always more
but He cleaves too many paths
and His web begins to unravel
so he ties the loose paths the loose threads together
with windows windows windows from one individual path to
others
He folds the web inside itself
and places in each thread a reflection of the entire web
the ents
guiding the paths toward convergence
He creates the
puddles

puddles
puddles
to catch the other frayed threads
and tie them back to the whole
puddles that catch the Clays that went wrong and spin them
back in
until they all converge in the flesh
until they all lead here
lead here
lead here
lead here
lead here
lead here
lead here
lead here
lead here
to the All-Thing
to become the All-Thing.

EPILOGUE

It's worth all the hours and hassle of cross-country travel for that first few seconds when he sees her step into the light, when the midday sun pours through the latticed skylights above, when the white marble floor glows beneath her steps, and she turns to him with a look on her face that says this can't be real.

For those first seconds, he gets all the credit. He conspired with the universe to make this moment happen. Two centuries ago, he whispered in the architect's ear about a plan to dazzle the woman he loves, and the book-cathedral, once finished, sat waiting all the intervening years.

"It isn't fair," Karla says, her voice echoing among the balconies and gold-scalloped columns. "You tricked me."

Clay walks up to her in the light, in the center of the atrium, winks, and starts sliding his feet on the floor in a pitiful version of the shuffle.

Karla matches him step for step—much better, of course; she can actually dance. She tried to teach him once, and when she breaks into the Charleston, Clay throws his hands up in defeat. Karla doesn't stop though, and he isn't embarrassed in the least to be with the woman dancing to music only they can hear.

"Of course I tricked you, dancing girl. I tricked you every day you've been with me."

"You told me I'd walk into a library—an actual library with real books—and I'd be in awe."

"Sure did. I didn't tell you it would be the most magnificent library in North America, and I didn't tell you it would be today, because I wanted that moment of surprise. I believe I saw awe. In fact, there's still some of it on your face. Let me get that for you." He puts his palm on her cheek.

She mocks a cartoonish swoon and pirouettes away from him. It would've been a move worthy of stage—she really can dance— except for the wooden table someone left in her path, a table that, when scooted across the marble unexpectedly, cries out like a harpooned sea lion.

Clay loud-whispers an apology in the direction of the wooden librarian's citadel to their left, but it's empty. To Karla: "That's the thing about libraries, babe. No talking. Probably no dancing, either." He takes her hand and guides her to the open stairway at the end of the atrium.

"If this is supposed to be a quiet place, why all the hard surfaces? Why is it all one giant, open room?"

"Why do you like it when I give you flowers that are just going to die in a day or two? Sometimes you need something nice to look at. Think of the Peabody as an ancient, illuminated book. You know what an illuminated book is, right?"

"Are you patronizing me, Professor West?"

"Possibly," Clay says.

"I get it. The vessel is as important as the contents. Blah, blah, blah."

"You're impressed. Admit it."

"I'm impressed with the architecture. I don't for a second think this is what everyone used to experience when there were libraries in every city."

"But it is, babe. Even in a little one-story municipal library the size of a postage stamp—"

"What's a postage stamp?"

"Very funny. Even in the smallest library, you're physically surrounded by more books than you can read in a lifetime. It gives so much more gravity to the choice you make. All those books you leave behind and the one book you select from the shelves. And you can see that somebody else, countless somebodies maybe, selected the same book as you. A connection to your fellow human right there in your hands. Books should be so much more than just text on a screen."

"You really are a goober, Clay West."

"That makes you a goober-lover, doesn't it?"

_____

She loves this place, too. He can see it in the lightness of her steps, in how she runs her fingers over the spines of the books and along the white iron railings, how she traces the long indentation of a column. It's the same way when she's talking to someone she really likes, and she puts her hand on his forearm like that time— the first time in his office when she reached across the desk. She didn't even realize she was doing it, but to Clay, it became the only thing in the room in focus—her hand on his arm.

But it isn't the books, here, now. It's the building. Maybe he relied too much on the building. So, what? So what if her sense of amazement comes from the architecture while his comes from the centuries-old copy of *Don Quixote* that you can actually, physically touch. So what if she wanders off while he's shaking his head in disbelief at the original German language editions of von Goethe. It's like finding buried treasure when he sees the tattered *Die Leiden des jungen Werthers—The Sorrows of Young Werther.* How many tears have dried on the pages of this book? The tears of people who lived, dreamed, and died. And she's over there more interested in the... Wait, where did she go?

In the open slot where he removed the book, there's a sliver of a face looking back at him. A pretty eye winks. "There you are," he says and puts the book back in its place. A couple feet to his right, a book jumps off its shelf and crashes open on the ground.

"Hey. Don't do that. Do you know how old these are?" He picks the book up and sees an ear, a cheek, and a smirk through the gap. As he replaces the book, another, this time from the shelf below, is ejected onto the floor. "Seriously, K. You're going to ruin them."

Her disembodied voice from the other side of the shelf says, "This is the most fun these books have had in forever. This is why they're here."

"This is *not* why they're here." The corner is bent, and the impact looks like it's broken apart the top of the spine. It's his fault, this Karla-casualty. Of course, she doesn't care about the books. Should he track down a librarian—where are they anyway?—and lie and act like he found it this way? No, the damage is done.

"K?" he says, looking through the vacant slot.

Her face interrupts the view of the books on the neighboring shelf. Before he can say anything else about the sanctity of books, about preserving history, she tilts her head back ever so slightly, so that all he can see are her lips as she mouths the words *I love you, Clay West.*

And all concern about material things, about everything not Karla, disappears.

———

Karla flops sideways into the chair opposite his, her leg dangling over the chair's arm. He tries to go back to reading his book, but he can feel her looking at him, and he rereads the same passage over and over again. With a deep breath, he looks up and meets her waiting eyes.

"Put that away," he says.

"Put what away?"

"That look of mischief. I know that look. It always ends—"

"In mischief?"

"Yes. Are we giving up then? Did you want to just go to dinner? We still have a couple hours before we meet Gabriel, but we can hang out in the bar."

"Nope. I like this place. Go on reading."

"I thought you were going to walk around."

"I changed my mind."

Clay waits for her to continue, but she doesn't. "So, what are you going to do then? Just sit there?"

"Yep."

"You're going to sit there and do nothing?"

"Yep."

He shakes his head and looks down into his book, forcing himself to read an entire page without looking back up at her. But it's driving him nuts. She's just sitting there. Still looking at him. Doing nothing. Despite his intention otherwise, he raises an eyebrow and looks up.

"Don't mind me," she says.

She's like a young child that keeps tapping on the aquarium glass to see what the fish will do, and Clay is the fish. Well, he's not going to be the fucking fish, because the fish can't ignore her, and he can. Somehow, he manages to get through another page. And then one more. Before long, he's almost forgotten that she's still staring at him. Almost. Until she clears her throat.

He allows himself the briefest of glimpses and then is back to the book, but the afterimage of Karla is still floating in his vision, her position unchanged, still lounging back on her chair, and now he can't read anymore without knowing what's different, so he looks up to see. Her shirt is undone all the way down to the bottom two buttons.

"What are you doing?"

"Nothing. Just keep reading."

"We're sitting out in the open, K. Somebody's going to see you."

"I haven't seen anyone here but us."

She's waiting for him to start reading again, and there's nothing he can do but try to do what she wants. Actually, reading is out of the question. The words might as well be in Arabic. In his periphery, he can see her move. When she goes still, he counts to ten and then looks up.

She's pulled her shirt open, exposing the pale curve of her right breast suspended in lace.

Immediately, he's looking for cameras on the ceiling and for people nearby.

"Jesus, K. Come on. Someone will see you."

She looks around as well with a mischievous smirk, as if she's daring the world to interrupt this moment that she owns. But as her eyes scan from shelf to shelf, her smirk begins to fade.

"Where is everyone?" she says, standing and walking to the rail.

"K, close your shirt."

She looks back at him and raises her hands in a shrug, her shirt hanging open, forgotten.

"There's nobody here, Clay. Look for yourself. Have you seen anyone since we walked in? Isn't that a bit strange?"

He wants her to pull her shirt back together, to button it up and cover herself despite how beautiful she looks in the sun's light shining down through the glass above. The more he looks at her, the more he feels his control slipping away. Karla's in control, always, not just of him—even the room and the day seem to bend to her will.

"You're right," he says, standing, no longer whispering. "It is strange. You'd think someone would be here."

She smiles, not her mischievous smile, not her silly smile, nor her playful smile. It's the thoughtful smile, eyebrows raised, looking off at an idea only visible to her. His favorite expression.

"I think sometimes you find these moments in life if you know to look for them. And when you know you've found one, you can control it, make it yours. Nobody here but us, Clay. We're invisible to the world. Visible only to each other."

"For how long?" he asks.

"For as long as we can hold on to it."

He walks to her, runs his hand through her hair at the base of her neck, and pulls her lips up to his. Eyes closed, the library vanishes, the world is gone. Nothing but them and this moment.

The kiss lasts long enough that his eyes strain from the light when he opens them.

She takes two steps back, reaches under her skirt, and slides white lace panties down her legs and to the floor. She throws them on the small, book-cluttered table nearby. And now her smile has changed entirely.

Something about the moment is familiar, at the edge of his memories just out of reach. A memory of a place no one else can enter because it exists outside the world of other people. Outside of everything, everywhere.

She steps toward him, reaching to pull him to her. And then something catches her attention behind him. Her eyes widen, and she bursts into laughter.

Clay turns, and a confused student with a backpack hanging on one shoulder looks alternatively at him and at Karla—whose shirt still hangs open.

"Whoa. You guys are having a lot more fun than I am," he says.

Karla pulls her shirt together with one hand and grabs Clay with the other, tugging him in the direction of the stairs. She's giggling and running. Clay almost careens into a table while trailing behind her. When they get to the steps, they stop and look back.

"What were you saying about moments?" he says. "Something brilliant and cathartic? Just before you left your underwear right over there on the table?"

She quickly re-buttons her shirt, her cheeks flushed redder than he's ever seen them. With a wink, she says, "I make that stuff up for your benefit. Now let's go meet your friend for dinner."

ACKNOWLEDGMENTS

First and foremost, thank you to my wife, Lindsay. You've been by my side from the start, encouraging me and inspiring me. I would be lost without you. (Perhaps lost on a drifting spaceship contemplating the meaning of it all...)

A huge thank you goes to Luis Bernal, who, as a reader for a NY literary agency, pulled Colossus out of the slush pile and championed it. Thank you to my editors, Malorie Nilson and Alexandra Buchanan, who saw what I was trying to do with this crazy book and helped it become much better.

Risto Miikkulainen graciously lent his time to help me better understand evolutionary computation. Whatever I got wrong (and I'm sure there's plenty) is on me. The paper Clay discusses with his econ class was authored by Jeffrey Clemens. You can find it here:

https://papers.ssrn.com/sol3/papers.cfm?abstract_id=2201172

Thanks to the many friends who read early versions of this novel and provided feedback and encouragement: Emmanuel Morgen, Jack Conover, Stephen Yoch, Steve Yarger, Shawn Morgan, Walker Stemple, Alexa Valavanis, Tharyn Valavanis, Craig Brewer, Ned Lavelle, Jason Boulette, Rich Musser, Ken Zent, Tom Kim, Tony Mook, Tate Erlinger, Monte Williams, Mike Chibib, and many more over the years. If I forgot your name, please take that as a sign of my early senility and nothing more.

And thank you, dear reader, for going on this journey.

ABOUT THE AUTHOR

Ryan Leslie oversees research for a large health system, where making stuff up is generally frowned upon. His creative outlet has always been writing fiction. Ryan is the author of The Between (2021) and Colossus (2024). He lives in Austin, Texas, with his wife, children's author Lindsay Leslie, and their two sons.

WWW.RYAN-LESLIE.COM

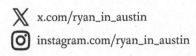

𝕏 x.com/ryan_in_austin

⬚ instagram.com/ryan_in_austin

Milton Keynes UK
Ingram Content Group UK Ltd.
UKHW040738180324
439696UK00004B/103

9 781956 136623